Land of Broken Promises –
By: Margaret Penfold
ISBN: 978-0-908325-19-1

All rights reserved
Copyright © Jan. 2016, Margaret Penfold
Cover Art Copyright © Jan. 2016, Brightling Spur

Bluewood Publishing Ltd
Christchurch, 8441, New Zealand
www.bluewoodpublishing.com

Names, characters and incidents depicted in this book are products of the author's imagination or are used fictitiously. Any resemblance to actual events, locales, organizations, or persons, living or dead, is entirely coincidental, and beyond the intent of the author or the publisher.

No part of this book may be reproduced or shared by any electronic or mechanical means, including but not limited to printing, file sharing, and email, without prior written permission from Bluewood Publishing Ltd.

Other titles by Margaret Penfold:

Land of Broken Promises series:
Patsy
Maftur

For news of, or to purchase this or other books, please visit:

www.bluewoodpublishing.com

Land Of Broken Promises:

Dalia

by

To Pat, thank you Marget Penfold

Margaret Penfold

Dedication

This work is dedicated to:
- An active member of a local synagogue who gave so much help but wishes to remain anonymous.
- All the marvelous writers at Leicester Writers' Club who have given so much support.
- The brave hearted men on PPOCA forum who have answered innumerable questions about their experiences in Palestine, and in particular to its former moderator, the late Graham Jenkins.
- Martin Higgins, the primary source for imformation on members of the British section of the Palestine Police.
- BPPA's honorary adviser in Israel, Michael Gottschalk.
- My friends of many cultures in Leicester, a city that rejoices in its diversity.
- Evelyn Hall who once again helped a sloppy writer with her copy editing.
- My offspring who have given me so much moral support, and;
- Last but not least to Bluewood Publishing for placing a triple bet on my work.

If you deem this work worthy of your praise, please vindicate my publishers' decision to print it by recommending the completed trilogy, the value of which is intended to be greater than the sum of the individual parts.

Part 1

Munchen, Germany 1933

Chapter 1

Dalia heard the knock as she was washing the breakfast dishes, not quite sure which cloths and brushes to use. The last servants, the loyal ones, had left the night before, in tears, six months' pay in hand. Mama had insisted they leave.

"The Brownshirts will return to carry out their threats. Remember what happened to Christine!"

Dalia wished her mother hadn't said that. She didn't want to remember, and diverted her thoughts to the uncertain future. How long before they found out whether they'd they be leaving Germany to live in Palestine, or be moving to Lübeck to stay with Granny and Grandpa?

A bell clanged. She looked up at the long row of bells, each with its own label, expecting to find the one marked 'drawing room' vibrating since her mother had taken herself off there after breakfast. It wasn't the drawing room bell, however, but the one labelled 'front door'. Had her father lost his key? Would he have brought news of Christine?

She dried her hands and ran up the wooden service stairs to the foyer, her footsteps echoing in a room now devoid of furniture and carpet.

When she was little, the foyer had been a favourite place. While Christine had sorted the post at a desk, she had sat on a thick rug in front of an inlaid ebony cabinet, tracing around intricate pearl pictures with her index finger and making up stories about the dainty ladies carrying parasols who trotted over a hump-backed bridge. She had looked up occasionally to see Christine set Papa's letters in neat rows on top of the chest and had accompanied her as she distributed the rest of the post, first to her mother, and then to members of staff.

Today, however, the post lay jumbled on the floor. She

stepped over it to unlock the door.

Beyond the porch, a courier straddled a motor bike. He held an international telegram in his hand. "You took your time," he sneered, "but what else would one expect from a lazy Judenknecht."

He'd mistaken her for a servant!

"How dare you speak to me like that?"

"Oh yeah, and who's going to stop me? Sign here, that's if you can write, of course." He handed her a notebook and indelible pencil.

She wanted to fling the book back at him, but realised the telegram was almost certainly important, so, her hand shaking with rage mingled with fear, she scrawled her signature and snatched at the telegram.

"A word of advice," the lad said as he kicked the bike into action. "Make yourself scarce before we get round to cleaning up this road."

She banged the door shut and stood in the foyer panting and shaking until she was breathing normally, before picking up the mail. One letter had a Palestinian stamp. With no chest on which to display mail, she decided to take it to her mother and knocked on the drawing room's thick mahogany door that led off the foyer. Normally she only visited that special room to be formally introduced to ladies on the various charitable committees her mother chaired. It was grown-up territory, both glowing with inherited opulence and decorated in the height of fashion. Friends and relatives used the cosier sitting room.

She had to wait for longer than she had expected before hearing her mother call, "Come in."

On entering, she stared around in shock. Despite everything that had happened recently, she wasn't prepared for the change. The large bay windows were devoid of curtains. The room looked larger, a different shape. It smelled different too. Bare wires hanging from the ceiling were the only reminder of the fairy tale chandelier she had admired so much. The Persian carpet Papa had once described as priceless lay rolled up, leaving bare boards. Pictures with strange cuboid shapes had disappeared, leaving lighter patches on the grey striped wallpaper.

Stacks of furniture, mostly family heirlooms, stood to one side, labelled 'SOLD'. A larger collection of more modern furniture still waited for purchasers.

Strong twine, scissors, and a large needle lay on the floor next to her mother, who was kneeling in the middle of the room surrounded by empty cabin trunks with freshly sewn lining. Piles of worn clothes, shoes, sheets and towels, scrapbooks, and toiletries lay beside three empty picture frames that had once held her parents' most prized paintings.

Her mother looked up, eyes puffy and red, almost as if she'd been crying. Holding her breath, Dalia gave her mother the telegram and watched her slit it open.

She breathed again when her mother smiled. "The hotel in Haifa's booked. Now we can only hope the Nazis agreed to make Palestine an exception to the emigration rules."

Dalia hoped they had. She would much rather go to Palestine than the USA, which had been her parents' first choice until they discovered that if they emigrated there they would have to leave behind not only their house and furniture but all their money.

Her mother opened the letter with the Palestine stamp. She read it and looked up. "Cousin Elsa says we can stay with her until we get settled in Palestine. Do you remember Cousin Elsa and her family?"

"No. All I know about them is they send us oranges and a photo every Hanukah."

"I'm not surprised. You were only two when they made their last visit, but I've kept every one of their Hanukah photos." Her mother reached out and picked up a scrap book from one of the piles. "Here's my Cousin Elsa's album."

Dalia took the scrapbook, flipping past pictures of people in clothes twenty years out of date until she found the more recent photos. The last one showed a family of five, a stocky, bearded man, a plump middle-aged woman, a younger woman holding a baby, and a handsome boy with wavy hair. Dalia had eyes only for the boy. Why hadn't she noticed how good-looking he was when she had seen this photo last?

Her mother looked at the photo and shook her head. "Those children are both so much taller than their parents but Cousin Elsa says that's usual for Sabras."

"Sabras?"

"Jews born in Palestine. They grow tall because of all the oranges they eat."

Dalia pointed at the boy. "What's his name?"

"That's Shimon," her mother said. "Cousin Elsa says he'll be meeting us off the boat if we go."

The door behind them opened. Dalia turned and saw her father. Before she could ask if he had news of Christine, her mother had jumped up and run past her. "Is the Transfer system in place?"

Her father put his arms round her mother and held her close. "Yes. I've signed the forms and collected the boat tickets."

"Did you phone your parents?"

"Straightaway." Papa dropped his arms and frowned. "But Mutter still refuses to come. She says she wouldn't have minded spending six months or so in New York visiting relatives, but she's not going to live permanently in a country full of strangers, flies and malaria."

"You must go over to Hamburg and have a serious talk with your father."

"I will, but right now let's have a look at where we are here." He looked around. "No sales today?"

Her mother laid her head against her father's shoulder. "Albert, I've been wasting my time here. Nobody wants to pay the right price—nobody."

Dalia watched her father stroke her mother's hair and crept out of the room still carrying Cousin Elsa's photo album. She would have to find out later if Christine had recovered from her ordeal at the hands of the Brownshirts.

She hated the Nazis for many things—making her leave home, spoiling her friendships, taking her scholarship, turning Germany into a land where her father couldn't earn a living, but most of all because of the awful way they had treated

Christine.

Upstairs in her own bedroom, the only room with all its furniture intact, she carefully lifted the last photo from the album and slipped it between the jacket and hardcover of her favourite book, 'Emil und die Detektives'. Her excuse for taking it, if found out, was that she wanted to recognise the boy, Shimon, when he met them.

Part 2

Palestine 1933 – 1939

Chapter 2

Three weeks after secreting that photo, Dalia sat on a deck chair on a liner, holding a pencil and note-pad, with her favourite book and a two-way dictionary on her lap.

They had sailed from Bremerhaven in the damp chill of autumn, but now summer had returned, with heat strong enough to make all passengers appreciate cooling sea breezes. Members of other Jewish families emigrating from Germany who surrounded her had made this side of the deck their own. A swastika on a red background might fly above their heads, but the ship's captain and most of the kitchen staff were Jews.

She was teaching herself Hebrew by translating 'Emil und die Detektives' from the original German. Since Germany was rejecting her family, the sooner she could reject its language, the better.

They were close to their destination. Every so often she looked up at her older brother, Werner. He was leaning against the railing, peering into the distance. Half-an-hour previously he had sworn he could see land where she had only seen another bank of clouds.

Glancing around to make sure her mother wasn't looking, she slipped out her stolen photo and gazed down at the boy she would soon see in the flesh.

Werner called out. "Dalia, it really is land. Come and see."

She stood up, dizzy with excitement. The smudge on the horizon now showed as tall hills, perhaps even mountains. They leaned against the rail together as the land came nearer and they headed towards a wide bay.

A range of mountains rose to the left. One, white-topped, soared high above the rest. Werner, who had placed himself protectively behind her, pointed towards it.

He spoke slowly and carefully in Hebrew because his vocabulary and grammar were still limited, although still streaks ahead of her. He had been learning Hebrew for three years at Zionist youth club while she had only begun when she turned twelve less than a year previously.

"The snow-capped mountain is Mount Hermon. The mountain in front is Mount Carmel. It is the end of a long ridge stretching many miles to the south."

Dalia sighed. Her brother had obviously been learning sentences from his copy of the Guide to Palestine. However, even if talking Hebrew didn't exactly add sparkle to their conversation, she knew they had to persevere. On boarding the ship she and Werner had vowed that, from then on, they would speak nothing but Hebrew to each other, even if they still had to speak German to their parents.

German, Werner had pointed out, wouldn't be the most popular of languages in their new home, but, currently, Dalia's main motive for studying Hebrew was that she might need it to talk to Shimon. She hoped, when she met him, and that would be in only an hour or so now, he wouldn't talk so fast that she wouldn't be able to keep up.

The engines burst into frenzied activity. She ran to the stern, wrinkling her nose at the stale air wafting from the ship's ventilators, leaned over the rails and watched the propellers churn a foam-flecked circle. The engines stopped thrashing and reverted to their rhythmic thud, thud. A new wake formed at right angles to the old. She made her way back to Werner and saw that they were approaching a curving breakwater. She shivered in excitement as she wondered whether Shimon was already on the quayside.

Beyond the breakwater, pale flat-roofed apartment blocks climbed the mountain slope. In contrast, rows of red-tiled houses occupied flatter ground where the breakwater joined the land.

A German woman nearby pointed towards one of these houses and said in excited German, "See, Nelly. Our home."

Dalia looked at her brother and whispered, "We've come

all this way only to be surrounded by Germans?"

What a difference eight months could make, she reflected. A year previously she had been proud to be German.

"Germans live in their own colonies," Werner reassured her. "Where we live will be one hundred per cent Jewish."

A small boat sped towards them. As it docked alongside she saw it sported a blue ensign with a Union Jack in the top left quarter and a silver badge bearing the words 'Palestine Police' on the right. Two men in smart navy uniforms and flat-topped caps climbed aboard.

A tannoy boomed across the deck. "Attention, please! Attention, please! All passengers must take passports and visas to the purser's office."

Everyone rushed below.

After shuffling in line for over an hour, their family eventually reached the purser's office. Behind them a queue wound its way along corridors and up stairways. Somewhere close a man cursed in German, grumbling at length that all these Jewish immigrants were turning the usually simple disembarkation procedures into a nightmare. The British should have arranged separate controls for residents and immigrants.

Dalia stuck her tongue out at him when her mother wasn't looking.

While her father waited politely to be called, Werner, eager to assert his independence, stepped forward and thrust his student permit at a policeman.

The man studied it before addressing him in English.

Dalia gave a superior smile when her brother gazed at him in consternation. Werner's Hebrew might be better than hers but he was worse at English.

"Atah medaber ivrit?" the policeman asked eventually in such a heavy accent that it was only when Werner nodded enthusiastically that she understood he was asking Werner if he could speak Hebrew. She listened carefully.

"Your student permit is only valid while you are studying in Palestine. When you finish your education you must leave the country. Understand?"

The policeman handed Werner back his permit. Her father stepped forward to show the policeman the German passport that covered the rest of the family.

"Your visa is valid for only three months. After that your family must leave Palestine."

She felt her stomach lurch as Werner translated for her parents. There was no way they could return to Germany where no one wanted them. Strangely, her parents seemed unperturbed.

Dalia had no time to dwell on the disturbing information, as the ship was already docking. She was about to meet Shimon at last.

She saw and recognised him while they were still coming down the gangway. He was in the crowd on the quay holding up a placard bearing the words in Hebrew, *ALBERT AND TRUDI LEITNER. WELCOME TO ERETZ ISRAEL.*

"There's Cousin Elsa's youngest," her mother shouted and rushed over to embrace him.

She stared. Shimon looked like a grownup and was even better looking than the boy in the family photograph. His tanned skin was smooth. He had a wavy shock of dark hair growing back from a square forehead, with just one unruly lock falling over an eye. He wore informal khaki trousers, an open-necked white shirt and sandals as if he were on a beach holiday.

Her father and Werner walked over in a more dignified manner than her mother, leaving her alone guarding the luggage. She watched her father shake hands with Shimon and point in her direction. She waved enthusiastically until she realised her father wasn't pointing at her but at their luggage. Shimon directed a heavily sunburnt porter in a long striped tunic and red flower pot hat to bring a trolley over. To her intense disappointment, he ignored her as he stood close, focussed on directing the porter in a strange language. She determined to make him notice her but couldn't very well interrupt while he supervised the porter.

Joined by her mother, she followed the loaded trolley to the customs desk. Her father and Werner showed passports again. The customs officer searched through the large trunks while Shimon stood by to translate when needed. Dalia slipped her arm through her mother's and felt her shivering, despite the heat and the heavy fur coat she had put on before leaving the ship. The customs officer found nothing but clothes, sheets and towels in the trunks and allowed them to leave.

She caught up with Werner and Shimon, determined to join in their conversation. "Shalom, Shimon, I am your cousin, Dalia," she started in her best Hebrew, but Werner contradicted her.

"He's not your cousin, Dalia. Your mother and Cousin Elsa are only honorary cousins. Shimon and I are discussing something important, so go back to Mutti. She may need you. Sorry about that, Shimon, you know what kid sisters are like."

Shimon glanced at her "I can't imagine they get in the way as much as older sisters, but Dalia, Werner and I really have something private we need to talk about before he joins the Youth Village."

Reluctantly, Dalia rejoined her mother. If only she could find some way to get rid of Werner. Well, he'd be off to school tomorrow. She hoped Shimon would still be around to see her parents and herself off at the station when they set off to stay with his parents.

Once outside the port gates, her mother removed her coat and handed it to her father who packed it carefully into the top trunk on the trolley. While her parents were occupied and Werner and Shimon were still in close conversation, she inspected her surroundings. They were in a large square decorated with bunting and posters proclaiming in English, Hebrew, and another language with strange writing, both a grand opening of the harbour the following Tuesday and a special showing of the film 'Cavalcade'.

At one end of the square workmen were erecting a huge grandstand. Buildings still under construction lined the sides. Her mother said something she couldn't hear because of banging hammers and yelling workmen. The noise from cars and taxis constantly hooting at camels, donkeys, and jay-walking pedestrians just added to the cacophony of sound.

To her annoyance, her father, Shimon and Werner strode

off behind the trolley. She was hurrying to catch them up thinking the boys couldn't discuss anything important while her father was with them but her mother called her back in a weak voice. She was frightened to see her mother panting and leaning against the side of a half-built shop front.

"I'm all right," her mother reassured her, "just relieved we got through customs."

Dalia watched Shimon stride confidently along the crowded street behind their porter. She couldn't understand why there were so many Arabs on the street. At least she guessed they were Arabs because of their strange head coverings.

Even men in expensive European suits wore elegant versions of the porter's red flower pot thing. Others, riding donkeys or leading camel trains and wearing dark cloaks and striped tunics, wore white head scarves fastened with black cord. More numerous, however, were men and boys in skull caps, larger and dirtier than the kippas her father and Werner wore on Friday nights. Many wore simple sackcloth tunics. Others were slightly better dressed in short black jackets topping baggy white trousers. They carried loaded baskets of vegetables or firewood on their backs and occasionally large items of furniture. She saw one man bent double under the weight of a piano.

She knew Arabs lived in Palestine from letters pioneering farmers wrote to the Munchen youth club, but the youth club leader had said there were only a few. Here, however, Arabs seemed to be everywhere. The only Jews she could see were women.

Now that was something she could ask Shimon about.

They caught up with their own men in front of the hotel where Cousin Elsa had booked rooms—a three-storey stone building with a rounded wall curving away from older houses further up the street.

"Cousin Trudi," Shimon addressed her mother. "I have advised Uncle Albert to leave any luggage containing valuables at the Left Luggage Office at the station."

"No," her mother protested, laying her hand protectively

on the largest trunk. "We must keep everything with us."

"Cousin Trudi, thieves target hotel rooms. It's far safer to leave valuables in Left Luggage."

Her father placed his arm around her mother's shoulder. "I think we should listen to Shimon, Liebling. He knows this town. I'll get the hotel porter to take in our hand luggage and small suitcases. You and Dalia can book in while Werner, Shimon and I take the trunks on to the station's Left Luggage Office and buy train tickets."

Her mother withdrew her hand reluctantly. Dalia turned to wave goodbye as the men set off again but Shimon was too busy talking to Werner to see her.

"Will we be seeing Shimon again before we leave Haifa?" she asked her mother.

Her mother looked at her, raising her eyebrows. "Dalia, you're far too young to be chasing after boys."

She felt her cheeks go hot. "I was only thinking about you needing to ask him things because we know so little about the country, Mama."

"You can rest easy on that score. We're taking him to a decent restaurant tonight."

She would get a chance to speak to him there if there was a train to Werner's school today.

An hour later, after showering and helping her mother unpack the hand luggage, she leaned over the balcony outside her parents' bedroom, watching the crowds below.

An ululating wail, the most weird, alien sound she had ever heard, disturbed everything. Taxis stopped abruptly. Their drivers, and sometimes the passengers as well, emerged onto the sidewalk, unrolled mats and knelt on them. Porters put down goods they were carrying or parked their barrows to do likewise, and so did the brown-capped shoe shine boys working outside the hotel entrance. Camel trains and donkeys stopped, still tethered to their owners who had also unrolled their mats.

In between the bodies raising and prostrating themselves on their mats, men in European suits and trilbies and women in straw hats, weaved their nonchalant way.

Dalia imagined the chaos if people had behaved like that in Munchen. Ten minutes later the street returned to normal.

Her mother came out onto the balcony to ask what dress she wanted to wear that evening. While they were discussing it, a mob of several hundred raced down the street and proceeded to throw stones at the police station opposite. Police came out with what looked like dustbin lids on their arms. Most carried batons but a few held rifles.

Terrified, she and her mother rushed into the bedroom and shut the french windows. Even with the windows closed, the shouts and screams were deafening. She huddled close to her mother.

"We would have been safer back in Munchen," her mother exclaimed.

A cockroach, almost as large as a mouse, scuttled across the black and white floor tiles.

Her mother gave a scream. "We never, never should have come."

Cracks of gunfire rang out, followed by yells of pain and the sound of running feet.

The bedroom door opened and her father and Werner came in.

Her mother threw herself into her father's arms. "Thank goodness you are both safe. How did you get through?"

"We were already in the hotel, talking to the receptionist, when the trouble started."

"I'll go and unpack in my room," Werner said, and left.

"We won't be leaving tomorrow," her father told her mother. "The trains have stopped running. Apparently, the rioting is even worse in Jaffa than it is here so I've rebooked our rooms for tomorrow."

"Not another night here with all that trouble outside!" her mother screeched.

Her father patted her mother's arm. "We're safe enough inside, Liebling. In any case, the worst seems over here, although Shimon said there's bound to be a curfew tonight so I didn't invite him for a restaurant meal."

Dalia clenched her fists. Now she wouldn't get a chance

to talk to Shimon.

"So where will we eat tonight?" her mother asked.

"I've booked us in for a meal tonight and tomorrow night. I've also left a message with Shimon's landlady inviting him here tomorrow night. I've persuaded the receptionist to put a camp bed in Werner's room so if there is a curfew Shimon can sleep over."

Dalia felt the outlook brighten. She would get a chance to talk to Shimon after all but it sounded as if Werner wouldn't be leaving tomorrow either.

She risked a brief excursion to the balcony. The fighting had stopped but the street seemed emptier than it had been and two ambulances stood outside the police station.

Shimon arrived for supper next evening in clothes similar to those he had worn when meeting them. He carried a well-worn leather jacket and goggles.

"You've come by bike," Dalia exclaimed.

"Yes," he replied briefly.

She examined him as he greeted her parents. His hair still flopped in natural waves over his forehead. In comparison to her father and Werner with their pomaded hair and formal clothes, he looked strange but, she decided, healthy, natural hair in a man was quite appealing. She imagined herself running her hands through the curls.

"What bike do you have?" Werner asked.

Shimon gave an enthusiastic description involving revs per minute and road speeds.

Her mother interrupted as they went into supper. "Now, Shimon, you can tell me what you're studying."

Shimon was as enthusiastic about his studies at the Technion as he had been about his motorbike.

"Irrigation is the key to success in creating our homeland," he told them earnestly over the barley soup. By the beef course he was discussing rock porosity. Over the almond torte, he considered in depth the problems of wilderness salinity, and all the time he waved his hands about, bending forwards as he strove to explain an issue, while shaking a stray lock from his eyes, or leaning back in satisfaction when he thought he had got a point over. There was no break where Dalia could ask why there were so many Arabs in Haifa.

If anyone else had gone on like that she would have thought it boring but she couldn't help admiring Shimon's passion for turning Palestine back into a land of milk and honey. If anyone could do it, she was sure he could.

Shimon and Werner retired to their room early.

As soon as they were out of earshot, her father exploded. "Conceited young whelp!"

She was glad when her mother defended him. "He'll grow out of it. I can remember you at his age. You went on all evening at my parents' house about Peter Behrens and Frank Lloyd Wright and hardly acknowledged my presence."

"It was only because your family's formality made me nervous."

Her mother laughed. "Exactly."

Dalia was determined to ask Shimon about the Arabs next morning at breakfast but by the time she and her parents went down, the boys had already departed. Werner had left a note saying Shimon was giving him a lift to his new school.

Chapter 3

They hadn't expected Cousin Moshe to meet them at Rehovot Station with an ox-drawn cart. He stood by it, stocky, muscular and sun-tanned, with a beard—greyer and bushier than in his photo. A wide leather belt held up loose fitting dark trousers, below a sweat-stained khaki shirt with a multitude of pockets. A floppy cotton hat covered his head.

Uncle Moshe must have noticed the look on her mother's face. "I considered buying a pickup last year, but the roads round here would ruin the axles."

Dalia understood what he meant when they started off and the cart bumped over a potholed dirt road. By the time Uncle Moshe halted the oxen to greet a shepherd noisily, in what she presumed was Arabic, her posterior ached.

The shepherd, in a full length brown and white striped tunic, had a lamb slung round his neck like a collar. A white scarf tied with a thick black cord covered his head and shoulders. With sheep and goats following obediently behind, he resembled a biblical illustration.

The shepherd must have noticed her gazing longingly at the lamb because he bent down, stroked one of his sheep, and murmured something, before gently lifting the lamb from his shoulders and holding it out.

"May I?" she breathed, scarcely believing her luck.

Cousin Moshe smiled. "B'seder. He's asked the mother's permission."

She placed the lamb on her lap, stroking him gently. The lamb made a little bleating noise. The ewe baa-ed reassurance. The ox cart plodded on and the lamb settled down as Uncle Moshe and the shepherd conducted an animated conversation.

Ten minutes later, Dalia had to give back the lamb when the shepherd led his flock off through an olive grove.

"That man's sons pick my oranges and a niece helps Elsa in the house," Uncle Moshe said.

Her father raised his eyebrows.

Uncle Moshe broke into a broad grin. "I know, I know. The Agency says we should only employ Jews. Of course we give precedence to the Olim, but at harvest there's work for all." His gaze challenged her father as he continued, "Some of us believe the way forward is to work hand in hand with the Arabs, not segregate ourselves."

The landscape changed dramatically. Ruler-straight rows of orange trees bearing baubles of green fruit, some already yellow and being picked, replaced tiny stone-fringed fields and scattered olive trees. A strange clanking noise came from somewhere among the trees. A delicious perfume wafted from the orchards.

Her mother commented on the scent.

Cousin Moshe explained, "Citrus flower and fruit at the same time."

"What's that funny noise?" Dalia asked.

"We tie tins to every irrigation pump," Uncle Moshe explained. "If the noise dies down we know the pump's stopped working."

They drove off the main road onto an even bumpier one, passing houses where women and children waved and ran over to greet them in Hebrew. Everyone seemed to know who they were and why they had come.

"Nearly home now," Cousin Moshe said. "You can see our house." He pointed to a large white bungalow standing on a low hill.

A few minutes later Cousin Elsa, exactly like her photo—plump, middle aged with grey plaits wound round her head—bustled out to greet them.

"Welcome, welcome," she called and led them through a wooden porch to a varnished front door. "You'll want to wash before you eat. Moshe, show the men the outside pump."

Dalia and her mother followed Cousin Elsa down a passage with five doors. Cousin Elsa flung open the end one as if revealing a palace stateroom. "Our washroom."

As they entered a stone-slabbed room complete with shower, bidet, flushing toilet and wash basin, Cousin Elsa continued. "For years I had to live with an outhouse in the yard containing only a bucket with a wooden seat. One good thing about it was Moshe fertilised my vegetables with night soil every week. Now our cesspit fertilises the fields just once a year and I have to collect ox manure for my garden."

After they had washed, Cousin Elsa showed them into a large kitchen containing a table loaded with a variety of homemade cakes and sweetmeats, including Dalia's favourite—coffee cake.

A back door stood open onto a yard where chickens clucked as they pecked the ground, a view only partially obscured by a closed secondary door of fine wire mesh.

Her mother exclaimed at a gleaming copper sink divided into two sections.

"I found a picture of one in a German magazine," Cousin Elsa told her. "Moshe took the picture to a Jaffa coppersmith." She turned on a tap and rinsed her hands before picking up a knife to cut the cake. "I still can't quite believe I have a kitchen with running water. We used to have a camel to haul water from the well. I had to carry the buckets into the house. Now a pump brings water indoors. When we first came, the house was little more than a partitioned wooden shed." She pointed to a table. "But come, you must eat. You've had a long journey."

Later, Uncle Moshe took her father and Werner round the orchards, vineyards and vegetable plots.

Cousin Elsa gave her mother and herself a tour of the recently extended house and finished the tour of three comfortably furnished bedrooms and a sitting room by saying, "So you see, Trudi, we live in civilised comfort, almost as if I were still in your house in Munchen."

Dalia wished Cousin Elsa hadn't mentioned the house where her mother, Werner and she had all been born. Her mother had cried buckets when they had left, but although her lips were pursed now, there were no tears.

The next few weeks, as far as Dalia was concerned, were bliss. Although Rehovot's residents worried because the winter rains were late, she enjoyed the warm weather, especially as she didn't go to school. Instead, she had half-an-hour of formal

Hebrew with Cousin Elsa each day and another half hour of Hebrew handwriting practice on her own.

For the rest of the morning, dressed in the oldest of her cotton dresses, wearing leather sandals bought from the local store, and topped off with a tembel (the trademark floppy hat of rural Palestinian Jews), she helped with domestic chores. She fed turkeys and chickens, swabbed floors, weeded and watered Cousin Elsa's vegetable patch which was dominated by the pale red of ribbed tomatoes and dark purple of aubergines. In the afternoon, she wandered through deliciously perfumed citrus orchards to the clattering of the ubiquitous irrigation system and stopped to practice her Hebrew with everyone she met.

When mule carts brought children home from school, she retreated indoors, reluctant to meet other girls of her own age and remind herself she was an outsider.

After supper, made with ingredients often more middle-eastern than German, while grownups sat chatting around the table with a bottle of home produced wine, she retreated to a bedroom decorated with posters and photos of motorbikes, wells, both ancient and modern, cisterns, hydro-electric stations, irrigation systems and pieces of machinery she couldn't recognise. All Shimon's books were in Hebrew but they too, judging by their illustrations, were about motor bikes, water sources and aquifers. She tried reading his books to improve her Hebrew and learned a lot. She decided that when she grew up, and after Shimon had laid water pipes to the arid Negev wilderness, as Cousin Elsa declared was his ambition, she would become a pioneer farmer in that wilderness.

Her parents were learning about farming as well. When her father wasn't travelling to Tel Aviv to get their finances sorted, he was out in the orchards with Uncle Moshe helping with the grapefruit harvest, and learning all he could about large scale vegetable growing. He was almost unrecognisable in his daytime working trousers and cheap cotton shirts, but, like Uncle Moshe, he changed back into formal wear for the evening meal.

Her mother worked hard, learning to shield food from

flies, heat and excess light, to keep cockroaches at bay with Shelltox, to erect mosquito netting round beds, to look after hens and grow fruit and vegetables in garden beds for home use rather than sale.

She worried, however, that her mother seemed less lively than she had been back in Munchen when she had spent her time organising charity work amongst her friends.

Oranges were ripening fast now. Uncle Moshe hired more Arabs and all spare hands were pressed into harvest work.

One afternoon, standing on a ladder with a basket, she found herself working the same tree as her father who was wielding a long cutting pole from ground level. They worked for a while in companionable silence until Dalia used the opportunity to broach her concern. "Papa, is Mutti not well?"

Her father placed the oranges he had cut into the basket before answering, "I think so many changes have confused her. I wonder if I've been selfish by becoming a farmer. Maybe I should have settled in Tel Aviv and worked in architecture until the Nazis are voted out of power and we can return home."

"Even if the Nazis lose an election, I don't ever want to go back to Germany," she replied. "I'm glad you and Mutti are now farmers."

Chapter 4

The following week Dalia's father went into Jaffa almost daily. To her surprise he exchanged their visitors' visa for a residential one with no difficulty. He opened an account with a local branch of Barclays Bank, sorted out his South African investments and assured himself that the Finance Transfer agreement between the Germans and the Jewish Agency really did work. With his financial position assured, he wrote to the Jewish Agency asking to view the property they were hoping to lease in Bereisheet, a Moshav settlement in the Hefer Valley, halfway between Jaffa and Haifa.

The Agency wrote back that Bereisheet's rabbi and Muhktar, Gideon Cohen, would meet them at Hadera Station the following week. She felt so happy. Her family would have a home of their own again.

Her mother insisted they dress up for the occasion. Her father wore a homburg, jacket and immaculately creased trousers held up by braces. A bow tie adorned his best cambric shirt. Her mother chose a silk afternoon frock designed in Paris that suited her trim figure and sleek cropped hair. Dalia wore a cotton school dress and a straw hat. They walked to Rehovot station to catch the train to Hadera, her father in black highly-polished shoes, her mother in a pair of blue court shoes and she herself in buttoned up school shoes, not nearly as comfortable as the leather sandals she had been used to wearing.

As their train approached Lydda station, Dalia leaned out of the window on the lookout for Werner, who had taken a day off school.

"He's here," she shouted as she spotted him standing on the platform in a khaki shirt with rolled up sleeves and loose fitting cotton trousers. He had also neglected to pomade his hair.

Her mother took one look. "My goodness. What sort of impression is he going to make?"

Once on board, Werner announced that his name was now Uri, and would his parents please introduce him as Uri to the person meeting them.

Dalia ran the new name round and round her head. "Uri, Uri, Uri." Dressed as he was now, the name suited him.

Her mother eyed her son in dismay. "But, Werner, your father named you after a dear friend who…" She didn't need to finish her sentence. They all knew that Werner Schmidt, her father's best friend, had died in the Great War.

Dalia worried her father would be angry, but he sat there, calm and thoughtful. "Do all the other boys at your school have Jewish names?"

"Yes, except for newbies like me."

"Sabras make fun of you because of your German name?" Abba asked. "You would fit in better with a Jewish name?"

Her brother gulped, then nodded.

"In that case," her father said, "I shall call you Uri from now on. Trudi and Dalia, try not to embarrass Uri by calling him anything else."

"I'll try," her mother replied, "but it will be hard remembering."

Dalia smiled. "I'm glad you and Mutti gave me a Jewish name, Papa, so I don't have to change it."

Uri scowled at her. "You must call our parents Abba and Eema now, not Papa and Mutti."

Dalia felt herself go hot. She should have thought of that herself.

"I suppose Uri's right," her mother said, but didn't sound as if she believed it.

They couldn't see the rabbi on the platform at Hadera so they went outside to find only a cart drawn by two mules waiting beneath a clump of tall eucalyptus trees. A burly man, in a dark blue shirt with rolled-up sleeves, a leather hat, and loose fitting trousers, sat on the driving seat.

The man jumped down with athletic ease and offered his hand to Abba. "Shalom." He switched to German. "I am pleased to meet you, Herr Leitner. My name is Gideon

Cohen."

This man was the rabbi!

Her father replied in careful Hebrew, "Shalom, Reb Cohen. I have brought with me my wife Trudi, my son Uri, and my daughter Dalia."

Reb Cohen smiled and held up work-roughened hands. "Shalom to you all." He turned to her mother, and reverted to German. "Frau Leitner, you come from Munchen. My wife continues to cook Bavarian style."

Dalia held her breath, worried Eema would answer in German, but her mother used her limited Hebrew. "I have missed good Bavarian cooking since leaving Munchen."

Now it was her turn. She was flattered when Reb Cohen addressed her in Hebrew. "Dalia, my daughter Ruth will be happy to have a school friend of her own age if your parents decide to join us."

Hoping a quick response would indicate fluency in her new language, she asked. "Is the school large?"

"Large enough. It's an all-through school here in Hadera that we share with several kibbutzim. I've just dropped off our pupils."

He turned to her brother and again spoke in Hebrew. "Uri, I understand you are a pupil at agricultural school?"

"I am, sir."

Reb Cohen let down the cart's tailgate and hooked on a short ladder. The skirt of Eema's best frock was somewhat tight for climbing ladders, but she made no fuss, climbing up with Uri's help and seating herself on a bench. Abba hitched up his immaculate trousers before sitting next to her mother. When they were all on board, Uri pulled up the ladder and fastened the tailgate. Reb Cohen cracked his whip.

As they plodded on dirt roads through neat citrus orchards where harvesting was in progress with not an Arab worker in sight, Reb Cohen pointed at the landscape.

"This was all malaria swamps when the first settlers made Aliyah. Now it's the most densely populated area in Palestine. Bereisheet is on the fringe. We have an Arab village next to us."

As they approached Bereisheet she could see gates, guarded by a young man in uniform holding a shot gun.

Reb Cohen called out, "Shalom, Mikhail," as the young man let them in. "The government pay our young men to be part-time community police," he explained. He drove the cart down an avenue lined on each side with overhanging eucalyptus trees.

Beyond the trees, citrus groves gave way to ploughed fields, which in turn gave way to vegetable fields, sheds and byres. They reached a tee-junction. An elliptical drive lined on the outer edge by bungalows, enclosed a dusty oval, mostly bare soil with a scattering of dead grass. It contained a few sheds at one end and a large stone building at the other.

Reb Cohen halted the cart on the oval. Two young women in white blouses and blue slacks emerged from a shed, called out "Shalom" and unhitched the mules.

Uri unfastened the cart's tailgate, put the ladder in place and jumped off the cart without using it. He stretched up his hand. "Come, Eema."

Their mother hesitated.

Uri said, "You'll find it easier, Eema, if you turn around and climb facing the cart. I'll catch you if you fall."

Gingerly, their mother stretched one foot down. Her father held her hand and she climbed down. When she reached the ground she looked ruefully at her white cotton gloves.

A middle-aged, wiry woman in a crisp cotton frock came running out of one of the bungalows. "Shalom, and welcome to Bereisheet," she called in German. "Gideon, why are you keeping these people outside? They have had a long journey. They must come in and have coffee. My name is Miriam Cohen and I'm married to that man who has brought you from the station. Come in now."

As Dalia followed her mother and Miriam Cohen to the rear of the bungalow, she heard Reb Cohen say to her father and Uri, "We men wash our hands at the pump to leave the bathroom free for the ladies."

Miriam Cohen ushered her mother and herself through the kitchen door, touching the mezuzah as she did so. As with all Palestinian houses she had seen, it had an inner door of wire mesh to keep out flies. On a scrubbed pine table in the kitchen stood six china mugs, a pot of coffee, and a magnificent Black Forest gateau.

Passing through the kitchen without pausing, Miriam showed Dalia and her mother into a washroom nowhere near as luxurious as Cousin Elsa's, but it did have a flush toilet and a sink with a cold water tap.

Back in the kitchen with coffee and moist slices of cake, Miriam regaled them with the history of the previous owners of the bungalow they were about to view.

"Such a tragedy! A nice couple, Lech and Ania, founder members, so young, so full of enthusiasm. Didn't have much capital but used all they had on animal stock and sheds. Last year, we had an epidemic of scarlet fever. Everyone else except Lech pulled through. Poor Ania. She had two children, and a third on the way. We all did our best to help, but when her third child arrived, she sold everything back to the agency, and returned to Poland. More cake?"

Her mother politely declined a second helping and glared at Dalia to make sure she did the same, although Uri managed to sneak a second helping.

Reb Cohen showed them around the property they had come to look at. They followed him next door into a yard surrounded by outbuildings.

"We build our animal sheds immediately behind our houses so we can keep an eye on them. Being close to the hills we get jackals, foxes, even hyenas digging under the fence, but Lech built a fully enclosed chicken pen, complete so your hens will be safe. There's also a goat shed and byre with a hayloft for two cows."

"Cows? We have pastures?" Abba asked.

"We keep our cattle inside for the most part."

They walked beyond the animal sheds into a field filled with rows of vegetables. Narrow to start with, the field widened the further they walked. A chicken-wire fence separated it from a freshly ploughed field.

"We all grow the same main crops each year," Reb

Cohen explained. "Last season we grew wheat in our top fields. You'll still have time to sow, Albert, if you move in soon. If you delay, the Agency will do it for you and charge."

The path terminated at a locked gate in a heavy metal fence.

"Second line of defence, in case of trouble," Reb Cohen explained.

He took out a key and unlocked the gate. An orange tree almost barred their way. "Now here is where you make your profit."

"Why is the tree so close to the gate?" Dalia asked.

Reb Cohen smiled. "If someone's firing through the perimeter fence, that tree affords cover while the gate's being unlocked."

Her mother clutched her father's hand.

Dalia was surprised to see two men harvesting the oranges.

"They're Agency employees," Reb Cohen explained. "Our co-operative will market their oranges but the Agency will take the profit."

Beyond the citrus trees, tall iron posts more than twice her father's height supported thick mesh wire, angling at the top first outwards and then downwards. Beyond that was a hedge of prickly pear.

"No Arabs could get through that, Liebling," her father commented to her mother.

Reb Cohen shook his head. "Fences like that are strong, but not impregnable, as several kibbutzim found to their cost in twenty-six. Our older lads patrol the perimeter every night."

"Have you had many attacks?" her mother asked, her voice squeaking a little.

"Not attacks as such," Reb Cohen admitted, "but several attempts at theft."

"You shoot the thieves?" Uri asked.

Reb Cohen looked horrified. "Certainly not. We call in the police. We installed a telephone for our nurse, so we're not completely cut off from civilisation."

"Could we see the house now?" her mother asked.

"Of course," Reb Cohen said. "It's very basic, I'm afraid." He produced a bunch of keys. "I'll leave you to look around on your own. When you've finished, please come around to our house for lunch." He turned to Uri. "Would you like to come with me, get some experience working on a private farm?"

Uri's face lit up. "Thank you, yes." He followed Reb Cohen across the field to a gate in the low boundary fence separating them from the Cohens.

Her mother was silent as they walked back to a dilapidated wooden bungalow. Abba unlocked the back door and pushed back the inner mesh.

Beyond the animal sheds there was a small evil-smelling corrugated iron shed. Her mother opened the door and immediately turned away, her face white. Abba hurried after her and put his arm round her shoulders.

Dalia went inside. The tiny room was buzzing with flies, most hovering over a packing case on which lay a wooden lavatory seat case. Presumably, the packing case hid a bucket. She remembered what Cousin Elsa had said about the contents of a lavatory bucket being useful for fertilising vegetables and her stomach heaved.

When she caught up with her parents, her mother was examining the Mezuzah on the back doorpost. "It seems in good condition. At least it doesn't need replacing."

The room they entered was empty apart from a wooden sink. A waste pipe led from the plug hole out through the wall but there were no taps.

The bungalow had only two other rooms, the larger with two blanket-covered camp beds presumably used by the men harvesting the oranges, the other containing baskets of oranges.

Miriam Cohen came scurrying around the side of the house. "What do you think?"

Her mother shuddered but made no reply.

"There's a lot to be done," her father replied slowly, "but I have the capital and the know-how."

"Good. I've just come to say dinner's ready."

Reb Cohen and Uri were already in the Cohen's savoury smelling kitchen. Dalia raised her eyebrows. She hadn't seen Uri wearing a yarmulke since his Bar Mitzvah. Her father also pulled a yarmulke out of his pocket and placed it on the back of his head before Reb Cohen gave the pre-meal blessing. Her mother looked more cheerful when Miriam dished out hearty helpings of a typical Bavarian meal—liver dumplings, sauerkraut and mashed potatoes.

Her father asked many questions during the meal. What had Reb Cohen paid for his electricity generator and septic tank? Was it possible to buy clay mud for cob walls? How much should he pay workmen?

After the meal, Miriam shooed them into a sitting room that doubled as Reb Cohen's study. While the grown-ups and Uri talked about the price of wheat and grapes, and of this year's first citrus shipment that had sold so badly because of pale skins, Dalia inspected the books lining the walls, mostly theology books written in German, Hebrew, French, and Arabic but interspersed with farming manuals also in a variety of languages.

More interesting were the framed photographs on the mantelpiece. In one, Reb Cohen and a boy with an impish face stood in front of a tractor. In another, a girl with a smooth, placid face and a single thick plait of fair hair, bottle-fed a lamb.

Miriam Cohen saw Dalia looking at the photos. "Those are my children. Josh has another two years to go at university but Ruth is the same age as you, Dalia. A pity you have to leave before she comes home."

Half-an-hour later, while her mother stayed to help Miriam with the dishes, Dalia joined her father and Uri in a conducted tour of the moshav.

"Think of Bereisheet as a giant bagel divided into segments," Reb Cohen said as they walked out of the front door. "The houses and the segments of land behind each are all privately owned. We work our farms individually but plan and market as a co-operative." He pointed to the sheds on the central oval. "Those are all jointly owned and include storage barns, stables, and a small general store. The large building at the other end is a synagogue, which serves as a fortress, kindergarten and community hall.

"Every family contributes to purchasing communal items such as tractors and the mules. Eventually, we hope to have our own primary school, a purpose-built community centre, a hospital, and even specialist shops."

They returned to the Cohen's house for a last cup of coffee before walking to the bus stop outside the settlement gates.

Dalia was anxious to find out what her parents thought about Bereisheet, but they occupied themselves with finding out how Uri was getting on at school.

Uri made his farewell when their bus came into sight and he started hitching back to school. "See you all at Hanukkah."

The bus to Hadera was crowded. They had to stand all the way, not conducive to conversation. The station platform too was crowded, and she didn't know who would be listening. However, in an empty first class compartment she burst out. "Are we going to live in Bereisheet?"

Her mother turned to her father. "I'm sorry, Albert. I know Elsa and Moshe found Rehovot just as primitive when they first came out, but they were younger. I can't cope without a bathroom."

"I wouldn't expect you to, Liebling," Abba said, putting his arms round her. "I felt so sorry for you today, but if the house had been different, would you be able to live in Bereisheet?"

"Oh, yes. Miriam was saying they have a wonderful choir and women are allowed to join it. They have a sewing group and a library. The school sounds fine for Dalia, too."

"Those are the important things, Trudi," her father said. "I can do up the house before you move in so long as you and Dalia don't mind staying on at Rehovot for a few extra weeks. We'll use our South African investments to build a new kitchen and bathroom and, thanks to the Transfer Finance agreement, we can use our German capital to install a sewage system and an electric generator. We'll draw up a set of rough plans together tonight and you can take your time choosing kitchen and bathroom equipment while I get the building done in Bereisheet."

Her mother burst into tears. "Thank goodness I'm married to an architect, and a man who understands finance."

"No, Trudi, I'm no longer an architect. You're married to a farmer, and I'm married to a farmer's wife. We made a promise to Uri, remember, to help create a homeland, dunam by dunam, and goat by goat."

Dalia sank back into her seat, glad that her future was settled. It was just as well she was being given extra time to get her Hebrew up to scratch before she started school, but she would miss her father.

Chapter 5

The day after they visited Bereisheet, the drought broke with a deluge of rain, which continued for weeks. Lorries were unable to get through. Oranges for export went bad. Every farmer in Rehovot was frantic with worry. Work on their own house at Bereisheet was held up because building material couldn't get through.

Cooped up in a house full of stressed adults, Dalia would have gone crazy if it hadn't been for the anticipation of the Hanukkah and all the shifting of furniture and improvisation of sleeping arrangements that entailed.

Her father, along with Uri, Shimon, Cousin Elsa's daughter, Shayna, her husband Shlomo and little Hadassah had all promised to be in Rehovot for the first two days of the festival, and despite road conditions, they made it!

The first evening of Hanukkah was extra special. Uncle Moshe, who never went to synagogue, chanted the traditional Hanukkah prayers while she held her menorah as she stood between Uri and Shimon, her nostrils revelling in the aroma of traditional potato fritters and barley soup.

Despite dark clouds and heavy rain, Dalia woke on the second day excited at the prospect of spending a whole day in Shimon's company. Uri had agreed she could work alongside him and Shimon. Today she would impress Shimon with her new orange-picking skills.

She almost danced into the kitchen to help Cousin Elsa prepare breakfast and eagerly waited for Shimon and Uri to put in an appearance after they had finished milking, but when Uri came in with Uncle Moshe, there was no sign of Shimon.

"Where's my son?" Cousin Elsa asked.

"He received a note from his girlfriend," Uncle Moshe said. "Her father's sprained his ankle. She's asked Shimon to help out."

Shimon had a girlfriend? Dalia hugged her stomach before walking over to the sink to get a drink so no one would see how close she was to tears.

"Which girlfriend is that?" Cousin Elsa asked.

"The eldest Salomon girl."

"Oh, her! Deigned to visit her family for Hanukkah, has she? Didn't think we'd need our Shimon here?"

Uncle Moshe opened out his hands. "Elsa, David Salomon needs help more than we do. Dalia is perfectly capable of showing her brother how to pick oranges."

Even Uncle Moshe's tribute to her harvesting skills couldn't cure a wounded heart. Dalia spent a miserable morning working alongside Uri.

"Why so miserable, sis?" Uri asked.

She gave the cold and rain as an excuse.

Uri scoffed. "Farmers have to get used to that."

She revived when Shimon returned in the early afternoon but her relief was short-lived. He had only come back to change out of mud-covered work clothes and carry Uri off on his motorbike, ostensibly to return him to school but, in reality, she suspected, to go off to a wild party with that horrible Salomon girl.

The sky cleared. She accompanied her parents on a pre-supper stroll around the settlement. Determined not to spoil precious time with her father by brooding over Shimon's absence, she did her best to contribute to the conversation. "Uncle Moshe says oranges are Palestine's most profitable crop. I wish our orange groves at Bereisheet were bigger."

Her mother glanced at her father. "I'm glad to hear you say that, Dalia, because we're giving you a special Hanukkah present."

She looked up in excitement. Was it an orange tree or her very own goat?

Her father's response couldn't have stunned her more if they had presented her with a whole herd of goats. "We've bought you an orange grove further up the coast near Haifa."

She owned an orange grove! She tugged a plait, and composed her face to that of a responsible landowner. Initial excitement changed to fear. "I don't want to live on my own."

Her mother reassured her. "It's all right, Dalia. You don't

have to live there, not until you're grown up. We've arranged for the current manager to stay on."

"Are you buying Uri an orange grove too?"

"We don't need to," her father said. "When Germany comes to its senses, and Uri has finished his agricultural training, your mother and I will return home and Uri will take over the Bereisheet holding. If you, too, decide to stay on in Palestine, we want to make sure you have a home of your own."

Dalia was horrified. "I don't want to stay in Palestine if you're not going to be here."

Her mother smiled. "I suspect when you're older you might change your mind. Anyway, when your father retires we'll spend winter here, so we're looking at a vineyard for sale in Tiberius, where we can build a small bungalow. It will be useful when your grandparents visit. Between whiles, we can let it out as a holiday home."

"Returning to the subject of your birthday present," her father said. "Next week, I'm taking you with me to close the deal at al-Tira."

* * * *

In the taxi on the way to al-Tira, a lawyer and her father talked in German about business. She could tell this lawyer was Arabic because he wore a red fez instead of a proper hat.

When they arrived, she stood by the taxi in front of a stone-slabbed veranda attached to a primitive stone bungalow, feeling out of place and insignificant. She hoped her father would renovate this unprepossessing building before she grew up.

People were sitting on the veranda as if at a cafe. A tall, middle-aged Arab in a brown striped suit and red fez and an elderly stout gentleman wearing an expensive looking grey chequered suit and fez had small cups of coffee and glasses of water in front of them. On the other side of the veranda, drinking cloudy lemonade, a girl about her own age, French by the look of her elegant frock and patent leather shoes, accompanied a large, middle-aged Arab woman in an embroidered blue thob.

The stout gentleman came over to speak and made a long speech in, presumably, Arabic. Her father's lawyer interpreted it into flowery Hebrew.

The stout man beckoned over the French girl. She moved across the veranda in a dignified almost grown up way.

The lawyer said in Hebrew. "Dalia, please meet Maftur al-Zeid, the great granddaughter of the present owner and this gentleman's grandniece. She would like you to have lemonade with her."

So this girl, Maftur, was not French but she had a friendly smile. Was the woman in a thob her grandmother?

"I will be honoured," Maftur said in English, "if you would sit with me."

Dalia's English might be better than her brother's but she wasn't sure she could carry on talking English all morning. French was her favourite foreign language. Her French teacher in Munchen had been kind even when other teachers were being horrid. "Est-ce que vous parlez Francais?" she asked hopefully.

Maftur gave a delighted smile and answered in beautiful French although rather too fast for her comfort.

"Mais oui. My mother and I speak French all the time."

"I speak French better than English, but not as good as you do," Dalia replied, ashamed her French was so hesitant.

An Arab woman in a grey thob came over and poured her a glass of lemonade.

"Dalia," Maftur said, "may I introduce your manager's wife, Umm Ibrahim."

Dalia came out with her one Arabic phrase. "Salam wa aleikum."

The woman's face lit up. "Wa aleikum ah salam."

Maftur indicated the Arab wearing the keffiyah. "That is your manager. This citrus grove is to be your dowry, yes?"

Dalia felt uncomfortable with that description. "Dowry? No. My father wants me to have a home of my own when I grow up."

Maftur drew her eyebrows together. "You will run this orchard yourself?"

"Only when the manager chooses to retire. That is part of the agreement."

The answer seemed to please Maftur, but she wished her father hadn't accepted that condition. She didn't want Uri knowing she had an Arab manager.

Maftur introduced the woman beside her. "This is Zubaiyda. She used to be my nurse."

Umm Ibrahim went into the house and came back with two greaseproof bags, two small bottles of lemonade, and two straws.

"For our picnic," Maftur explained. She looked at her watch. "We have one hour. I will show you your orchard."

They wandered up a muddy path, but today, instead of rain, blue sky appeared between the rows of trees. Open orange blossom exuded perfume.

They came upon a group of workers on ladders, picking oranges which they placed in a wicker basket balanced on the head of a woman standing with hands clasped in front of her, her head tilted slightly to the left to offset the basket's tilt. When the basket was full, one man climbed down his ladder, took the basket from the head of the living statue, and replaced it with an empty one. For some reason, it reminded her of Christine standing with that dreadful poster round her neck on her last day at school. Jewish workers wouldn't treat a woman like that. She didn't want Arabs in her citrus orchard.

She followed Maftur until they came to a couple of benches and a table. They sat on one of the benches to eat sticky sweet baklava filled with almonds.

"What do you think of your grove?" Maftur asked.

"It's beautiful and looks well cared for but I didn't like the way the workers were treating that woman. I shall speak to my father about it and see if he can get other labour."

Maftur gave her a smile. "I'm so glad. I hadn't realised my great-grandfather employed migrants. I'm sure the manager will be pleased if your father insists on employing Palestinians. Hauranis are hard workers but cause trouble wherever they go."

Dalia suspected that by 'Palestinians' Maftur didn't mean Sabras.

Maftur looked around with a satisfied air. "I've always wanted to picnic in an orange grove," she continued, "and now I've done it."

"When I'm grown up, I'll invite you to a summer picnic here," Dalia promised.

* * * *

Dalia's mother said it was her four-poster bed she missed the most. Three generations of her family had been born in that bed. How could the Nazis allow them to use their German capital to buy as much agricultural and kitchen machinery as they wished, yet refuse to let her bring over a bed her family had owned for seventy years?

Cousin Elsa was unsympathetic. "You want to count yourself lucky, my girl. Jews leaving Germany for any other country than Palestine have to forfeit all their money as well as their goods."

Dalia accompanied her mother and Cousin Elsa when they went to replace basic items of furniture from a department store in Tel Aviv, a fast growing Jewish suburb of Jaffa.

While walking to Tel Aviv from Jaffa bus station they passed a second-hand shop displaying a bed almost identical to her mother's old one. On impulse, her mother went inside and bought it, shocking Cousin Elsa by paying the asking price. Her mother also bought a set of rush chairs and a pine kitchen table that could have dropped out of a Van Gough painting. They would, she said, give her new kitchen a real farmhouse feel and would contrast happily with the ultra-modern kitchen equipment coming from Germany.

Before leaving, her mother added ceramic mugs, a Dresden dinner service, and copper pans, arranging to have everything delivered to Bereisheet on the day they left Rehovot.

Cousin Elsa told everyone in Rehovot that dear Trudi was only playing at being a farmer's wife and it wouldn't be long before she regretted not buying something more practical.

On a hot day in April, Dalia and her mother left Rehovot. In a taxi, getting stuffier and warmer by the minute, consumed by her own anxieties, Dalia only half-listened to her mother harping on about the furniture, worrying that her father wouldn't know where to place it if it arrived before they did.

She was dreading starting school the next day, consumed by year-old memories of the afternoon when she had first felt an outsider.

It had started so happily. She had left the classroom after school, brandishing her essay with its attached first prize certificate, the heels of her high-laced school boots tapping out a dance on stone tiles of the corridor, her thick plaits bouncing against the back of her lime green jersey dress, her best friend Gertrud shouting, "You did it, Dalia!"

Then Eva's sneering voice in the cloakroom, "At least mine was all my own work."

Everyone turned to stare. Eva pressed on. "Don't you lot ever listen to the wireless? All Jews cheat. Gertrud, does your father know you're friends with a Jew?"

Everyone shuffled their feet, staring at the ground. Gertrude made no reply. Eva swept past, smirking. Dalia bolted indoors to hide shameful tears, waiting until everyone had gone.

She caught the tram alone, staring out of the window, streets lined with small shops, Brownshirts holding up banners. Gertrud's father was with them.

"Don't buy goods from a Jewish Shop. All Jews Cheat."

Banners writhed, turning into blood-red snakes marked with dark swastikas, forked tongues licking out towards her.

She heard her mother's voice, "Wake up, Dalia! Here, take my handkerchief. Your forehead's covered in sweat."

The taxi driver pulled up behind a pantechnicon. Looking out, Dalia saw the front door of their new house completely blocked by the frame of her mother's bed. Her father and two removal men stood by it, arguing.

While her mother paid the taxi driver, her father came over. "Trudi," he burst out with no preliminary greetings, "that bed won't fit through any door. I'll have to saw it in half."

"No," her mother wailed, "it's an antique."

"We're sleeping in it, not selling it," her father snapped. "I'll put it together again once it's inside."

Dalia flinched. It wasn't like Abba to be so irritable. She felt happier when her father's tone softened.

"You won't be able to tell the difference, Liebling, once the bed's made up. Go in and admire your new kitchen."

Her mother ran around the side, biting her lip. Dalia chased after her. As her mother opened the doors, a strong smell of coffee wafted from the kitchen.

Her mother put her fingers to the mezuzah on the doorpost before kissing them and peeking inside. "It's magnificent," she breathed.

Dalia peered over her shoulder. A whiff of fresh baking mingled with the aroma of coffee.

The new kitchen was at least twice the size of the old one. A solid fuel stove sat next to a small electric one where steam spurted from beneath the lid of a pulsating coffee percolator. Blue checked curtains hung from a large kitchen window.

Her mother called "Shalom" and they stepped inside.

Taps above a large ceramic sink indicated they now had running water, and by it, attached to the wall, was an electric water heater. Next to the sink stood a Kelvinator refrigerator just like Cousin Elsa's. A cloth matching the curtains covered the pine table. On it stood the ceramic mugs her mother had purchased and a plate of what looked like Bavarian sugar cookies.

"Shalom," a voice answered as the door on the other side of the kitchen opened. "I was just taking coffee to the men," Miriam Cohen said as she walked in. "What do you think of your kitchen?"

Her mother shook her head in wonder. "It's even better than I had hoped. I can't believe you've made up the curtains and tablecloth. I was intending to do that once I had set up my new sewing machine."

"They didn't take long," Miriam said. "I thought it would be a nice surprise. You'll want to use the bathroom before coffee. You'll be impressed. Your Albert has done a wonderful job."

They went out into the lobby. Dalia opened the front door and peered out. Her father and Reb Cohen were examining the bed frame now sawn in two, while holding mugs of coffee. The pantechnicon had left.

The new bathroom that lay beyond the bedrooms was similar to Cousin Elsa's. Her mother looked delighted.

Back in the kitchen, they had hardly picked up their coffee and bitten into a crisp cookie when another voice called, "Shalom," and a tall, slim woman, probably in her mid-twenties, entered the kitchen. Her dark hair was smooth, and cut into a bob two inches above her shoulders. She carried a loaf of bread.

Dalia had got used to people in rural Palestine just shouting 'Shalom' and walking into a house without waiting to be invited, but she could tell her mother found it disconcerting to have it happening in her own home.

"Thelma Goldstein," Miriam Cohen said. "I wondered where you'd got to."

Thelma Goldstein held out her hand. "Frau Leitner, I'm delighted to meet you. I've brought you a loaf." Thelma Goldstein's Hebrew accent was less guttural than Miriam Cohen's. "I'm your neighbour on the other side."

Her mother shook Thelma's hand. "I'm Trudi Leitner, Thelma Goldstein, and this is my daughter Dalia."

"Pleased to meet you, Dalia. Just call me Thelma. We don't stand on ceremony around here."

"That goes for me too," Miriam Cohen said. "Where's Johnny, Thelma?"

"Outside the back door in his push-chair. He's asleep, so I get a break."

She took an empty chair and Miriam pushed over a mug of coffee and the plate of cookies.

"Trudi, I hope your family can come over for a spot of

dinner at one o'clock, although I'm sure you are dying to use your magnificent kitchen." She looked around in admiration. "You Germans make such wonderful kitchen machinery. When we've got our small holding in profit, I will consult you and Miriam before planning my new kitchen."

"Your crops are doing just fine this year, Thelma," Miriam said, "and you've got all that extra money from Jack wiring this house. Jack's a qualified electrician, Trudi, very useful. Thelma and Jack have been with us for just over two years. Before that they lived in Manchester in England. They honeymooned in Palestine four years ago, and vowed to make Aliyah as soon as they could afford it."

"Do you like it here, still, Thelma?" Dalia asked.

"Oh, yes, everyone's so kind, and with a wonderful nurse on site I know Johnny's safe."

"Was he born here?"

"Yes, a proper little Sabra."

As they drank coffee and ate cookies which tasted like the ones Cook had baked back in Munchen, Dalia realised her mother was concentrating on the noises from the inner part of the house, rather than the stream of information pouring from Miriam. Her mother, however, succeeded in staying still and polite until Miriam and Thelma left, then she hurried to the larger of the two bedrooms. Dalia followed.

Her mother pushed against the bedroom door but it struck something before it was fully open.

Looking over her mother's shoulder, Dalia saw Reb Cohen squashed against the far wall holding two halves of sawn bed-frame together, while her father screwed short slats of pinewood across them. She retreated into her own even smaller room, almost filled by a single bed. At its foot, there was just space for a very small pine table and a bentwood chair. She stared in disbelief. The table held her Rheinmetall Super typewriter! How had her parents managed to smuggle it from Germany?

She ran to her parents' bedroom. Her mother had somehow managed to squeeze inside.

"My typewriter! Thank you! Thank you!" she shouted

from the doorway. "How did you get it here?"

Her parents exchanged amused looks.

"Don't ask questions, Liebling," her mother said.

If it hadn't been a physical impossibility, she would have run into the room and hugged them both.

Chapter 6

That first afternoon in Bereisheet, Dalia's father took her and her mother on a conducted tour of the small holding. He showed off their maize, already six inches tall.

They were on their way to the orange grove when Dalia heard the gate between their field and the Cohens' clang and turned to look. A blonde girl, the same height as herself, but sturdier, was running towards them.

"Shalom, Ruth," her father called. "Back from school already? It must be later than we thought."

"Shalom, Albert. I've come to ask if your Dalia would like to visit." The girl skidded to a halt, clasped her chin in dismay, obviously remembering her manners. "Shalom, Trudi Leitner. I hope you like your new home." She turned and gave Dalia a radiant smile. "Dalia, I have so been looking forward to you coming. I could hardly concentrate at school all day. Would you like to come over and have a glass of lemonade?"

As Dalia hesitated, her mother answered for her. "Ruth, thank you. That will be lovely. Dalia, run along now. I'll make sure your school clothes are ironed ready for the morning. If you're not back by supper, I'll collect you."

Dalia followed Ruth to the Cohens' house. Ruth obviously wanted to be friends but…? Memories of Gertrud and her fits of crying and apologies during that last summer term in Munich flooded her mind. Would this daughter of a rabbi also be torn between two loyalties when she discovered Dalia's family weren't all that religious?

"My mother says I should tell you about our school," Ruth said.

Dalia didn't want to be told. She didn't want to think about school. She was saved from having to reply, however, by a large black and white cat that stalked out of the Cohens' cowshed and brushed against the back of Ruth's legs.

Ruth bent down and picked it up. "This is Blitz. Lightning fast at catching mice. Come on, Blitz. I'll get your milk."

Dalia followed Ruth into the kitchen. At their 'shaloms', Miriam Cohen looked up from the saucepan she was stirring.

"Shalom, Dalia. Ruth, there's lemonade in the icebox and if you're intending to give that cat milk put the saucer outside. There's cookies in the tin, but don't eat too many or you won't want supper."

Dalia watched, feeling uneasy while Ruth saw to the cat, filled a jug with lemonade and placed cookies on a plate.

"We'll go to my bedroom," Ruth said. "We can talk in peace there."

Ruth's bedroom was larger than Dalia's. A floral bedspread matched ruffled curtains, a dressing table supported a threefold mirror, and there was still space for a wardrobe, desk, chair, and small bookcase. A rag rug with colours matching the curtains lay on a quarry tiled floor. It was a room that cried out for pictures of flowers and trees. Instead, posters on how to treat burns, use splints and tie bandages decorated the walls. Books on first-aid and home-nursing jostled with bound copies of a Hebrew children's magazine.

Ruth set the tray on the desk and pulled out the chair. "Which do you want—chair or bed?"

Since Dalia didn't know the correct etiquette for sitting on a bed, she opted for the chair and observed the way Ruth jumped onto the bed and sat on it cross-legged.

"The first thing you need to know about school," Ruth began, "is that it's at Hadera, so grownups have to take it in turn to drive us there. You'll like it at our school. The girls from other moshavim are friendly and our teacher's nice. I've asked her if you can have a desk next to me, and she said yes."

Dalia felt torn between gratitude and anxiety. Ruth was forcing her into a best friend situation which would probably end badly.

Ruth continued. "A new school will open at Pardes Hannah soon. Our fathers have already registered us. It's much nearer than the one in Hadera, so we'll be able to cycle."

"Do you know anything about it?

"It's not just an agricultural school. It will have *Bagrut* classes in other subjects."

"What's *Bagrut*?"

"Exams you take when you're sixteen or older. The lowest levels allow you to leave school, the highest let you into university."

Dalia's eyes drifted to the magazines on Ruth's bookshelves. "Have you read all those?"

"I have. You may borrow them if you like."

Dalia was glad she had come.

That night, in bed, she read stories from Ruth's magazines until her mother came in and switched off her light. "You've school in the morning, remember."

She'd been desperately trying not to remember. Past events played repeatedly in her mind as if in a series of horror cartoons.

Her teacher breaking the news that she couldn't take up her scholarship to senior school.

Her agonised wail. "Why not?"

Frau Krenz's shame-faced answer. "They're not admitting Jews this year."

Leaving the classroom, racing to the tram stop, Christine not there to meet her. Gertrud's father, grasping Christine's arms. Around Christine's neck a placard, *I am a sow. I only work for Jews.*

Eva and her friends hurling insults. No sign of Gertrud.

Christine's neck expanded and covered a black sky but the figure on the crucifix was Christine. Above her head a golden scroll, *I am a sow. I only work for Jews.*

"Help us. Help us!"

"Dalia, wake up."

She opened her eyes.

"You've been having nightmares again," her mother said, "but we're safe here in Bereisheet now."

When Dalia woke next it was to the smell of baking pretzels, but the thought of school lay too heavy on her stomach for her to appreciate food. A cold shower brought her a little more to life. She dressed, went into the kitchen, drained a glass of orange juice and toyed with pretzels and cheese while her parents discussed their livestock plans.

Ruth arrived.

Dalia picked up her lunch box, her satchel, and her PE bag, kissed her parents goodbye and attempted a cheerful smile as she followed Ruth to the mule wagon.

* * * *

The mule wagon was filled with boys and girls between the ages of six and fourteen.

When they arrived at the single storeyed school, the boys raced off to join informal games of football already in progress in the bare dirt playground. The girls wandered straight into their classrooms.

Ruth showed her to her desk before introducing her to friends in the same side of the classroom. Another set of girls congregated on the other side. The two groups ignored each other.

A bell rang outside and, to Dalia's consternation, boys bounded in, scuffling and shouting. She hadn't expected a co-educational class. Ruth's friends made a great show of ignoring the boys, but girls at the other end of the room turned to smile or wave.

The teacher entered. Everyone stood up straight behind their desks. Dalia copied the others, grateful to Ruth that she wasn't standing at the front waiting for the teacher to allocate her a desk. That ordeal was bad enough in an all-girls' class, but to have boys staring at her too, she wouldn't have known where to look.

After everyone returned her 'shalom', the teacher called the register. Dalia gritted her teeth. Would she have the courage to bring her presence to the attention of the teacher? But her name was called, already slotted into its correct alphabetical position, so she was able to reply "Present, Line Löwenstein," as the others had done.

The teacher looked up and smiled. "Welcome to Year Eight, Dalia Leitner," and moved on.

At break, she played hopscotch with Ruth and her friends

at one end of the dirt yard. The other girls from their class played skipping games at the other end of the yard with girls from another class. In the centre, the boys resumed their football.

She asked Ruth about the other girls in the cart on the way home.

"They're kibbutzniks," Ruth said. "They think they're better than the rest of us, but they aren't. They don't believe in the Bible and their parents keep getting divorced."

Dalia felt shocked. She had never met anyone before who didn't believe in the Bible. Even Nazis believed in the Bible, although they also believed in the false bit Christians had added on.

For the next few months, she found schoolwork hard. A teacher gave her extra lessons in Arabic and extra homework so she could catch up.

She and Ruth did as much of their homework as possible in the jolting mule cart taking them home from school. However, while it was just possible to make jerky notes in pencil in rough books, all homework involving neat handwriting had to be fitted around feeding hens, milking the nanny goat, and weeding vegetables. One way or another she and Ruth organised things so they could work together in Ruth's bedroom.

Gradually, Dalia began to get into the swing of her new life. The event that most helped change her outlook from negative shame at being German to positive pride in being a Palestinian Jew was the 1935 Maccabiah Games.

Maccabiah fever swept through the school from the beginning of January. Even the teachers gave priority to games and PE lessons. Pupils with relatives participating in the qualifying rounds held their heads high. Pupils with relatives selected to take part in the finals basked in reflected glory but the ten pupils, who had been selected to take part in the callisthenics display on the final day, were the ultimate heroes.

Dalia enjoyed her share of glory when Cousin Elsa wrote boasting that her Shimon was participating as a guest in the Bulgarian motorcycling display. Even kibbutzim girls came up to talk to her when she claimed Shimon Mabovitch as her cousin. At last she felt an insider and almost a Sabra.

On the final day of the games, the community at Bereisheet went en masse to Tel Aviv in two hired charabancs. They were lucky. In contrast to the dark skies that had graced the earlier days, the sun shone warmly in a sky the blue of a starling's egg. When they reached Tel Aviv, they found every shop, firm, home, radiator cap and horse harness displaying Zionist colours. Flags of the fifty nations taking part hung from electric standards but there were no swastikas. At the opening day parade the German contingent had been the only one to march without a flag.

Dalia, her parents, and the Cohens left the charabanc to meet up with Uri, Cousin Elsa and Uncle Moshe at Shayna's flat before walking down to the Levant Fair Ground.

As they stood on the pavement opposite Shayna's flat waiting for the traffic to move on before crossing the road, they heard music growing steadily louder and, from a side street, came a strangely dressed all-male band, marching jauntily and banging drums and tooting horns. The men wore black stockings, white skirts and blouses topped by elaborately embroidered thigh-length red jerkins. Equally elaborate embroidery decorated their black boots. Behind them trailed a Tel Avivim crowd of all ages, dancing and waving their arms.

Through a gap between two coaches, Dalia saw Shimon wearing hefty leather boots, goggles, and a leather jacket rather smarter than the one he had worn in Haifa. He darted out of the entrance to Shayna's flat, and joined the crowd following the band.

"You'd have thought that young man would have been at the stadium by now, instead of chasing bands," her mother said, staring after him.

When they had eventually managed to dodge their way through the heavy traffic, they found Uri already in Shayna's dining room drinking coffee. Shimon, he told them, had given him a lift from school.

"That was good of him seeing it's off his route from Haifa," her father commented.

"He had business at the kibbutz," Uri explained.

"He has business at too many Kibbutzim," Cousin Elsa snapped as she pushed in a trolley bearing cups, plates and an extra-large black forest gateau. "We don't pay good money to send him to the Technion to have him racing around the countryside visiting all his girlfriends."

Behind Cousin Elsa, a heavily pregnant Shayna held little Hadassah's hand.

"What was the band that passed your door just now?" Dalia asked.

"Bulgarians. Their team haven't won a single point in the games, but their band has made their contingent the most popular here. We've so many Bulgarians in Tel Aviv, and they follow that band everywhere, begging them to stay in Palestine."

"Well, they can't," Cousin Shlomo said. "Every foreign games participant had to promise they would leave Palestine before their visas expired."

"There are more important things than broken promises," Uri said.

Everyone, except her father, looked at him in horror.

Her father spoke up. "I suspect what my son means is that if someone's life is at risk a promise can be disregarded."

"But no Bulgarians can claim their lives are at risk by returning home," Shlomo stated.

Two hours later Dalia was with Ruth and Werner amongst the fifty thousand people gathered in the fairground built on sand dunes between the sea and the River Yarkon. The beat of surf on the nearby beach served as a background to the noise of the crowd.

She dutifully cheered the Maccabiah exercises and subsequent athletic finals, waiting impatiently until at last the motorbikes roared on with Shimon amongst them. Although he didn't take part in the acrobatic show pieces, he raced through rings of fire with the best of them.

Dalia cheered herself hoarse.

Highlighted by the rays of the setting sun, the British High Commissioner gave out the prizes and congratulated all the competitors on their sporting spirit.

Night snuffed out the last remnants of light. Illuminated by dramatic flares, the national contingents marched by the podium. Lord Melchett, the Maccabiah president, pinned a ribbon on each standard and appealed to all non-Palestinian athletes to show the spirit of the Maccabiah movement by honouring their oaths to return home.

In the event, many delegates remained as illegal immigrants but the Bulgarians were the prime offenders. None returned to Sofia. Dalia was certain that Shimon had organised their disappearance.

Chapter 7

At the beginning of the summer holidays Dalia and Ruth received their bikes and decided to make use of their new-found independence by joining a Youth Club in Pardes Hanna. Dalia fancied *Hashomer Hatzair*, partly because she and Uri had both belonged when they lived in Munchen and partly because membership led to a chance to join Haganah at the age of fifteen.

Ruth shook her head. "HH is a Commy club for kibbutzniks. I fancy Scouts."

"My parents wouldn't have let me and Uri join a Commy club."

"It might have been different in Germany."

"I'll write to Uri and ask him about the club in Pardes Hannah."

Uri replied by return of post. "Tell Ruth HH's Socialism is Bible-based, nothing to do with Marx."

"You're really set on joining HH, aren't you?" Ruth said.

Dalia bit her lip. "I don't want to break friends with you, Ruth, and scouting sounds fun, but I want to join Haganah when I'm fifteen."

Ruth took a deep breath. "All right. I'll ask my father if I can join."

Dalia felt a wave of relief wash through her. "I'm so lucky to have you as a friend."

Against Ruth's expectations, Reb Cohen had no objections to Ruth joining *Hashomer Hatzair*. His only stipulation was that she and Dalia cycle to and from the club together.

Once enrolled, they discovered, as Ruth had expected, that Kibbutzniks heavily outnumbered Moshavniks. However, after mixing with Kibbutzniks on rambles, judo, rock climbing, and the washing up rota, they discovered, to their surprise, that not all kibbutzniks were atheistic, out-of-control political zealots. By the end of their first camp they had made friends with two kibbutzniks, Leah and Esther.

Leah was serious, short and sturdy. Esther was flighty, tall and slim, but nevertheless the pair had been friends almost from birth. Dalia envied them. They both had parents who took it for granted that their children would grow up to be pioneer farmers. Dalia's mother, on the other hand, expected her to take a degree at Hebrew University, marry a graduate, and settle down on her citrus grove in al-Tira to produce literary novels and a clutch of grandchildren.

By the time school re-opened for the autumn term it was clear to everyone in the region that the citrus harvest was going to be poor that winter. After the losses of the previous year, everyone in Bereisheet feared the worst. To Dalia's dismay her father started talking about moving to Tel Aviv and starting an architecture practice. Her mother was all for it. They discovered, however, that although the crop was poor, what fruit they picked fetched better prices than before, and this year there were no transport delays because the government had surfaced the coastal road.

Since he had done better than expected, Dalia's father, once harvest was over, hired unemployed Jewish labourers to enlarge their existing bedrooms and add a proper bedroom for Uri whenever he came home, which wasn't as often as they would have liked since he now had a steady kibbutznik girlfriend.

Soon Dalia revelled in a room with space for wardrobes, bookshelves, and a larger desk. She and Ruth now divided their homework time equally between their two houses and often invited Esther and Leah to join them in sleepovers.

Her father also built three seaside type chalets at al-Tira, and for a week of each summer vacation, her mother took her and up to four of her friends there for a holiday. Umm Ibrahim cooked their breakfasts and evening meals, leaving them free to walk with packed lunches to nearby small deserted beaches, or to go on mountain rambles reminiscent of those the family had enjoyed in the pine forests of Bavaria. Their one regret was that their grandparents couldn't get a permit to join them for a winter holiday as they had hoped. They didn't have time for more than one holiday so they didn't make use of the bungalow in Tiberius, but it brought in a steady income as a holiday let and the grapes there made a small profit too.

Back in Bereisheet, Dalia pursued the club's ideal to create a fertile, independent Israel from swamp and desert. While she milked cows at dawn, fed chickens before breakfast, sorted eggs before cycling to school, and weeded vegetables in the evenings, she knew she was not just doing family chores but preparing herself for life on a pioneering kibbutz.

Once a week, HH organised rifle practice in a soundproofed section of the enormous basement area beneath the school, off bounds to all pupils during the school day.

Without telling her parents, and swearing Ruth to secrecy, Dalia, along with Esther and Leah, persuaded eleven other HH members to join them in creating their own youth brigade dedicated to setting up a kibbutz in the wilderness. They agreed to prepare themselves by going on to agricultural college as soon as they had passed their lower level *Bagrut* exams.

By Passover, however, Dalia realised all her plans to switch to agricultural college at the end of the academic year would go for nothing if she allowed her parents to dictate the subjects she took for lower level *Bagrut*. She considered digging in her heels and refusing to follow her parents' advice but realised they held the winning cards. She had to have their permission before applying for agricultural college. She consulted the HH leader on alternative routes into pioneering farming and discovered the Hebrew University offered degree courses in agriculture for people who stayed on at school to take upper level *Bagrut*. These courses, the HH leader told her, would be useful for people intending to become brigade leaders. She told Leah and Esther about them and told them what she was intending to do. They, in turn, took it to their kibbutz, who promised to support them. The rest of the brigade, less academically inclined, decided to stick with agricultural college, but agreed it would be useful to have three graduate members responsible for administration when eventually they founded their own kibbutz. They insisted on adding vocational typing and book-keeping to higher level

Bagrut subjects. They also recommended that Dalia, already fluent in English thanks to Thelma Goldstein's tuition, take English as a main *Bagrut* subject since it would be useful when dealing with government agencies.

Dalia left the brigade meeting euphoric. She would have no difficulty in convincing her mother qualifications in typing, book-keeping, and English were useful assets for both an author and the owner of a citrus grove.

Now she used her English and secretarial subjects as an excuse to type up stories about tough but beautiful heroines who fell in love with Haganah commanders, (all bearing a remarkable resemblance to Shimon Mabovitch). These heroines played no passive role, but rode out into the wilderness to rescue their beloved when kidnapped by notorious gangs such as the Black Hand Gang led by Sheikh Izzedin al Qassan Sheik. The stories had to change a little when the police killed the real Sheikh Izzedin al Qassan Sheik and most of his followers in the autumn of 1935, but they remained the same in essence, although the balance shifted from adventure to romance as her body rhythms changed.

After one HH meeting she was startled when Leah's brother asked her out on a date to see 'Captain Blood' at the weekly bioscope show. She was not particularly attracted to Reuben, nor any other boys at school, come to that. They were all so immature compared to Shimon Mabovitch. However, she was flattered to be asked and wanted practical experience of romance. She told Ruth she was going on a date and tentatively brought up the subject of sexual behaviour, a subject they usually avoided when alone together.

"Ruth, how far would you let a boy go when out on a date, if you liked him?"

Ruth's response was firm. "Just a kiss on the lips at the beginning, and not much more than that, even if I continued going out with the same boy for a long time. I'm saving myself for my wedding day."

Dalia didn't want to risk Ruth's disapproval, so determined not to let any boy do anything he could boast about afterwards. It was easy to keep her resolve on that first date. Reuben seemed even more nervous than she was when he pecked her cheek before she mounted her bicycle to go home.

During the following months, however, she went out with several more boys and found it increasingly difficult to ward off the overtures of the more confident, her randy body almost taking over. Only the fear that Ruth might learn about any boy getting to second base kept her on the straight and narrow. By the time she and Ruth turned fifteen, they had earned the nickname 'The Ice Princesses' and only the most daring boys now asked either of them out. They were both conscious that they had a reputation to live up to.

* * * *

In April 1936, Dalia and Ruth spent the evening before their first political rally creating a white banner with slogan in blue, *'Self rule for Eretz Israel'*.

The rally was to take place at the funerals in Tel Aviv of three Jews killed by Arab highway robbers.

While they were making the banner, Uri paid an unexpected visit home, explaining with a patronising smile that he had come to protect his mother and sister.

Their father looked up from his chair and raised his eyebrows. "Protection? From what?"

"The Irgun. They're out to make trouble at the funerals."

Their father gave a sceptical smile.

Next morning, however, Uri's predictions appeared more credible when they heard that armed Jews, presumably Irgun, had entered a roadside shack during the night and deliberately gunned down two innocent Arab workmen.

Bereisheet residents arrived in Tel Aviv in an old-fashioned charabanc. It parked in a piece of waste ground close to the cemetery. A cordon of police encircled the area—whether to protect the mourners from Arabs or ensure there was no trouble from the Irgun, Dalia wasn't sure. Dalia had never seen such a huge crowd outside a sports stadium, even in Munich.

The sun's heat reminded her that summer was almost on them so she was grateful when her father bought lemonade from one of several street-sellers from Jaffa. A group of shoeshine boys too were doing a roaring trade. The street-sellers and shoeshine boys were the only Arabs present at this Jewish event.

Dalia was proud of her big brother's presence when he helped her and Ruth hold up their banner while the speaker, David Ben Gurion, chastised the government for failing to provide protection against highway robbers.

"It doesn't take much time to murder three men in cold blood but it does take time to drag rocks and oil drums across a main road and ambush ten cars. Where was the police presence in this notorious black spot? We call upon the government to instigate hourly patrols along that route."

Most cheered his speech but a group at the back chanted, "British out. British out, out, out," and threw stones at the police. While the police defended themselves, a larger section of the crowd surged towards Jaffa.

Dalia saw Jewish youths grab hold of the shoeshine boys and begin beating them with stout sticks. Two older men punched a lemonade seller to the ground and proceeded to kick him until the police pulled them off.

One end of the banner flopped. She looked sideways. Uri held Ruth by the arm. Uri grabbed her arm. "Drop the banner and walk fast," he shouted. "We're going back to the charabanc—NOW."

Reluctant to lose the banner, she kept a firm grasp on it. From behind, her mother ordered. "Do what your brother says."

In front of her, Ruth's father and brother, Josh, protected Miriam Cohen from the frantically jostling crowd, attempting to leave the cemetery all at once.

Reluctantly, she dropped the banner and started forward. In the distance, above the surrounding din, she heard the chants changing to, "Arabs out, out, out."

While climbing aboard the charabanc, she saw men running back along the road chased by a group of police.

They waited in the car park. Shouts grew louder. Bereisheet residents returned, panting, beads of sweat trickling down their faces, but unharmed. Only the Goldsteins had not returned.

Shots sounded out.

"We must leave now," the driver said, his knuckles showing white on the steering wheel.

Reb Cohen stood up, opened a door, and jumped to the ground. "I'll wait for the Goldsteins. We'll take a taxi home."

Her father stood up. "There won't be any taxis. I'll take them to Shayna's." He too left the bus.

The charabanc slowly reversed.

"Stop!" Reb Cohen banged on the outside of the door. "Jack and Thelma are here."

Dalia could see them now. Jack was carrying Johnny who was crying loudly. Thelma was limping. The heel of one shoe was missing.

The charabanc stopped. Her father took Johnny while Jack and Thelma climbed inside. He handed the small boy to Thelma and he and Reb Cohen jumped in.

Dalia bit the back of her hand as they left the coach park heading towards the main road, expecting an attack when they reached Jaffa, but all remained calm along their route.

Back at Bereisheet, she hurried indoors before her parents had even left the coach, just wanting to run to her room, lie on her bed and cry into her pillow. However, in the kitchen, a comforting smell of Shabbat chicken soup, left simmering on low heat, reminded her that Eema would need her. She sank into a chair, shaking uncontrollably.

Her parents and Uri came in. Her mother, who had seemed so calm on the bus, was dabbing at her eyes. Her father laid his arm across her mother's shoulder. Her mother put her hand on his and squeezed it. They sat around the kitchen table in silence until her father said, "We must milk before Shabbat. Uri, will you help? You, Dalia, stay with your mother."

Her mother stood up. "Dalia, you lay the table while I get out the matzo balls."

Dalia worked in a daze. It wasn't until her mother had lit

the candles and was reciting the Shabbat prayer that the jagged peaks and troughs of her emotions smoothed into Shabbat peace.

* * * *

The day after the funeral Dalia and her mother had arranged to help with little Hadassah's fourth birthday party, catching the Jaffa bus as soon as Shabbat ended.

"Please, Eema, phone Cousin Elsa. Tell her you won't be going," Uri pleaded. "There are sure to be reprisals for what the Irgun did."

Dalia willed her mother to agree but she shook her head. "No. I promised Cousin Elsa we'd help out. Shimon will meet us at the bus station, so we'll be all right."

Dalia looked up. Shimon was at his sister's? That changed everything.

Uri thumped the table. "One man against a mob! Eema, you and Dalia mustn't go."

Her mother drew herself up. "Uri, Dalia and I aren't hothouse flowers. Shayna needs our help. She has a ten month old child to look after as well as Hadassah, who can be quite a handful when she puts her mind to it."

"If you insist on going, I'm coming with you until you meet Shimon," Uri stated.

Shimon was at the Jaffa terminal. Uri, instead of staying on for the return journey, left with them, carrying her mother's case. Shimon gave her a smile and took charge of her overnight case. She stood next to him. This, she thought, was going to be a lovely walk.

Uri spoilt it all by saying, "I need to speak to you, Shimon. Can we go ahead a little so we can talk in private?"

Dalia felt like screaming as she accompanied her mother, too far behind the boys to hear what they were saying, Still, she consoled herself; she would have the whole evening to speak to Shimon because Uri couldn't stop for long at Shayna's or he'd miss the last bus home.

To her dismay, however, Shimon didn't even enter

Shayna's flat. He and Uri put down the overnight cases by Shayna's front door and sloped off.

Shimon called over his shoulder. "Tell my mother to expect me when she sees me."

Dalia felt her shoulders slump.

Cousin Elsa opened the door. "I didn't see you at the funeral yesterday," she greeted them.

"I didn't see you either," her mother said.

"We were with the Rehovot party but Shimon took me straight back to Shayna's once trouble started. I'm glad he did. Shayna was frightened out of her wits when we arrived. A rowdy mob had poured down her street about half-an-hour before we arrived and we kept hearing firing all evening. Things were even worse this morning. The usual man delivered her ice, but had only reached the next block when about twenty Irgun overturned his donkey cart. Shimon called out some of his friends, but by the time they arrived at the scene the thugs had gone. Where is Shimon, by the way?"

Her mother shrugged. "I presume the Agency needs him. He said he wasn't sure when he'd be back."

"Huh, so the Agency is more important than his mother, now! Ah well, we can't stand here talking all night. We've work to do."

Dalia and her mother were awakened at dawn the next morning by an excited little girl asking if it was time for her birthday yet. After everyone had watched her open her presents and they had finished breakfast, Shayna put both children down for a nap and announced she was taking their new car into Jaffa to pick up ice cream.

"Go with Shayna, Dalia," Cousin Elsa ordered. "We need more bread."

Excited at the prospect of a car-ride, Dalia watched Shayna swing the handle of the baby Austen until the engine caught. "I wished I lived nearer so you could teach me to drive."

"It won't be long before your father buys a car," Shayna prophesised. "He'll teach you."

"I don't know so much. He's saving to build a house on

the Jezreel plot for when Grandpa retires."

"If your grandparents had any sense they'd leave Germany right now."

Outside the ice cream factory Shayna paid one urchin a piastre to keep an eye on the car and hired another to carry the icebox. Dalia expressed surprise to see her leave the car's windows down.

"You wouldn't want to get back in if I closed them," Shayna told her.

The bakery was two doors down from the factory. Dalia stood in a short queue enjoying the aroma while the baker pulled fresh loaves from the oven. Two women in front of them chatted in Arabic. Mindful of her pending Arabic exam, Dalia seized the opportunity to listen in.

One woman claimed that Jews had killed four Arabs in Tel Aviv.

Someone behind corrected them. "No! It was three Arabs in an orange grove on the Salameh Road."

Another woman announced, "It was definitely three. My husband has gone to the police station to view the bodies."

An eruption of distant shouts interrupted the conversation. One woman turned to stare and said in slow and distinct Arabic. "You look like a Jew from Tel Aviv. Tell us what happened."

Dalia mustered her oral Arabic. "I heard no trouble last night." But, she thought, listening to shouts getting louder, there might be trouble now.

Everyone looked incredulous. She was relieved when the baker called out, "Right. Now, who's first?"

By the time Dalia had bought her bread, the shouts sounded close. She rushed back to the car.

Shayna, already in the driving seat with the engine running, shouted, "We must get home fast."

As they turned the corner from the factory, they saw a crowd of Houranis, blocking sidewalks on both sides of the road.

When they caught sight of the car, the mob began chanting in Arabic, hostile mouths opening and shutting only a few inches away. Dalia recognised the Arabic word for murderers. A boy in front threw a stone. It whizzed towards them, crashed onto the car bonnet, gouging a trail in Shlomo's immaculate paintwork. A hail of stones followed, clanging on the roof, bouncing off the sides. Terrified, Dalia hid her head on her lap. Just as well. One stone, flying through the open window, hit her shoulder blade. She yelped in agony. The car jumped forward as Shayna stamped on the accelerator. Dalia yelped again, thrown backwards, her bruise bumping against the backrest. She clamped her fingers around the bottom of the seat and glanced sideways. Shayna was hunched over the steering wheel to protect her face, while her hands clenched the rim. Outside on the pavement, faces leered at them. The car left the mob behind and Shayna sat up straight. The whole incident had taken only a few seconds but it took far longer for either of them to regain their equilibrium.

"Please, say nothing to my mother," Shayna said, as Dalia lifted the ice cream from the car.

Shayna let them in and retrieved a note from the lobby floor. She read it aloud.

"Sorry, Eema and Shayna, urgent things to do. Don't let Cousin Trudi and Dalia try to get home tonight. The buses won't be running. Uri and I will come over tomorrow. Shalom, Shimon."

"You'd have thought he would have come in and told you instead of posting a note," Dalia said.

Shayna gave a shrug. "Typical of my brother. Too scared to face Eema. I'd better get on. Our guests will be here soon. At least having to play the clown will put a stop to Shlomo going on about his new car's ruined paintwork."

While Shayna served coffee and biscuits to adults, Dalia was so occupied helping her mother and Cousin Elsa mop up spilt jelly and dropped ice-cream, that she hadn't time to dwell on the pain in her back or sulk over Shimon's non-appearance. If any noise came from Jaffa, it couldn't compete with the childish shrieks of laughter at Shlomo's antics, or wails when someone fell over or spilt lemonade on their best frock.

When they stood at the door to wave goodbye to the

departing visitors there appeared to be more plumes of smoke than usual spewing from Jaffa's foundry chimneys and they could definitely hear shouts. Disturbing noises continued well into the night.

They didn't realise how bad things really were, however, until Shimon and Uri turned up next morning bringing a family of four and an emergency billeting order from the Jewish Agency.

Thanks to the Jewish Agency laying on armed escorts and special buses starting from Tel Aviv, however, Dalia and her mother returned safely to Bereisheet.

Chapter 8

1936 was a momentous year for the Leitner family. They became eligible to apply for Palestinian citizenship. Gazing at the family's new passport with the acronym for Eretz Israel preceding the word Palestine, Dalia felt that so long as no one opened it to where it showed her place of birth she could pass for a genuine Sabra.

Busy concentrating on revision for lower level Bagrut in the relative calm of the Hefer Valley, the chaos that swept through much of Palestine that year had little impact on Dalia and Ruth. They were closer than they had ever been that summer term, only too conscious that this was the last time they would be sharing most experiences.

When the exams ended, Ruth left for Haifa and a preliminary course with *Magen David Adom*, the Jewish equivalent of the Red Cross. Dalia, more intent than ever on becoming a pioneering farmer, continued agricultural training with the brigade and HH.

At the end of one strenuous day spent harvesting wheat, the HH leader handed her an envelope containing the typed aims and ideals of Haganah, together with the words of an oath to be learnt by heart. He instructed her to keep all contents secret.

A week later, he handed her a note inviting her to an interview in the school basement the following afternoon.

She felt her stomach muscles tighten as she opened the basement door and found herself in a room smelling of damp concrete. A dim electric bulb suspended from the low ceiling spotlighted a rickety wooden chair.

"Be seated," a voice boomed from in front.

She obeyed, the chair rocking beneath her weight, her eyes slowly adjusting to the surrounding gloom. Three hooded figures faced her from behind a trestle table.

The first figure asked about her loyalty to Eretz Israel. Conscious of an embarrassing squeak in her voice, she regurgitated a well-rehearsed answer. When the second examined her on her attitude to discipline, she felt a little more confident. By the time the third questioned her willingness to suffer discomfort during training, she was answering almost normally.

She waited for the next question but the examiners fell into an unnerving silence. A dripping tap sounded louder, the smell of damp concrete grew more pervasive. Her palms felt moist.

The light went out.

From behind, unseen hands pulled her upright, turned her sideways, and pushed her forward.

She envisaged her nose crashing into a wall, her feet stumbling over machinery, her body toppling into a pit, and she took a deep breath. This was the real test, she realised, the question and answer session mere ritual. She forced a leaden foot to move, and walked steadily forward, chin tilted high, until hands halted her.

A door opened to reveal two lighted candles in the centre of a blue cloth-covered table. At one end lay a leather-bound Bible, at the other an ancient pistol, both reassuringly familiar symbols of Haganah.

A bright light aimed at her face dazzled her, forcing her to close her eyes.

A deep voice ordered, "Place one hand on the Bible, the other on the pistol."

She groped forward, until her hands felt the edge of the table. The odour of hot wax filled her nostrils. The fingers of her left hand fumbled sideways until they touched grained leather. Her right hand found the pistol's cold muzzle.

"The Bible and the gun, the two principles by which we of Eretz Israel defend our homes," the voice intoned. "Lift your hands and turn around."

She opened her eyes to profound darkness.

"Walk forward seven paces."

No hands guided her now. Sweat dropped from her face as she took each step.

"Now, by the Supreme Conscience of Zionism, make

your allegiance."

With swollen tongue filling her mouth, she blundered through the memorised vow. "I will remember always that our purpose is to provide security for those who work for Eretz Israel. I will regard Haganah as the servant of this purpose and not its master. I promise to beat off attacks, but will not let the smell of blood go to my head." She finished, drained of energy.

The voice boomed, "I now declare you one of us."

Dalia's shoulders sagged in relief. With difficulty, she prevented herself falling. A door swung open onto a well-lit room filled with a cheering band of older HH members crowding behind her hooded interrogators. She wiped the sweat trickling into her eyes as they removed their hoods, revealing Esther's older sister, Ruth's brother, and Shimon Mabovitch. Her already labouring heart thumped even faster.

Shimon stepped forward. She felt him kiss her cheek and, in ecstasy, heard him say, "You're already an impressive shot, young Dalia. Now we'll start training you in earnest."

All this while, the news from Germany had been growing worse. The numbers of Jews trying to emigrate exceeded the numbers the British allowed into Palestine. Boats carrying refugees without permits routinely ran aground on Palestinian beaches. By the time the police arrived, the passengers had disappeared. Bereisheet played its part by sheltering these illegal immigrants until Haganah could disperse them around the country.

In July 1937, the Peel Commission, set up by the British after the 1936 Arab Rebellion, published its findings, which overturned all the brigade's preparations to turn wilderness into fertile ground.

The British Government approved the commission's suggestion that Palestine be partitioned, with Palestinian Jews receiving the fertile Sharon and Jezreel plains, while Palestine Arabs received the Nablus triangle and nearly all the wilderness. To make the plan work there would be a forced transfer of 225,000 Arabs and 1,250 Jews.

The disappointment of Jews at the loss of promised territory was as nothing compared to that of the Arabs deprived of most of their agricultural land. Violent Arabic opposition to both British and Jews escalated, causing Haganah to boost its military activities. The extra firearm practices, to a certain degree, compensated Dalia for the trashing of her plans to become a pioneer farmer.

The practices meant long hikes with fellow Haganah members to isolated training sites and an increased number of firearm competitions. As a bonus, she received occasional glimpses of Shimon when he turned up on his motorbike to distribute weapons and observe her squad in action. His presence stimulated her competitive spirit and, when he presented her with the junior regional trophy at the last exercise of 1937, she basked in his approval.

A few days later Shimon turned up at Bereisheet, to assess the settlement's capability for self-defence in the event of a serious attack. He asked if Dalia could show him around. Dalia, overwhelmed by the request, had difficulty answering his questions as he examined the perimeter fence, the stacks of stones in the orchards ready for throwing at would-be invaders, and the stone synagogue where mothers and children could hole up until police arrived.

Returning from their orchard, he stopped to lean against the gate. "Tell me, Dalia, have you heard of Mossad el Aliyah Beth?"

Dalia, conscious of his strong frame so close that she could smell his not unpleasant body odour, stuttered, "I-is that what you belong to?"

Instead of giving a direct answer, Shimon tapped the side of his nose. "Mossad el Aliyah Beth" he continued, "is an organisation devoted to helping all Jews enter Palestine, but especially those from Germany. I'm telling you because they desperately need typists in Tel Aviv and Haifa."

Shimon smiled, causing instability in her legs, contractions in her stomach, and a strong desire to rush into his arms.

"Dalia, I know you want to be a farmer. I know being a typist is not the most glamorous job in the world, but a loyal Haganah member sacrifices personal preferences for the good of Eretz Israel."

He placed a hand under her chin, tilted her face, and gazed straight into her eyes. She realised he was waiting for her to say something. She thought of the farming plans the brigade had had to set aside. Perhaps this was what Eretz Israel really needed from her. She heard her voice, unnaturally high, say, "I'll make learning shorthand and typing my priority." She thought of Ruth who had recently been offered a placement in a Haifa hospital and added, "But I'd like to work in Haifa not Tel Aviv."

"That's the girl. Anyone would take you for a Sabra!" Shimon gave her another searing smile. She wanted desperately to reach up and kiss him.

"But remember," he warned, "keep the reason for your career change a secret."

"Of course." No one would learn anything from her, whatever methods of torture they might use—except, "May I just tell my friend, Ruth?"

"No. No one at all."

She nodded. "B'seder." But her excitement diminished. Where was the fun of doing something adventurous if she couldn't talk about it with her best friend?

Shimon took his hand from her chin and glanced at his watch. "I must hurry. I promised Eema I'll be in Rehovot for supper." He jumped on his motor bike and roared off.

She watched his bike career off, wondering what difference it would have made if she had seized the initiative and kissed him.

* * * *

"A typist yet with your *Bagrut* results? You listen to me, my girl. You go to university. You get proper qualifications."

Dalia sat through her mother's tirade, arguments ready. After all, she'd had a whole year to prepare them. "Eema, an author needs to experience the real world."

Her father supported her. "Dalia's right, Trudi. A year working in a cosmopolitan port like Haifa could do her the world of good. She'll have Ruth there to keep her steady."

Eema snorted. "A port yet. Next she'll be training to be a sailor, you see."

Fleetingly, Dalia considered asking Shimon if Alia Beth had vacancies for crew members on the ships that brought in illegal immigrants, but was mature enough now to realise one could only take romantic ideas so far. She wrote to Shimon the same evening.

A fortnight later she received a letter informing her she had an interview with Max Zeider, head of the XL Agency in Haifa.

The day before the interview, the Irgun exploded bombs in Haifa Suq, killing twenty-seven Arabs and leaving seventy-five wounded. Her mother tried to dissuade her from going for the interview.

"Haifa is far too dangerous. I won't have you living there."

"Yet you'd be happy for me to go to university in Jerusalem, and that is even more dangerous," Dalia retorted.

Max Zeider accepted her onto his Agency books. It turned out he was not only head of the XL Agency but also chief organiser for Mossad el Aliyah, or Shai as it was now being called. He told her she could join Shai, provided she promised to keep her membership secret. However, he warned, "All Shai members must pass the scrutiny of British security checks so you must stop all activities connected with Haganah and resign from the brigade."

Dalia nearly walked out of the interview. The cost was too great. Only the prospect of disappointing Shimon kept her in place as Max ordered her to fill in an application form for a job in the typing pool of an import/export firm in Haifa.

Having to tell the brigade the next day that she was deserting them without explanation was the hardest thing Dalia had ever done. Esther guessed there was something behind this abrupt resignation and persuaded Leah not to pass judgement, but the rest of the brigade snubbed her completely.

It was easier terminating her membership of the local Haganah squad, since moving to Haifa was an adequate excuse.

By the end of July she was in digs halfway up Mount Carmel, and working conscientiously with an eye to earning a good reference.

Part 3

The Haifa Years 1939 – 1941

Chapter 9

It was not the best time to be in Haifa. Arab Nationalist and Zionist extremists vied with each other as to who could produce the worst outrage. At least one episode of violence occurred daily. Irgun concentrated on placing bombs in markets and cafes, while the Arabs focussed their attention on public transport. The result was constant curfews.

Dalia wouldn't have minded the disruption to her leisure activities so much if she enjoyed her work, but she hated the monotonous job that took up almost all her waking hours, and lived for Friday afternoons when her father took her home for Shabbat in the Austin Seven he had bought especially to ferry her to Haifa and back.

While summer lasted, she and her family spent most Saturday mornings on small beaches near her grove at al-Tira. The manager's wife cooked them a magnificent evening meal which they would eat in a four metre square mesh fly-and mosquito-proof shelter that her father had erected in the grove. When Ruth was off duty, she squashed into the car with them and sat on Uri's lap.

If it hadn't been for those family Saturdays, and the prospect of a monthly report back to Shimon at a local coffee house, Dalia would have revoked her Shai membership at the beginning of October and gone on to university in Jerusalem with Esther and Leah. It wasn't as if she could garner useful information from receipts for citrus and bully beef.

Her social life improved after six months. Her firm allowed her half a day off each week to attend a secretarial course. She had bridled when Max suggested she take the course since her skills were already superior to those of her colleagues.

"It's not about your typing," Max told her. "So far you've lived in an exclusively Jewish environment. You'll be no use to us until you get to know Gentile Palestinians. The secretarial college has the most diverse female membership of any Institution in Haifa."

There were Jews in the class she joined who looked and spoke like Arabs, Arabs who spoke French as well as any Parisian, Armenians who looked like Turks, and a solitary British woman, Patsy Quigley, who worked at Police Headquarters on Kingsway. She had already met two women attending the class, Golda Kaminer from the Hefer Valley's Haganah squad, and Maftur Nour al-Zeid, granddaughter of the original owner of her orange grove at al-Tira. Maftur invited her and Golda to join other students at a cafe on Kingsway after each lesson. She would have enjoyed those coffee sessions even without the hope that she might gain information useful to Shai. In the interests of Shai, Dalia particularly attached herself to the British woman, Patsy Quigley. Before long they were visiting the cinema together and, when the weather became warmer, going swimming after work.

Influenced by fashion conscious Maftur, Dalia took her own grooming in hand. She trained her auburn curls to sweep back and bounce between her shoulders, and pinned a beribboned boater on top of her head. She bought a geometrically patterned cotton pinafore dress, the latest fashion, and wore it over an organdie blouse.

Shimon stood and stared when she stalked into their meeting place on high-heeled sandals.

"My! You look almost grown up."

"I *am* grown up," she retorted. "I'm seventeen now."

In August, life in the export office became hectic.

"I'm putting in so much overtime, you wouldn't believe it," Dalia grumbled to Ruth. "All these war rumours. Everyone with relatives in Europe wants their orders processed the day before yesterday."

Threat of war may have been a mere irritation at work

but it felt more serious when she went home for Shabbat. Her father read out Grandpa's reply to a letter he had written, pleading with him to bring forward his retirement and sail to Palestine before war started.

Her father had taken his advice to retire early but her grandmother's doctor had warned her to avoid excessive heat, so they were waiting until the end of October to come over.

Her mother looked up from the sock she was darning, stood up, put an arm around her husband's shoulders and laid her cheek against his. "They'll be all right, Albert. After all, your father *is* German."

Dalia had only found that out that Grandpa wasn't Jewish two years previously. She had more or less come to terms with that knowledge now, thanks to Ruth who was the only person she had told. Ruth had pointed out being one-eighth Aryan didn't make her any different from the person she'd always been and, anyway, she was a real Jew because her grandparents had raised her father as a Jew.

Until recently, the knowledge had its brighter side. She had assumed her grandfather being a gentile would keep her grandparents safe, but she had heard rumours that Jewish spouses of Aryan Germans were being sent to labour camps. Looking at her father's eyes, she guessed he had heard them too.

The British declared war on Germany at the beginning of September. In the last letter her grandfather sent, postmarked Hamburg, he wrote that the Nazis had interned her grandmother. They wouldn't even tell him where the internment camp was. They had then forced him to take up his old job at the mint. He hoped Germany would win the war soon so he and her grandmother could settle back into retirement.

Strangely, the riots and bombings, which had made Haifa so dangerous over the past year, stopped when war in Europe started. Arabs and Jews even started using each other's buses again.

* * * *

At Simchat Torah, a fortnight before her eighteenth birthday, Haifa was safe enough for Dalia, Ruth, and other off-duty nurses to dance outside a synagogue near the hospital. Afterwards, her feet still tapping, she accompanied them back to the Nurses' Home. She was hoping to chat to Ruth over a mug of cocoa but Home Sister stopped them as they entered the building.

"Nurse Cohen, will you ask your friend, Miss Leitner, to phone Bereisheet as a matter of urgency?"

Dalia's stomach contracted. This could imply a family disaster. Rushing to the pay-phone in the Nurses' Home, she was surprised when her mother answered. She must have been sitting in the clinic waiting.

"My Dalia, my Dalia, such dreadful news." Her mother stopped.

Dalia heard her sobbing. She clenched the receiver, her stomach rolling over. "Abba?"

"No, Uri," her mother managed.

"Uri? Has he had an accident?" She looked at Ruth's face distorted with fear and tried to share the receiver.

Her mother answered. "No! It's the British. They've arrested Uri."

"What?" She and Ruth shrieked in unison.

"He's in prison, in Acre, where they do the executions."

"Why?"

Just another burst of weeping from the other end of the phone.

Dalia concentrated on being strong for her mother, "Eema, I'll come home straight away," she promised, but when Ruth gave a wail, she realised she would have to be strong for Ruth as well. Ruth obviously felt as much for Uri as Dalia did for Shimon.

Her father's voice on the phone now, calm. "Dalia, no need to panic."

She visualised him, standing by her mother, stroking her hair while he talked.

"I'll fetch you home on Friday as usual."

"What's Uri done, Abba?"

"Nothing, except learning to fight Nazis. The police arrested forty-two of our boys on their way home from rifle practice. They took them to Acre because it's the only prison with enough room. We wanted to tell you rather than have you read it in the papers."

The odd thing was that there was practically nothing in the Palestinian Post about the arrests that week, although everyone talked of very little else.

As she typed up invoices at work, Dalia tried to push to the back of her mind the knowledge that her brother was facing charges which could bring the death penalty.

On evenings when Ruth was off-duty, they met up to comfort each other and discuss efforts being made to get the group released. They learned eventually that Uri, with the rest of the squad, was to be tried in a military court.

Dalia phoned home the first day of the trial.

Her mother sounded distraught. "Dalia, we stood outside Acre barracks all day but the British bring their prisoners to trial in canvas-covered trucks, and only wives are allowed into the courtroom. Don't the British have mothers?"

Next Shabbat was hard. No one knew how the trial was going. Her mother was on the verge of a nervous breakdown.

Her father dropped her outside her digs on Saturday evening.

Shimon Mabovitch emerged from the shadows and pointed to his motorbike. "Climb on."

She hitched her skirt and swung a leg over the pillion, clinging tightly to his shoulders as the bike lurched forward. Any other time she would have been in seventh heaven, but now she just wondered where he was taking her and why.

Shimon slowed the bike to a halt outside a row of small shops on the summit of Mount Carmel.

When he had helped her dismount, he said, "Uri asked me to make sure you and Ruth are with your mother when the British announce the verdict tomorrow."

"How did Uri get the message out?"

Simon tapped the side of his nose as he led her into a coffee shop. "Make sure you and Ruth take time off work."

"How do we get there?"

"I'm taking you both."

"You can't get two passengers on your motor bike."

"I'm borrowing a car from a wealthy Arab friend."

She thought of Patsy and wondered if Shimon had befriended the Arab on behalf of Shai.

"Is he useful to us in any other way, this friend?" she asked.

Shimon smiled gently and pulled out a chair for her at a vacant table. "Ahmed al-Zeid and I met at the Technion. We've a lot in common. We both want independence from the British and both believe Arabs and Jews can live in a shared Palestine."

"There's no room for both!" Dalia exclaimed.

Shimon raised an eyebrow. "Here's a story I read when I was little, about refugees from Persia who fled to India."

A waitress, in a frilled white apron over a black dress, interrupted to take their order.

Shimon continued when the waitress had left. "Their spokesman visited a local ruler to ask if they could stay in his kingdom. The king served them coffee and waved his hand at the densely populated countryside surrounding his palace. 'As you can see, there is scarcely room for my own people'.

"The Persian spokesman filled his cup with coffee until it reached the brim, then took a large spoonful of sugar and trickled it into the full cup. Not a drop overflowed.

"'See,' he told the king. 'Sugar has not displaced the coffee but made it taste richer. Combining the talents of our two peoples would create a more prosperous kingdom for all.'

"The king agreed to let the Persians in and the two peoples have lived in harmony ever since."

Dalia frowned. "Our science teacher showed us that trick, but whenever I tried it, coffee always splashed over."

The waitress returned with a silver coffeepot, china cups, milk, sugar, and petit fours on a lace-covered tray. Dalia felt as if she was back in a Munchen teashop.

Shimon poured the coffee, filling his own to the brim. He trickled in sugar slowly without slopping a drop. "See, it works if you go slowly."

"But we can't afford to take things slowly," she retorted, "not with all the refugees needing shelter."

Shimon leaned back. "About Monday. We've heard from a reliable source that the British will be handing out harsh sentences."

Dalia covered her cheeks with her hands and whispered. "Hanging?"

Shimon laid his hand on her arm "No, not the death sentence. The British can't afford to upset American Jews, but the verdict will be worse than most expect."

Dalia took her hands away from her face and clenched her fists. "I hate the British."

He raised his eyebrows. "And how many British do you know?"

She stopped to think. She couldn't count the Goldsteins from next door since they were also Jewish, so no one, really, except Patsy Quigley from Secretarial School whom she rather liked.

"See, you don't hate the British," Shimon observed quietly. "You hate the system they run and you're quite right to do that. Now drink up and we'll take a walk to the Park."

They stood side by side at the bottom wall of Allenby Park looking across the bay to Acre Castle shimmering in the moonlight. A chilly wind blew against the mountain, making her shiver. Shimon put an arm round her. She felt ashamed. Here she was achieving her heart's desire at the cost of her brother's freedom.

She shook off his arm. Turning to face him, the dismay on his face told her what she had done.

"I'm sorry. It's only… Oh, I didn't mean…" She burst into tears. Why did this have to happen at the wrong time?

"B'seder," Shimon muttered. "I'll take you home."

She was conscious of the gulf between them as they walked back to the motorbike in silence.

Midday on Monday, Ruth and Dalia stood with their parents in a crowd of friends and relatives outside the mesh gates of the military barracks. As soon as he delivered them,

Shimon and Ruth's brother Josh had joined a group of young men on the other side of the crowd.

The barrack gates opened. The trucks that had brought the prisoners to the barracks drove out with armed soldiers guarding their canvas covers.

Dalia screwed her eyes shut to prevent tears rolling down her face. The prisoners had not been acquitted.

A solitary female figure walked slowly down the long drive. The sentry opened the gates again. The woman, the wife of one of the prisoners, stood outside, her mouth moving, but no sound emerging. The hushed crowd waited.

"Ten years," the woman managed at last. "Ten years with hard labour."

Beside Dalia, her mother yelped like a wounded dog and would have fallen if her father hadn't held her up. Dalia seized her mother's free arm. Miriam Cohen fetched out a bottle of smelling salts and held them to her mother's nose. As they led her to the shade of an olive tree, she realised Ruth was in almost as bad a state as her mother.

She, however, was too angry to cry. What sort of people could steal ten years from the lives of forty-three young men whose only crime was trying to defend their country against Nazis? Was there anything to choose between the British and the Germans?

Chapter 10

1940 was not a happy year. From the slopes of Mount Carmel, Dalia, bitter and frustrated, observed police launches escorting clandestine refugee ships into Haifa harbour and felt more useless than ever.

Her father struggled on the farm without Uri. She was at the point of leaving her sterile job at the import/export company when Haganah persuaded her father to employ two Romanian illegals.

The war against the Nazis was going badly. Germans captured France. Italy, with an airfield on Rhodes, within flying distance of Haifa, entered the war.

Giza Barat handed out blackout material to all her lodgers, cleared out her cellar and brought in benches. As some compensation for the subsequent air-raids, the lodgers came to know each other better and Dalia began to feel more at home.

She stayed at her boring job until October when the XL Agency ordered her to apply for a more potentially useful situation at Police HQ on Kingsway.

"I won't get the job. Not now my brother has a criminal record," she protested to Max.

He shook his head. "The British are coming round. Next week they'll announce a reduction in your brother's sentence. Your friendship with Patsy Quigley will pay off."

She was called for interview.

On the day of the interview, she had to push her way through an angry crowd protesting at the detention of two boatloads of refugees. She wished she could join them. Only her love for Eretz Israel helped her endure their insults and carry on.

An Arab constable escorted her to a door labelled 'Superintendent's Office'. He entered without knocking.

A middle-aged woman looked up from a typewriter and spoke into a tube. "Miss Leitner is here now, sir."

A voice boomed back. "Send her in, Mrs Jones."

Mrs Jones pointed to a door at the side of the room. "Please go through."

A balding man, with too many wrinkles for his upright posture, sat behind a cluttered desk. He took off his glasses to peer at her and put them on again to glance in an off-hand manner at her application. He looked up and offered her the job. Without waiting for her response, he picked up a folder, raised his hand, recited the Official Secrets Act mechanically, and ordered her to swear to abide by it.

She was unprepared for this. Her whole motive for applying for the job was to pass on secrets but she couldn't back out now. Her stomach tensed as she perjured herself.

A police inspector entered the room with a bulging file. The superintendent transferred his attention to the newcomer. "Yes, Inspector?"

"Sir, the refugee data."

Dalia peeped sideways at the reporting officer and recognised him as the policeman who had visited Bereisheet three years previously when Arabs had made a minor attack on Bereisheet.

"The thing is, sir," the inspector continued, "the medical authorities need this information. The CMO has asked for a copy. I know Mrs Jones is overwhelmed so I've sifted out the most sensitive material. Can the rest be typed up in the general office?"

The superintendent frowned. "Miss Boutaji and Miss Quigley are up to their eyeballs with the new food regulations." He held out a hand and flicked through the papers, pulled a face, and held them uncertainly. His face cleared and he passed the bundle to Dalia. "You may as well start work at once Miss...er." He paused and looked down at her application. "...Miss Leitner. Inspector Monteith will show you the ropes."

She gave a gasp. "But I haven't resigned from my present job. I'll need to give notice."

The superintendent shrugged. "Our need is greater than their's. Don't worry, I'll see that they send any pay you're owed."

Bewildered and clutching the papers, she followed

Inspector Monteith down a dark corridor into a room labelled 'General Office', her stomach still insisting it was in shock.

Compared to the enormous, crowded room at the export firm, the police general office was minute. It held only two women, one of whom was Patsy Quigley. Patsy smiled at her reassuringly.

The other woman stood. "Welcome to our world, Miss Leitner. My name is Leila Boutaji. I'm the office supervisor."

Miss Boutaji led her to a desk furnished with a turn-of-the-century typewriter. Dalia seated herself at her new desk. The inspector bent over and spread the papers over her desk. She was conscious of a powerful masculine smell, combined, in an exciting way, with the oily odour of Brylcreem.

"These are the refugees' medical notes. We need, in triplicate, a list of surnames in alphabetical order, with a column for place of former residence and another for medical comment. Here's a list of recognised abbreviations."

Only when he straightened did she dare glance up to observe his tanned skin, sensual fleshy lips, and soft, blue eyes—the countenance of a John Barrymore, with perhaps just a dash of a Douglas Fairbanks. She forced her gaze away and fixed it on a metal bin packed with screwed-up carbon flimsies.

Inspector Monteith was still speaking. "Sounds complicated, I know, but you'll find it obvious once you start. I'm working in Inspector Sutton's room for the rest of the day. Bring the list there when you've finished."

When the inspector left, the two women came over.

"Welcome again," Miss Boutaji said. "Please call me Leila, and I hope you'll allow me to call you Dalia. You already know Patsy. It was she who persuaded Mrs Jones that you were as good as your application."

"I was the only applicant?"

Leila laughed. "No. We had over fifty, but security turned down the rest. They would have removed your name, too, if Mrs Jones hadn't persuaded the superintendent to bypass them. Now I'll show you the cloakroom and ladies' toilet."

On her return to the office Dalia looked through the refugee data, and realised she had, at last, something to take to

Shai if she could smuggle it out.

After typing each page, she tucked the used carbon flimsies between blank sheets at the bottom of her work.

When she had completed her task she asked Leila for directions to Inspector Sutton's office.

On the way there, she stopped at the ladies' toilet to secrete the flimsies down the front of her knickers, sadly conscious that the carbon would ruin her best underwear. The first thing she'd do back at digs would be to make a pouch from leftover blackout material.

When she reached Inspector Sutton's office she found Inspector Monteith and a civilian in a crumpled suit and thick glasses poring over sheets of paper. Inspector Monteith gave her a welcoming smile, skimmed through her work, looked up, and smiled again. "Wonderful, Miss Leitner. I don't know how you managed it so quickly."

The demonstrators were still blocking the entrance to Khayat House so the office staff stayed inside. The other two shared their packed lunches with her.

"What are they protesting about this time?" Patsy asked.

Leila looked at their door to make sure it was shut. "The refugees on the list you've just typed. They'll be protesting again when they find out the commissioner's requisitioned a French liner to take them off to Mauritius. With their usual tact the British have renamed the ship 'Patria'."

"Poor people!" Dalia commented.

"Why do you say that?" Patsy asked. "Mauritius is a nice, quiet place to sit out the war. Many British are away from home in far worse places."

"Don't start on politics," Leila ordered. "Men are far more interesting. Dalia, you've already attracted the notice of the most eligible bachelor on the force."

Patsy gave a dramatic sigh. "Unfortunately for us maidens, Peter Monteith's a 'Born again Christian'. You'll have to watch out for other British officers though, Dalia. They'd have your knickers down before you could shout 'No'."

"Well, most would," Leila agreed, "but not Sour-face Sutton. In other ways he's the worst of the lot."

Patsy elaborated. "Inspector Shaw considers everyone else either an idiot or a sinner. He'll always find something wrong with your work. Make sure your desk is piled high when he comes in."

The bit of gossip about the Patria gave Dalia an excuse to contact Shimon on the special number he'd given her.

"News already?" he commented. "That was fast work. See you in half an hour at the café you use when meeting Ruth."

At the cafe Shimon took the flimsies. "We've heard rumours. You've done well to contact me so quickly," he observed when she had finished telling him about the Patria. "We may have time to disable the Patria before she sails."

The next day Dalia typed memos asking British policemen to volunteer for the task of accompanying the refugees. She was given the task of pinning a map of the Indian Ocean and Mauritius and a call for volunteers to guard the refugees to the police notice board in the canteen.

"Plagued with tropical diseases, Mauritius," one of the policemen crowding round the map observed. "You'd not catch me volunteering." He pinched her bottom. "I'd rather stay here, round you, darling."

Only the prospect of losing a rewarding job prevented her from slapping him.

* * * *

Three weeks after starting at Khayet House, Dalia arrived at work to find Patsy had been called away. After Leila had divided the pile of work into two instead of three, Inspector Sutton came in carrying an overflowing folder.

"I don't need these until lunch-time but I must have the lists I handed in yesterday by eleven, ladies."

"It won't be possible. We're short-staffed today, Inspector," Leila informed him.

"You'll just have to work harder, then. Won't you?"

Soon after he left, an ear-splitting, earth-shaking explosion sent papers flying. Both Dalia and Leila dived under their desks and waited for the air raid siren. Footsteps tramped down the corridor. All went quiet. Still no siren. They crawled out and began retrieving papers.

The superintendent entered the room, his face grave. "Ladies, the ship taking refugees to Mauritius has capsized."

Dalia caught her breath. The previous evening she had watched police escorting a long line of captured refugees on board the 'Patria'. If they were drowned, was it all her fault?

She was barely conscious of the superintendent continuing. "The Red Cross has set up a relief canteen. I've signed dock passes for you both if you want to help."

Overwhelmed with guilt, Dalia followed Leila down to the docks. The Patria was a giant autumn leaf floating on water with blobs swarming over and around. A hammering of pneumatic drills drowned other sounds. As the two women drew nearer, the blobs on the leaf resolved into men in bathing suits and pullovers using drills. Divers, in more fearsome gear, held up limp bundles.

The canteen was a shed at the back of the quay. The organiser, a well-padded British matron, welcomed them into an oasis of peace. "I need someone behind a counter," she told Leila. She looked Dalia up and down. "And you look sturdy enough to carry water to the medical tents."

On her journeys to and from the pump, Dalia watched boats bringing in victims. Waiting soldiers covered the survivors in blankets and rushed them on stretchers to medical tents, but lifeless bodies they wrapped in sheets and laid out in neat rows. Dalia hurried past those rows. On glancing over to the Patria, she noticed a man who looked like Inspector Monteith, passing a child-shaped bundle to men on a tug.

After six hours, the Red Cross organiser sent Dalia and Leila off duty but told them they could return for a second shift later, since searchlights would enable rescue work to continue after dark.

"What a target this would make in an air raid," Leila commented when they returned to the floodlit harbour, but thankfully the night sky remained silent.

Arms near to breaking point, Dalia continued to ferry

water in buckets hour after hour, more and more guilt-ridden as the lines of sheeted bodies lengthened.

Shai must have found a refugee on her lists willing to smuggle a bomb into the hold. They would have expected the liner to sink gently to rest on the comparatively shallow harbour bottom, not capsize, flooding half the cabins.

On what she hoped was her last trip she found Inspector Monteith seated on the cold slabbed ground, his head against a wall, his chin dark with unshaved stubble, a look of despair on his face.

He pointed to a long row of tiny sheeted forms, his answer almost a moan. "Those children—we were too late."

The canteen was waiting for water, so she hurried on to the field kitchen full of police rescuers taking a break. Leila, behind an urn, urged a cup of tea on her.

"There's someone outside who needs one even more," Dalia said. "Can you sweeten it well?"

"No problem," Leila replied. "Apparently the NAAFI hasn't heard of sugar shortages."

She found Inspector Monteith where she had left him. She shook his shoulder and forced the mug into his hands. "Drink this."

He took a sip of the treacly brew, gulped it, and handed her the mug with a tremulous smile. "Thank you," but he remained slumped on the floor.

"Inspector Monteith," she said as if addressing a new Haganah recruit after a hard exercise. "Go home and change out of those wet clothes."

The inspector rose, gave a mock salute. "Orders received and understood, ma'am."

He headed unsteadily for the exit.

It was two am before Dalia returned to her digs. She dreamed of heavy buckets dragging her down into dark green water full of children with accusing eyes.

Chapter 11

The morning after the Patria disaster, Dalia walked wearily to work, her arms and back stiff and sore. She pushed through an enormous crowd surrounding the police headquarters. This time she had no urge to join the protesters chanting anti-police slogans and waving banners. No one who had seen police climbing off the Patria, exhausted after hours of rescue work, could lay the blame at their door.

Two days later Inspector Monteith entered the office. Instead of a bundle of papers, he carried a bunch of yellow carnations. For Patsy, she thought. Patsy's father was still in hospital in Jerusalem but off the danger list. A nice gesture! Instead of stopping by Patsy's desk, however, the inspector laid the flowers on hers.

He whispered. "Thank you for the cup of tea, and the telling off."

He left, and both Leila and Patsy teased her over a conquest. She hadn't time to explain as she had arranged an extra meeting with Shimon.

She was carrying the carnations when she reported to Shimon who was already at the café.

With no preliminaries, she hurled her question. "Did Shai use the information I passed to capsize the Patria and murder those children?"

Shimon glared. "Haganah would never sabotage a ship with passengers on board." He eyed the flowers in their expensive gift-wrap and raised his eyebrows. "And who gave you those?"

In a provocative mood, Dalia shrugged. "My new boyfriend."

Shimon frowned. "Do I know him?"

"A British police officer."

Infuriatingly, Shimon appeared unperturbed. "My, but you *are* becoming a most effective agent, little cousin. Perhaps being a displaced German rather than a Sabra helps."

If the coffee had arrived she would have hurled it at him.

He stood up. "I take it you have no more important intelligence to impart today so I'll get to a more urgent meeting on time." He stalked out.

For the next two evenings Dalia kept to her room, trying to forget her misery by writing stories. She was typing a paragraph, where the despised newcomer heroine rides across the desert with blazing guns to rescue an arrogant pioneer from marauding Bedouin, when Giza, her landlady, banged on the bedroom door.

"Dalia, telephone!"

She rushed downstairs and picked up the receiver. "My mother's sent you a cake," Shimon's code for a meeting.

She forced her reply through tense lips. "I'll fetch it right away."

When she reached the cafe, Shimon was at his most professional.

"That other boat, the one in quarantine," he asked, without preamble. "What do you know about it?"

"The passengers are to be kept in Athlit until the authorities find transport."

Shimon nodded but said nothing. She noticed a peculiar gleam in his eyes and felt uncomfortable.

"Aren't you going to congratulate me?" he asked at last.

She opened her eyes wide. He hadn't managed to...? "Uri? He's free...?"

Shimon's expression changed. "Sadly, no."

Another silence. His lip twisted to one side. "You obviously don't keep in contact with your family as efficiently as with the British. No phone conversation with your mother yet? Mine phoned her as soon as I told her."

"What are you babbling about?"

"My engagement, of course."

Her stomach lurched. "Engagement? When did it happen?"

Shimon laughed. "You make it sound like a nasty accident. Yael has done me the honour of accepting my proposal."

From deep inside she found the strength to fake a smile. "Congratulations, and who is this Yael?"

Whoever she was, she wanted to boil her in hot oil before throwing her from the top of a cliff.

"The Sabra my mother has been nagging me to marry ever since I left Technion. You'll come to my engagement party, won't you? Your parents are driving down."

"Of course."

She would make sure that plague, dysentery or influenza incapacitated her first; preferably all three. She managed to add the appropriate words, "I hope you will both be very happy," before glancing pointedly at her watch. "Well, if there is no real business, I'll be on my way. I do have a social life of my own."

"How could I forget? However, there is something I need to tell you. Haganah are pulling me out of Shai. You have a new agent, Aaron Schmidt. He'll contact you."

* * * *

Inspector Monteith, in mufti—dark gabardine over grey flannels—accosted Dalia after work the next evening. "Miss Leitner, I was wondering…"

Waiting for him to finish his sentence, she watched his face turn pomegranate red. Her own breathing quickened.

"That is," he continued at last, "would you care to accompany me to the cinema tomorrow evening? There's a repeat showing of 'The Story of Louis Pasteur.' I missed it the first time round."

"Thank you, Inspector Monteith," she began, "I've seen it already."

Loyalty to Shai, backed up by a desire to show that rat Shimon Mabovitch that she could do without him, intervened. She continued in a rush, "But it's really worth seeing again."

He regained his composure. "What time shall I meet you, Miss Leitner? Would it be more convenient to have a meal beforehand? In a kosher restaurant, of course."

"That would be easier," she replied, conveniently overlooking the early supper that Giza Barat cheerfully laid on for anyone needing it.

"Say about seven?"

She nodded.

"I'll call for you tomorrow." He turned away.

She entered her digs, fizzing with guilty excitement. Later in the evening, she wondered if he'd attempt to get her drunk as a prelude to seduction.

The next evening when he met her in the hall, he gave a little whistle. "Whew, Miss Leitner, you look wonderful."

In the restaurant, renowned for the excellence of its cellar, Inspector Monteith waved the wine list away. "Orange juice?"

"No, not orange juice. 7-up, please."

The inspector ordered fresh orange juice for himself. "One of Palestine's greatest luxuries," he said, lifting his glass with its frothy cap.

Dalia gave a wry smile. "I'm sick of oranges. We can't export now, so I brought a whole sack back to Haifa."

"Your parents grow oranges? I thought they were refugees."

She didn't tell him the oranges came from her own grove at al-Tira but explained how her father, a successful architect, had turned to farming when they left Germany.

Eventually she asked, "What made you come to Palestine, Inspector?"

"Please, call me Peter."

"Right, Peter, why are you here?"

"Jobs were difficult to find during the depression and I've always wanted to travel."

"Do you ever think of going home?"

"I did once." Peter's fingers knotted his napkin. "I met a girl, while on furlough."

"What was she like?"

He smiled, a faraway look in his eyes. "The sweetest girl you could imagine. Her name was Penelope." He pulled the knot out of his napkin and tugged the ends as far apart as they would go. "She was an actress. My parents disapproved and my mother made no attempt to hide her feelings." He crumpled the napkin in one hand. "Oh, Dalia, I have wanted to talk about Penelope for so long. It's something you can't talk about to a chap. You don't mind, do you?"

Since this Penelope was obviously not still around, she said, "No, please go on."

"Penelope and I became engaged despite my mother's disapproval. I started applying for jobs in England, but my mother refused to come to our wedding. Penelope suggested I return to Palestine." He dropped the napkin on the table and gripped his hands together. "She took a short contract with a touring company, promised to join me in six months, hoping to persuade my parents to come to Jerusalem for Easter and a spring wedding." He went silent once more.

"What happened?"

"She walked through a storm to unheated digs." He lowered his gaze. "Caught pneumonia. Didn't pull through."

Dalia searched without success for a suitable response.

Peter spoke again. "For a long time nothing was worthwhile. Then I became Born Again in the Blood of the Lamb and my life had meaning again." He gave a lop-sided smile. "The only thing I miss is being able to talk about Penelope. Thank you so much for listening to me."

After the film, he asked. "Would you come to the pictures with me again next week?"

Despite having learnt nothing of use to Shai, she agreed. A connection with a British Police Inspector might impress her new line manager.

* * * *

Aaron Schmidt was a stocky bald man in black jacket and pressed trousers. A more complete contrast to Shimon you couldn't get.

After listening to her report without interruption, he commented, "You probably won't learn much from such an experienced police officer. However, Inspector Peter Monteith is close to someone else we're keeping an eye on, a Mr James Shepard, so even if he lets nothing slip, persuade him to invite you to British social events."

Dalia guessed Peter would rather spend time alone with her than take her to meet friends, but perhaps she could persuade him to take her to the New Year's Party on Mount Carmel. All the British Palestine Police seemed to be going and many British civilians.

Wheedling an invitation from Peter proved no easy matter. By the twenty-third of December, she still hadn't succeeded. Over the preliminary meal, she chatted almost continuously about the New Year party, but Peter remained infuriatingly unresponsive.

He was quiet all evening and escorted her home after the film saying hardly a word. When they reached her digs, he shook her hand and thanked her for a pleasant evening. She turned to go in, fumbling in her clutch bag for her key. Suddenly Peter's hands were on her shoulders, turning her round, pulling her towards him. He bent his head, kissing her hard on the lips. She stiffened in surprise. Before she had recovered sufficiently to kiss him back, he had released her, apologising profusely, his face almost purple with embarrassment. He loped off into the darkness before she had collected herself together sufficiently to call after him.

She found her key and groped her way upstairs, too shaken to hunt for the light switch. As she undressed she tried to make sense of the incident. She might have been a bit slow responding but she hadn't exactly fought him off. So why had he run away?

The next day, Christmas Eve, both she and Patsy planned to leave work by three-thirty since Christmas and Hanukkah coincided that year. Luckily, Leila, as a Greek Orthodox Christian, celebrated Christmas in January, so someone would be in the office on the twenty-fifth. All the same, everyone worked extra hard to leave nothing urgent undone.

At 2.30pm a crowd of British policemen invaded the office, waving bottles of Gold Star and white wine. Somewhat bemused, Dalia accepted a glass of luke-warm white wine from one police constable while watching another hang mistletoe from the light bulb before dragging Patsy under it and kissing her to a chorus of cheers.

Dalia emptied her glass and a constable immediately refilled it. Another took her by the hand, and begged her to go to the party on Carmel with him. She emptied her glass again.

Peter entered the room. Ignoring the man talking to her, he seized her wrist and steered her through the door. Overcome by surprise, she made no resistance.

"Dalia." Peter's words spurted like steam from an overheated radiator. "I'm so ashamed. If only you weren't so beautiful! Nothing like last night will happen again, ever. Please don't stop going out with me. I need you."

She exploded with anger. "Your needs, your feelings!" she shouted.

Peter let go of her arm and stepped back. She drained her glass, placing it on a ledge beneath a notice board and put her hands on her hips. "Don't my feelings matter?"

He looked even more contrite. "I'm trying to apologise…"

She interrupted. "For the wrong thing. It's not proprieties I'm talking about, Peter, it's my feelings." She stamped her foot, beating her fists on his chest before lifting up her face. "Kiss me again."

Peter flung his arms around her and obeyed, then released her without warning and placed his hands on the sides of his head. "No, Dalia." His voice almost a moan. "No! This isn't the path the Lord has chosen. The Lord owns my life now, Dalia. I can't be unequally yoked."

"Who said anything about yoking?" she retorted. "I'm only nineteen. Let's just enjoy ourselves."

His eyes widened. "Oh, Dalia, I'm already corrupting you."

"So you don't fancy me?"

He looked down at his feet. "Dalia, if you are the woman He has chosen for me, He will find a way to tell us. Meanwhile, I promise to control the lusts of the flesh, but please, remain my friend. You're the only person I can talk to about Penelope."

She'd had enough. "Peter, someone has just asked me to

go to the Mount Carmel New Year's Party. I haven't given him an answer. Will you take me?"

"Dalia, I can't. Second Chosen don't do things like that."

She turned and walked back to the office.

"Dalia," Peter pleaded from behind, "don't leave, please. We can go out to dinner instead." He seized her arm.

She turned to face him.

"Uh-hmm." A cough behind had them springing apart. Inspector Sutton stood there, back straighter than ever, chin tilted high. "Inspector Monteith, I need to discuss an urgent matter with you."

Dalia escaped back to the typing room. She could almost smell Leila and Patsy's curiosity.

"So, is Inspector Monteith taking you to the Carmel party?" Leila whispered.

She snapped, "No!" clasped her hands together and bit a finger. She took a deep breath, before continuing. "It appears it's against his religion."

Patsy nodded. "The Second Chosen have their claws well and truly into him."

"What is this Second Chosen?" Dalia asked.

"One of many fundamentalist Christian groups in Palestine. My parents belong."

She felt slightly nauseous. After scanning the room without success for the young man who had asked her to the dance, she collected her coat and went outside to wait for her father. It was raining but the fresh air revived her.

Once home, the aroma of vegetable soup and traditional potato latkes, part of every Hanukkah Dalia could remember, wafted through the kitchen. Events in Haifa no longer seemed important.

She stood next to her mother and wished Uri was with them, as she watched Ruth holding her brother's menorah. It had been two years since she had held Uri's menorah at Hanukkah. Reb Cohen chanted traditional Hanukkah prayers and blessings. The table in front of them, covered in white damask, gleamed with polished glasses and cutlery. She had a lot to be thankful for.

Before returning to Haifa she confided some of the tangled details of her involvement with Inspector Monteith to Ruth, without, of course, any mention of Aliyah Beth and Shai.

Ruth adopted a tough approach. "Ditch him. He's getting in the way of you finding a good Jewish boy."

Dalia knew that. What she needed was something to stiffen her will-power.

Peter was outside Giza's lodging house when she jumped out of her father's car, lugging yet another sack of unsaleable oranges.

"Dalia," he said, after her father had driven off, "I had to see you. I know I promised to take you out to dinner on New Year's Eve, but my friend Jim has been sent abroad. He asked me to spend New Year with his family. After all he and his wife have done for me, I can't refuse."

If Jim Shepard had left the country, Shai didn't need her going out with Peter. She dug her nails into her palms, and kept her voice level. "That's fine, Peter. I hope you enjoy yourself."

She inserted her key into the lock of the lodging house door. Behind her, Peter said, "I'm off duty tomorrow night. Shall we go to the pictures?"

"No. I'm busy. Goodbye, Peter."

Chapter 12

Inspector Monteith was on unexpected leave when Dalia went into work on New Year's Day. A notice on the bulletin board said he was being transferred to Tarshiha near the Lebanese border.

Patsy, who occasionally worked on documents in Mrs Jones's office, had overheard Inspector Sutton conferring with the Superintendent and was indignant on her behalf.

"They're trying to split up you and Peter."

"They needn't have bothered. We've already split."

Life in Haifa that winter was bleak until her mother phoned with wonderful news. Without fuss or fanfare, the British had released Uri and all his squad.

Dalia rushed around to the Nurses' Home only to find that Uri had already visited Ruth and, what was more, had proposed.

"Isn't it wonderful?" Ruth trotted around, unable to sit still. "He's received my father's blessing so we're choosing my engagement ring before picking you up tomorrow. He's borrowing your father's car to take us back to Bereisheet."

"Isn't this all rather sudden?" Dalia asked, alarmed for her friend.

"Not really," Ruth said. "I'm so glad I can now tell you what's been happening. I felt awful but Shimon said I had to keep it secret because you worked for the police. He wouldn't take me unless I promised."

"Take you where?"

"To the experimental agricultural station where Uri worked. Uri asked Shimon to take me up once a week. All the girlfriends were doing it. There's a gap in the fence. The prison staff turned a blind eye. That's when Uri and I agreed to get engaged. We didn't think it would be this soon, though! Prison has changed Uri, Dalia. He's a lot more caring and thoughtful."

"But shouldn't Uri settle back into normal life before rushing into engagement parties?"

Ruth twiddled with an imaginary engagement ring. "That's how we planned it but here's another secret. You are not to tell anyone because we haven't told your mother yet. We don't want to spoil the engagement party for her. Your father knows, though."

Dalia's stomach tensed as Ruth twiddled with that imaginary engagement ring again.

"Told her what?"

"The Agency has ordered Uri to join up."

The next afternoon outside the Khayat building, Uri bounded out of the Austin 7 with a broad grin. A radiant Ruth stepped out of the front passenger lifting her left hand high in the air to display a diamond ring, then slipped into the rear of the car.

Dalia hugged Uri, indifferent to the wolf-whistles of passing policemen. When she joined Ruth she hugged her too and duly admired the ring.

Back home, she found her mother and Miriam already had next evening's engagement party well in hand and were preparing to light the two Shabbat candles together. It was the happiest Shabbat Dalia could remember.

At sunset on Saturday she joined the other women of the moshav in a frenzy of activity. An hour after Shabbat her mother stood back in the synagogue that doubled as a community hall surveying tables covered in coffee, chocolate, and vanilla gateaux, a broad smile on her face. "Nu, you'd never think there was a war on."

Her duty done, Dalia snatched a few minutes with her brother and father, while Ruth went off to change into suitable clothes. She listened to Uri describing the new farming techniques he had learnt in prison and wished she could help put them into practice. If only Shai hadn't forced her to resign from the brigade.

She was catching up with gossip when Reb Cohen summoned Ruth and Uri to the platform. The babble died down. Dalia gazed around at her old school friends as they held up their glasses to toast the couple. Those who weren't already married were flaunting engagement rings. She was the outsider, yet again.

Speeches over, she left the hall. Outside, bright stars shone with hardly a flicker. She shivered in her party frock. A cow mooed in one of the byres. In all the excitement, had anyone remembered to milk the animals? She walked briskly across the green.

Inside the cowshed, staring at cows that needed no attention (her father must have seen to them while she was helping with the catering), she felt lonely. In the past, Ruth would have come running after her when she left the party, but not tonight, of course.

The next morning, long before anyone else was awake, her father drove her to Haifa.

"I have to tell your mother about Uri's call-up when I return home. Wish me luck, Dalia," he said, before driving back to Bereisheet.

* * * *

A few weeks after Uri had joined the army, Dalia found Peter waiting outside her digs after work, ashen faced, with red-rimmed eyes, and shaking hands.

She hardened her heart. "Well? What brings you here?"

"Please," Peter muttered, "I have to talk to someone. I'll go mad if I don't. Please."

"Can't you take your troubles to Mrs Shepard?"

"Dalia, I can't."

"Why not? She's the wife of your best friend."

"Dalia, please." His face had all the hurt expression of an injured child. She resisted the urge to run up and comfort him, but couldn't bring herself to send him packing. She was curious too. What was it Peter couldn't tell Mrs Shepard?

"Just for half an hour," she said, telling herself she was doing this for Shai.

Peter led her to a café with seats so high-backed they created private booths.

He peered around to make sure the adjacent seats were empty before bursting out, "Dalia, last week I murdered two men."

"You what?"

"My squad—we shot two Arabs."

It didn't make sense, that upsetting him so much. He was a Palestine policeman. Killing Arabs came with the job. Well, ordinary Arabs, of course, not people like Maftur.

"Why can't you take that to Mrs Shepard?"

"Because Jim has gone missing somewhere in the Balkans. The men we killed were spies, doing for the Axis what Jim does for the Allies."

Although that gave her something to report to Aaron, Dalia felt sorry for Jim Shepard's wife. Her tone softened. "All right, Peter, tell me what happened."

His story juddered out. "We've been shadowing this hashish smuggler—a man owning a few donkeys, a very minor German agent." Peter pushed his hair back. "He met up with the Mufti's top man. We weren't expecting that. I went in with the handcuffs. The hashish smuggler pulled a knife." Peter clenched his fists. "My squad shot both men although the Mufti's man had already surrendered. They did it to protect me, Dalia. I'm to blame. I was in charge."

"So what did the authorities say?"

"We didn't tell them. We buried the bodies on the mountainside."

"L'Azazel!" Dalia was shocked. "All bodies, even those of your worst enemies, should be treated with respect and returned to their families."

Peter placed his head between his palms and kept his eyes on the table. He gave a deep breath, obviously trying to calm himself. "Both men were Muslim. They had to be buried before nightfall. We did what we could. We faced them east. One of my Muslim men said washing didn't matter because they'd died martyrs. Our Muslims said prayers." He banged his fists on the table. "I tried to pray too, Dalia, but I had their blood on my hands and the words sounded wrong. The soil was shallow. We had no spades. The best we could do was pile rocks on the graves so animals couldn't get at them."

"And what about their families, Peter? Their mothers,

fathers, wives, children, wondering why they haven't come home. Never being able to grieve properly."

Peter seized her hand. She thought about pulling it away but in the state he was in, wasn't sure what effect that would have.

"We couldn't take them to Haifa. The Mufti's man comes from a powerful Syrian family. It's vital we don't antagonise Syrians."

They sat in silence. After a while Peter raised his head. "Dalia I'm so grateful you listened and we're friends once more."

In his vulnerable state she couldn't bring herself to say they weren't friends, so couldn't refuse to meet him outside the cinema the following week when he would be on leave in Haifa. At least that would please Adrian.

Peter was keeping their place in the queue when she reached the cinema. His face glowed with excitement. "Dalia, you won't believe this, but Jim's home. We'd almost given him up. We had too little faith in our Lord."

"Where was he?"

"All over Eastern Europe. He returned on the last convoy from Athens."

More information for Adrian.

During the ice cream break, Peter confided, "You don't know how much Jim's return means to me, having someone with whom I can share my problems."

So she had only been a substitute for Jim! Why was she feeling disgruntled? It was what she wanted, wasn't it?

Looking awkward outside her lodging house, he announced, "There's a globe-trotting American from Hollywood speaking at the New Covenant Hall next Thursday…"

She waited, allowing time for his embarrassment to grow but instead of "So I'll be with Jim," she heard, "Will you come with me?"

To hear an American from Hollywood? Wow! She might even contact Mr Shepard there. How could a good Shai member do anything but answer, "I would enjoy that."

"Seven-thirty, then?"

Peter paused and fixed his gaze on her hair. "Oh, and by the way, it's one of those occasions when you wear a hat."

A hat? So it was going to be a posh do! Back in her room, she ransacked her wardrobe. She had no fashionable hat. Her dresses were all distinctly dowdy.

Her bank balance, however, contained money for an emergency. This was an emergency.

She ran out of the house to the nearest public phone and dialled the Shai number.

"You told me to keep an eye on Jim Shepard," she informed Aaron when they met next day. "He's back in the country. I may meet him on Thursday."

"Dalia, that's wonderful. It's vital we find out what this man is up to."

Next Thursday Dalia saw the admiration in Peter's eyes as she posed halfway down the stairs to display her new dress and hat to full advantage.

"My, but you are beautiful."

She ran on down, satisfied by the compliment.

As they walked downhill, she envisaged the New Covenant Hall, a miniature version of the grandiose YMCA, with an interior full of gilded statues, jewelled crucifixes, and suspended ostrich eggs.

She was soon disillusioned. Close to the dry stone boundary wall surrounding a simple Baha'i shrine, Peter stopped outside the wooden porch of a rusty corrugated iron building. "Here we are."

The interior was scarcely less dismal than the exterior with a scuffed wooden floor, dark brown walls and curtain-free, frosted glass windows set well above eye level. The only adornments were a painted, crimson banner bearing gold-brushed text in English, 'For God so loved the World that he gave his only begotten Son', and painted tablets bearing an English translation of the Torah's Ten Commandments.

A British soldier handed them faded cloth-covered books. Another ushered them past rows of soldiers, sailors, and airmen to seats behind a cluster of drab civilians. Several turned their heads, nodded at Peter and stared curiously at her.

She removed the hatpin from her inappropriately frivolous hat. A look of almost horror filled Peter's face.

"Keep your hat on," he whispered.

She opened the book she had been given. It contained Christian songs. Peter had tricked her into attending a Christian service. She felt angry, even if Shai could benefit.

"Where are the Shepards?"

Peter pointed to a row in front of the soldiers. A group of Aussies in the second row obscured her view.

An elderly woman in an ancient felt hat, who had been drooping in front of an upright piano, straightened her back and thumped out Beethoven's *Pathetique*. Two men emerged from a side door and walked onto a raised platform. One, elderly, white-moustached, and balding, she recognised as her bank manager. The other, clean-shaven, dapper in ecru linen, strutted beside him.

The bank manager introduced his companion, who appeared to have spent his entire life, apart from a month each year in Hollywood, crossing and re-crossing the Atlantic in his Lord's Service. He finished by announcing a hymn. The woman at the piano pounded keys. Everyone stood.

The congregation made up in volume what it lacked in melody. By the third repeat of the chorus 'Will you let him save you now? Will you take his loving hand, Pilot to a better land; will you let him save you now?' she was competent to join in but didn't as she suspected blasphemy, although why that would make a difference to someone like her, unsure that God existed, she couldn't think. Nevertheless, she felt uncomfortable.

The bank manager ordered everyone to close their eyes. He proceeded to thank the Almighty for Saints who had returned unscathed from battle, to request the safety of the allied armed forces, listing each military front in turn. Cries of "Yes, oh Lord, yes!" punctuated his prayer. Another blasphemous hymn before the star turn.

The American performed well. His voice caressed and soothed, as depicted the blissful wonders of heaven. His mood changed and he thundered the torments awaiting unbelievers. He twisted his body and banged the floor as he described the agonies of a fiery hell. Then it was back to cooing and sweetness as he pleaded with the audience to come forward and be saved that night.

Before the American had finished talking, five women in white standing in the back row sang softly, "Oh please say yes. Say yes. Say yes. While He so gently, so patiently knocks: oh, let Him in tonight."

Against the musical background, the American spoke of mothers back home in England praying for their sons' safety. He went on to wives, fiancées, sisters, fathers, criss-crossing the platform as he talked. How much greater still, he asked, than family was the love of Jesus? The music, in a way she could not explain, seemed to make sense of it all.

The evangelist drew his oration to a close. The overhead lights went off, leaving only the platform lit. The singing became slightly louder, the tune still more hauntingly beautiful. The American beckoned to the congregation.

From the front of the hall, just visible in the gloom, a hefty marine stumbled into the aisle. Soldiers, sailors, and airmen, singly and in pairs, followed, walking towards the platform as if hypnotised. Peter turned his head. Even in such dim light, she detected his love. Her thighs clenched. She wanted to hold him close, kiss him passionately and shout, "I love you too."

She stood to relieve her tension. Peter's hands urged her on, out into the aisle. Her logical self, lurking at the back of her mind, muttered, "I don't believe I'm doing this," but she joined a fair-haired nurse in front of the platform.

The singing died away, the evangelist asked each new convert individually. "Do you give your life to the Lord Jesus?"

She was last and wanted to scream, "I made a mistake," but staring into those large, round eyes, she meekly answered, "Yes."

The evangelist gave thanks to the Lord for those brands saved from the burning and invited the new converts into the back room. That should have been her cue to hightail it back to her seat, but she envisaged Peter's disappointment, and followed the rest.

In the back room the atmosphere was uncompromisingly prosaic. Army privates, imitating recruiting sergeants, took names and contact addresses before rapping out a brief blessing and handing over each recruit to a counsellor.

Her counsellor, a curvaceous woman with hair braided into a bun beneath a nondescript hat, took hold of her hands and folded them between her own, before kissing her on the cheek. Despite her dowdy dress and lack of makeup, the woman was beautiful.

"Praise the Lord that at last you have opened your heart to Jesus, Dalia Leitner," the woman said. "I have prayed for this moment. My name is Addy Shepard."

So at least one thing had gone to plan. She had contacted Mrs Shepard.

"I expect you are wondering what happens now," Addy said. "The next step is to show the world that you have been born again, and immerse yourself in the word of God."

Addy led her to two seats at the rear of the room. She fished into a capacious handbag and brought out a book bound in soft black leather. "Here is the Holy Word of God for you to keep. Spend at least half-an-hour each day reading it. Since you are already familiar with the Old Testament, I suggest you concentrate on the New Testament. I will answer questions you may have. Please come to my house twice a week, starting tomorrow evening. Peter will show you where I live."

"It's Shabbat tomorrow. I go home," Dalia started and the enormity of what she had done overwhelmed her. She had given up her right to Shabbat. She had thrown away an identity she had inherited from hundreds of generations. "My digs are closed from after breakfast Friday until sunset Saturday," she added.

"You'll have to stay with us. I'll move my girls back into our bedroom. They're used to it. They slept there while Jim was in the Balkans." Addy stood and tapped the shoulder of a small man in thick spectacles, who was talking earnestly to a soldier. "We're going back to the hall, Jim. We'll see you there."

Dalia stared at the civilian. She had seen him at Khayet House with Peter. Was this insignificant man in a shabby brown striped suit the spy Aaron was so anxious she contacted?

Peter strode over and seized her hand.

Addy included them both in her radiant smile. "I imagine you two want to be left alone. I'll expect you both for supper tomorrow."

Dalia followed Peter. Once outside, he threw his arms around her and hustled her into the deep shadows around the side of the building.

Someone in the small house next door to the hall hung a lamp outside their door. It shone above the foliage and cast a dim light on Peter's face. He drew her to him. She clung to him for comfort, trying to make sense of what had happened that evening.

"Oh, Dalia," Peter said at last. "I knew the Lord would find a way. Now at last we can get engaged."

His words pushed her back into reality. She was not the heroine of a Hollywood romance. Kisses did not change everything, however handsome the kisser. She drew back, trying to block out Peter's presence as she thought of her mother, her father, Ruth and Uri. She must retract her conversion even if it meant short-changing Shai.

Peter flung his arms around her, burying his face in her neck. She made a final effort to assert control over her body but burst into tears instead.

"I am a Jew," she sobbed as she pushed Peter away. "I want to go on being a Jew."

Peter stroked her hair. "Dalia, you don't have to stop being a Jew just because you're a Christian. Our Lord never stopped being a Jew."

But she wasn't a Jew by religion but by heritage. Converting to Christianity would have been no problem if it had just been a matter of religion, but being Jewish was part of the cement that bound her to parents and friends.

"Peter, Christians may allow me to remain a Jew, but to

Jews Christianity is blasphemy."

She looked up and could see he didn't understand. It was as if he missed a mental layer. Waves of lethargy left her body limp.

Peter had his hand under her chin, gently forcing her face up into the dim light. He looked into her eyes. "Dalia, darling, you'll see things more clearly once you start bible study. When you finish work tomorrow, we'll buy your engagement ring at Silbigers."

She wanted to scream that they were not engaged but a voice at the back of her mind said restoring Peter to a whole person again was equally important. It was her mission to restore the missing layer. Another section of her mind lent its support. She would never get close to Mr Shepard if she rejected Peter. Eretz Israel was more important than any individual.

They walked back to the lodging house. Outside the door Peter said, "I gather you're spending tomorrow night with the Shepards. Pack your bathing costume and walking clothes. We may go swimming on Saturday. Oh. And don't forget to tell the superintendent tomorrow that you're changing your day off. It's probably too late to change this week, you'll have to take a day from your annual leave."

"I can't go into work next Saturday either," she said. "We have to go Bereisheet so you can ask my father's permission to get engaged. I'll have to take another day off my holidays."

They indulged in another long kiss. After Peter had turned the corner, she raced to a public phone. After leaving Aaron a message, she left another for her parents with the nurse at Bereisheet saying she would be spending Shabbat with friends.

Chapter 13

It seemed odd not to be going home that Friday. She plucked her eyebrows, powdered her face, and applied lipstick in the women's restroom. Carrying her overnight bag, she met Peter at the jewellers.

He asked the assistant to show them a tray of diamond rings but she was enthralled by the colours and cuts of other stones on display.

The assistant held out a sparkling red ruby. She pictured fresh blood glinting in the sun. "No, not red."

She tried on an opal. Waggling her finger, she watched its pink mutate to shades of green and blue.

"An opal is unlucky unless it's your birthstone," the assistant warned.

Peter laughed. "We, who have received the Lord Jesus into our hearts, have left superstition behind. We will let that opal symbolise our faith in the Lord."

A cloud crossed the sun. The opal turned dead and grey. Dalia tugged off the ring, ready now to choose a diamond, but Peter was already at the desk writing out a cheque.

Outside the shop he placed the opal ring on the second finger of her left hand.

They caught the bus to central Carmel. The Shepards' house was only one storey high but couldn't be described as a bungalow. With tower and parapets surrounding a flat roof, it was too castle-like.

Jim and Addy Shepard seated them on a veranda, under a wooden canopy. An Arab maid brought in tea and biscuits and glowered at her the whole time she was serving.

At dusk, Peter and Jim went off to play in the dining room with Evie and Clare while Addy led her into a shabby sitting-room. All Dalia retained from that first study session was Addy's emphasis on Second Chosen women never wearing makeup.

Before Peter left, the Shepards announced that they were

going for a ramble to Khayet Beach the next day and Peter and Dalia would be more than welcome to join them.

The next morning, woken by Evie and Clare attempting to collect their clothes quietly from a cheap wardrobe, she found herself in a narrow room, on a lumpy mattress spread over a turquoise painted iron-frame bed. There was no dressing table, no mirror in the room.

"Sorry, we didn't mean to wake you," Evie apologised.

The children left. Dalia opened her overnight bag. When packing it the day before, she had decided the close fitting twill shorts and blue shirt she usually wore for rambles would not go down well with the Shepards, so had settled instead for a home-made dirndl skirt, white blouse, ankle socks, and floppy tembel hat. She had forgotten her sturdy sandals so would have to ramble in the court shoes she had worn the previous day. The house had no running water so she had a cold rainwater shower. On returning to the bedroom she took her vanity mirror from her purse and stared at her drab unpainted face, wondering if this was how she was going to have to look for the rest of her life. She unrolled her haversack and put in her bathing costume, towel and water bottle.

Peter arrived with pitta bread still warm from an Arab baker, butter from the NAAFI, and a jar of honey. They ate breakfast sitting around the table on the veranda, and Suzanna, still glaring at her, brought in tea and coffee.

After breakfast Peter stuffed her haversack into his rucksack. Addy and the children, eight year old Evie and six year old Clare, carried their own haversacks, but Jim weighed himself down with a large rucksack containing the main picnic items. He untied a smooth-haired terrier that answered to Dandy from a nearby tree and put it on a lead. The adult Shepards picked up stout walking sticks, reminding Dalia of her parents setting out to ramble in the Black Forest before Hitler took over.

The back lane behind the Shepards' house led to an as yet undeveloped area of the comparatively flat but rocky mountain top, but it was already marked out with building pegs.

Jim let Dandy off the lead. He constantly scampered out

of sight, running back to check its owner was still in existence before racing forward again.

They reached a goat track that sloped steeply to the foot of the mountain where an emerald carpet of deceptively peaceful citrus groves stretched to sand dunes lining the sparkling blue Mediterranean. Dalia knew those citrus groves hid camps where allied troops trained for the desert war. Further south, illegal immigrants languished in a concentration camp.

While the children negotiated the goat path on their backsides, and the Shepards used their walking sticks, Dalia, in her unsuitable shoes, even though she was holding Peter's hand, slipped and slithered. Eventually the path widened between rocky walls. A stink of rotting flesh assailed her nostrils.

"What is that awful smell?" Addy asked.

Dandy whined and bounded up the rocks above the path and howled. Jim whistled. The animal climbed down reluctantly. Jim put it on a lead, but it strained forward, whining, trying to drag its master up the side of the mini-gorge.

Dalia felt Peter's hand tremble as he cleared his throat. "We killed a couple of smugglers around here some time ago, but we built a huge mound of stones over them. Nothing could have dug them out."

Jim handed the dog's lead to Addy and clambered up the rocks. Clare hid her face in her mother's skirt. Evie wandered off until called back by her mother.

Jim shouted, "Didn't you bury them before piling on those stones?"

Peter shouted back, "We hadn't any spades."

Jim climbed down. "You may have kept out the jackals but you left chinks for flies. You should have found a cave and blocked the entrance."

Addy hit the ground with her stick. "Jim, hurry up. This is not a fit place for children."

Dalia let Addy go ahead with Clare and Evie as she waited for Peter.

When he came up his face was white and drawn. "I'm

sorry, Dalia, I didn't realise we were so near Haifa when we caught up with those smugglers."

They reached the citrus groves, and a wave of homesickness swept over Dalia. She should be home, not out here.

When they reached Khayet Beach, the cashier refused to allow Dandy in. Jim argued but lost the dispute. He found a shady bush and tethered the dog.

Dalia was grateful to see rows of changing booths. She hadn't been looking forward to undressing in public.

The cool booth smelled of seaweed. She sat in her bathing costume on the sand-sprinkled seat, her arms huddled round her thighs. She'd thought she'd known all about death and violence but that stench on the mountain had brought home all the sordid aspects of death. She wanted to comfort Peter but, if she were honest, needed him to comfort her.

She stood up, folded her clothes, and opened the door. Peter stood outside. She flung her arms around him. He kissed her gently and drew her, not towards the sea, but to the rear of the bathing station. She leaned back against the hut as he bent towards her and kissed her harder, his tongue exploring her mouth, his hands slipping down her bathing costume straps, exposing her breasts.

Sliding her hands down the length of his body, she closed her fingers around the cord of his trunks, drawing him towards her.

"Peter, Dalia, where the heck have you got to? The children are waiting for you." Jim's voice came from somewhere close.

Peter pulled away, and Dalia hastily pulled up her straps.

"Oh, Dalia," Peter whispered. He stepped back a pace. "Oh, my darling, I do so want you. Go on down to the sea with Jim, dearest. I'll see you there."

He turned and hurried off towards the fence separating the site from undisturbed sand dunes.

Dalia found herself shaking with excitement. She could still feel the thrill of Peter's mouth on her body. She wondered how far they would have gone if Jim hadn't called them. She took a deep breath, straightened her costume and attempted to step sedately between the huts. "Peter is feeling sick after that experience on the mountain," she told Jim. "He needs a little while before he joins everyone."

"The idiot should have thought of that two months ago," Jim replied.

She felt sure now that she loved Peter. The way things were going they should marry as soon as possible.

After the inauspicious start, the rest of the day at Khayet Beach went well as she and Peter played with Clare and Evie and enjoyed the picnic the Shepards had brought. They were the happiest hours she had spent in Haifa.

She was disappointed, however, when Peter insisted she return on the bus with Addy and Clare while he walked back up the mountain with Jim and a very reluctant Evie.

"I'll meet you at ten tomorrow to take you to Sharing," he promised before he went off.

* * * *

Dalia wasn't looking forward to a return visit to the dingy Second Chosen hall, although intrigued by the mysterious Sharing ceremony.

To avoid answering awkward questions at her lodgings, she dressed for the office as usual before going down to breakfast, but afterwards removed make-up and dressed in dowdier clothes. When it was time to meet Peter, she slipped downstairs and closed the front door quietly.

Peter, waiting outside, hooked her arm onto his and gave a satisfied sigh. "I have been waiting for this moment so long, the two of us going to Sharing together!"

She would rather they were off to the beach or anywhere else where they could continue what they had started behind the changing booths.

Outside the hall she stared in dismay at the sight of clusters of people in elegant clothes.

"They all look so different today," she burst out.

"Of course, they're in their Sunday best," Peter replied.

He looked her over. "Never mind, sweetheart, you look beautiful whatever you're wearing."

Jim came rushing over. "Dalia, would you mind if I take Peter off?"

She did mind but, without waiting for her reply, Jim led Peter around the side of the building. People threw her curious glances and she was conscious again of inappropriate attire. She went into the hall, looking for Mrs Shepard, but the chairs, now arranged in a number of small circles, were occupied by groups of children.

She beat a hasty retreat and moved into the shade of a fig tree growing in a dry-stone wall. A pair of bulbuls, pecking at ripening apricots beyond the wall, reminded her of Bereisheet, and by association, her parents. She worried about her parents' reaction to her conversion. It was all very well telling herself that her grandmother had married a gentile. At least her grandmother had been able to bring up her father as a Jew. Her children would be brought up Second Chosen.

Peter and Jim returned. Peter's cheeks glowed an angry red.

Jim looked sad as he said, "The Spiritual Guides have asked to see you, Dalia."

She clutched Peter's arm but he shook his head. "They insist on seeing you alone, sweetheart. I'll wait here."

She followed Jim through a door at the rear of the hall and found herself in the backroom where she had met Addy on Thursday. Men, in best suits, sat in rows, bibles on their laps, facing a single empty chair. She recognised Inspector Sutton next to her bank manager, Mr Manners, in the centre of the front row. Jim Shepard slipped into a side seat.

Mr Manners waved her to the lone chair. She regretted more than ever her shabby dress.

Mr Manners addressed her in a pious tone. "Miss Leitner, you came forward on Thursday to give your heart to the Lord, for which we give praise." He paused while other men chorused Amens. "Recently, after much prayer, we have adopted the practice of receiving converts on active service into immediate fellowship."

His tone changed as if addressing an overdrawn customer. "However, you, Miss Leitner, are not on active service nor are you 'a brand plucked from the burning'. You, the seed of Abraham, already have a covenant with the Almighty. Before we take you into fellowship, you must understand the difference between the Old Covenant and the New. It is the opinion of the Spiritual Guides that you should receive adequate instruction in the New Testament before entering into our fellowship. Our Sister in the Lord, Adelina Shepard, will provide this instruction."

Mr Manners paused and glanced at Inspector Sutton. "Until you are baptised and received into the fellowship of Saints, you and our brother in Christ, Peter Monteith, may not enter into a state of holy matrimony."

Time stuck focussing on a single silent frame, a boardroom photo of complacent men in pressed suits. Movement returned.

Jim Shepard stood, forestalling her indignant response.

"Dear Brothers in Christ, the Lord has commanded me to speak. This young soul—" he glanced at Dalia and gave her a brief smile "—made a courageous decision when she let the Lord into her heart. She forsook her parents and friends, a sacrifice few of us have had to make." He looked at Inspector Sutton who flushed and averted his eyes. "Being a babe in faith," Jim continued, "Miss Leitner should be treated as we treat our young children of the flesh, and although she may not participate in Sharing, she should be allowed to sit with us in fellowship."

A serious looking man with a tidy toothbrush moustache called out in a heavy Arabic accent, "Amen, Brother Shepard. The Lord our God is a merciful God. He tempers the wind to the shorn lamb."

Mr Manners drew himself up even straighter and stared the man down.

Jim resumed his seat and Inspector Sutton rose.

"Brethren in Christ, we agreed after much prayer that we need to test this young person's faith."

"Amen to that," Mr Manners intoned. "Now let us pray

again."

The men knelt on the rough, wooden boards. Jim beckoned her to follow suit. She hesitated, wanting to storm out, but Shai needed her close to Jim, so she dropped to her knees, cursing under her breath when she heard a gentle zing and felt a ladder in one stocking run from knee to thigh.

On the other side of the wooden partition children sang, "One door, the only one, and yet the sides are two. We're on the inside, but which side are you?"

So long as she was an insider for Peter she could stomach being an outsider to these pompous Spiritual Guides.

Mr Manner's lengthy prayer ended.

Jim rose to his feet and escorted her outside. Peter rushed to her side.

"I'm sorry, Peter," Jim apologised. "Len remains convinced that Dalia only converted to marry you."

Peter tucked her arm into his reassuringly. "We both know that's not true, sweetheart."

Evie and Clare skipped towards them. Jim waved them away. Dalia watched them droop over to the bus stop on the main road.

"Dalia," Jim said, "I am afraid you have to sit on the back bench during Sharing."

Peter glared. "Then I'll sit with her."

Dalia felt confused, unsure why they considered the issue of where she sat more important than the wedding ban. She watched Addy step off a bus, resplendent in dark patterned silk. Evie and Clare ran and clung to her. Mr Manners approached. The children let go of their mother's hands and walked slowly back.

Peter led Dalia into the hall. The chairs had been re-arranged yet again, this time into two concentric circles surrounding a table that held a still life arrangement of earthenware jug, silver chalice and cottage loaf on a wooden platter. Most people seated in the circles were well-dressed civilians with a sprinkling of men and women in uniform. She recognised some as fellow converts from Thursday evening.

Peter led her to a bench at the rear of the hall. Jim and

his children settled in the inner circle. Addy came in a few minutes later and waved at her before joining her family.

A man in the outer circle stood and, in broken English, asked everyone to join him in prayer. For the next hour and a half, men from both circles stood to announce hymns, which the congregation sang without the aid of a piano, say prayers or, while holding open bibles, to ramble on about pomegranates on the bottom of priests' robes and prophets burning dung. Others shouted Hallelujah and Amen at frequent intervals. The women only opened their mouths to join in the singing.

Halfway through the service Mr Manners walked to the central table and broke the loaf of bread with his fingers before passing the plate to a man in the front row. The plate passed from hand to hand. Adults took a crumb and ate it. Jim left his seat when the plate reached him, and brought it over to Peter. The two men each took a crumb. Jim returned to his place and passed the plate on. The last person to receive the bread returned it to the table. Mr Manners poured wine into the chalice. That too went the rounds, everyone taking a sip, Jim again leaving the circle to bring the chalice over to Peter.

Mr Manners gave out notices about women's meetings and forthcoming baptisms, after which the programme resumed its previous impromptu style, with Mr Manners intoning a blessing to close the meeting.

On the final Amen, Peter sprang from the bench and dragged her outside.

"I'm not coming here ever again," Dalia stated.

Peter took both her hands. "Of course you're angry, sweetheart, and so am I. You needn't attend Sharing again until you're baptised, but Sunday evening gospel services are different. Mrs Shepard has invited us to supper after tonight's service, so we have to go." He put his arm around her and kissed her hair.

She had to keep in touch with Jim Shepard, so compromised. "Okay! But no Sharing, you promise?"

"Promise. Not until the Spiritual Guides let you sit in fellowship."

"What about our wedding?"

"That will be hard, but the Lord will give me the strength to contain myself. I promise not to give way to my baser instincts again until we are married."

She wanted to ask, "Do I have to restrain my baser instincts too?" but, while cold sober, couldn't bring herself to voice that thought aloud.

"Come on," Peter said. "I'll take you out to lunch and then we can go for a walk until it is time for the Gospel Service."

Addy brought both her children to the gospel service.

"Where's Jim?" Peter asked.

Addy rolled her eyes dramatically, and put a finger to her lips. "Tell you later."

Peter nodded. "I hope he won't be away as long as last time."

Back on Mount Carmel, Addy told them, "Jim's been sent to Iraq but don't say anything to Suzanna. She's loyalty itself, I'm sure, but who knows whom she meets on her Sundays off."

"You're right to be cautious," Peter agreed. "Even Christian Arabs are dithering about loyalty to the Allies now the Nazis are doing so well."

Before they left, Addy arranged that while Peter was in Tarshiha, Dalia should come for bible study on Monday, Wednesday, and Friday evenings.

"You'll be back next Saturday to come to Bereisheet?" Dalia asked Peter as they walked to the bus stop.

"Of course."

Chapter 14

Tuesday, Dalia reported back to Aaron. He was delighted when she informed him Jim Shepard had been sent to Iraq.

"We knew there was something big going on when troops from Nathanya drove brand new cars up the Jordan valley, but we weren't sure whether they were about to invade Iraq, or fight rebels."

Dalia wondered whether sometimes Shai welcomed new information just for the sake of it. "How does my information help?"

"Now we know British troops will be thin on the ground here, we can take a few more risks. We may even be able to get chaps of our own included on this Iraqi excursion to help bring in refugees held up in Iraq."

On Thursday she went to see Ruth. It was high time to tell her about her engagement. Ruth was on evening duty but had a ten minute break about nine p.m. She went up to the hospital armed with a studio photograph of Peter in uniform and sat outside the ward staring ahead at the corridor's white wall tiles. The smell of carbolic was strong.

She caught her friend as she came out. "I need to tell you something, Ruth."

Ruth sank into a chair opposite.

Dalia thrust Peter's photo under her nose. "Peter and I are engaged."

Ruth studied it closely. "He looks sensitive, your Peter, and very handsome, but are you sure about this, Dalia? You, of all people, marrying a gentile?"

Dalia returned her friend's gaze without flinching, her chin high, and said, "Yes," but wondered if she was being truthful.

Ruth gave her a hug. "Dalia, I am so happy for you. When are you planning to marry?"

"Not until September."

"Oh, I am going to Egypt at the end of July! I hope I can

get leave to come up."

"You'll have to. You're my chief bridesmaid. Oh!" She put her hand to her mouth. "But you may not want to be. Things are a bit more complicated than I told you."

Ruth sighed, and settled into a chair. "He isn't in the middle of getting a divorce, is he?"

"No, nothing like that. You may think it's worse, though." She felt her fingernails bite into her palms. "He's a fundamentalist Christian, Ruth." She looked down at the black and white floor tiles. "And this is the bit you'll hate. We can only marry because I converted."

Ruth sat up straight, her face a mask of disbelief. "You! You've converted to Christianity!"

"Yes."

"But why? Not just so you can marry this Peter?"

"Ruth, I can't explain what happened." She banged the arms of her chair in frustration. "One minute I was sitting, listening to this weird American preacher. The next I was walking down the aisle being saved."

Ruth nodded. "I've heard of that happening, but," she added comfortingly, "the conversion wears off once people remember who they are."

"If it does, I lose Peter. The worst part is, Ruth, I have to be married in the Gospel Hall."

"That's something your mother won't appreciate."

"I know. What shall I do?"

Ruth stared thoughtfully at Peter's photograph. "Say nothing for a while. Sometimes things resolve themselves."

Dalia screwed her face up. "You mean Peter and I may never marry? Oh, Ruth. That's what I am afraid of."

* * * *

Dalia removed her engagement ring in the car on the way to Bereisheet. "Best not let my parents see it until you've asked my father's blessing."

There were only the four of them around the table that lunchtime, the Rumanian illegals having discreetly taken themselves off to friends at a nearby kibbutz when her parents had warned them of the visit by a British policeman. Conversation was mainly instigated by her mother, interrogating Peter in broken English about his family and upbringing. Dalia learnt that Peter's father was a solicitor in Cumbria, that Peter had gone to a local grammar school, and had joined the Palestine Police after meeting the ex-Palestine policeman and author Douglas V Duff.

After lunch Peter asked Dalia's father if he could have a word in private. While the two men walked around the farm she told her mother that Peter had asked to marry her and she had accepted.

Her mother jumped up and punched the air repeatedly as she strode round the kitchen, letting fly a long tirade including phrases like. "I knew we shouldn't have allowed you to work in Haifa!" and "To think a child of mine is marrying a goy!"

"Granny Leitner did," Dalia pointed out, but it went unheard.

Eventually, her mother sat down heavily at the kitchen table. "Do you love this man?"

Dalia nodded.

"When do you expect to marry?"

"In autumn."

That at least reassured Eema that she wasn't pregnant.

Her mother abruptly transformed from tragedy queen to efficient organiser and picked up paper and pencil from the sideboard. "We'll have our friends from Rehovot over for the wedding. You'll want your old school friends, plus their husbands, children, and fiancés. Everyone from here, of course.

"But Eema."

Her mother ignored her interruption. "How many people will this Peter of yours want to bring over? You must find out as soon as possible. We'll have to have it outside. There'll be at least three hundred guests. If we have it early October we won't need marquees."

Dalia, who had been trying to interrupt calmly, now shouted, "Stop."

Her mother looked up, startled.

"Eema," Dalia began, and burst into tears.

Her mother put down her paper and pencil. "Child! What is this?"

"Oh, Eema," Dalia started again and couldn't go on.

"Speak. Tell me, what is wrong?"

"It's just..." Dalia took a deep breath "...we won't be getting married in Bereisheet."

"You want to marry in England? You think this war's going to be finished by autumn? No way!"

"No, Eema," Dalia tried again. "Peter wants us to marry in Haifa, in the Second Chosen hall."

"So," her mother flashed her eyes. "He wants to choose where to get married, but his parents are in England. You leave it to me, Dalia. I'll tell him."

At this juncture her father and Peter entered the kitchen. Neither looked happy.

Her father glanced at her mother and raised his eyebrows. "Trudi," he said in Hebrew, "the four of us had better sit down to thrash this thing out."

Her mother sat at the table, twisting her fingers. When they were all seated, her father continued. "Trudi, Dalia has informed you that Peter has asked my blessing on their betrothal."

Her mother nodded.

"Dalia, you explained the complications?"

She shook her head. "She wouldn't listen."

"Trudi," her father said gently. "Peter told me that Dalia has converted to Christianity."

Her mother gave a screech. "Dalia, tell me this is not so."

Dalia looked at her mother. She didn't want to hurt her. She looked at Peter. She didn't want to lose him. She burst into tears, ran to her bedroom and slammed the door, but knew sooner or later she would have to face everyone, so she might as well make it sooner. She returned to the kitchen.

Peter was huddled in his chair.

She looked at her mother. "I'm sorry, Eema, but what Abba said is true."

Her mother burst into tears and pushed her hands forward as if shoving her away. "Leave this house."

Her father remained calm as he usually did when her mother got into one of her furies. He, too, spoke in Hebrew. "Dalia, your mother and I will never stop loving you, but in making this decision you have turned your back on your family. If you visit us again before your wedding there will be nothing but strife between you and your mother. You will say things to each other that will be hard to forget.

"Peter," he said, changing into English, "there is time between now and the wedding. It may be that you will find it within you to compromise and take Dalia as a Jewish wife as my father did with my mother."

Peter sat up straight. "Sir," he stated almost apologetically, "that will not be possible."

Her father nodded. "Dalia," he continued, still in English, "unless you decide to marry as a Jew, for the sake of peace, please stay away from Bereisheet until after your wedding. After your wedding, I will welcome Peter to my house as a son-in-law and hope you will invite me to your home."

Oh, dear, wise Abba. How he must be hurting and yet he sat there so calm, so reasonable. Dalia breathed in hard, stood up, and kissed the top of her mother's head. Her mother flicked up a hand as if brushing off a fly. Dalia kissed her father on the forehead. That close up she could see the effort he was making to keep back his own tears.

She hugged him. When she pulled away, Peter held out his hand to her father.

Her father took it and said, "Please think things over."

"I will pray for a resolution," Peter replied.

Dalia picked up her things and walked to the car. They drove off in silence, tears streaming down Dalia's face. When they reached the main Haifa road, Peter stopped the car and wiped her face with his handkerchief.

"Dalia," he said, "your father is a remarkable man."

She sniffled. "I know, and I am an ungrateful daughter."

"No!" Peter protested. "You did what you had to. Your father recognises that."

"My mother doesn't."

"But as your father says, she will come round once we are married." He pulled the ring box out of his pocket.

"I don't want to put it on!"

"Please! Your father didn't withhold his permission."

Slowly, he drew the ring out of the box and placed it on her finger. In the shadow of the glove compartment, the opal showed an ominous grey.

Chapter 15

With Peter back at Tarshiha, Dalia couldn't bring herself to go to the gospel service after work that Sunday. She phoned to arrange a meeting with Aaron instead.

He was delighted that she would be visiting the Shepard's house regularly.

"Mr Shepard doesn't leave sensitive documents at the office," he told her. "Seize every opportunity to hunt for papers. If you find anything, contact us immediately."

She couldn't think how she could wander unnoticed through the few rooms in the Shepards' house.

She kept her bible study appointment with Addy on Monday, and explained she had been too upset by her mother's reaction to her engagement to attend Gospel meeting the previous night before.

Addy was sympathetic. "Peter came to Sharing before returning to Tarshiha. He told us what happened. We are your new family."

After the inevitable prayers for guidance, Addy said, "I've been thinking. Why don't you stay with us both Friday and Saturday nights? I know you won't be coming to Sharing on Sunday mornings until you're baptised, but you would do me a favour, keeping an eye on the roast and putting in the rice pudding at the right time. Sunday dinner's always over-cooked when Jim's not here to take the children to Sunday school."

Dalia had hoped to spend next Sunday morning swimming and sun-bathing at Bat Galim, but a Shai agent couldn't turn down the opportunity to search the house.

"That's so kind of you."

The following Sunday Dalia discovered Jim's papers. They were spilling out of a folder in the Shepards' communal bedroom; a hotchpotch of diagrams, handwritten memos, and typewritten documents. She concentrated on the text. The bulk concerned British plans for Palestine in the event of a German invasion. Those, she thought, would interest Aaron the most.

She started making notes and realised she should have put on the meat and potatoes half-an-hour earlier. She interrupted her note taking again for the rice pudding. By the time she had to pack away and lay the dinner table she hoped she hadn't missed anything important.

Aaron glanced through her notes at their next meeting.
"No diagrams?"
"Yes, but I didn't understand them."
Aaron waved a hand. "No matter, I'll be bringing a photographer and communications expert. When can you let us in?"

She had not anticipated that. It was one thing for her to search the house, quite another to allow strangers in. Her conscience pricked as she thought about Addy's kindness, but she couldn't let down Shai.

The following Sunday she let in Aaron and his two accomplices. While they went through the papers deciding what to photograph, she basted the meat and put the rice pudding into the oven.

Locking the back door, she sat at the veranda table.

The hinges of the back door squeaked. She checked the key in her pocket. As a warning to Aaron, she called loudly, "Who's there?" and stepped into the dining room.

Suzanna was in the kitchen. Seeing her, the maid slapped her hand to her mouth, eyes wide open, the very picture of guilt.

"What are you doing here?" Dalia asked in as stern a voice as she could muster, while blocking the door with her body to prevent Suzanna moving through.

Her voice obviously wasn't stern enough because Suzanna dropped her hand and retorted, "I might ask you the same question."

Dalia had to keep conversation going until she was sure Aaron and his team had escaped. "Mrs Shepard invited me to stay overnight. She left *me* in charge this morning and said nothing about you returning."

Suzanna moved forward until they were almost touching.

"If it's any business of yours, which it isn't, I've come to pick up presents for my brother's new baby. Let me pass."

Dalia marched into the dining room and leaned against the door leading into the dormitory, listening for sounds on the other side, while watching Suzanna enter the curtained-off cubicle that served as her bedroom. The maid emerged carrying an embroidered baby gown.

"You have what you want. Now leave," Dalia ordered.

Suzanna, however, glared and turned towards the dormitory.

"I have to collect Mrs Shepard's present as well. You may watch me if you suspect I am a thief."

All was quiet in the next room so Dalia opened the door. She cast a quick look around the room. There was nothing to suggest intruders had paid a visit. The documents were back in the folder, looking tidier than when she had found them. Suzanna walked past her, and stooped to open a sewing box from which she pulled out a matinee jacket wrapped in tissue paper.

Dalia reported the maid's visit when Addy returned home. If anything was missing there would be another suspect beside herself.

"So she found the matinee jacket I knitted. That's good," Addy commented. "I hope it washes well. With the wool you get nowadays you can't tell. Talking about washing, what do you do about your laundry?"

"I'll have to sort something else out now I'm not going home every week."

"Bring it with you, sorted into whites, coloureds and delicates. Suzanna can wash it with ours."

That solved another problem, but even as Dalia gratefully accepted the offer, she wondered how much more of her life Addy would control over the next few weeks.

It turned out Addy took over her wedding, much as her mother would have done. "We must get you baptised before the rains start so we can have the wedding reception in the garden. What are you doing about bridesmaids?"

"There's my friend Ruth," Dalia said, "and..." she

hesitated. She couldn't ask anyone else she knew or her conversion would be all around Bereisheet. Her mother would never forgive her for that. "What about your daughters?"

Addy beamed. "They'd love it."

Peter wrote to her every day. He, too, was in organising mode.

My dear, darling Dalia, my sister in the Lord and bride to be,

I praise the Lord you and Addy are hitting it off so well. It makes me feel less guilty being away so long.

Don't let Addy spend any money on our behalf. The Shepards are the soul of generosity but haven't two piastres to rub together now inflation's gone through the roof. They're civilians and have to buy everything on the open market. I'm able to get stuff through the NAAFI. Ask Addy to send me a list of things needed for the wedding. I'll also pay some money into your bank account for things like the wedding cake and flowers.

She kept Peter's letters, tied with ribbon, under her pillow. She took them out and read them for comfort whenever she felt miserable. She felt even more in love with Peter when he was away than when he was with her.

Jim returned from Iraq, obviously far from well. Almost immediately he became involved in something else very hush-hush that kept him out of the house to all hours.

While convoys of trucks filled with Ghurkhas rolled through Haifa all day on the way to the Syrian border, he succumbed to yellow jaundice. Despite Addy spending the best part of the day with him at the hospital, Dalia's bible study classes continued. She no longer felt it strange to go down on her knees and pray with Addy. At the end of July, after listening to Addy's account of her progress, the Spiritual Guides finally named a date for her baptism.

My own darling Peter, Dalia wrote. *You'll be over the moon to learn I am to be baptised at the end of September, on Addy's birthday. That makes our wedding the first week in October. Be sure to book your leave, so I can get the invitations out. I'm so excited now. I found a beautiful second-hand wedding dress. It took most of my savings but you will agree it's worth it when you see it. An Armenian dressmaker is altering it to fit. I've put in an order for the wedding cake.*

Oh, Peter, I do love you so.

Despite her letters, Dalia still had misgivings. She felt like two people, one half the Dalia Leitner who wanted to save as many refugees as possible and see Jews create a fertile Eretz Israel, the other the head-over-heels in love fiancée of a British Christian policeman. The one thing she didn't delude herself about was that she had actually become a Christian.

The Friday after she'd posted the letter telling him of her baptism date, Peter walked into the police office with work to be typed. It was all Dalia could do to stop herself jumping up and hugging him.

"Have you set the date yet?" Leila asked.

"The first Saturday in October," Peter said.

"I hear congratulations are in order for you, too," Peter said.

"Yes, my mother insists I leave work so she can train me to be a proper housewife before my wedding in November."

"I'll soon be the only one in the office with any experience," Patsy said.

Jim had returned from hospital, very weak and somewhat cantankerous, but Addy decreed that while Peter was in Haifa for the weekend, they should have a serious discussion about the wedding.

"Who'll be marrying us?" Dalia asked.

"The Lord," Jim replied. "Only God makes a marriage. The service is merely a celebration. The civil part takes place at the High Commissioner's office. We can get that over with the week before, in your lunch-hour perhaps, Dalia? Peter has plenty of time to apply for the licence. Addy and I will be witnesses."

"What about invitations to the proper wedding?" Addy asked.

"I'll see to those," Dalia said. It was her wedding, after all.

Jim bit his lip. "Show me your mock-up and I'll get them printed. You mustn't put our address on them, you know that, don't you?"

"Why not?"

"Security."

"But how will people know where to go?"

"Just say that the wedding service will take place at the Second Chosen hall and there will be a reception afterwards," Addy said. "We'll tell people after the service."

Her parents wouldn't come to a Christian wedding, she was sure, but they might come to the civil ceremony. She'd speak to Addy afterwards about putting the civil ceremony on the wedding invitations. Addy could deal with Jim's objections.

"All sounds tickety-boo," Peter said. "I'll take three weeks' annual leave starting the Saturday of the baptism so I'll be in Haifa for the civil ceremony and we can have a fortnight's honeymoon. How do you fancy Tiberius, Dalia?"

"I'd love it."

The next Thursday, when Dalia went to work, she received a note from Peter. He was in Haifa overnight. Did she fancy dinner out?

It would be good to meet up, just the two of them, away from the Shepards. She'd tell him about the full-dress civil ceremony she and Addy were planning. She couldn't get over how firm Addy had been with Jim about adding the civil ceremony to the wedding invitations in case Dalia's parents and friends wanted to attend.

The telephone rang. The new girl, Michelle, Leila's sister, answered it. "For you, Dalia." Michelle had her hand over the receiver. "A man."

"Peter?"

"No."

Dalia rose from her typewriter, her stomach suddenly queasy. Who, apart from Peter or Addy, would ring her at work? No one from Shai. Had something happened to Peter, to Uri, to her parents?

She took the receiver. "Hello."

"Jim Shepard here."

Instant relief. Probably just something to do with her baptism.

"I need to speak to you urgently." Jim's voice sounded aggressive. "I can't talk over the phone. Meet me in the café opposite the Post Office at twelve-thirty." He hung up.

Dalia had an uneasy feeling. What had Jim to say that he couldn't tell her on the phone? After that, she couldn't concentrate on her work. Suppose the Spiritual Guides were postponing her baptism and Peter insisted on changing the wedding date? She had already posted invitations to the civil ceremony to her parents and Ruth. Ruth had applied for leave.

By the time she left the office, her eyelids felt bloated and her mouth dry. Peering through the café window, she saw Jim, stiff-backed, his lips pressed hard together.

As she seated herself opposite him, instead of a conventional greeting, Jim mouthed, "Mossad el Aliyah Beth?"

She felt the blood drain from her face and wished she still carried a powder compact to hide behind. "What are you talking about?"

The waitress arrived and took their order. Jim drew his handkerchief from his top pocket and wiped first his glasses and then his forehead.

After the waitress had left, he said wearily, "Stop the nonsense." He drew a paper bag from his jacket pocket and held it out. "You won't deny this is yours?"

She looked inside and saw the embroidered handkerchief she had included with her laundry. It still gave out whiffs of Lily of the Valley, so Suzanna hadn't yet washed it. What, though, had it to do with Shai?

She stared at Jim, wondering what he wanted her to say. He stared back as if the hanky explained everything. Seconds dragged on to minutes. The waitress brought their coffee. She picked up her cup, sipping gingerly at the hot liquid, determined that Jim should make the next move.

"You left it in my briefcase," he said at last. "I've had your background investigated thoroughly since."

She was well and truly confused now. She had bought the handkerchief after searching through Jim's papers.

"Dalia, I'm giving you the chance to resign," Jim ground out, "to leave Haifa without ruining Peter's career. If you've any feeling at all for him, that's the least you can do."

He stood up, leaving his coffee untouched. "That's all I

have to say."

She wanted to scream, shout, and burst into tears. Instead, she sat in the café, finishing her coffee, thinking—now it was too late—of questions she should have asked, if only to learn how much he knew.

She gazed around the crowded cafe. Anyone could be spying on her. Contacting either Aaron or Max immediately was out of the question.

She made her way back to work, sought out Mrs Jones, pleaded a severe headache, and caught the bus to the top of Mount Carmel. She sat on a seat in Allenby Park, deserted at this the hottest time of the day, sobbing while flies buzzed round the outside of her head and everything whirled inside.

A young mother with a pram sat on the seat beside her. She stood up and found herself walking automatically towards the Shepards' house. She must confess everything, or nearly everything, to Addy.

In the Shepards' living room, she explained that she belonged to an organisation whose sole purpose was to help Jews escape from the Nazis and settle in the Promised Land. "That's not wrong, is it?"

"My dear, of course not. The Lord has obviously called you to do this work, so how can it be wrong?"

Dalia felt a wave of relief. She had Addy on her side. She took a deep breath. "Jim doesn't see it your way."

"No," Addy answered. "He wouldn't. Nowadays his undercover work seems more important to him than the bible."

"Undercover work?"

Addy clapped a hand to her mouth. "Forget I said that. Let's concentrate on your difficulties. We must pray this through."

Dalia had endured enough instruction by now to know the drill, but, after kneeling, all she could come up with was a heartfelt, "Help me, Lord."

"Better sometimes just to listen than to speak," Addy comforted, so they spent another ten minutes kneeling in silence.

"Let's go to the Good Book for guidance," Addy said eventually. While Addy was fetching her a spare copy from the bookshelf, Jim came in. He stopped at the door and glared at them both.

"I'm taking the dog for a walk," he announced.

Addy resumed her place on the settee and opened her bible at random. "The Lord has guided us to Ephesians."

They ploughed through both the first and second epistles to the Ephesians. Nothing seemed pertinent, although, Addy claimed, the reference to the Commonwealth of Israel was significant. It had been a mistake, coming here, but it was already growing dark by the time she escaped. She walked to the main road and found a path leading behind houses to the unspoiled hillside that sloped steeply to the lower leg of the Stella Maris Road.

Cicadas, oblivious to her misery, scraped a continuous high-pitched chorus. The moon, like a divine searchlight, silvered the blacked-out buildings of downtown Haifa. In the foreground, the apartment block, where Peter lived, loomed tall against a backdrop of corrugated sea. Dalia remembered that Peter had asked her to phone after work. She had to see him if only to find out what Jim had told him.

She sat on a patch of sweet-smelling thyme, plucked two weed leaves already slightly damp with dew, and placed them on her swollen eyelids. Slowly, she counted to five hundred before removing them and walked down a goat track in her office clothes, conscious of thorn bushes shredding her stockings and pulling threads from her dress.

She knocked on Peter's door, shouting, "It's Dalia."

The door opened wide and Peter enveloped her in his arms, took her into the living room, and seated her on a sofa. "My poor, dear darling, whatever is the matter? Why didn't you phone?"

Coherence was a problem but after a while, Peter interrupted gently. "You're trying to tell me that you've been reporting to Shai and Jim has had a go at you?"

Dalia found it impossible to speak.

Peter hugged her again.

"But, darling, I guessed about you and Aliyah Beth. I *am* a detective, you know! Some of us in the British Police aren't entirely heartless. We ignore refugees entering illegally once they're living in Jewish settlements. What I can't understand is why the deuce Jim is making this fuss."

Reluctantly, and only because she was sure that Jim would tell him anyway, she confessed to reading his papers. She omitted the bit about letting in Aaron and his companions.

"Well, that was a bit naughty, but darling, it's not as if you were selling information to the Germans." He kissed her hair. "I can see that you may have to give up your job, but that won't matter. You'll be leaving when we marry, anyway."

She looked up at him in a daze. "You still want to marry me?"

"Of course, sweetheart."

He let her go. His face contorted. "Oh Dalia, I... If Jim talks to the authorities they'll stop us marrying. I must speak to him."

"Peter, will they send me to prison?"

"It won't get as far as that but..."

The telephone on the table near the sofa rang. Peter picked up the receiver, listened, and put his hand over the mouthpiece. "It's Jim."

Dalia felt sick, certain Jim would turn Peter against her.

Peter continued his telephone conversation. "She's sitting right beside me, very, very upset. Why all the fuss, Jim? You know we agreed that we weren't worried about connections with Shai. If you report this nonsense to the authorities they'll put a spoke in our getting married."

Jim said something.

Peter exploded. "Of course we're still getting married."

Dalia breathed a sigh of relief.

Peter listened again, then shouted angrily, "Security risk. What security risk? You, yourself, gave her clearance when she applied for the job."

Sounds on the other end of the line grew louder. Peter was now obviously forcing himself to calm down. "Look, Jim, can't we just forget this ever happened?"

More from Jim.

Peter put his hand over the mouthpiece again. "Dalia, he says he'll not report you so long as you hand in your resignation tomorrow."

"But I can't do that without giving a reason."

Peter relayed the message and listened again.

"Jim says tell them you need time to get ready for the wedding."

"But if I haven't got a job I can't pay my landlady."

Peter relayed that message too, adding, "The Spiritual Guides wouldn't approve of her moving in here."

"Jim's talking to Addy," Peter told her, keeping the receiver to his ear.

After a while, he handed it over, saying, "Addy wants to talk to you."

"Oh, Addy," Dalia burst out, "I don't know what to do. I could go home, I suppose, but my mother will go on and on about my getting married in a synagogue and there will be such ructions we may never be on speaking terms again."

"Jim and I would love you to stay with us until the wedding, Dalia. It'll make things easier all round getting everything arranged. Now hand the phone back to Peter. Jim wants another word."

Dalia sank back against the settee cushions, wanting nothing more than to fall asleep. When Peter put down the phone, however, she roused herself to throw her arms around his neck. "Thank you, thank you, my darling."

"It's the Shepards you should be thanking. Addy is really putting herself out for you and Jim is risking his entire career. Now come, I'll drive you back to your digs."

At the end of the week Dalia moved out of Giza Barat's lodging house. Patsy helped her carry her things downstairs, including her heavy typewriter.

Dalia didn't dare tell Giza Barat she was only leaving because she couldn't afford to stay in case Giza embarrassed her by offering to let her have a room free until she found another job. Instead, she handed her a wedding invitation and hugged her.

Peter had a taxi outside. He piled in Dalia's luggage and directed the driver to his flat.

Dalia set out her books and typewriter in a space Peter had cleared in the living room so she need only take clothes to the Shepards.

When she arrived on Mount Carmel she was surprised to find Addy going through an exercise book with Suzanna.

Suzanna was arguing about one of the exercises. "You can't measure three times the square root of two accurately, so why didn't they measure a side that wasn't an irrational number and ask me to work out the hypotenuse."

"Evie," Addy said in an irritated voice, "take Miss Leitner through to her bedroom and show her the wardrobe space you've cleared."

Evie looked sulky but led the way into the small bedroom. "There's no room in Mum and Dad's bedroom for my treasure box, so I've had to leave it here," she said, pointing to a tin trunk at the bottom of the wardrobe. "It's private, so please don't look in it like you did Daddy's briefcase."

At supper that night after Suzanna had served the food and glared at her as usual, Dalia asked, "Why's Suzanna working at maths?"

"Addy's trying to get her up to matric standard," Jim replied.

"Unusual thing do be doing with a servant," Dalia commented.

Addy looked embarrassed. "Dewya's not really a servant. She helps with the housework to pay for her tutoring. She is aiming to go to missionary college in London."

"She wants to be a missionary?"

"That's the role the Lord has chosen for her, although the silly girl has picked up the notion that she would rather be a government nurse."

Dalia realised she was not the only one whose life Mrs Shepard was organising.

Chapter 16

Dalia needed to contact Aaron to reassure him she had not abandoned Shai just because she was marrying Peter.

The problem was Addy was sticking to her like a tick and Jim had expressly forbidden her to write to anyone. She had to attend Sharing, but was still confined to the back seat. The only time she had to herself was the daily half hour meditation period Addy insisted on.

An idea occurred to her when she and Addy passed the XL job agency on their way to a fitting for her remodelled second-hand wedding dress.

During her next meditation period, she tore a page from the notebook Addy had given her for bible study and scribbled a brief note to Aaron.

The next time they went for a fitting, she limped for a while before stopping by the agency door. "Wait, please, Addy, I've a stone in my shoe."

Leaning on the door, she slipped her shoe off. While giving it an ostentatious shake, she surreptitiously slipped her note through the letterbox.

When Mr. Manners announced that the army had taken over the banks of the Jordan so the baptismal site would have to be changed, the other twenty-one baptismal candidates expressed bitter disappointment. Dalia, however, won oversight approval by declaring public witnessing was more important than geographic location.

The night before the baptism, the Shepards had invited Peter over for a special prayer meeting. They had agreed on eight o'clock but he had not arrived by nine.

"If you are marrying a British policeman, you'll get used to being kept waiting," Jim told her. "We'll start without him."

They were in the lounge, on their knees in prayer, when Evie flung open the door, wearing an air of self-importance. "Superintendent Fielding is on the phone, Daddy. He says he has bad news, and it's very serious."

Jim followed Evie out of the room.

"This is it, Dalia. The invasion," Addy said. "We'll have to get you evacuated with us. I'll tell the authorities you're the children's nanny."

"No," Dalia said. "I'm staying in Palestine to look after my parents."

"Peter should be your first concern, dear. You must forsake all others."

"But I can't forsake my parents!" Even if they have forsaken me, she thought.

"The bible tells us…" Addy didn't finish her sentence. Jim had returned, his face pale, both hands gripping his bible.

"Dalia, you are going to have to be brave."

"Peter?" she screeched, just before her hand slapped against her teeth. "He's been killed?" she whispered through open fingers.

"No-o," Jim answered slowly. "But he has been very, very badly wounded." He paused. "He's been shot in the stomach." Jim's voice sounded now as if on the other side of glass. "I've ordered a taxi for you and Addy."

She followed Addy out of the room to get her coat. This was the worst thing that had happened in her life, so why wasn't she crying?

In the taxi, Addy prayed all the way to the hospital, but Dalia could not join in. A vision of Peter lying on waste ground, blood and entrails mixing with dust and weeds left no room for prayer.

At the hospital, Peter lay between sheets only marginally whiter than his face. She hid her face in his bedcovers.

"He's full of morphine," a nurse told her. "Don't worry if he doesn't recognise you."

Dalia placed a hand on Peter's chest and continued to kneel, not praying, just trying to pour the excess of her own life into Peter.

"Penelope," Peter called out. "Penelope darling, you've come."

She pressed her forehead into the white bedcover. "Peter," she whispered, "it's Dalia. Dalia's here waiting for you."

A nurse tapped her gently on the shoulder. "We're taking him to theatre now, dear."

Porters wheeled the bed out of the room, down a long corridor.

"No further." A nurse restrained her gently. Dalia stood staring at closing double doors until a nurse led her back to Addy.

"I've phoned Jim to let him know what's happening," Addy said, knitting needles clicking as she worked on a half-finished pullover. "He'll come down tomorrow when he's parked the children at Sunday School." She put down her needles. "Let us pray." For once she didn't kneel.

Dalia closed her eyes and listened to Addy pleading for Peter's life, but still couldn't pray herself. Eventually, Addy stopped and resumed her knitting.

Outside the window, black night gave way to grey sky over a leaden sea. The sun peeped behind the mountain. Crests of waves glowed orange. The sea turned blue. A nurse brought cups of tea.

A British doctor entered the room, asked to speak to Addy outside. Dalia kept her eyes on the sparkling water.

Addy returned, a handkerchief pressed to her eyes. She whispered, "He's passed into glory. The Lord giveth, and the Lord taketh away. Blessed be the name of the Lord."

The cruel sea still sparkled. Everything else was still, except her lips. "Where's Peter? I want to see him."

She turned her head and concentrated on a nurse's white overall, her lips still moving. She walked behind the white into white, to a white Peter on a white bed surrounded by white walls. As she pressed her head onto his still chest, her throbbing temple seemed to meld into it. If she stayed long enough, they would become one. His heart would beat again. Someone tried to get between them, someone in white.

"He's mine," she told the dead Penelope and flung her arms round Peter to hasten the melding process.

Masculine arms tugged at her back.

"You're too late," she told Shimon and tightened her arm

round Peter, keeping the all-important contact between her head and his chest.

Something pricked her arm.

A blur of sobbing, the musty smell of a shoddy-filled mattress, an occasional shuffling to a bathroom next door, and a no longer hostile Suzanna bearing unwanted food. Addy prayed by her side. She was in a taxi again. Addy walked beside her into a building resembling Barclays Bank.

British policemen placed a large box, covered in a police flag, on a trestle.

"Where's Peter?"

"Shh," Jim Shepard hissed.

"Peter's in glory," Addy whispered. "Only his body's in that coffin."

People praying, kneeling as if at Mrs Shepard's house, except they had comfortable cushions for their knees. English versions of Jewish prayers, not the rhythmless ramblings of the Second Chosen. Chanted responses reminiscent of a synagogue service.

Police carried the box outside.

A taxi again.

The sun blazed down. Khayet Beach, where Peter had so nearly made love to her, lay beyond the wall. The mountain where he'd buried two smugglers loomed behind. Close to her feet a damp pit leading to Sheol.

The policemen lowered the box into the pit. A single trumpet wailed a forlorn tune. Peter had descended to Sheol to marry Penelope. The treacherous ring on her hand sparkled. She pulled it off and flung it away. It landed in the pit. Why had she given Penelope her ring? She leapt forward to retrieve it, but Penelope barred the way. She lifted her arm and hit her hard. Penelope fell back, rising again as Patsy.

"Dalia," Patsy said, "I am so sorry."

Addy intervened. "Miss Quigley. I am afraid only true believers can offer comfort to Dalia in her hour of sorrow. Dalia dear, it is time to go."

* * * *

More blur, more tears, a sodden pillow, light followed by dark, followed by light, followed by dark.

An urgent voice. "Dalia, pull yourself together and listen. This is important."

She forced open sore eyes. Addy sat on the foot of her bed.

Dalia placed her hands on her eyes, and moved them up to lank and greasy curls. "I must wash my hair."

"Dalia, listen. Do you know where Peter left his will?"

"A will, a will, a will o'whisp?"

"A will, a legal document, Dalia. Pull yourself together, girl."

She knew nothing of any will, but Addy continued to sit there, talking as if it were important, while pushing in recalcitrant hairpins.

"Peter made a will leaving everything to you, but the police say they haven't seen it. They're using the one that's been in their files since he joined the force."

There pops another hairpin.

"Unless we find the new one, the police will auction everything in his flat and send the proceeds to his parents. Even if we can't find the will, we need to retrieve your things."

Her things? Her typewriter. Peter had her typewriter. "I want my typewriter."

"We'll go and get it."

As she sat on the bus, her fingers caressed the smooth metal of the key Peter had given her. It made him seem less dead.

Police tape, enforced by a padlock, sealed Peter's front door. Her key was as dead as Peter.

Addy sighed. "We'll have to call in at Police Headquarters."

The Arabic sergeant at the front desk was new.

"I want to see Miss Quigley in the typing office," Dalia told him.

"Sorry, Madam. Miss Quigley left last week."

Addy, in her most haughty British voice, demanded to speak to the superintendent. The sergeant ordered another policeman to usher Addy through.

"Take a seat, Miss, while you wait," the sergeant said.

Addy returned. "Dalia, have you any receipts? The superintendent will only let you take your things if you can provide receipts."

"My parents bought my Rheinmetall Super typewriter in Germany back in nineteen thirty-two."

Addy placed her hands on her cheekbones. "Oh, your typewriter? There's bad news on that score. The army has requisitioned it. If you have a receipt they'll pay you the money."

First, the British had imprisoned Uri, then sent Peter off to be killed. A stolen typewriter was a minor crime.

She slumped back on the wooden chair, trying to retreat into the blur again, but Addy stood over her.

"The rest of the stuff is still there, Dalia. Even though it's been catalogued ready for auction, the police will let you have anything that belongs to you, just so long as you produce a receipt."

"My name's in some of my books," Dalia muttered. Books she could replace, but not the typewriter.

"I'll go back and ask about the books," Addy promised.

"Eema and Abba will know…" But Addy had already left.

Where were Eema and Abba? They must have heard about Peter. It would have been on the wireless, in the paper.

"Sorry to be so long, Dalia. The superintendent insisted I stop for a cup of tea. He tried to help. He telephoned the legal department but they say a name on a flysheet is insufficient evidence. They need receipts."

"It doesn't matter."

Nothing mattered now.

* * * *

"Dalia," Addy said the next morning, "Suzanna has handed in her notice. I'm going to be stuck running this house by myself. Jim and I…" She stopped. Her cheeks turned red.

"Well, until you find yourself a proper job, Jim and I wondered if we could make you a small allowance in return for you helping me about the house."

It took a while to sink in. Addy was planning to turn her into a domestic drudge like Suzanna. She stood up, walked over to the bedroom window and opened it, but because of the blackout, the exterior shutters were closed.

"Only the sort of things you would do for your own mother," Addy pleaded.

Her own mother? Why hadn't her mother contacted her? She closed the window and turned around. Addy was gazing down at her shoes. Addy who had stood up for her against Jim, was now the only person in the world who cared about her.

"All right. Just for the time being, until I get myself sorted."

Addy leapt up and kissed her. "You won't be plunged in at the deep end," she promised. "Suzanna will show you how we do things, while she works out her notice."

After lunch, she followed Addy into the tin-roofed kitchen attached as an after-thought to the house

"Dalia and I will prepare the salad tonight, Suzanna," Addy said.

Suzanna shrugged and bent down to scoop potatoes out of a straw bag.

Addy primed the pump that stood in the middle of the kitchen and drew a bowlful of water. She stirred in a spoonful of permanganate crystals, went to the refrigerator in the dining room and brought in a lettuce. "You tear off the leaves and leave them to soak for half an hour."

The phone rang in the dining room. Addy handed the lettuce over and left the room.

Suzanna began to peel the potatoes. "They've made you take my place?"

Addy poked her nose around the door. "Suzanna, make me a pot of tea, please. I'm simply gasping. Dalia, you'll have finished the lettuce by the time it's made. Bring the tea through to the lounge and we'll have a bible reading."

"Looks like you'll get better treatment than me," Suzanna

said.

As Dalia entered the lounge with the tray she asked, "Addy, where do you collect your letters?"

"The main Post Office," Addy replied. "Why?"

"Has there been anything for me?"

Addy shook her head. "Nothing."

Her parents didn't want her. She couldn't go home.

During the next few days, Suzanna thawed towards her as they worked together in the kitchen.

Addy went to the auction in Peter's flat and returned with a bundle of photographs. Dalia took a long look at the photograph of herself and Inspector Monteith at Kayak beach. How happy they had looked, but had Peter all along still been grieving for Penelope?

That evening over dinner, Jim said, "Superintendent Fielding asked me to see him today."

"What did he want, dear?"

"He told me Inspector Sutton suspected you, Dalia, of having been planted in the typing pool by Aliyah Beth."

Dalia sat there trembling.

Addy gazed at her husband. "So?" she queried softly.

Jim leaned back. "He said that, since Dalia no longer worked for the police authority, he was inclined to let sleeping dogs lie but he might have to arrest her if she ever worked in Haifa again or socialised with people working in strategic areas."

"Jim," Addy said, "you must write to the Spiritual Guides in Jaffa and ask them to find Dalia a job."

That night Dalia woke sweating from a nightmare. Penelope, all in white, pointing to red anemones sprouting from a wound in Peter's side as he hung crucified, Penelope shouting, "See what you've done!"

Damp sheets twisted around her legs as she tossed and turned, untangling the dream's message. She spent the next two days drifting mechanically from one domestic task to another while allowing herself to accept that, as far as Peter was concerned, she had been second best.

There came a day when she woke more clear-headed than

she had been since Peter's death. She lay in bed, reviewing her time in Haifa and anything she had gained from her experiences.

She had learned about the way the Mandate worked, useful knowledge in a future struggle for independence, but could now revert to her earlier ambitions.

She would find a well-paid secretarial job in Tel Aviv and save for tuition fees to take a degree course in agriculture.

While she cooked breakfast, she tackled Addy. "I'm grateful for the way you have cared for me when I most needed it, but I can manage on my own now. Tomorrow I'm going to Tel Aviv to find a proper job."

"You will be constantly in our prayers," Addy replied. "I'll give you a good reference and Jimmy will give you a letter of introduction to the Spiritual Guides in Jaffa."

A letter of introduction was something she didn't need, but she didn't want to hurt Addy, so said nothing.

The next morning she picked up her packed bag, stared hard at the studio portrait of Peter on the windowsill, and turned her back on it.

At the bus stop, she tore up Jim's letter of introduction and placed it in the Used Ticket bin.

Her first port of call was her bank. To her amazement, her account showed a large positive balance. Studying the details, she saw her orange groves at al-Tira, worthless since the outbreak of war, had made a huge profit. She had heard someone at the Hebrew University had invented a way of producing fuel from orange juice, but had not realised the personal implications.

Finding a seat in the marbled hall, she assessed her changed circumstances. She could apply to University straight away.

She rushed to the Post Office and sent a telegram giving Poste Restante, Jerusalem, as her address, and walked back to the bank.

She wrote a cheque to the Shepards, more than enough to repay them for all they had spent on her, and drew out cash for a month's living expenses and the bus fare to Jerusalem.

While the cashier was counting her money, a clerk approached and handed her two letters. "Miss Leitner, the manager said we should give you these when you next came in."

Letters from Mr. Manners? Setting new dates for her baptism, no doubt. She was about to throw them unread into a trash bin but something made her look at the envelopes. Ruth's handwriting! Her mother's!

She tore open her mother's letter written three weeks previously.

Dalia darling,

We're going mad with worry. We heard the terrible news about your Peter. We tried and tried to get in touch with you but Giza has no idea where you are. We heard that you were staying with a British family, but no one, not the Post Office, not the police, not the bank manager, will give us your address, so I am leaving this note with your bank as Ruth suggested. Please forgive my nagging ways and come home. We all love you so much.

How could she have been so stupid? How could her parents have known Addy's address? Even the wedding invitation had only named the Second Chosen hall.

She rushed to the counter and asked one of the bank staff if she could use their telephone. She left a message with the nurse at Bereisheet asking her mother to phone the bank. While waiting, her feet bouncing uncontrollably on the floor, she opened the letter from Ruth.

Dearest Dalia,

Uri and I are so sorry about your Peter. I came up from Alexandria to look for you. Where are you? Your parents are desperate to find you. I spoke to the brother of one of the nurses I knew at Haifa who works at your bank, and he explained the situation to the manager who gave permission for our letters to be kept in your bank file. Please write as soon as you get them.

A bank clerk approached. Her mother was on the phone.

"Dalia, hah," her mother panted, she must have run all the way across the common. "You wait right there in the bank. Your father's on his way to collect you. The Romanians are killing a chicken. Miriam is busy baking."

Dalia's throat constricted. She couldn't reply.

Her mother continued. "Dalia, my love, please forgive me. I have been nearly dead with worry. Nu, say you are all right. Please say you are all right."

"I'm all right now, Eema," she managed.

"Good, you stay right there. I must get back to the cooking."

Dalia commandeered one of the comfortable bank chairs in front of a writing desk and concentrated on gaining control, but lost out when her father arrived. She clung to his neck, laughing and crying at the same time.

"Hush," her father soothed as he led her out to the car. "You are back with us now."

Once he was driving, he kept up a stream of conversation—news of Josh, Ruth and Uri, and a description of the harvest—until she calmed down.

She told him about her decision to study at the university.

"Your mother and I will drive you to Jerusalem tomorrow," her father said. "The Romanians can cope with the farm for a week. We will stay at a hotel until you settle in, help you buy your study materials, and sort out your clothes if you have to start lectures straight away. And we'll make sure we know where you're staying before we leave."

Part 4

Student 1941 – 1942

Chapter 17

The last day of her first full term at the Hebrew University and Dalia was the only female agricultural student left on campus. The other women in her year group all belonged to one Pioneer Brigade, so their placements had been booked even before they had started their course. They had gone for their briefing en bloc the day before.

The tutor had had to make special arrangements for her, eventually placing her in the same location as Leah and Esther, now in their final year. She wasn't sure how she felt about this. She had met up with Leah and Esther again on the campus and they had been friendly, but she was no longer part of their brigade.

After her briefing she joined Dov, an intern doctor from the neighbouring Hadassah Hospital, who had been waiting for her. He was a long-time friend of Uri. She suspected her brother had asked him to keep an eye on her. She hoped he was the only one on Mount Scopus who knew she had been engaged to a British policeman.

He took her arm. "Dalia, I have something I need to talk about with you. Let's take a walk where we can't be overheard."

She experienced a surge of panic. While grateful for his friendship, she was not ready for a romantic entanglement. Her unease deepened as they walked downhill and he invited her to sit on some rocks under a group of pine trees. The view of the old city walls across the valley was a clichéd romantic setting.

She scanned his face but, to her relief, saw no embarrassment, rather a flush of suppressed excitement.

"This is all hush-hush, Dalia, but Haganah have recommended me for full-time training in a new resistance unit created by the British. I'm not sure what it entails, except I have to give up my job at the hospital. I'm not too happy about that."

"Oh Dov, I'm so glad the British are facing reality at last. Stopping the Germans winning must take precedence over anything else. I'd have joined a resistance unit like a shot if they'd invited me. I wish I hadn't had to leave Haganah."

"I'll drop the word that you're available. They'll snap you up. After all, you were one of their best shots. The people in command will know why you had to leave." He looked at his watch. "If you're going to catch the Jaffa bus we must leave now. I'll come with you to the bus station."

On the bus that zigzagged away from Jerusalem down to the Mediterranean coast, Dalia turned her thoughts to the holiday ahead.

Ruth had written to say she would be home for Passover. Dalia was so looking forward to seeing her again. If only Ruth had been in Palestine when Peter died!

As the bus approached the terminal, she saw Ruth waiting for her and, beside her, Uri, smart in military uniform.

Uri had his arm slung casually around Ruth's shoulder. For a brief moment Dalia let slip a mental barrier and allowed herself to wish that she and Peter had had that easy kind of relationship. She hastily blocked the thought and hurried to the front of the bus. Her heavy canvas rucksack bumped painfully against her back as she jumped onto the pavement.

"Hi, Carrot tops," her brother greeted her.

She had received so many compliments on her auburn hair since growing up she no longer resented the nickname. She spread out her arms and managed to encompass both Uri and Ruth.

"How did you two wangle leave at the same time?"

"My Ward Sister doesn't mind us swapping rotas when our boyfriends get home leave," Ruth explained. "Here, Uri, aren't you going to take your sister's heavy rucksack?"

"She shouldn't have brought so many books. She can practise practical farming at home rather than reading about it." All the same, Uri lifted the rucksack off her back and put his arms through the straps as he strode off. "We left Abba's car parked up by the Post Office."

They walked single file through streets smelling of spiced chick peas, open sewers, and exhaust fumes, pushing their way through crowds swarming round fruit and vegetable stalls that made narrow streets even narrower. Conversation was impossible while they concentrated on avoiding donkey droppings and banana skins.

Eventually they emerged onto the broad, tarmacked Jaffa/Tel-Aviv road.

The Post Office, a huge cuboid, built in layers of pale pink and white stripes, always reminded her of one of those Liquorice All Sorts of which the British were so fond. Her father's baby Austin looked minute parked in front of it.

Uri deposited the rucksack on the front passenger seat. "Okay, girls! You get into the back and start gossiping. Don't mind me. I'll concentrate on the driving."

Inside the car, Dalia embraced Ruth as Uri swung the starting handle and jumped into the driver's seat. When the car started, Dalia let Ruth go and settled back against the utilitarian upholstery.

Ruth gazed at her. "You're looking so much better than when I last saw you."

"I feel better now I'm back on track. How do you like what you're doing?"

"I love Alexandria. People say it's quite different from the rest of Egypt but I haven't had time to go anywhere else, so wouldn't know, but people of all sorts mix together and everyone is so kind."

"What's the job like?"

Ruth's enthusiastic smile faded. "Heartbreaking, but I wouldn't want to be doing anything else. We get patients straight from the front. I can cope with the amputees. We train them to use artificial limbs, but strapping young quadriplegics break my heart."

Dalia knew Ruth was thinking *What if it happened to Uri?* She watched her friend shake herself and stretch a smile back onto her face. "Talking of patients! We admitted Shimon

Mabovitch last week, dehydrated and with a broken right arm, but still full of himself."

"Did you fix him up?" She was annoyed at allowing anxiety to put a squeak into her voice.

Luckily, Ruth showed no signs of noticing. "Yes, and helped him write his letters. Not only that, but yesterday, when we came up from Alex, we had to ask your father to pick us up at Rehovot instead of Hadera, because Shimon, if you please, had ordered Uri to deliver a letter to his mother."

Without turning his head, Uri joined in the conversation. "Shimon has three weeks' sick leave coming to him, so now Eema's *kvetching* that Cousin Elsa will have her son home for the whole of Passover, and I have to leave before it's over."

Ruth laughed. "You know what your brother replied, Dalia? He only asked your mother if she wanted the Germans to break his arm so he could get sick leave too."

Uri returned his attention to driving as he negotiated the car past a slow-moving army convoy.

Ruth took advantage of his preoccupation to lower her voice. "Did you know that Shimon is no longer engaged to that Yael?"

"I'd heard it was because he had joined up," Dalia answered in what she hoped was an off-hand manner. "I gather the break-up didn't particularly upset Cousin Elsa."

Ruth laughed. "No. There are plenty more nice Jewish girls about. For a start, one not sitting a million miles away."

Dalia shrugged. "I had my chance and blew it."

Ruth stared at her accusingly. "You never told me." She lowered her voice still further. "Incidentally, Uri wasn't the only one Shimon asked to by-pass the censor. He told me to give this to you." She put her hand in her bag and brought out a letter.

Dalia kept her face impassive but couldn't prevent her stomach contracting. "What does it say?"

"I don't know. He didn't ask me to write this one."

Dalia tore open the envelope and with difficulty scanned the scrawling first page.

Greetings, Dalia. I must apologise for not writing before. I didn't know about Inspector Monteith until Ruth told me. My post hasn't caught up with me yet.

He continued with formal condolences. Why Shimon should think he had to bypass the censors for those, she couldn't imagine. She turned the page over.

I can't leave it there, Dalia. I want to apologise for being so angry about the accusations you made in nineteen-forty. I couldn't believe them then, but they may contain an element of truth. It's not something to broadcast, of course, and it certainly wasn't intentional. You're not to blame for it, though. Decisions were taken independently of your information.

Dalia put the letter down, recalling the quarrel sixteen months previously. She had been railing at herself, as much as at Shimon, when she had charged Haganah with sabotaging the Patria. What had really infuriated her had been Shimon's indifference to hints that she was dating Peter.

Despite Shimon's reassurance, if Haganah had sabotaged the Patria with passengers aboard, her report was responsible for the deaths of nearly three hundred.

Ruth nudged her. Dalia opened her eyes and read the anxiety in her friend's face.

"What's he said to upset you?" Ruth asked.

"Nothing. I was just remembering Peter, that's all." She skimmed through the rest of the letter quickly. "Shimon would like to see me while he's on leave. Wants to take me out to supper."

"You'll go, won't you?"

"I don't suppose it can do any harm," Dalia replied, her mind still far away, on a quayside in Haifa.

Uri called out. "Hey, you two, we're nearly home. Start smiling. You don't want your mothers worrying."

Both Dalia and Ruth knew enough to take the warning seriously.

The blacksmith's younger son was on gate duty. "It's good to have your brother home, no?" he greeted Dalia as he swung open the stout iron gates.

"Yes, and a double bonus to have Ruth. How's your brother doing?"

"Still stuck with guard duty at Sarafand."

Uri drove on and pulled up outside their house.

In the Leitner kitchen the table was set out for the Sabbath meal.

Her mother threw herself around Dalia's neck. "It's so good to have all my family home."

Dalia noticed her father's glance at the door of the bedroom he had built for her grandparents. She gently disengaged herself from her mother's arms and went to hug her father.

"I'll take myself off home and help my mother light the candles," Ruth said. "Then we'll all come over."

Dalia counted the place-settings. "Aren't the two Romanians eating with us tonight?"

"No. They're visiting friends. To be honest, I'm glad they won't be here while we're spring-cleaning for Passover. They've no idea what clean means. Not surprising since they haven't seen their mothers since they were fourteen."

Uri and her father watched while Dalia and her mother lit five candles and recited prayers in unison. Although she did not believe in the existence of the Deity to whom the prayers were offered, Dalia took comfort from words that had passed from one generation to another. She wondered if her mother believed, but that was not a question she would ever ask.

After Sabbath ended, Dalia joined her mother in a frenzy of cleaning. It was not that they had been particularly observant back in Germany, but the sight of her first large cockroach had persuaded her mother that some traditional customs were worth keeping, even to the point of superstition.

By four o'clock on Passover Eve, even her mother was satisfied they had removed the last crumb. The Leitners and Cohens congregated outside the Leitners' back door drinking tea and eating luxury chocolate biscuits from paper bags.

The moshav nurse strode around the corner. "Your Cousin Elsa's on the phone. She's in a bit of a state. Wants to know if you've seen or heard from Shimon. He wrote he'd be home for Passover but hasn't arrived and she's heard nothing."

Her mother left with the nurse. When she returned, she

said, "Elsa's convinced Shimon is still in hospital or has died of his wounds."

"Shimon left the hospital on his own two feet," Ruth assured her. "The doctors sent him back to his unit with a medical note advising he would be unfit for active duty for another six weeks. Apart from an arm in plaster, he was fine."

"If Shimon suffered amnesia after his hardships, then the British could have shot him as a deserter," Miriam said.

"That sort of thing happened back in the First War," Ruth said. "Nowadays the British look more closely at medical reasons. Has Elsa Mabovitch thought to contact the army?"

"She's afraid because Shimon bypassed the censor."

"He'll turn up," Dalia prophesied.

When, however, days then weeks passed without news, everyone became worried. Elsa phoned the army saying a friend had told her Shimon had been given sick leave. They said Shimon had not been posted missing. His letters had probably gone astray.

Chapter 18

Shimon Mabovitch, seriously underweight, one arm in a sling, his kitbag over the opposite shoulder, was struggling through an outer section of the fifteen-mile stretch of tents that made up Geneifa camp. Sand blew in his face, tent sides bulged out as if attempting to attack him, and the sound of flapping canvas almost drowned the howling *khamseen*. His mind was whirling as wildly as the sand.

An hour earlier, he had learnt that two-thirds of his comrades were dead and the army had disbanded his commando unit.

Now, despite an MO having signed him off on sick leave, he had been ordered to attend a briefing with full kitbag at an admin hut on the edge of the camp.

When he found the hut, an orderly took his name and rank, ticked a list, and directed him to an inner room.

The smoke-filled interior was dark after the brilliance outside, but as his eyes adjusted, he made out an aisle between rows of occupied benches leading to a platform where an officer sat ramrod straight in a chair behind a trestle table.

Shimon walked down the aisle, came to attention in front of the table, and saluted.

The officer picked up his pencil. "Sergeant Mabovitch?"

"Sir."

The officer placed a tick on a paper in front of him. "Good. You're the last. Take a seat."

Looking around, Shimon recognised six survivors from his disbanded commando unit plus several other faces from his Haganah days. He eased his kitbag off his shoulder and clashed his good hand, Palmach style, with each comrade.

The officer moved to the front of the table and introduced himself as Captain Buck. "You may be wondering why I have called you here," he said, and looked around the room before adding, "You all have at least two things in common."

Shimon stared around. At a guess, everyone present was a Palestinian Jew. If so, what other attribute did they share?

Captain Buck left no time for guessing games. "You are all fluent in German and have all exhibited courage in unconventional action, essential aptitudes for our new unit. Life in it will be no picnic. Your task will be dangerous to the point of suicide. Moreover, you will forfeit all leave, be forbidden to communicate with your families or even other servicemen, and, what some may consider more critical, you will not keep Shabbat. You may feel you have already contributed enough to this conflict. If so, leave now without recriminations. I want volunteers only."

Shimon owed it to all his dead comrades to stay. He looked around. No one had moved.

The captain continued. "I warn you, if you stay to hear what I tell you next, you forfeit the right to leave."

Another pause. Still no one moved. Shimon wished the officer would cut to the chase.

Captain Buck moved back behind the table and as he walked he changed—gone was the stiff military step, his movement becoming fluid. He slid into his chair and leaned back. When he spoke, his linguistic style had changed as well.

"Right. I'll now tell you about myself. I was with the Punjabis. Took one in the leg and was captured by the Krauts at Gazala. I speak the lingo like a Blackshirt, so I liberated an Afrika Korps uniform and bluffed my way through the lines. Like taking candy from a baby. That's when I got this idea. Sent it up the flagpole with HQ. They liked it, so here we are. We're calling this unit 'The Special Interrogation Group' though that's not what you'll be doing. We're turning you into Krauts, Afrika Korps from helmet to boots. You'll march like Germans, eat like Germans, swear like Germans, think in German, and even dream in German, because if the Germans find out who you really are when you're on the job, your number will be up."

Shimon breathed out slowly and closed his eyes, thinking it through. He could see this working.

The door opened. All heads turned as two people entered

the room, one an ATS private and the other a middle-aged Jewish padre. The woman carried a candle. They walked down the central aisle and stood in front of the table.

"With your permission, Captain Buck," the padre said, indicating the candle.

The captain stared, a look of bewilderment on his face. Understanding dawned. He gave a sardonic smile. "By all means, go ahead."

When the woman had lit the candle and the padre had intoned a prayer, the two left, closing the door behind them.

The captain pointed to the candle. "It will be Shabbat in less than eighteen minutes. Two trucks are waiting to take you to your new base. The journey will last over an hour."

Most kibbutzniks wouldn't be too worried but Shimon saw a few troubled faces. No one, however, protested.

"Incidentally," the captain continued, "I asked the censors to hold back all mail you posted during the past week. They will destroy letters informing their recipients that the writers have Passover leave."

Shimon wished he had used the official post to write to his mother and Dalia.

* * * *

Dalia had been clearing stones from the kibbutz's newest field since first light. Her back ached, her shirt stuck to her skin, and she hated the rough feel of her hands.

Standing to stretch her back, she saw the supervisor walking down the track towards her. She wheeled her partially full barrow towards the stone pile already beginning to look like a wall. By the time she returned to her patch, the supervisor was there.

"How's it going?" he asked.

"The worst job I've ever had."

The kibbutznik lifted disparaging shoulders. "Pioneering farming you want, pioneering farming you got. You moshavniks have been lazing about too long on German tractors. Your hands may be dirtier now but your soul is cleaner."

Dalia was tempted to ask if her father should have handed over his assets to the Nazis rather than opting to buy goods needed to make Palestine prosperous. However, she needed this man to give her a good grade so bit her tongue.

"You can knock off now," he growled, "but mind you're not late back."

Dalia heaved herself upright and headed up the track towards Esther and Leah at the top of the field. She heard Leah call, "Dalia, over here."

An arm beckoned through the drooping branches of the weeping fig, where they had left their water bottles. Her spirits lightening, she ducked through the leathery leaves into moist shade.

Dumpy Esther and willowy Leah sat leaning against the fig tree's pimply bark. Esther had her water flask to her lips.

Leah was examining her nails. "However am I going to get these back in shape?"

Dalia picked up her own water flask and couldn't stop drinking until she had emptied the flask. "I hadn't realised how thirsty I was."

Esther's brow puckered. "You can die from dehydration here. Leah and I take a few sips every half-hour."

"First thing I'll do when I leave here is visit a manicurist," Leah said. "What are you looking forward to most?"

Esther looked wistful. "Time to read."

Dalia rubbed her aching back. "A massage."

"That Dov Goldberg would jump at the chance to give you one," Leah teased.

She felt herself stiffen. "I don't want to get close to a man again, ever." She regretted the hostility in her tone even before she had finished speaking. "I'm sorry," she apologised, "I didn't mean it like it sounds."

"That's all right," Leah said, but she and Esther stared at the curtain of leaves in front of them, and the silence lengthened.

"I'll tell you about it sometime," Dalia promised at last, "but not just yet. The wounds are still raw."

She hoped that sounded like just another romantic breakup.

Esther stood up. "Come on. We want to give ourselves time to digest lunch before starting again."

They trudged up the hill still in uncomfortable silence and entered the community hall. The radio was on as usual. People sat at tables calmly discussing the price of tomatoes and their soil's suitability for wheat growing while Golda Meyerson talked about the deliberate murders of Jewish civilians in Europe and described the terrible conditions in the labour camps. How could they? Her thoughts flew to her grandmother. Were occupants of internment camps any better treated than the ones in the labour camps? She shouldn't be here picking up stones by hand. She should be fighting Germans, should have joined up like Shimon Mabovitch. She felt a now familiar stab of painful emotion. Where was Shimon?

Someone tapped her shoulder. Dov Goldberg!

"What are you doing here?"

"Acting as messenger boy. You're to report to Kibbutz Mishmar Ha'Emek the day after tomorrow."

Her anger evaporated. Mishmar Ha'Emek! Rumoured to be the unofficial headquarters of a hush-hush resistance unit.

She stood on tiptoe and kissed Dov on the cheek. "Are you staying for lunch?"

"No. Too many others to contact. I'll see you at Mishmar."

* * * *

The small boy had wavy dark hair that reminded Dalia of a miniature Shimon. The Muhktar of Mishmar Ha'Emek ordered him to take her to the Palmach.

"What is Palmach?" she asked the child when the Muhktar was out of earshot.

His face took on an expression of awe. "Haganah's top fighters."

He led her to a cave, the entrance camouflaged as a

donkey stable complete with fresh dung and accompanying odours. He conducted her around a section of rock at the back of the stable, and pushed aside a heavy goat-hair curtain. She found herself staring at bales of straw.

"You have to go around the straw," the child said. "Remember to shout 'Shalom'." He ran back.

Dalia stepped carefully around the bales into dusty smelling darkness. Memories of her initiation into Haganah flooded back. She took a few tentative steps forward, brushing her hands against prickly straw walls, before rounding more bales into an orange glow. One more turn and she was in a room illuminated by a bright electric bulb. Facing her, sat a row of figures in dark clothes, the lower part of their faces hidden behind black scarves, holding rifles trained at her. She stood paralysed with fear, less because of the guns, more because of what was beyond—a German officer sitting upright behind a table.

The German officer raised his helmet. "Hey, Dalia. Come on up and enrol." Shimon Mabovitch grinned broadly, obviously relishing her reaction.

Whether it was the immediate shock, or the sudden release of months' long pent-up anxiety, but a wave of anger fiercer than any she had yet experienced overcame her. Not usually foul-mouthed, words now tumbled out of her mouth as if she had been Sabra born.

"You!" she yelled. "Haven't you had enough fun letting your own mother think you were dead for weeks on end, without trying to scare the shit out of the rest of us?"

Shimon had the grace to look crest-fallen. "Dalia. I'm only dressed like this because I'm leading a course in infiltration, and I went to see my parents yesterday."

The figures in the foreground lowered their rifles. One removed his mask, exposing himself as Dov. "I'm sorry we frightened you, Dalia, but you gave us a fright too. Mac told us everyone was already here and you didn't shout 'Shalom'. Anyway, welcome to the Palmach."

Still glowering, she looked harder at the two men sitting next to Shimon.

A silver-bearded, stocky man of about fifty, wearing a battle blouse with enormous breast pockets, was Yitzhak Sadeh, a kibbutznik famous for leading night raids against Arabs before the war. She had assumed the younger man dressed as a British army captain was another Palmach member in disguise, until he lifted his head from papers he was studying and she recognised him as a genuine British army officer, a close friend of the Shepards, Lieutenant McIntyre. He'd been a lieutenant when she'd known him but, judging by the three stars on his shoulder, he was now a captain.

"Name, please?" Captain McIntyre asked in English.

She hesitated briefly, unsure how to address him. She wasn't going to 'Sir' him. Hierarchy played no part in Haganah culture. "Dalia Leitner."

He stared at her. "Dalia Leitner?" he repeated slowly. "Of course." He looked at her again. "I'm so sorry about Peter."

She wasn't sure how to reply.

He turned back to his list. "But you shouldn't be here. You're down for wireless training in Jaffa."

"I was ordered to report for combat training."

"No, you're definitely down for wireless. You should be there, being billeted."

She had never volunteered for wireless training. She straightened, prepared to argue.

Dov intervened. "Typical admin *balagan*, Mac. I recommended her for sabotage training. If only the Germans were as inefficient as the allies."

"Who recommended me for wireless?"

Yitzhak Sadeh consulted his notes. "Head office."

Dov turned to Yitzhak Sadeh. "Tell him, Yitzhak. Tell him. Didn't I recommend Dalia for her firearm skills?"

Yitzhak immersed himself in his paperwork.

Captain McIntyre replied in his place. "Sorry, Dov, but we need wireless operators even more urgently than crack marksmen. Dalia, I'll give you a lift to Jaffa after lunch."

Dalia breathed in heavily. "I know nothing about wirelesses."

Yitzhak Sadeh looked up. "That's why we're training

you." He returned to his papers.

Dov gave an exasperated shrug. "If Yitzhak says you're doing wireless, then I guess you're doing wireless. We'll meet up after your training."

Dalia wasn't giving in that easily. "Jaffa's too far from Bereisheet to travel daily."

"You'll be found a secure billet," Captain McIntyre assured her.

She'd rather find her own billet. Shimon's sister lived in nearby Tel Aviv.

Dov shouted, "Stow weapons, comrades. We're off."

Everyone else rushed to pegs screwed into the rock and hung up their rifles.

An outsider once again, Dalia asked, "Why no guns on a training exercise, Mac?"

He gave a wry smile. "The army provides the official weapons. Not enough, but at least they're legal."

Dalia clenched her jaws. The military had sent her brother and other Haganah members to prison for carrying rifles, now the military was arming them!

The cave emptied as men sauntered out in twos and threes.

"Miss Leitner," the captain continued, "would you mind going over to the kibbutz and telling them there will be three of us for lunch, not two?"

After delivering her message, she asked for directions to the public phone.

She phoned the operator and asked to be put through to Shlomo's dental surgery where Shimon's sister worked as the receptionist for her husband. Dalia told her that she needed a bed for an indefinite period.

"So long as you don't mind sharing a room with Hadassah," Shayna told her, "you'll be welcome."

"I've found myself a billet," Dalia informed Captain McIntyre at lunchtime.

He shook his head. "That's not allowed. The wireless course is hush-hush. We choose billets carefully."

"I'm staying with Shimon Mabovitch's sister."

Captain McIntyre smiled. "Okay. I'll drop you off. But first I'll pop into the Officers' Club to let the organiser know."

He ushered her into a military car and took his place in the driver's seat. Dalia, noticing a Christian bible on the dashboard, resigned herself to a prayer meeting somewhere en route. However, Captain McIntyre didn't once enquire about her spiritual welfare or suggest they stop to pray. Instead, as they drove through the green wheat fields of the Jezreel valley, and then on through the rocky thorn-covered slopes of Wadi Ara, he kept her in fits of laughter with exaggerated anecdotes of his experiences in Cairo.

In Jaffa, Captain McIntyre nipped into a former German hotel where the course was taking place before driving her to Shayna's apartment.

Shayna was home alone.

Sitting on an opulent settee with cups of coffee and generous slices of moist coffee cake, Shayna explained, "It's Shlomo's chess evening, and Hadassah and Ephraim are at junior Youth Club."

"Little Ephraim old enough for Youth Club already!"

"He's eight now. I wouldn't have let him start until he was nine, except our Hadassah is so responsible I know he's safe."

"You're making me feel old, Shayna."

"And so I should. You should have found yourself a nice Jewish boy by this time and settled down."

Dalia hastily changed the subject. "And how is your mother keeping?"

"Better now she's seen Shimon but she was in such a state before."

The outside door opened and Hadassah came in shepherding Ephraim.

How she's grown, Dalia thought, still only eleven and already her body is showing signs of puberty.

The girl stopped to stare when she saw Dalia.

"You want a glass of milk and a cookie before going back to Club, Hadassah?" Shayna asked.

"I'm not going back if Dalia is here," Hadassah replied.

"She knows more about pioneering farming than I can ever learn at Club."

Dalia raised her eyebrows.

"Her grandmother's been singing your praises," Shayna explained. "According to Eema, you are a cross between Supergirl and a maven."

"Me?" Dalia almost squeaked in surprise. "I thought Cousin Elsa wanted nothing to do with me after the Haifa balagan."

"Your brother dropped enough hints about your real activities to persuade my mother you were leading a second exodus from Europe single-handed, and that you are currently transforming Eretz Israel back into a land flowing with milk and honey."

A role model now, Dalia thought, as she settled down to answer Hadassah's questions about pioneering farming and defence skills, while Shayna checked Ephraim into bed.

Part 5

The Guerrilla Fighter, 1942

Chapter 19

The next morning Dalia enjoyed the fifteen minute walk that took her from the international modernism of Tel Aviv through Jaffa's mediaeval Middle East, into turn-of-century Germany.

In obedience to the instructions Mac had given the day before, she knocked on the staff entrance of the Officers' Club. An Arab kitchen porter let her into a kitchen redolent of frying bacon after she had given the pass phrase, "It's a good morning."

An Arab waiter showed her to a stone stairway leading down to a roughly planed wooden door. Feeling slightly uneasy at the thought of meeting strangers, she walked into a whitewashed cellar, decorated with murals of vineyards and bunches of grapes. Four trestle tables covered the flagstone floor, each labelled with a letter of the English alphabet and surrounded by six chairs. On each table except the one labelled 'A' stood small machines, resembling miniature orange squeezers. A lieutenant and sergeant from the Signals Corps sat on table 'A'. Civilians sat around the other three. She recognised most from Haganah exercises. The sergeant took her name and motioned her to a chair beside a woman she recognised as a Tel Aviv hairdresser whose boyfriend had been imprisoned by the British at the same time as Uri.

A shout came from behind her, "Dalia, you made it."

Patsy ran over from a door at the side, hugged her, and sat down beside her.

She looked strained, Dalia thought. The climate in Cairo hadn't done her any good.

"You don't know how upset I was yesterday when you turned up late for billeting! I gather from Mac that you know the person we billeted you with." She emphasised the word 'we'.

She got the message. "Yes, by a strange coincidence, Shayna's my honorary Cousin Elsa's daughter. But what are you doing here? I thought you were in Cairo?"

"I was, but they made me billeting officer here. I'm so glad to see you. When you didn't turn up yesterday I thought I'd be with complete strangers."

More people drifted in. Toni Huss, a friend of Shimon's, came over. "Any news of Shimon?"

"I can tell you haven't come straight from Rehovot, Toni! Shimon turned up at his mother's the day before yesterday. Cousin Elsa will have decorated the whole settlement in bunting."

"Is that your Cousin Elsa's son?" Patsy asked. "I met him briefly when we worked in Haifa."

Dalia glanced over at the hairdresser, relieved she was deep in conversation with another woman. She didn't want everyone to know about her sojourn in Haifa.

"Yes, he went missing but he's turned up now."

Why did that upset Patsy? Her friend's eyes glistened before she took out a handkerchief and blew her nose.

The lieutenant rose. "Welcome to the course. I'm Lieutenant Hemming and this is my colleague Sergeant Harris. If you are wondering why you have been chosen for this course, someone, somewhere, has recommended you as having both intelligence and deft fingers. Before you leave, we will have transformed you into world class efficient wireless operators because your lives, and the lives of the units you will work with in the event of invasion, may depend on the speed of your transmission. In England, operators need four months training before they transmit at the speed we need. In Palestine, the Jerries may not allow us that time. Therefore, we start at once."

Dalia was glad she was paired with Patsy. They had worked together well both in the Police Headquarters and on first-aid courses.

As this course progressed she found herself enjoying it. A

great deal of her enjoyment, she realised, sprang from impressing her male colleagues.

She became the fastest coder on the course, but that wasn't all. In the third week when they were taught to dismantle and reassemble wirelesses at speed she again excelled.

While studying diagrams of circuits, she thought back to the drawings she had dismissed as incomprehensible when searching through Jim Shepard's papers the previous year. She realised now they had been plans to co-ordinate Palestinian Resistance wireless communications in the event of an invasion.

While she packed away on the last day of the course, looking forward to a farewell party at their favourite cafe that evening, Lieutenant Hemmings tapped her on the shoulder.

"Would you stay behind after class, please?"

Instinctively, she jerked her shoulder away.

The lieutenant flushed and muttered, "Sorry, it's official business."

She felt her own face redden as the lieutenant hurried off.

"What's that about, I wonder?" Patsy commented.

She shrugged. "Wish I knew!"

Patsy tucked her chair under the table. "I'll freshen up. See you in the café."

While Dalia hovered uncertainly by her table, Captain McIntyre entered the room. "Good afternoon, Miss Leitner."

She raised her eyebrows. "Are you the reason I'm waiting here?"

He smiled. "I guess so. Lieutenant Hemmings and Sergeant Harris have informed me of your prowess so I would like to send you into the field straight away. I don't know for how long, and I can't guarantee your safety. How do you feel about that?"

"If it contributes to the war effort, I'm happy."

"Thought so. Before I go any further, though, I have to swear you in under the Official Secrets Act."

Dalia glanced up.

If the police and army failed to communicate, that wasn't

her business.

She took the oath again.

* * * *

Dalia was ready and waiting when Patsy picked her up shortly after midnight. They picked their way down the steep external steps by Patsy's shaded torchlight. The night was warm and the torch drew a cloud of nocturnal flying insects.

"Why do we have to start out at this unearthly hour?"

"We don't want to be driving through the Negev in the midday sun," Patsy replied.

Dalia experienced a surge of excitement. At last she would visit the most arid region of Palestine!

Their vehicle was a Ford pickup with a camouflaged canvas cover. She settled into the passenger seat, while Patsy pulled an OS map from under the driving seat and switched on her torch, shielding the beam with her hand.

"We take the coast road to Gaza to pick up fuel and supplies before heading off towards Beersheba. When we reach here..." she placed a finger about halfway along the road joining Gaza and Beersheba "...we turn right onto an unmarked track. It should be light by that time. We drive along a sort of plateau, aiming for a spot here, code-named Zamzum." Patsy dragged her finger until she reached a knot of contour lines.

Patsy started the car and concentrated on avoiding late night revellers, no easy task in the blackout. She talked again once they were in the country.

"Jim Shepard discovered Zamzum."

Dalia felt a spasm of alarm. "We're not meeting Jim there?"

"No. He's nothing to do with Zamzum now. When the balloon goes up, he'll be stationed at Magog."

"Magog?"

"Our HQ."

Conversation ceased when slow convoys of army trucks and anti-aircraft guns on the coast road forced Patsy to focus on driving. Three hours later, Patsy was waving a petrol voucher in front of the Gaza quartermaster. The sergeant took his time checking their credentials over the phone while both girls fumed.

"We can't be too careful nowadays," the sergeant told them by way of apology. "There's been a pile of stuff nicked, blatant as you like. It's down to an outfit called the Stern Gang. They often use Jewish women as a distraction."

"Abraham Stern was killed last February," Dalia pointed out.

"His gang carries on though, the police say. They reckon it's his sister running their show now."

"Well, we're not the Stern Gang and we're in a hurry," Patsy reminded him in her best British accent.

It was dawn before they had crammed tins of gasoline into spaces between the radio components and picked up supplies from another section of the depot.

Patsy relaxed when they were finally under way again. "Fancy that sergeant thinking we might be terrorists!"

Remembering the Patria, Dalia turned away.

The rising sun revealed a bleak landscape of stones, boulders, and seemingly dead thorn bushes. How on earth, Dalia wondered, could she ever have been so daft as to contemplate farming in terrain like this?

After the initial impression of utter desert, she saw a bird of prey hovering, a mere dot in the sky. Something, large enough to provide it with a meal, must live between the dry rocks.

The sun rose higher. Even though they had both windows down, the air was unpleasantly warm. The car began to bounce even more uncomfortably than the pot-holed state of the dirt road warranted. Beside her Patsy cursed as she diagnosed a puncture and pulled the car to a halt.

"We're already far later than planned, thanks to those idiots in Gaza," she muttered as she pulled out a tool case.

Dalia stood beside the wheel, handing over levers. The sun blazed down. The track ahead shimmered with false promises of cool water. To add to her discomfort she found herself a target for hundreds of tiny mosquitoes.

When they set off again, Patsy reminded her to watch out for signs of their turn-off. She noticed a two meter wide scar on the roadside that appeared to have been caused by a skidding lorry. Nothing on the other side of the scar indicated a track but all the same she drew it to Patsy's attention.

Patsy got out and examined thorn bushes beside the scar. Broken branches formed an inconspicuous cross. "Well spotted. It would have been just our luck for a shepherd to have brought his goats along and destroyed the sign."

They bumped across sloping dirt that gave way to bare rock. The ground flattened out. Several miles further and they turned almost at right angles to run parallel to a wadi. As Patsy twisted to avoid a large boulder, Dalia gave an involuntary yelp of pain. Patsy stopped the car.

"I'm all right," Dalia reassured her. "I laid my arm along the window to steady myself. I didn't realise the metal was so hot."

"That must be why the desert rats take off the doors," Patsy said. "That's a savage welt you've got there, though." She fetched out a first-aid kit from under the seat and handed it over before starting off again.

"You leave a burn open to the air," Dalia reminded her, "so I won't need a bandage and I won't put iodine on either. It hurts too much already."

By the time the pickup drew to a halt above a rocky ridge pocked with caves, the welt had inflated into a blister and she felt dizzy and slightly sick, but the sight of Dov walking up a narrow path towards them took her mind off the pain. She remained in her seat while Patsy jumped out. Dov waved at her before introducing himself to Patsy who handed him a bundle of papers.

More people walked up to help move boxes. Patsy came to the window and handed her a list of the wireless parts. Dalia, her arm really painful now, left the truck, holding onto the door frame.

Cosseting a box of fragile valves, she followed Palmach members carrying other wireless parts to a cave, closer to the top of the cliff than the rest. It had a scrupulously clean rock floor and whitewashed walls. As she deposited the valves gently in a corner Dov came in.

"Dalia, your arm!" he exclaimed. He handed over his bundle of papers to a member of the Palmach team. "Take these, and check everything else. Dalia, come with me. That wound needs urgent attention."

He led her down the path to another cave, the interior of which resembled a pharmacy, took cotton wool from a cocoa tin and poured on surgical spirit.

"In the wilderness, even the slightest wound must be tackled immediately," he warned, as he dabbed gently at the blister. "Every cut and graze turns septic if left unattended." He looked up to emphasise his point and, for the first time, she noticed his beautiful brown eyes. "About the wireless," he said when he had bandaged the wound. "I'm sure the British have given you their frequencies, but Haganah HQ has another. When the wireless is up and running, you have to contact them to set up a schedule."

A kibbutznik, who had been at school with her, entered and smiled. "Welcome to Palmach, Dalia Leitner."

So, she was part of the Palmach team! Dalia felt like bursting into tears of joy, but restrained herself.

"Food and ammunition all checked, Dov," the kibbutznik said, adding, "Pity they didn't send more arms."

"Your first messages to Haganah, Dalia," Dov said, when the woman had left, "will be to request they negotiate with the British over the use of personal weapons."

"Personal weapons?"

"Just so. We need more than the few rifles and pistols the British have allocated."

A gong sounded from below.

"Time to go down to the mess. After lunch, Dalia, you must sleep. There'll still be time to check wireless parts before Patsy leaves."

She followed Dov down the narrow path past a small cave full of clucking hens to the largest cave where tables and chairs filled the centre and tidy piles of tinned provisions filled every cranny. The savoury smell of chicken noodle soup filled the air.

Chapter 20

Right from the start, everyone at Zamzum treated her as a full member of the Palmach team, and invited her to all weaponry practices and sabotage exercises. She felt very much part of the team.

The wireless was temperamental and she was the only trained wireless operator on site. If Rommel invaded, she would be on duty twenty-four hours a day. She took her concerns to Dov. He sent a message to Magog. Within a few days Headquarters wirelessed back. Zamzum could have a superior wireless and a second wireless operator at some indefinite time in the future.

The desert war continued with little change. Resigned to missing the start of the academic year, she wirelessed a message to her department head via the Jewish Agency and received a reply that she could resume her course when her war service ended.

She was checking breakfast bread in the clay oven they had built outside the canteen when she heard a truck drive up and come to a halt at the edge of the plateau. She looked up and saw two figures emerge from it. One looked like Patsy, although from canteen level it was impossible to be sure. She persuaded another Palmach member to take over the bread and walked up the path to greet the visitors.

It *was* Patsy, looking a lot less strained than she had been in Tel Aviv. The man with her was Toni Huss.

"Toni's the second operator you requested, and I've brought you a new wireless," Patsy told her.

Dalia was delighted. Toni would have been her first choice if she had been consulted. In addition to mastering skills speedily, he was a brilliant improviser.

Dov and other team members joined them. Patsy handed Dov the paperwork. Dov shuffled through it and passed on the list of radio components.

"I'll see you in the canteen at breakfast," she told Patsy as she carried off glass valves she didn't trust anyone else to handle.

She had checked the components and was starting to break down the old wireless for Patsy to take back when the gong sounded. She found Patsy in the canteen, changed and washed.

"You look well."

Patsy beamed. "That's because I've heard from Tim."

They picked up hunks of freshly baked bread, plates of corned beef hash, and mugs of coffee laced with condensed milk.

"Oh, I'm so glad about Tim. Is he all right?"

"He was very badly wounded and was in a German field hospital for weeks but he's been put back together again and is now a POW in Italy."

"At least you can stop worrying about him being in the middle of the fighting."

They concentrated on their food but chatted freely over coffee.

"Dov tells me that you are Zamzum's champion shot," Patsy remarked.

Dalia let out a sigh. "Guerrilla tactics and domestic chores, that's all we do. Here I am, with a full water tank, thanks to the British Army, in an ideal location to practice arid farming, and I'm banned from planting."

Patsy smiled. "I guess having green plots around the site might draw the attention of occupying Germans."

"I know, but it's such a waste. Now, tell me, what's going on in the outside world?"

"Well, Maftur's husband joined up, so she's back in Haifa with her in-laws and working in the Post Office there. When this is over we must ask her to organise a reunion at Edmonds."

"Tempting, but I'd rather not risk coming face to face with Jim Shepard in Haifa."

"I thought you were close to the Shepards."

Dalia couldn't tell Patsy about *Aliyah Beth*, so she merely shrugged and replied, "I upset them when I left without being baptised." This, of course, was true.

"Bully for you," Patsy said and leaned across the narrow trestle table to hug her. "I never thought Christianity was right for you." She gave a huge yawn. "I'm sorry. Driving through the night takes its toll. I'll have to get some kip."

After Patsy had wandered off to the women's dormitory, Dalia returned to the wireless cave and stripped down the old wireless set.

Toni joined her in the late afternoon and together they began assembling the new wireless and studying its peculiarities. They had been concentrating for over an hour when they heard the rumble of a combustion engine.

Dalia stretched painfully stiff muscles and lifted eyes aching from studying the cramped handwritten instructions that had accompanied the components.

"Two vehicles in one day! We're becoming as busy as Jerusalem."

She was about to complain that Haganah hadn't notified them of visitors when she realised that, with the old wireless taken apart and the new one not set up, they were cut off from the outside world.

"Who erases wheel marks after visitors leave?" Toni asked.

"Dov makes up a squad."

"I hope I'm not in the party. I'm whacked."

"You won't be. Our priority is to get the wireless working. I wonder who the visitors are, though."

She stood up and went to the cave entrance. Dov, passing her on his way up to the cliff top, greeted her in a friendly fashion and hastened on. She stepped onto the outside ledge and gazed up at the plateau. Behind Patsy's carefully camouflaged pickup, the windows of a military staff car blazed orange in the last rays of the setting sun—another reason, she realised, for removing vehicle doors in a war zone.

She watched Dov greeting two men. From this top cave she could see one was an army captain she didn't recognise and the other, of all people she most didn't want to meet, Jim Shepard dressed in filthy khaki shorts and a torn shirt that stuck wetly to his back. She backed into the shadow of a protruding rock and watched him move to the rear of the car. A private jumped out of the driving seat and opened the car's trunk. He and Jim hauled out what, at first, looked like a sheepskin rug. Only when a dangling head and legs appeared did she realise it was a dead sheep. Toni came out as the two men placed it in front of Dov like a sacrificial offering.

Dov examined the animal's hide, shook his head, grabbed a work knife from his belt and expertly amputated a haunch. He skinned it and handed it with a flourish to Jim, who took it back to the staff car.

"What's that about, do you think?" Dalia muttered.

"If I were to make a guess, I'd say mutton stew tomorrow."

"Make a nice change. After this, I don't want to see another tin of corned beef or pilchards in tomato sauce for the rest of my life."

They returned to the dark cave.

Toni rubbed his eyes. "My eye sight isn't as good as yours, Dalia. I'll pop over to the mess and fetch a lamp."

"No. You go and explore the place while it's still light enough outside. You can bring me a lamp if I haven't finished by dark."

She was glad to be alone. Seeing Jim Shepard had brought back bad memories. She struggled to calm herself as she studied the wireless manual.

She met Toni's questioning eyes. "I came into contact with Jim when I worked for another Haganah project. Not something I can talk about, so please don't mention it to the others."

She made sure to keep out of the way until Jim had left.

* * * *

Friendly relations with local Bedouin were vital to their mission. Once a week, Dov paid a day-long visit to the Bedouin permanent camp a mile or two from the mouth of the side wadi, taking his medical equipment.

He complained that Bedouin women wouldn't let a male doctor examine them. When desperate for medical assistance, they trekked to Beersheba because there was a female nurse.

She offered to help, telling him in Arabic that she had a basic knowledge of the language. He quizzed her about her first-aid qualifications. She listed certificates she had achieved at school on Haganah courses, and with the Red Cross. He made her demonstrate how she would deal with a sprained ankle and a broken arm and then invited her to accompany him on his next medical visit.

She was delighted. The excursion would make a welcome break from the monotony, and provide an opportunity to chat to Dov in private, something she had missed since joining the Palmach squad.

She met him in the first-aid cave well before dawn, when it was chilly enough for her to have slipped a pullover over her cap-sleeved blouse. In the dim light of a paraffin lamp, Dov inspected her tight-fitting shorts and floppy *tembel* hat. He held out a full-length long sleeved Gaza thob. "This will cover your arms and legs."

"I'm not walking for miles in that."

"You needn't wear it until we are almost in sight of the camp."

"Why should I dress like an Arab?"

"Bare arms and legs offend Bedouin. I want the Bedouin women to respect my female assistant."

"So that's why we had to radio Magog for blue thobs. Toni and I assumed they were disguises needed for sabotage missions."

"We may still use them for that."

He folded the thob and tucked it neatly into her haversack. "Right. Now let's go."

Dawn was breaking when they turned into the main wadi. More a valley than a wadi, she thought. Even six months after the last rainfall, it was by no means a lifeless desert. Lizards scuttled out of their way on the path, clumps of tamarisk sprouted from the valley bottom. The seemingly dead chalky-white snails clinging to dry grass stalks would return to life in

November.

Remains of ruined houses and crumbling terraces on one side of the wadi provided evidence of a former Arab village.

Dov explained it had only been deserted after the Turks had conscripted all able-bodied men and demanded exorbitant taxes. The villagers had used the Zamzum caves as their burial plot.

After walking for half-an-hour, Dov called a halt. Dalia removed her pullover and tugged the thob over the rest of her clothes.

A few minutes later, they came into sight of the Bedouin camp, a collection of small goat-hair tents and tethered nanny goats surrounding a much larger tent. To Dalia's amazement tiny fields surrounded each tent.

Bedouin grew crops! Was that why the British had placed the Negev in the Arab section of Palestine when they had proposed partition? If primitive Arabs could grow crops here, Jews with their superior tools and education could do even better.

Dov noticed her surprise. "Before the Great War," he told her, "most of Europe's breweries imported barley from the Negev and Judean wilderness."

A black-robed, white-keffiyahed Bedouin with golden threads incorporated into his iqal strode out to greet them.

Dalia listened in amazement to the flowery compliments rolling off Dov's tongue in response to the Sheik's opening statement. The light of a lamp shining in Dov's face reflected the virtue in his heart.

After enquiries about the health of each other's families, the Sheik led them to the large central tent, which Dov told her was called a zigg, and indicated they should sit on cushions laid out on a carpeted floor. A woman, with a veil hiding the lower part of her face, served honey cakes and cups of strong coffee. The coffee contained even more sugar than caffeine. Dov requested that Dalia be allowed to stay with him while he conducted his surgery. He wanted her to give out pills so he could concentrate on diagnosis and treatment. The Sheik gave the request grave consideration and agreed, so long as Dalia was not visible when men were treated.

The Sheik remained in the zigg to supervise the session. Dalia sat behind a goat-hair curtain slightly to the rear of Dov. From there, although unable to see him, she distributed pills under his verbal direction.

At noon, they broke for lunch. The men of the tribe sat on a carpet around a large dish of carved lamb and spiced rice. Dalia, treated now as an honorary but inferior man, sat with them. Before they ate, the serving women provided brass bowls of water in which lemon slices floated so they could wash their hands. After that, everyone scooped food from the same dish using only their right hand. The headman plucked the sheep's eyes from the pile of meat and offered them to Dov, who ate them with a great display of enjoyment. There were occasions, Dalia reflected, when it was an advantage to be someone unimportant.

Before the meal ended, Dov asked the Sheik if any of the women and female children would like Dalia to treat them. He offered to sit where he could not see the women but would be available to offer advice if Dalia needed it. After due deliberation, the Sheik agreed.

So, late in the afternoon, after they had treated the men, a woman conducted them across the camp. Dalia noticed that each tent opening, regardless of its position in relation to the Zigg, faced east.

"Do the tents face this way to help your prayers?" she asked the woman guiding them.

The woman giggled. "No, bad robbers come from Transjordan, so we make sure we see them."

A long queue of women and children had already formed outside the tent where she was to work. Dov remained outside under an awning. Dalia sat on the inside of the tent close to him.

For the rest of the afternoon she worked non-stop, pausing occasionally to ask Dov for advice and to listen to his slightly muffled answers. The most common complaints she had to deal with were gummed eyes and ears, but impetigo came a close third.

As she applied eye drops, ear drops, and gentian violet, Dalia felt she was accomplishing a job more worthwhile than any she had yet undertaken. She also realised, as she chatted to the women, how little she knew of Arabic rural life, and felt ashamed that she had never once talked to the Arabs who lived in the village adjacent to Bereisheet.

She asked where they got their water from so, after she had seen all the patients, one of the headman's wives conducted her down a slope to the lowest section of the wadi and showed her a series of holes, called thamilas, covered by large flat stones.

"At dawn we remove the stones to collect drinking water, and cover them before we leave to protect the water from sun and mosquitoes."

The sun had set by the time they headed back to Zamzum, but a bright moon lit their way. Once out of sight of the camp Dalia swapped her thob for her pullover and they sat on a rock to talk over the day's happenings. When Dov put his arm around her, it felt more natural than she had expected. During a lull in their conversation, he bent his lips to hers. He kissed her gently at first and then with passion. He put his hands under her tee shirt to undo her bra and it felt right, but even so, she laid her hands on his arms to stop him, making sure she smiled as she did so. She had learnt her lesson after Shimon's sulk. "You want me kicked out of the Palmach because I'm pregnant?"

Dov grinned. He reached down into his medical pack and pulled out a packet of french letters. "It's surprising what the British consider essential military equipment."

She smiled back and put her arms around him. "B'seder, but please don't expect too much from me. It will be my first time."

He pulled back in surprise. "But, I thought…" he stopped, obviously not sure how to go on.

She knew what he was thinking. "Yes, I was engaged, but Peter did not believe in sex before marriage."

She pushed Peter to the back of her mind, something surprisingly easy to do, but why was Shimon struggling to come forward in her mind? It took so much effort to force him out, she found herself trembling. To gain time she spread the thob across a larger, flat-surfaced rock, before helping Dov strip off her clothes. She lay down on the thob, but feeling she might give the impression of an unwilling sacrifice, held out her arms.

The foreplay was as delicious as she remembered with Peter, but this time when her legs spread apart of their own volition, there was no frustration, nor did she have to suffer frantic expressions of guilt. Dov was gentle and loving throughout. When he pierced her she experienced a little pain, but that was only to be expected. Other women had told her it always hurt the first time, and at her age her skin must be tough.

A few minutes after climax, Dov moved off her and sat up. "Well. Was it that bad?"

"No," she said, gazing up at him wishing it was light enough to see his expression more clearly. "You were wonderful. I'm sorry if I did it wrong. I'll be better next time."

Dov's mouth broke into a smile. "I'm glad you are contemplating a next time."

She flung her arms around him and kissed him. "Oh, yes."

She could not bring herself to say she loved him. She knew she was not in love, but she badly wanted his love. She smiled up at him reassuringly and, hoping the moon was lighting her face, said, "I think I could get to enjoy it."

"Good," he replied, "because I enjoyed making love to you."

She avoided his eyes. "There's something I ought to tell you."

"I thought there might be. Your strong streak of honesty is one of your many virtues."

She hesitated, trying to put her thoughts into words that wouldn't be wounding. "I like you, Dov. You are the kindest man I've ever met and I want you for my best friend, but I don't think I'm in love with you. Not because of anything I dislike about you. It's just I don't think I'm capable of falling in love."

She felt ashamed saying that last bit but he had complimented her on being honest.

The moon was shining on Dov's face now. She observed him carefully, afraid she had hurt him, but he was laughing. "We'll strike a bargain, shall we, Dalia Leitner? We won't fall in love but we'll be lovers and the best of friends, faithful to each other until one of us falls in love with someone else, when we'll part with no recriminations. I suggest, though, that it would be sensible for neither of us to fall in love with anyone until the war's over."

She could live with that. She flung her arms around him and kissed him hard.

They walked back to Zamzum hand in hand. Dov told her how much medicine meant to him. "But even so I had an underlying feeling that somewhere there was a particular task I had been born to undertake. Since coming to Zamzum I've realised what that task is—to work with people who really need me, people like the Bedouin."

Dalia told him how she had always wanted to be a pioneer farmer but had given up that ambition to become a secretary at Shai's request. She didn't mention Shimon's part in that decision. "After Peter's death, I realised where my true loyalties lay and resumed my dream to make the Negev fertile."

"But why the Negev? You'd never seen it until you came to Zamzum."

"As a child I listened to Shimon Mabovitch lecturing us for hours about ways to bring water to the Negev."

Dov laughed. "I understand. I've also endured Shimon on that subject."

As they turned the corner into their own wadi, the singing around the camp fire near the main cave sounded louder and more cheerful than usual.

Toni came running down to meet them. "Hey!" he shouted. "You two, have you heard the news? Monty has Rommel on the run."

Chapter 21

The good news continued. The Germans in North Africa remained in retreat. What with that, and an allied task force invading Morocco, the risk of Nazis capturing Palestine receded. Everyone at Zamzum expected the British to transfer the Palmach to the Eighth army.

Dalia was manning the radio when Magog sent the anticipated order to close down Zamzum. That was a relief. Now she would be able to continue her studies. Relief turned to rage when she realised the full significance of the rest of the message. Palmach members had to leave all personal weapons in camp when transport arrived next day. No one was to leave the camp carrying weapons.

Dalia seethed with anger. The Palmach had revealed their illegal weapons in good faith when the British needed them. She should have known better than to start trusting the British.

When Dov read out that order, everyone shouted at once.

"I'm not leaving my rifle behind."

"My gun belongs to my *kibbutz*."

"No way do I hand over my revolver to the British."

Dov brought the meeting to order and chaired a heated debate.

Someone suggested they bury their personal weapons for collection later but Dov pointed out the army now had the new Polish metal detectors. The favoured solution was to radio the Jewish Agency for a vehicle to collect their personal weapons before dawn.

Toni proposed that first they remove serial numbers from all weapons. "It will confuse the issue. We can explain that we removed the serial numbers in case they fell into enemy hands."

The next morning every Palmach member endured a rigorous body search before being allowed on the transport trucks. The British were petty enough to confiscate every smuggled item of food but at least they had the grace to use ATS personnel to search the women.

"What will you do now?" Dalia asked Dov once they were seated on a bench in the truck.

"Apply for a job being advertised for Head of Outpatients' Unit at Beersheba. What will you do?"

"Return to university and work like mad to make up for time I've lost."

Dov smiled. "I'll buy a motorbike and disturb your studies."

* * * *

Dalia had been back at college three weeks when she found a note pinned to her haversack inviting her to a meeting at Kibbutz Mishmar Ha'Emek. No reason was given.

Dalia arrived bemused by the cloak and dagger atmosphere surrounding her summons. When she entered the cave she found benches covering the floor. Grave-faced Palmach leaders, including Dov, occupied the front benches. There were no British on the platform, only the Palmach commander, Yitzhak Sadeh, looking much older than when she had last seen him, and another man she recognised as Yitzhak Tabenkin, head of the Kibbutzim Union.

Puzzled at the Union leader's presence, Dalia took a seat on a bench occupied by Toni Huss and other members of the Zamzum team.

Conversation died as Yitzhak Sadeh stood up. "Comrades, it is my sad duty to inform you that the British have ordered us to disband."

Yitzhak waited for the clamour to cease before continuing. "However, that is not the only message in the communication I received from the British. As you know, when facing a common enemy, we did not hesitate to disclose the weapons we could muster in event of an invasion. The British kept a list of them all. They told me that the number of weapons recovered from our bases does not tally with their records. If they do not receive those weapons they will send police to search the homes of all Palmach members."

Dalia joined in the general gasp of angry disbelief followed by an even louder hubbub. This time the commander did not wait quietly for it to die down but thumped on the table.

"Like you," he continued, "I'm angry, but I've had time to go beyond anger and consider the future. Yitzhak Tabenkin and I have come up with proposals. One: we do not disband but go underground. Haganah will provide us with weapons and other equipment. Do you find this acceptable?"

Loud cheers answered his question.

"Now I will hand you over to another Yitzhak who will explain the rest."

Yitzhak Tabenkin rose to his feet. "The two main difficulties with an underground Palmach are that you have no funding and your platoons have to train in secret. *Kibbutzim* leaders have already discussed these issues and drawn up a plan. The larger *Kibbutzim* are each prepared to host a Palmach platoon and supply them with food, accommodation, and resources. In return, the kibbutzim will ask the platoons to defend them and assist with agricultural and maintenance work." He stared around the room.

There was some muttering but no voiced dissent.

"After consultation with your commander, we decided that if you agree to this proposal, every month each Palmach member will spend fourteen days labouring for the kibbutz, eight days undertaking military training, and enjoy up to seven days pursuing private activities."

People were still too angry to be in a mood to accept the plan straight away. The ensuing discussion was heated, each person arguing from their own viewpoint.

Dalia, who considered the plan did not cover part-time members such as students, put her point forcefully but calmly. Dov, who as a practising doctor was in a similar position, supported her. Yitzhak Sadeh agreed to train part-timers.

Toni Huss asked what they should do about surrendering weapons.

"Officially," Yitzhak Sadeh informed him, "I have to

order members to surrender all weapons on the British list. I have a copy of that list. You need to check if the British have enough information about your weapons to justify an arrest."

Yitzhak's statement caused such consternation that it seemed as if the meeting would break up in disarray, until Dov shouted out a proposal. "After we have handed in our weapons, let's discover where the British store them and recapture them."

Cheers broke out. Dov's proposal was carried unanimously. Yitzhak Sadeh named a date for platoon leaders to plan the mission. The meeting closed.

Dalia approached Yitzhak Sadeh and asked if her first training session could take place in the Passover holiday. He made a note of it.

Dov came over. "Shall I hitch back to Rehovot with you?"

She accepted the offer with alacrity. "How's the job going?"

"I still visit manage to visit the Bedouin encampment near Zamzum on horseback once a week, since I'm making it the basis for a paper."

"Will the Palmach include you in the mission to retrieve our weapons, even though you're working full time?"

"I should hope so, seeing it was my suggestion."

"Please, please, if you find a Rheinmetall Super typewriter hidden anywhere in the British stores, it's mine."

Dov raised a questioning eyebrow.

"The British army stole my typewriter in Haifa last year."

Part 6

Back on Track 1943 – 1944

Chapter 22

In March Dalia received her fourth letter from Patsy. She had thrown the previous ones away unopened, still furious with the British. Her anger had simmered down. It wasn't Patsy's fault that the British had betrayed the Palmach, so this time she opened the envelope.

Dear Dalia,

I don't know if you received my other letters as I have had no reply. Just in case you haven't, I'll tell you once again I can't begin to tell you how sorry I am about the disbanding of the Palmach and the unfair way they confiscated your weapons.

The closure has affected me too. I have to leave my job before Easter but have managed to find another in Cairo.

I'll be on leave in Jerusalem for a fortnight until Bank holiday Monday. Maftur is organising a reunion of our secretarial group. It would have to be in the evening, for people at work, and not a Friday evening, of course. I hope you can make it. I am enclosing Maftur's address in case you're interested in going to the Reunion. Her married name is Shawwa.

I will have a car so could drive you to Haifa from Rehovot and back the next day.

Incidentally, do you remember telling me once that you would love to make the desert fertile? I have something I would like to discuss with you.

Lots of love,

Patsy

Dalia put down the letter, puzzled by the last paragraph. What did Patsy want to tell her that she couldn't put in a letter, or was she just whetting her curiosity so she'd agree to meet her? She'd like to attend the re-union. Haifa CID was unlikely to find out if she spent just one night in Haifa.

Internal letters weren't censored so she wrote to Maftur saying she had heard from Patsy, was interested in a reunion, and had no afternoon lectures on Thursdays.

Maftur sent a postcard by return of post.

Dear Dalia,

How wonderful to hear from you. You will need somewhere to stay in Haifa. My mother-in-law would be very happy to offer you a bed. Patsy will be sleeping over too. Will Thursday 26th March be all right?

Love,

Maftur

That was kind of Maftur but she was a little hesitant about accepting, never having been in an Arab house. She knew everyone slept on mats on the floor all in the same room and, as for food, the whole family sat on cushions scooping up meat and rice with their bare hands from the same dish. Still, it would be an experience. She wrote back accepting Maftur's offer, and wrote to Patsy saying she would be glad of a lift to and from Haifa, suggesting they meet up at the Hebrew University canteen and break the return journey with a meal at Bereisheet.

After posting the letter, she worried about Patsy's car. She wouldn't want Palmach members to see her climb into a British army vehicle.

On the day of the Reunion Dalia waited outside the university canteen. She was relieved when Patsy arrived at the wheel of an uncamouflaged Ford. Although she'd kept telling herself Patsy couldn't help being British and wasn't responsible for her country's actions, she felt awkward. Patsy's straight-backed posture indicated she too was feeling uneasy. Dalia contented herself with a simple Shalom and made no attempt to hug her former friend or even shake her hand.

Patsy looked around, to make sure no one was able to overhear. "Please, Dalia, can we still be friends, despite all that's happened? Both Mac and my boss fought tooth and nail against the orders, but London overruled everything."

Still feeling unsure, Dalia replied, "I know you weren't responsible, Patsy, but you can understand how angry I feel?" It wouldn't help, however, to let Patsy dwell on how angry she had been, so she added, "Anyway, what is it you have to tell me about making the desert fertile?"

"Do you mind if we wait until we're on the way to Haifa? It's a bit delicate."

They walked over to the canteen in silence and queued at the counter for meatballs and rice. As soon as they sat down, Patsy said, "Did you know Tim is alive and in a POW camp in Italy? If the British invade, I hope my new job will bring me closer to him."

"Patsy, I am so glad." Without thinking, she sprang up and hugged her friend.

After that, while they were eating Patsy regaled her with tales of life in Cairo. With the threat of invasion over she no longer had to work overtime. Her mother had visited her and they'd enjoyed picnics in the desert and tennis in the sports ground at Gazera.

Dalia's malaise had evaporated by the time they collected their coffee, but when Patsy asked if she still kept in touch with the handsome Palmach leader who had run the Zamzum base, she felt awkward as she replied, "We're going out together."

Patsy held up her thumbs. "Well, that's something positive to come out of Zamzum and, while on the subject of that, it's what I want to talk to you about in the car. Come on. Let's get started."

She had to wait until Patsy had manoeuvred her way onto the main coast road before Patsy assuaged her curiosity.

"Remember saying that you thought Zamzum would be a suitable site for experimenting with arid farming if it had a water supply? I've heard that the army didn't rip out the water tank, after all. This winter's rain should have re-filled it."

"That would have been useful information if it weren't for that stupid British law."

"What law?"

"You must know it! The one saying Jews may not live in, or even camp overnight, in Arab designated territory."

"But you camped there for more than one night last year."

"The British turned a blind eye to many things then. It's back to normal now."

"There'll be a loophole somewhere," Patsy said. "There

always is."

"Only if it suits the British."

Patsy kept her eyes on the road, pressing her lips close together.

Dalia tried desperately to think of a safer topic of conversation, but they were approaching Haifa by the time she said, "I've never visited an Arab family. I'm looking forward to learning about their culture."

Patsy laughed so much she wobbled the car on the road. "Dalia! We're staying with a friend, not doing a field course in anthropology."

She bit her lip in embarrassment and remained silent until they reached the house where Maftur's in-laws lived.

Maftur's mother-in-law welcomed them with plump dignity. A servant served mint tea and home baked honey cakes and, in her magical way, Maftur soon had both of them at their ease, laughing as they reminisced over shared experiences.

Afterwards, Maftur showed them to their sleeping quarters. They had a bedroom each. Dalia's room held a five foot wide cream upholstered bed piled high with embroidered cushions and a burgundy silk coverlet. An electric reading lamp with a chrome and red glass stem and a pale rose-coloured shade stood on a white bedside cabinet. On one side of the room, a Japanese decorated porcelain ewer and bowl occupied a red marble wash-stand next to an arched double-mirrored white wardrobe. So much for everyone sleeping on the floor, all in one room!

The dining room where they had a meal before setting off to Edmonds was another surprise. The table and chairs were European in style but less heavy than her mother's furniture had been in Germany. The table was laid British-style. A servant came in with onion soup and crisp toast. That was followed by lamb cutlets and a green salad.

Dalia felt ashamed when she thought back to what she had expected.

"Maftur is learning to cook English dishes for my son. We sent him to school in England, you know." Mrs. Shawwa explained, when Patsy congratulated her on the cuisine. "We usually eat French style, as my cook was brought up in Beirut. Sometimes, though, when my husband is nostalgic, I cook us the Saudi Arabian dishes I learned from my mother."

Patsy laughed. "It seems, Mrs. Shawwa, everyone in Palestine learns cookery from everyone else."

Later, the reunion in Edmunds proved a great success. When the communal session finished and the company broke up into smaller groups, Dalia seized the opportunity to talk to Golda Kaminer who was back in Hadera, working in her father's citrus export business.

Afterwards, as she walked back uphill to the Shawwa's house, Patsy asked, "Would you mind, Dalia, if tomorrow we started off an hour later than planned? Jim Shepard wants to see me."

She felt her stomach churn. "I need to leave Haifa tonight."

Patsy reassured her. "It's nothing to do with what you're afraid of. It's about a job Mr Shepard may offer Maftur. If she gets it, she and Ismail can live together for a fortnight every month."

"You can have a lie-in while we're gone, Dalia," Maftur put in. "I'll ask my mother-in-law to let you have breakfast in bed."

Breakfast in a gorgeous bedroom propped up on soft pillows. Dalia hadn't known such luxury since leaving Munchen.

* * * *

A few days after her surprisingly pleasant break, Dalia hurried out from the last lecture of term, eager to be on her way to a three day Palmach exercise. She found a note from the local Haganah rep pinned to her rucksack in the locker room.

Change of plans. Do not attend exercise. Return straight home and await further orders.

Her clenched fist scrunched the paper. She guessed what

had happened. The course organiser had been told to cut down on numbers and had given precedence to full time kibbutzniks, although the Palmach had agreed to include her on training sessions during university vacations. They were as bad as the British at keeping promises.

She went shopping in Jaffa before catching the bus on to Bereisheet. Nothing like buying new clothes and shoes to make one feel happier.

By the time she arrived in Bereisheet her spirits had lifted. They became even higher when Ruth looked in after supper and ran to hug her. "I'm so glad to see you. Your mother told me you wouldn't be home for another three days."

"I'm thrilled to see you too. But what are you doing here?"

"I'm on transfer leave. We're not needed in Egypt now the army have moved west. Come over to our cowshed to look at our latest arrival."

"Nu, what sort of novelty is a new-born calf for an agricultural student?" her mother asked. "You want to talk in private, you can use Dalia's bedroom."

Dalia, though, recognised the hidden message behind Ruth's invitation. How often when they were still at school, had they retreated to the hay loft to share secrets? She followed her friend outside and was not surprised when they reached the cowshed that Ruth suggested they climb the ladder.

Once in the loft, Ruth picked up a pitchfork and tossed the hay to one side, making her sneeze. When she opened her eyes Ruth was shining a torch on a typewriter identical to the one the army had requisitioned from Peter's flat.

She stared at it in amazement. "How did it get here?"

"Your good-looking friend Dov called this afternoon in his father's car."

"Dov Goldberg?"

"Yes."

Dear Dov, Dalia thought, as she gazed at the typewriter. *He remembered my request.*

"He looked disappointed when I said you wouldn't be here for another three days," Ruth went on. "He asked me to hide these things." She pushed aside more hay to expose the corner of a wireless. "He wrote a note and asked me to make sure I gave it to you when you returned."

She handed her a sheet of paper and held out the torch. "Here, you'll need this."

Dalia shone the torch on the paper.

Dalia darling,

I know how disappointed you will be about the course and I shall not enjoy it nearly so much without you, but since you were not complicit in our little venture you are the ideal person to caretake this wireless. If it's any consolation, we retrieved your typewriter. Please would you break down the wireless and find the components a really safe hiding place. The cow loft isn't good enough. I hope to see you soon. I'll write first, though, to let you know when I'm coming.

Love, Dov.

Before her parents were up the next morning, Dalia fetched the typewriter down from the hay loft and set it in its old place in her bedroom. She had never told her parents that the army had requisitioned it. They would assume that she had taken it to university. She examined it carefully. It lacked the initials she had scratched on it. However, it was in better condition than the original.

After breakfast, she and Ruth returned to the loft. While Dalia broke down the wireless, Ruth wrapped each component separately in newspaper and oilcloth.

In the afternoon, Dalia dug trenches between dill plants growing behind the cowsheds, and buried them. Before leaving, she sprinkled radish and lettuce seeds over the trenches.

She was back at Rehovot at the start of term when her mother phoned through to her digs, leaving a message that the British army and police had raided Bereisheet and ransacked their house.

She hurried home, ostensibly to comfort her mother, but mainly to check on the wireless.

"Oh, my darling, those British," her mother spat out. "They brought a thousand Indian troops into the Hefer valley. They searched everywhere in Bereisheet, pushed their way into my kitchen, with not so much as a 'by your leave'. Oi, look there!" She pointed to where soldiers had pick-axed the floor of the pickle store. "They turned everything upside down, my onions and gherkins, all ruined." She dragged Dalia to her bedroom and pointed to the cracked tiles. "See your room. Every bedroom, it's all the same."

With relief, Dalia noted the typewriter safely in position on her table. "Did they examine that?"

"You would not believe it. They were all for taking it away, until I showed them the receipt."

Dalia gazed at her mother in astonishment. "You kept the receipt for a wireless you bought in Germany ten years ago?"

Her mother looked embarrassed. "We didn't like to tell you when you were young, but the typewriter you had in Palestine wasn't the one we left behind. Your father bought a new one after we arrived, using the Finance Transaction Scheme."

Dalia didn't know whether to laugh or cry. If only she had known that her mother had that receipt when she and Mrs Shepard had called in at the police station. Once again, she cursed the bank manager who had failed to pass on her mother's letter. How fortunate, however, that the soldiers hadn't bothered to check that the number on this typewriter matched the one on her mother's receipt.

Her mother was still moaning about the floors. "Those tiles were expensive. Made in the German Colony, so we can't replace them. The moshav committee asked the Agency to put a complaint in to the courts, and your father has written to our lawyer on his own account."

Dalia made appropriate noises of sympathy. "Did the soldiers find anything, anywhere?" she tried cautiously.

Her mother allowed herself a smile of triumph. "Ha, all those wretches found were the useless arms by the synagogue. I don't know why the boys buried them. They were legal. The rifles we bought from Haganah are still safe in the citrus grove."

Dalia went out to the vegetable field. The radishes and

lettuces she had sown amongst the dill were almost hidden by weeds.

Chapter 23

Dalia was listening to a lecture on the practicalities of arid farming, and taking notes in a desultory fashion, when the lecturer grabbed her attention by describing the difficulties encountered by a team of Jewish scientists conducting an agricultural experiment in the Negev.

Her hand was the first to shoot up when he invited questions. "Surely, by the terms of the nineteen thirty-nine White Paper, Jews aren't allowed to settle in the Negev."

The speaker looked over his spectacles at her. "The government gave permission for a temporary experimental station, not a settlement."

Patsy, bless her, had been right. There was always a loophole.

As soon as the lecture finished, she rushed to catch a bus into Tel Aviv and raced to the Jewish Agency. She told the receptionist that she wished to discuss a subject too sensitive to divulge to any but the most senior officials.

After a frustrating two hour wait, a young man conducted her to an interior office, where she found a middle-aged lady, who didn't appear at all like a senior official until she opened her mouth and introduced herself as Gal Sieff. She asked Dalia to give a brief résumé of her problem.

Dalia explained that she was a third year undergraduate studying agriculture of arid regions, but, for a few weeks, had been part of the Palmach unit manning a guerrilla base in the Negev. The British still rented Zamzum from the Bedouin and had left its rainwater tank *in situ*. She wanted to do her final paper on the suitability of the site for an experimental agricultural station. She mentioned that one of the pioneer brigades, waiting for the Agency to allocate them a site, had graduates who had specialised in farming arid soil and might be willing to trial a project.

Gal Sieff took notes and promised to contact the British-run agricultural research station asking permission for a group to visit Zamzum with a view to assessing it as a suitable site for an experimental farm.

"If the government gives your brigade permission and they decide to go ahead with the project afterwards, I must have their preliminary plan by mid-January."

Dalia found Leah and Esther weeding between young vines on the southern kibbutz where she had done her first farming practice. They continued working while she stood sweltering in the blazing sunshine, describing Zamzum and suggesting it as a possibility for a pioneering site. She explained the legal loophole.

Esther straightened up. "If the brigade is agreeable we could take a look. Most members, however, have set their sights on a regular watchtower and stockade kibbutz, so it may be difficult to persuade them to look elsewhere. How do we get there?"

"I'm for anything that will get us away from here," Leah said. "Stay for lunch and show us Zamzum on the map."

"It's not marked on any map."

Esther frowned. "How do we get there?"

Dalia rubbed her hand against her forehead, itching in the dry heat. She was sure she would recognise landmarks if she saw them, but how to describe them accurately? She would have to go with them and realised that was what she had intended all along.

"I'll guide you, so long as we don't set out until the rainy season."

"We'll call a brigade meeting," Esther said, "and invite you to the meeting."

At the brigade meeting members listened politely as she described Zamzum's potential as a site for arid farming but she detected a certain lack of enthusiasm and resumed her seat feeling despondent. After Leah stood and made an ardent speech on the political advantages of gaining a foothold in the Negev, the brigade voted unanimously to undertake a preliminary exploration.

She decided not to tell Dov about Zamzum until the brigade had government permission, but wrote to Shimon, not mentioning Zamzum by name, but enthusing about a potential site in the lot of his namesake, describing in detail the caves and modern water tank.

In August, when Dalia was back in Bereisheet for the summer vacation, the Jewish Agency sent Esther an official permit, allowing the brigade to carry out a survey.

Dov paid her a visit. She announced triumphantly that she was to guide a pioneering brigade to Zamzum after the first rains.

His reaction came as an unpleasant surprise. "You? Their guide?" He glared at her. "You've covered the journey once, by car. You'll get them lost. Everyone will die of thirst. If you're serious about visiting the site, you'll need someone like Toni with you. My knowledge of the area is pretty good too. Between us, Toni and I would be infallible."

Dalia blinked back tears of frustration. Dov was right, but she badly needed a reason for the brigade to include her. "You can't spare the time."

"I'm writing a medical paper about the Bedouin, remember? That will justify my trip. As a Palmach commander, I can also persuade Yitzhak to let Toni skive off kibbutz duties to research a project that may prove invaluable to the whole Yishuv."

Dalia resigned herself to defeat. "So I won't be needed?"

"Of course you'll be needed. *I* need you. No one is going to tell you to stay away just because you've recruited Toni and me as extra guides." He put his arms around her and kissed her. They moved away to a hollow in the citrus grove that her father had dug as a redoubt after a minor Arab attack in nineteen thirty-eight.

Even while they made love, Dalia planned her next letter to Shimon, telling him the Agency had given her former brigade the go-ahead to explore a site in the Negev.

* * * *

At the end of October Dalia, Dov, and Toni joined the brigade for the hike from Gaza to Zamzum. They spent the first day walking along a pot-holed track, lined at increasingly infrequent intervals with Arab villages. At night they camped within sight of a village that, Toni informed them, was the last before Zamzum.

While filling their flasks at the village well the next day, Dov ordered, "Draw enough for three days. We may have water problems at Zamzum."

She whispered to Leah, "It's strange how everyone accepts Dov as leader even though he's not a brigade member."

"No, but he's a Palmach commander. A hero to our lads."

Obviously the secrecy surrounding the Palmach was being eroded.

They trudged on. Toni told them when they needed to turn off the track. How did Toni know where they were? She saw no clues and felt ashamed of her presumption in offering to act as guide.

When they arrived at Zamzum, she rushed down the path almost invisible from the plateau to check on the camouflaged tank. It was almost full. She bent down, sniffed, cupped her hands and took a cautious sip. It was odourless and tasteless. She jumped up displaying the V sign.

Dov was furious. "Poisons are not always immediate in their effects." He insisted no one else drank from the tank that day. "We will use the stored water tomorrow if Dalia displays no ill effects by morning."

She wondered how else he had planned to test it.

They sat in a circle close to the water tank to eat their rations. The initial, excited chatter died down into tired but contented silence. Dalia surveyed the dust-coloured landscape devoid of tree or bush lying under a wide blue canopy, as if the creator had abandoned a barely begun hand-tinting of a sepia picture.

She ran her fingers through a pocket-sized patch of earth and turned over a grass seedling with probing white roots. She stared at the water tank, imagining the spirits of the former village inhabitants approving the proposal to bring the wilderness back to life for longer than a brief spring. Everything that had happened so far had led to this moment.

The next day she and Dov paid a visit to the Bedouin camp, leaving to the brigade and Toni the task of mapping out areas that had sufficient soil for planting.

As she donned the thob Dov had brought, she experienced a wave of nostalgia for a time when the Palmach had accepted her as a full member of their squad.

The Bedouin were delighted to see Dalia accompanying Dov and set up an impromptu feast. Afterwards, she questioned the Bedouin women closely about their agricultural practices, making notes for her dissertation.

She and Dov made the most of their time together on the way back to Zamzum so she arrived back in a more relaxed state.

She tensed again when, after supper, the brigade retreated to a cave to decide whether to take on the site. She, Dov, and Toni collected dried thorn bushes, lit a fire and then lay on their backs staring at stars bright through the dry desert air.

Dalia looked towards the cave from which the brigade showed no signs of emerging. "It's a bit like waiting for a baby to be born."

"How should I know?"

Did she detect a note of bitterness in Dov's tone?

When, eventually, the brigade joined them, Dalia sat beside Esther, leaving Leah to take her place between Toni and Dov.

Esther smiled at her. "We've agreed to apply for permission to create an experimental station, and, Dalia, the brigade unanimously voted to invite you to join us when you finish your course. We would also like to speak to Dov."

Dov looked up. "Me—what for?"

"Would you consider becoming honorary medical adviser to the brigade?" She smiled.

Toni sat up, his face glowing in the firelight. "Only Dalia and Dov receive invitations?"

Esther picked up her mug of coffee and stared thoughtfully over its rim at Leah.

"No marriages, no children for three years," she reminded him, "and you've no experience of arid farming."

"But your brigade could use a fluent Arabic speaker."

Esther raised an eyebrow. "You haven't had time to think things through."

Toni shook his head. "I have. I've listened for hours to Dalia saying what she'd like to do here. I've read up about arid farming and have a few technical ideas."

"You've no need to make a hasty decision, Toni," Esther said. "In a week or two, we'll be better placed to know if we can afford to take on another member. In Dalia's case it's different. She's been training for something like this and needs to know what she's doing when her course ends."

Looking at Leah's face, Dalia felt Esther and the brigade would be in for a tough time if they didn't recruit Toni.

Chapter 24

The brigade received the permission for their experimental agricultural project at the beginning of January in 1944. Dalia wrote to Shimon, who had been posted to Italy, telling him the brigade would soon be moving to a site in the Negev, and both Dov and Rachael, the brigade's leader, would be writing to keep her filled in on the project's progress as she was using it for her degree dissertation.

At the end of February, when spring was at its colourful height all round Rehovot campus, her pulse quickened when she received a letter with an Italian stamp. When she turned the envelope over she saw the sender's name was not Shimon Mabovitch but a Mrs. T. Craine. She turned back to the front to make sure it was addressed to her, and recognised Patsy's handwriting. What undercover work was the woman up to now?

She opened it to find the censor had had a field day. The first paragraph, though, was clear and shocked her to the core.

Dear Dalia,

I'm in Italy. I'm allowed to tell you that now, and guess what? I'm on the last day of my honeymoon. I've married my ex POW boyfriend, and am deliriously happy.

Dalia felt a pang of dissatisfaction. She was used to attending local functions and finding nearly everyone of her own age already married but had expected Patsy, at least, to last out the war without tying herself down.

She couldn't imagine the career-orientated woman, who had spent all those evenings in Haifa at the Technion library when she could have been going out and enjoying herself, meekly settling down to become a housewife.

She continued reading the letter and, a paragraph or two further down, received a shock of a different kind.

You'd never have guessed in a million years who Tim's best man was. Only your cousin, Shimon! He organised a boozy stag night, by all accounts, but got Tim to the service in time.

The rest of the letter described Patsy's wedding day and honeymoon, although the censor, for some obscure reason, had blanked out almost all details of the honeymoon. Towards the end Patsy mentioned Shimon again.

You will be pleased to know that Shimon received your letter about ▓▓▓▓▓▓ on the morning of the wedding. He went on for ages about it.

Well, if Shimon had enjoyed her letter so much why hadn't he replied?

You must tell me yourself all about it but please miss out details of soil tests. I heard as much as I needed to about loess and soil salinity at the wedding reception!

Dalia laughed out loud. So typical of Shimon.

Shimon told us you are still going out with Dov. I hope you are as happy with him as I am with Tim.

A few days later, Dalia received another letter with an Italian stamp. This time it was from Shimon.

Dear Dalia,

Thank you so much for the vivid description of your expedition to the Negev. Applying for a government permit to use the location for agricultural research was a brilliant idea. I am so glad your friends' brigade succeeded in their request. Please keep me up to date, especially if they succeed in growing plants there. Can you also send me news of the other pioneering project in the Negev?

Did Patsy tell you I was best man at her wedding? Tim Craine is a great chap and we had a riotous night before the wedding. Some ▓▓▓▓▓▓ troops joined us and we ended up under some gum trees at four o'clock in the morning singing Waltzing Matilda. I got Tim to the club in time for the wedding ceremony though.

I hope your dissertation is going well.

Please give my regards to your brother when you write. Ask your mother to reassure mine if no one hears from me for a while.

With my best regards,

Shimon

She wrote back at once with details of her dissertation and of Toni's experiments with water conservation since he had joined the brigade.

* * * *

Dalia didn't tell her parents that she was joining the farming project in the Negev until the end of her final year.

Her mother's reaction was as she expected. "Uri, sent off goodness knows where, and now you, off to hide yourself in the wilderness. What happens if your father dies? If I die? Would either of you attend our funerals?"

Her father took her announcement more calmly. "Your mother and I had hoped you would settle down to running your orchards in al-Tira, but it's your life. You have a good manager, but maybe, before you leave, you can stay there for a while?"

Dalia was quite prepared to spend all summer in her orange groves if that would make her father happy.

"I'll teach you to drive before you leave," he continued. "When this war ends, jeeps will be two a piastre. You may be able to drive home occasionally."

After only a few lessons her father declared her fit to take over the wheel. He sat beside her while she drove all the way to al-Tira and left, promising she could drive back the following Friday when she returned home for Shabbat.

Dalia enjoyed working alongside Mr Said, her Christian Orthodox Arab manager. He was an authority on growing and marketing Jaffa oranges, the main crop in her citrus groves, although she had a few grapefruit and lemon trees as well. Once he had become used to her, and realised that she understood Arabic, Mr Said proved quite communicative. He told her that his family had been in citrus growing ever since the German Templers at Sarona, and Wilhelmina had developed the world-famous Jaffa orange towards the end of the nineteenth century. That piece of history surprised her. She had assumed that Jews had created the citrus industry.

Not so, Mr Said informed her. The European Jews had based their citrus growing colonies on the ones the Templers had set up.

As she went through the business books, and followed Mr Said around the peaceful groves, she felt she could safely leave him in charge while she worked at Zamzum.

"How long before you expect to retire?" she asked.

"If convenient to you, in about five years. I wish to live in Haifa so I can watch my great-grandchildren grow up."

That timing suited her. Zamzum would be established, and she could step out of pioneering gracefully, knowing she had made a solid contribution to Eretz Israel.

She felt she deserved a real holiday before leaving for the Negev and where better than here at al-Tira near the sea. A holiday on her own, however, didn't appeal. She was wondering whom she should invite to stay, when she received another letter from Patsy, this time bearing an Egyptian stamp.

It contained unexpected news. Patsy was expecting a baby and, in consequence, had lost her job in Italy. She was returning to Palestine to stay with her mother, until she could get a berth back to England. Did Dalia know that Maftur was expecting a baby too, and had left her hush-hush job to return to her in-laws in Haifa?

Dalia invited both Patsy and Maftur to al-Tira for a fortnight.

After receiving replies from both women accepting her invitation, she cadged the car from her father for the whole period. It was a holiday none of them would forget, not just because of how much they enjoyed it, but because of the way it ended.

Every day Umm Ibrahim packed them a lavish picnic, and she drove her friends down to one of the many small, almost deserted beaches along the coast line, which, because Palestine was a mandated area, not a colony, the allies had failed to mine.

Both Patsy and Maftur had received assurances from their doctors that swimming was a healthy exercise for pregnant women.

Pregnancy suited both her friends, Dalia reflected as she watched their contented faces. She envied them their unquestioning love for their husbands and their joyful anticipation of motherhood. If only she could be so certain of her relationship with Dov.

On the last morning of the holiday, Dalia chatted with

Patsy in the dining shelter while waiting for Maftur to persuade the manager's wife to join them.

"I'm in two minds about going to Zamzum now," she confessed to Patsy. "I hadn't realised how much I would enjoy being here."

"If this were my place I wouldn't leave it. How I envy you being able to bring up your children here."

She wondered whether Patsy's baby had been conceived intentionally. "Tell me, are you really pleased to be having this baby or are you just putting on a brave face?"

While Patsy explained how happy she was, she heard the rumble of trolley wheels as Maftur and Umm Ibrahim pushed it along the path, chatting away in Arabic. It didn't take long to set the steaming dishes on the table.

While she poured freshly pressed orange juice into glasses, Patsy took a camera out of her bag and snapped it two or three times. Umm Ibrahim said something to Maftur who explained the manager's wife wished to take a photo of the three of them.

Dalia put her arms round Maftur and Patsy's shoulders and Umm Ibrahim took their photo. As they sat down to enjoy their meal they heard a car turning into the drive. Dalia raised her eyebrows, but Umm Ibrahim shrugged. The car was a taxi. Dalia ran forward to wave it down before it went on to the empty house, and saw two women sitting on the back seat dressed in traditional Arab costume. They were crying.

Some crisis in her manager's family? She turned towards Umm Ibrahim but it was Maftur who came forward, her face ashen, calling in Arabic, "Not Ismail? Please Allah, not Ismail."

One of the women called back, "La! La, Abu Ismail."

Maftur and the women in the taxi spoke together in Arabic too rapid for Dalia to follow. Umm Ibrahim, her face drawn in shock, translated into halting English.

"Those women, they are servants from Maftur's house. Two men, fellaheen, came to her father-in-law's office this morning. They shot him. Maftur must go back for the funeral."

Later that evening, after they had helped a shocked Maftur pack and had seen her depart, Dalia sat outside with

Patsy. Political assassinations were rife amongst all Arab parties, Patsy assured her. Dalia hadn't realised the bitterness existing between Arab political parties. The British had worried for years that Abu Ismail was too blatant an Anglophile to survive long, Patsy said, but he had not listened to advice and had continued speaking out against the Grand Mufti who was now in Berlin supporting Hitler.

"What about Maftur's husband, Ismail?" Dalia asked. "Is he in danger too?"

Maftur's Ismail was far more discreet than his father, Patsy told her, but his English schooling would tell against him so Maftur was worried sick. She wanted to join Ismail in Transjordan but unfortunately his camp had no married quarters.

The next morning, Dalia dropped Patsy off at Athlit station. She wondered if she would ever see her two friends again. Patsy was waiting to return to England and Maftur to move to Jordan.

Dov phoned the manager's office the next day. He had a week's leave. Could he spend it with her at al-Tira?

"So long as you set up your tent at the other end of the grove from where I'm sleeping, otherwise you'll scandalise the Saids into resigning."

"I've something I need to talk over with you, but I'm running out of coins so it'll keep until I see you."

Their first evening together, they sat out under the orange trees, sipping glasses of chilled white wine.

"You could be in a different world here," Dov commented.

"Perhaps too much so," she replied. "I was almost tempted to stay, until the real world intruded last week."

She told him about the murder of Maftur's father-in-law. "Before it happened, I felt so contented here in al-Tira. Patsy thinks the assassins were thugs hired by people who want Palestine to become a Muslim state again so perhaps a viable partition is the only way we can have a true homeland. We'll need the Negev. But you came here to tell me something."

"Yes. I hope you'll be pleased. The government have

agreed to pay me a small salary to oversee the building of a clinic at Zamzum and to conduct a surgery there once a week. The local Sheik has offered to put all medical equipment under his clan's protection, so there'll be no worry about theft. They'll pay the brigade to build the clinic in collaboration with the local Bedouin. The extra cash will make a huge difference to the brigade's work."

"That's wonderful—a stone structure—one step nearer to Zamzum becoming permanent."

"There's just one snag! We start building at the end of September. I know I promised to hike down to Zamzum with you after the first rains, but the latest I can make it is early September. It will mean travelling at night and resting in the middle of the day. Will you be okay with that?"

"I can't say I like the idea, but it's preferable to making the journey on my own. I don't know how I'd manage if I had an accident on the last stretch."

"Talking of accidents—Zamzum being so cut off from civilisation worries me. I'd be happier if it still had a wireless set."

"Should I take the one buried in Bereisheet?"

He shook his head. "We couldn't transport it to Zamzum unless we stole a jeep and we wouldn't get away with that."

The week after Dov returned to Beersheba, Dalia took Ruth to al-Tira before she started a new job at the Hadassah hospital on Mount Scopus. Dalia's father lent her the car once again.

Like Patsy, Ruth found it difficult at first to understand why Dalia was abandoning her own paradise, for back-breaking toil in the wilderness.

Having to explain helped Dalia get her own thoughts straight. "We have to prove to the government the land is capable of supporting a much greater population than it does at present. If I stay in al-Tira I'm just maintaining the status quo but, if I help make the wilderness productive, we add extra land."

"What does Dov say to that? Doesn't he want to settle and raise a family as soon as the war's over?"

"We don't talk about the future."

"You're not like me and Uri. We can't stop dreaming of what we'll be doing after the war."

"Will you carry on nursing?"

"Of course not. I'll settle down to being a farmer's wife and having lots of children."

They arranged to have lunch together in Jerusalem before Dalia set off for Zamzum.

Chapter 25

Dalia was obsessed with finding a way to transport the wireless to Zamzum. Inspiration came while driving her mother to Tel Aviv. She noticed that although there were far fewer military vehicles on the road now the war had surged west, growing prosperity had brought a big increase in donkeys and mules carrying goods to and from those villages perched on hill-tops away from tarmacked roads. A mule could carry the wireless to Zamzum and, once there, help transport produce to Beersheba.

She returned to the agricultural institute to read books on mule management before visiting Bereisheet's oldest resident, known to all as Uncle Ozzie. He had been in charge of Bereisheet's mules before mechanisation and still kept retired mules on his plot. He agreed to go with her to the nearest livestock market.

On the appointed day, her father drove her and Uncle Ozzie to the Arab village hosting the market. They left the car on the outskirts of a field crowded with tethered donkeys, mules and camels, where men haggling with loud voices were almost drowned out by the animals' braying and harrumphing.

Even to Dalia's untrained eyes, most animals appeared in poor condition with dull coats and rheumy eyes. She was drawn to a tawny mule whose hide had a healthy sheen. Tentatively, she put out her hand, knowing she risked a painful bite, but the mule let her stroke his neck and seemed to enjoy it.

Uncle Ozzie examined the mule carefully for signs of saddle sores and eye infections but found none. "This mule has been well treated. He should be safe."

He haggled on her behalf with the owner, an equally elderly Arab in a striped tunic and white keffiyah. Apart from their clothes, the two men, one Arab, one Jew, looked remarkably similar as they sat cross-legged opposite each other.

"His name is Hod," Uncle Ozzie told her. "It is

obstinate, of course, but not as obstinate as most, and for a mule he is very good-tempered. You will not normally need to muzzle him, which is as well, since being muzzled is the thing he hates most."

The owner insisted that if she bought the mule she must also buy the set of tough leather panniers, saddle, muzzle, and reins that lay beside him. That suited Dalia as she would have had to purchase those items, anyway.

Once Uncle Ozzie had negotiated a satisfactory price, he showed her how to saddle her mule and check the straps. Her father helped her into the saddle. Uncle Ozzie showed her how to let Hod know when she wanted him to turn left, right, or stop. The saddle didn't seem as uncomfortable as she had expected and she quite enjoyed the jolting movement. Her father and Uncle Ozzie, in the Austin, dawdled after her as she rode Hod home, the car stopping at frequent intervals to allow Uncle Ozzie to show her the best way to get Hod going again when he stopped to chew at dry grass, or how to prod him into action when he stood still to reflect on the mysteries of the universe.

Back at Bereisheet she phoned Dov and told him of her purchase.

"Dalia," he exclaimed. "You're a genius."

* * * *

Dalia received a telegram to say Patsy had had her baby, and had called him John. She took the bus up to Jerusalem and lunched with Ruth in Ben Yehuda Street.

"Next time I see you, the war could be over and Uri demobbed," Ruth said, as they sat down to an uninspiring wartime menu of corned beef fritters and chips. "You will come back for my wedding, won't you, Dalia?"

"Of course! Don't you dare get married without me. Give me plenty of warning, though. They only collect mail from Beersheba once a week."

After their meal, and before Ruth returned to Mount Scopus, Dalia told her she was going on to the government maternity hospital in the Russian Compound.

Ruth grinned despite the sadness they both felt at parting for an indefinite period. "Mind how you go this afternoon. Holding a new-born baby can make you broody."

Dalia shook her head. "Brigade rules. No marriages, no babies, until either the project ends, or Zamzum turns into a settled community."

"Commitment's one thing, what happens is another!"

Bearing Ruth's warning in mind, Dalia was relieved to find baby John asleep when she entered the maternity hospital in the Russian Compound.

Patsy, a shining picture of contented motherhood, peered into the cradle, a dreamy smile on her face. The rather too red-faced baby gave a little yawn and crinkled his eyes but didn't open them.

"Perhaps he'll wake later, and you can hold him," Patsy offered in consolation.

A few minutes later, Maftur walked in to the ward.

"You haven't come all the way from Haifa in your condition?" Dalia exclaimed.

"No. The Emir's granted Ismail indefinite, compassionate leave so he's able to run the Jerusalem office again."

"Doesn't Ismail's mother mind you moving away?"

Maftur smiled happily. "My mother-in-law's living in Nablus with Ismail's sister."

"What about you, Dalia?" Patsy asked. "Are you ready for your sojourn in the wilderness?"

Dalia told them about Hod and how useful he'd be carrying produce to market.

"I'm so proud of you," Patsy commented. "You're doing something really inspiring. I wish I could visit you at Zamzum."

"Perhaps we could visit together, Patsy, when both our babies are born," Maftur suggested.

"It's not quite the same journey as swanning down the Seven Sisters to Tel Aviv," Dalia pointed out. "Neither your husband's car, Maftur, nor your mother's, Patsy, is tough enough."

"We couldn't do it anyway," Patsy said. "By the time our babies are old enough to survive such an excursion, I'll be back in England. Once the military have organised my passage I'll be an illegal immigrant if I stay."

Dalia couldn't keep a note of bitterness out of her voice as she said, "They won't lock you up in Athlit though."

Patsy pursed her mouth before answering, "They might well do that. The Admin would just jump at a chance to prove themselves even-handed. The only thing that would stop them is Tim being on active service. Putting a British soldier's British wife in prison for staying with her mother wouldn't look good in the English papers."

The door opened and a middle-aged ward sister came in carrying a tray of tea and biscuits. Maftur took the tray, placing it on the bedside table, and started pouring the tea while the Sister peered into the cradle.

"He's asleep again," she complained. "He was asleep last time I came."

Patsy gave a mock scowl. "My mother's been yo-yoing in and out every two hours even though she doesn't work in the maternity unit."

"It's my official tea-break," Sister Quigley said, "so I'm entitled to visit my daughter."

Dalia looked at the Sister again with more interest. While working with Patsy in Haifa, she had sensed her friend was not on good terms with her parents. She seemed at ease with her mother now, however.

Maftur handed a cup to Mrs. Quigley, saying, "I put in your usual spoonful of sugar," and Dalia felt an outsider once again.

"Umm Pat," Patsy said, "I don't think you've met my friend Dalia. She's going pioneering next week."

Mrs. Quigley held out her hand. "I'm delighted to meet you, Dalia. I have heard so much about you. Your orange grove sounds delightful. I don't know how you can bear to abandon it for the desert."

Dalia, feeling patronised, corrected her. "Wilderness,

Mrs. Quigley, not desert. In spring the Negev's full of wild flowers. You should see it, but Patsy says that she won't have time to visit Zamzum before returning to England. Will you be going with her?"

"I wouldn't get travel priority. I'll return for furlough after the war, of course, but plan to stay in Palestine until the end of the mandate."

As casually as she could, Dalia asked, "Have you inside knowledge of when that will be?"

Mrs. Quigley looked puzzled. "They agreed in nineteen thirty-nine that it would be nineteen forty-seven, didn't they? Do you think the war may have changed that?"

Dalia turned to Maftur. "It won't be long before it's your turn, chick. Are you still determined to have your baby at home?"

"Of course. Aziza's well settled in, and my mother will come up nearer the time. My doctor will hurry over from Jerusalem if the midwife needs him."

"We always used to have our babies at home when I was young, but I'm glad little Johnny was born in hospital. I guess grandmothers are more nervous about these things than mothers."

"I wanted to have Johnny at home," Patsy explained. "I could have registered him as Palestinian, then they couldn't chuck me out."

Dalia wanted to get off the subject of babies. "Have you heard anything from your Tim, recently?"

"Not for a while," Patsy replied. "I'm sure I will though. My mother used her magic to get a message through to the Major. He will pass the message on to Tim somehow. I suspect, from what I saw in Italy, that Shimon and Tim are working together. You haven't received any hints?"

"I've heard nothing for weeks."

Part 7

Pioneer Farmer 1944-1946

Chapter 26

Her last day in Bereisheet! Dalia scurried outside after supper to dig up the wireless components, wrapped them in hay, and stuffed them into the panniers. She placed the panniers beside sacks filled with alfalfa and carrots.

Long before dawn, she fetched Hod from the field where she had tethered him. He came willingly which she hoped was a good sign. She saddled him, lifted on the panniers, and tied the sacks over them, slipping the still unused muzzle into one of the sacks. They would need it in Zamzum if the brigade used Hod to carry equipment through crops.

She packed jerry cans of water and her heavy rucksack into her parents' car. She would tie the water onto Hod when she reached Gaza, but was allowing herself the luxury of riding to the station instead of walking beside a fully-laden mule. She mounted and set off, leaving her parents to follow at a more respectable hour.

Hod, clearly relieved to be out and about, behaved beautifully. The sun rose, high-lighting the yellow of ripe lemons in the citrus groves. A few oranges were beginning to turn colour. The scent of blossom, opening to provide the second harvest, wafted through the air. The clang of warning tins attached to the irrigation pumps rang out.

Riding past these reminders of all she was leaving, she thought about her parents and, for the first time, wondered if she was being unforgivably selfish by carrying the radio. Once she reached Hadera, she would not be dealing with compliant settlement police. If an Arab or British policeman took it into his head to search her possessions, she would face a long gaol sentence. She remembered the agony her parents had experienced when the British had arrested Uri. She rode on, outwardly calm but mentally flustered.

When she arrived at Hadera, with still an hour before the train left, she found Dov already there.

The station-master delivered his instructions. The stock car in which Hod would be travelling stood in a siding. They must remove everything Hod carried apart from his harness and muzzle him before taking him into the stock car. The panniers and sacks could remain on the platform until the train arrived.

Dalia experienced a wave of panic. How could she leave the panniers unguarded?

Hod was a model of docility while they removed the panniers between them. They were too heavy to carry. Dov seemed unaware of her reservations so she had to leave them while she led Hod to the siding. Trouble started when she tried to put on the muzzle. As soon as Hod saw it he began bucking and kicking. She'd never have coped alone, but Dov held Hod's head, while she struggled to place the muzzle over his braying jaws.

Once the muzzle was on, Hod stood with legs splayed apart and refused to budge. Dov borrowed a mop from the waiting room. While she hauled from the front, he pushed the mop's soft end against Hod's rump, dodging vicious kicks with the agility of a Cretan bull-dancer. An audience of *fellahin*, laughing and calling out mocking remarks in Arabic, did nothing for her self-esteem. To her horror she saw a British police constable enter the station and stand next to the panniers. She found it hard to concentrate on Hod, until she realised the constable was enjoying the show they were putting on so much he had no time for anything else.

The station-master shouted that the train was due in and they must hurry, but Hod was still only halfway up the ramp.

The train whistled and roared into the station, belching smoke and obscuring the panniers. Her panic increased. Rail workers uncoupled the guard's van. The train gave a jerk and the guard's van rolled back beyond the junction.

Two rail workers arrived to remove the ramp. Dov pleaded with them to wait.

A shunting engine puffed impatiently down the siding. The driver yelled at them.

She gave a desperate haul, but nothing happened. An elderly Arab came out of the stock car and whispered in Hod's ear. Hod's legs moved. Dov prodded and she led Hod into the car, three stalls of which were already occupied by two cows and a donkey.

From behind Hod, Dov jumped to the ground. She called "Panniers" but didn't think he'd heard. The workmen removed the ramp. The shunting engine connected violently with the stock car and caused Dalia to topple backwards.

The car jerked to and fro as the shunting engine moved it onto the main line. Railway workers connected it, first to the goods' van and then to the guard's van. She could see the platform again. The constable still stood next to the panniers. Dov strolled towards him and casually lifted the panniers away from the policeman's feet. He hoisted them into the goods' van before returning for the sacks.

She turned her attention back to Hod, still refusing to move towards his cubicle. The elderly Arab came to her aid again by whispering another charm into Hod's ear.

Once she had tethered Hod and slammed the cubicle door shut behind him, she resolved to relinquish all responsibility for him once they reached Zamzum.

Her father was on the platform now, carrying the jerry cans of water. Her mother followed him into the station, carrying her rucksack. Dalia jumped onto the platform and ran over to her parents while Dov took the water and rucksack to the goods' van. For the next ten minutes she endured her mother's alternating kvetches and tearful embraces. The guard waved his red flag. A porter started up the platform, slamming doors shut. She jumped into the goods' van.

As the guard blew his final whistle, her father shouted, "We'll miss you, Dalia, but your mother and I are proud of what you are attempting."

She looked round for Dov, but he wasn't there. She was about to panic when he emerged from the animal truck carrying Hod's muzzle. "I don't care if it is against railway regulations, but I couldn't bear to see that animal so unhappy. The donkey owner agrees. Go and talk to Hod now. I'll guard the panniers."

On opening the door of Hod's cubicle she was amazed to find he had once again become the docile animal she had ridden from home.

At Gaza, Hod allowed her to lead him out of the truck without fuss and down another ramp to ground level at the end of the platform. He stood quietly while she and Dov replaced the panniers, saddle and sacks, and tied their tent to the saddle.

Under blazing sun, they walked a short way out of Gaza before setting up camp under the shade of a clump of eucalyptus trees. Later that afternoon, once the worst of the midday heat had passed, they set off again, leaving the main road to take a track that zigzagged between villages. They stopped for a meal in the middle of the night, and carried on by moonlight.

They reached an Arab village two hours after dawn. She had just enough energy to tether Hod, water and feed him, before dropping into an exhausted sleep in the tent Dov had erected.

She woke, stiff and sore, in the late afternoon, hating the thought of yet another night march. She managed it, and was in slightly better shape than the previous day when they stopped at another village before mid-morning to sleep again. Before they left the village that second evening, they bought a mountain of barseem which they piled so high onto Hod that he resembled a moving haystack.

Stumbling along pitted rock in the moonlight, Dalia watched the monstrous shape plodding across a colourless world, in which humans were fleeting irrelevancies. She wondered why she was expending so much energy on a project, so meaningless in the infinity of eternity. Only pride kept her from curling up on the ground and telling Dov to leave her to claim her own oblivion.

Just after dawn, they reached the edge of the plateau above Zamzum. Members of the brigade raced up the cliff path to greet them.

"A miracle," Leah said, stroking Hod's soft nose. "Just when we were wondering how we were going to carry our crops to market."

Toni took Hod's halter. "I'll take him down to the water tank."

"Be careful, Toni," she called. "There are delicate radio valves amongst the hay in the panniers."

Esther caught hold of her, staring at her with her eyes open wide. "Radio?"

Dalia nodded, triumph overcoming weariness. "Yes, the agency have loaned us a wireless."

Esther breathed out. "Two miracles in one day."

* * * *

Late in the afternoon, Dalia woke from a long sleep on a comfortable camp bed beneath mosquito netting. Esther brought her a hot drink.

"Coffee, real coffee," she exclaimed at her first sip.

"Our one luxury," Esther replied with a smile. "But you'll have to get used to drinking it black."

"Where do you get it from?"

"A police friend at Beersheba buys it from the NAAFI. We make a monthly trip there to collect our post and buy fruit and veg. With the mule you brought, that chore will be so much easier and we'll be able to market our surplus produce."

"Surplus produce, already?" Dalia asked, between sips of coffee. Surely, even before the war, coffee had never tasted as good as this.

"Onions and tomatoes," Esther stated proudly. "I'll take you on a guided tour."

Still sipping the wonderful coffee, Dalia stood and moved to the cave entrance. What a difference in less than a year. She watched people rolling back old bed sheets and curtains from two-metre square gardens bounded by low stone walls. She counted sixteen.

"Why the covering?" she asked as they walked down.

"There can't be that many birds about?"

"Toni's idea," Esther answered. "The sheets conserve moisture, besides shading the crops in summer and protecting them from frost in winter. We aim to make ourselves self-sufficient by next year. We compost all waste, including sewage," Esther explained. "The tomatoes were a bonus crop provided by the sewage."

"Self-sufficient? That's a tall order. Who set the target? The Agency?"

"No, the British. The Agency helps us cheat to meet it."

"Cheat? What do you mean?"

"Last winter our rainfall was above average but if the rains fail next year, they'll sneak water in and fill our tank. They'll carry on subsidising us, too, if we need it, without letting the British know. It's important we exceed the Bedouin's level of production if we're to be allowed to settle here."

When they reached the wadi floor, Leah was weeding one of the miniature beds. She scooped a handful of soil from an area outside the cultivated plot, and let it slip through her fingers in a thin trickle. She leaned over a wall and collected moist, much darker soil, and gently moulded into a ball. The granules clung to each other and refused to run through her fingers. "See the difference compost makes to soil structure?"

"Impressive. I can't wait to start working out here."

"I'm sorry but I haven't included you on the gardening rota," Esther said. "We need every spare pair of hands to get the clinic finished by the contract date."

"I can't see any building going on."

"No. Dov insisted we erect it in the main wadi so the Bedouin don't have to enter territory populated by half-naked women."

Two days later, once she had the wireless set up, Dalia, clothed in a long-sleeved blouse and full-length skirt, went down to the main wadi which she had always considered more of a valley than a wadi. Its sides sloped gradually. The stone-strewn floor was comparatively level and covered by thorn bushes that, although grey now, would green up after the first rains. The occasional acacia tree grew in cracks between rocks.

Dov had chosen a spot on the slope to reduce the risk of damage by flash floods. Members of the brigade who had acquired basic building skills were erecting cavity walls of local stone and infilling them with pebbles and soil.

Dalia joined a workgroup composed of both Bedouin and brigade women collecting stones in large woven baskets which they took to the builders. The work, although similar to the job she had been allocated on her first college placement, was made more enjoyable because she was part of a team. Zionists and Bedouin women socialised during refreshment breaks.

With the walls completed, Esther contacted the Jewish Agency in Tel Aviv and a sturdy truck brought in materials and qualified professionals to fit the roof and put in windows and doors. They finished the building before the first rains.

From then on, Dov rode over once a week with a nurse and another female helper to conduct a medical clinic. They arrived the previous evening to share a meal with the brigade and would usually ride back to Beersheba late the following afternoon.

The first time the medics arrived, Dalia ran out with Toni and Leah to greet them and see to their horses. While she watched Dov dismount she heard his nurse call out, "Dalia, fancy seeing you here!"

She looked up and recognised Suzanna Haddad, Mrs. Shepard's former maid.

"You two know each other?" Dov asked.

"We worked together for a short time in Haifa," Suzanna said as she leapt off her horse and caught Dalia in an embrace.

Dov looked surprised. "You never told me you'd been a secretary, Suzanna."

"I wasn't. This was when I was working for Mrs. Shepard."

Dalia was uncomfortable with the way the conversation was going. Working as Mrs. Shepard's domestic had been the all-time low of her life.

"It's a long story, Dov. Meanwhile, Suzanna, let me take

you and..." she looked expectantly at the elderly woman with Suzanna, a Bedouin judging by her half veil.

"Sorry, Dalia, this is Ruhksana Tayi. She organises me, and makes sure the most urgent cases are given priority. I don't know how I'd cope without her."

"Let me take you and Ruhksana up to the women's dormitory so you can wash after your journey. I'll see you later, Dov."

Suzanna raised her eyebrows. As they walked up the path, she asked, "Dov's your boyfriend?"

"I guess so."

"When are you getting married?"

"Not before the war ends."

"That shouldn't be long now."

Dalia experienced a flash of panic. Another line of conversation she didn't want to pursue. She wanted the war to end, of course, but not to settle into bland domesticity with Dov so soon.

"What about you and Sa'eed?"

Suzanna twirled the end of her scarf and smiled. "So you've heard about my engagement?"

"Patsy Quigley wrote. She heard it from her mother. You know Patsy and her husband are back in Palestine with little Johnny?"

"No!"

"She's staying with her mother while her husband's on a course in Jenin. He's been transferred to the Palestine Police."

"Oh, Missus Quigley will be pleased. She missed her grandson so much. I must invite them to our wedding when we've set a date."

"When's that likely to be?"

"Not until Sa'eed receives his degree and finds a permanent teaching job, and when I've completed a midwifery course."

The next morning everyone in Zamzum accompanied the medical party down to the main wadi to wish them well. A huge crowd of men and boys waited outside the clinic. Every man of the tribe had come for the morning clinic, the majority with the most minor of complaints, and they had all brought gifts, either live hens or a cockerel. There was even a pair of goats from the family of a man who was genuinely ill with jaundice. Esther promptly assigned an extra two male first-aiders to assist Dov.

By the time Dalia and the rest of the brigade returned to get on with agricultural tasks, women and children were already camping out under goat-hair awnings on the other side of the clinic for the afternoon session.

Esther took three women off afternoon agricultural duties. Dalia was one.

When she and her two companions had pushed their way through the crowd to the nurse's room at the back of the clinic, they found Suzanna painting a woman's cheek purple.

The district nurse gave them a bright smile before setting the bottle of gentian violet onto an ashlared rock serving as a table and throwing the used brush into an enamelled bucket of diluted Milton. She greeted the next patient bearing a note with instructions from Dov.

Dalia donned a white overall and received the patient Ruhksana directed her way. Dov had diagnosed this one as having a sprained ankle. She unrolled an elasticised bandage and from then on worked non-stop until the clinic closed.

That evening Dov donated the bulk of his live presents to the brigade. They agreed on a livestock breeding program to complement their agricultural experiments and reserved one cave for the purpose. They bought barley and other animal feed from the local Bedouin. Besides providing milk, the goats proved efficient compost accelerators of kitchen waste, and the chickens added much needed nitrogen to the desert soil.

Dalia enjoyed her subsequent turns on the clinic rota once she grew accustomed to the work, especially when the Bedouin women, led by the women who had been on the stone collecting team with her, lingered to chat after the clinic closed. When the Bedouin ladies shared their crop storage secrets and gossiped about their agricultural successes and failures, Dalia felt almost as much at home with them as she did with her Zamzum colleagues.

The introduction of livestock caused problems with jackals which gave her an excuse to practice her firearm skills, another enjoyable task. Before long she had organised firearms practices for everyone.

In return for the animals, the brigade presented the Bedouin women with seeds harvested from their successful experiment with a new hardy wheat strain. The Bedouin women received them excitedly, because, up to now, barley was the only cereal they had successfully grown.

She reported back on Bereisheet's progress to Shimon and wrote at length about Toni's contributions. He had planted apricot and almond saplings in small pockets of soil trapped in cracks in the rock on top of the cliff. Although left very much to their own devices, they seemed to flourish once he had devised self-watering devices for each tree. He asked people making the monthly journey to Beersheba market with Hod to collected discarded jerry cans on their return journey, and filled the oblong tins with water. He placed one beside each tree. Into the small opening at the top of each can, he inserted a length of worn rope encased in discarded bicycle inner tubing picked up at Beersheba. He placed the other end of the rope into the crevice above the sapling's roots.

He planted more trees in the narrow stone-walled terraces they were all creating and filling with kitchen waste, dung—both human and animal—and baskets of earth painstakingly scraped from beneath rocks. He placed large flat rocks over the saplings' root systems and more self-watering devices plus the ever useful muslin covering. Before the sun grew too hot each day, Toni persuaded the rest of them to rush around and cover the treasured plants with sheets. He removed them in the late afternoon. To everyone's astonishment, the trees in both cracks and terraces survived.

She wrote to Shimon, too, about their growing closeness to the Bedouin.

We're going to all the clan's weddings and funerals now. While the men get up to whatever men do, the Bedouin women conduct us brigade women around their plots so we can admire the wheat plants which are doing well.

Chapter 27

"The German Army has surrendered!"

Esther switched off the wireless. No one could hear the presenter anyway amidst the excited hubbub.

She brought them down to earth. "We can't all go home to celebrate victory with our families. Someone has to look after the livestock and plants."

Dalia envisaged the huge celebration party when Uri was demobbed. She wouldn't want to miss that. If Shimon were demobbed at the same time that would be an even greater party. Shimon would visit Zamzum during his demob leave. The thought of hiking back with him made her breathe more quickly. "I'll wait until my brother comes home," she offered.

Dov, who was spending two leisure days at Zamzum before going up to Jerusalem to hand in a paper on Bedouin medical needs, nudged her. "I wish you hadn't volunteered to stay. The celebrations in Jerusalem will be spectacular and there's something I need to discuss with you now this war's over."

"It's not completely over," she pointed out. "They're still fighting in the east."

"As far as Palestine's concerned, the war's over."

Once Esther had sorted rota changes to everyone's satisfaction, Dov asked Dalia to take a stroll with him. They left the others around the bonfire singing and climbed the path to the plateau. They sat side by side on a large rock in silence. Above them, the stars shone brightly. Below, the red glow of the bonfire silhouetted the heads of some people and highlighted the faces of others. The words of the Palmach song floated up.

Dov turned to face her. "Remember what we promised each other when we first got together?"

Dalia had not forgotten. She repeated the words. "We won't fall in love but we'll be lovers and the best of friends, faithful to each other until one of us falls in love with someone else and then we part with no recriminations."

Even as she recited, she was wondering if Dov had fallen in love with someone else. She knew of no eligible woman at the small eight-bed hospital in Beersheba, and it wasn't possible to have an affair in such a small community as Zamzum without everyone knowing.

"How do you feel about us now, Dalia?" Dov asked. "Do you still want no commitments? If you have changed your mind, I would be more than willing to change mine too. I want us to marry and settle down."

"Oh, Dov," she burst out, "apart from Ruth, you're the best friend I have ever had, but…" She broke off, unable to explain because she didn't understand it herself. Why couldn't she just marry him? Why did she always have to have the feeling at the back of her mind that there was something important she must do before settling down? "Please couldn't we continue as we are?"

Dov put an arm round her shoulder. "I would cheerfully go on the way we are, Dalia, if I were your age. If I don't start a family soon I'll be an old man before my children grow up."

"I don't want to marry yet," Dalia replied, "and before you ask, I don't know why. I wish I did."

"I was afraid of that." Dov stared down the cliff at the bonfire. There followed another long silence. He did not look at her when he broke it. "How would you feel if I met a girl who would marry me?"

"You've found one. Who?"

"No one yet. I've wanted you."

"A family is that important to you?" She watched the skin round his outspread fingers grow white as they pressed into his knees. She shrugged, looking away. "B'seder, feel free to chase after every nubile girl in Palestine."

"Dalia!" he started.

"Okay, that was unfair." She turned back and forced a grin. "It's all right. We made an agreement."

* * * *

It is not a good idea to work in the open during a khamseen anywhere, but it is a particularly bad idea to attempt to do so in the arid wilderness of the Negev.

Dalia was struggling in noontide heat to save plants that had already survived heat, cold and drought. As the withering wind blew beneath a blazing sun, she bent over yet another stone wall surrounding yet another door-sized plot.

She stuck back the end of frayed rope, which had slipped from the top of a gas can filled with dish water, unrolled a cotton sheet to protect the plot from scorching, and used stones to hold it in place before stretching up to wipe her forehead clear of salt and windblown dust. She lifted her floppy tembel a few inches from her head, to dry off perspiration-soaked hair.

That afternoon she was on clinic duty. Bandaging wounds in a cool stone building was vastly preferable to slaving outside in this heat, but she wasn't looking forward to it. Dov's leave had ended but he and his team hadn't spent last night at Zamzum. They had gone straight to the clinic that morning. Had Dov found a new girlfriend? She had no claim on him so it shouldn't make any difference if he had, but the thought of him with another woman hurt.

Normally she would have set off early to enjoy a few minutes alone with him between the morning and afternoon clinics but she decided to leave it until the last moment.

While trying to concentrate on her current task to leave no time for brooding, she heard footsteps coming down the path that bisected the chequer board of plots. Glancing up, she saw Esther.

"Dalia, I'm glad I caught you. I was afraid you might have left. You haven't forgotten Dov's put women's surgery forward an hour because of the eye inspection afterwards?"

"No, but I can carry on for another fifteen minutes and still be in time."

"Can you bring the mule back with you this evening? Toni's filling goatskins with water and will take them down but I need him back here. A local woman will distribute the water and tether the mule in shade."

Dalia was grateful not to have the task of persuading Hod to leave his cool cave. Fetching Hod home to his manger would be easy.

Esther glanced at her watch. "I'll take over here. You and Dov haven't seen each other for a fortnight so I guess you'll have a lot to talk about."

Dalia didn't confess that she would rather not talk to Dov but set off up the path. She passed Toni leading a heavily-laden, reluctant Hod. If she'd had to take Hod, she probably wouldn't have coaxed him out of the stable by this time. Although theoretically he was her mule, he responded far better to Toni.

In the women's dormitory cave she used half her 200ml water allowance to give herself a sponge wash and changed into a skirt and long-sleeved blouse before moving on to the communal cave. There she snacked on home-baked bread and home-grown tomatoes before setting off to the main wadi.

As soon as she turned the corner, she saw a huge crowd of women and children from several Bedouin camps sheltering under makeshift shelters pitched against the back wall of the clinic. A local woman was leading Hod round and pouring water from the goatskin bags into scavenged glass bottles.

Toni passed her on his way back. "Get a move on, Dalia," he called out. "Dov's started already."

She checked her watch. "But it's not one yet."

"No, but there's an impetigo epidemic and women from distant camps are taking all their aches and pains into surgery since they have to make the journey anyway to bring their children to the eye clinic."

The reason for the early start was plausible, but she suspected Dov's real reason was to avoid speaking to her.

She watched Toni carefully while asking, "How does Dov seem?"

"Fine. He handed in his dissertation okay, and seems to have enjoyed his vacation." His face showed no embarrassment, his tone matter-of-fact.

Perhaps everything was going to carry on as normal after all. She hurried on.

Once inside the clinic, she closed her eyes for a few seconds to accustom them to the lower light level, and became conscious of unusually stuffy air and the humming of numerous flies. Normally the stone-built clinic was pleasantly cool and, thanks to mesh inner doors and the judicious use of Flit between sessions, fly free. She opened her eyes to see the clinic crammed with people from outside the local wadi, many with running sores, covered in flies. She waved a greeting to Ruhksana who had obviously given up on her usual attempts to allow only a certain number of patients into the clinic at one time.

Dov poked his head out of his curtained-off alcove. He gave her an embarrassed smile before summoning the next patient. She knew at once what had happened.

Weighed down by a stomach filled with lead, her arms and legs sticky under long sleeves and a full length skirt, she willed herself into professional mode before entering the nurses' screened-off area.

Suzanna was unrolling a bandage for a woman with a sprained wrist. "Sorry we didn't come over last night, but Dov phoned the hospital to say he wouldn't be returning until late yesterday, so we made an early start this morning." She turned back to her patient.

Dalia donned a white overall and called in the next patient. She and Suzanna remained too busy for chit-chat until dusk.

Once the clinic was clear of patients and they were tidying up, Suzanna announced she and her fiancé had finally settled on a wedding date.

"My mother and Sa'eed's parents have it all planned. The church service is in Nablus on the last Sunday before Great Lent. Can you still go into a church now you've stopped being a Christian?"

Dalia looked around, hoping no one had heard. "Suzanna," she whispered, "I'd rather people didn't know I'd ever been with the Second Chosen but I'd love to come to your wedding. How does Great Lent translate by normal office calendar?"

"The wedding's on February seventeenth and I hope you can come to my Henna Party in Jenin the day before. Leila Boutaji is organising the bridesmaids and says she she won't have time to chat at the wedding in Nablus. Are you allowed to attend things on a Saturday?"

"My family's not that strict. We keep Seder on Friday evening but treat Saturday as a leisure day. If I can get to Jenin that Saturday, I'd love to attend your Henna Party and get together with Leila. It seems far longer than two and a half years since I saw her."

"Aunt Julia will put you up in Jenin on the Saturday night. That's where the bridesmaids are sleeping."

"I'll do my best to make it."

Dov poked his head around the door. "See you both at supper."

"You're staying tonight?" Dalia asked Suzanna.

"Yes. What with setting off so early and the extra eye clinic, it's been a long day, but I'm keeping you too long. You catch up with Dov. I can finish off here."

"I'm in no hurry. I have to take Hod home and he doesn't get on with Dov's horse."

By the time she had fed and stabled the mule, the gong was sounding for communal supper. She was glad there would be no opportunity inside the canteen for private conversation.

After supper, however, Dov approached her and suggested, in a higher-pitched tone than usual, that they take a walk. They strode up to the plateau in silence and sat on their usual rock. The stars in the enormous dark sky shone just as brightly as before, but she and Dov sat further apart and no one sang round a bonfire. In the distance, a hyena gave a sarcastic laugh.

"So," Dalia stated eventually, "someone has agreed to marry you."

There was no moon to illuminate the expression on Dov's face, so she heard rather than saw him kicking his feet against the rock and was glad the darkness obscured her own face.

"It's okay, Dov," she said at last. "We did make an

agreement. So who is she?"

The woman turned out to be another doctor.

"I don't know why I failed to appreciate her when we were students together, Dalia. Clara and I have so much in common. Her speciality is paediatrics, something Zamzum will need in the not too distant future. Don't tell anyone else, though. I don't even know whether Clara will agree to marry me, and if she does whether she will want to live in the Negev."

Dalia forced a smile, even though she realised he couldn't see it. "You're a right, cunning conniver, picking a woman you know the brigade can't reject."

During the next few weeks she told no one about her split with Dov. She remained silent during the heated discussion that preceded the brigade's decision to allow official engagements between members. (A motion to allow marriages was narrowly defeated.) When anyone expressed surprise that she and Dov weren't announcing their engagement, she just shrugged.

The full extent of the Nazi inflicted horror in Europe now came to light. Ashamed of dwelling on personal woes in view of the most appalling tragedy anyone had ever heard of, she vented her pent-up anger in diatribes against the British. They refused to allow into Palestine the one hundred thousand Jews languishing in allied holding camps only marginally superior to Nazi concentration camps.

Esther told her that she was getting prematurely worked up. "Wait for the fighting to finish in the Far East before expecting the British to expend energy on our affairs."

As she listened to the wireless in the evening, she learnt that all over the rest of Palestine, Jewish citizens were preparing and building homes for displaced Jews, something they weren't allowed to do here in the Negev. As far as she was concerned, the project now lacked its proper purpose. Although she still worked hard on the soil it was without her former enthusiasm.

Chapter 28

Dalia was on friendly terms with everyone in Zamzum, but without Dov had no one with whom she could be entirely open. Dov was the only one apart from Shimon and her brother who knew that she had been a spy working for Shai. He knew that she had first dated a British police inspector in the hope of gaining useful information. Unlike most of her friends, he knew she had never betrayed her Zionist ideals.

She dreaded people finding out about her engagement to Peter Monteith. She still wasn't sure why she had agreed to marry him. Had she really thought that being so close to a British police officer would help Shai, or had she persuaded herself that she had fallen in love when all she had felt was sexual infatuation? If she wasn't sure of her own motives, how could anyone else understand? She had loved Dov more than she had loved Peter, but knew it wasn't the monogamous lifelong love both Ruth and Leah seemed so certain of.

The weeks passed with the British still keeping out the displaced Jews of Europe. Dalia was on the point of resigning from the brigade to find work more immediately useful to the establishment of a Jewish state, when a message arrived from the Jewish Agency. It ordered Toni to transfer immediately to a kibbutz close to Rehovot. If she left now, Zamzum would be without a wireless operator. She had to stay.

The day before Toni's departure, she raged, "What's so special about this kibbutz you're going to that they have to poach members from a genuine pioneering project? They think—" She stopped abruptly, realising how much like her mother she sounded.

Toni looked at her wide-eyed. She had a horrible feeling he too was comparing her to his mother.

"Dalia." He used the same conciliatory tone Uri adopted when their mother ranted. "Dalia, please don't be angry. You think I want to leave Leah? The Palmach needs me. Ask no more."

She took in seven deep breaths. "Sorry! Who would you suggest I train as your replacement?"

"I'm glad you asked that. Leah wants to learn. She says it would give us even more in common."

So Dalia initiated Leah into the mysteries of radio operating. Leah was a good pupil but since there was little time to spare for her training, Dalia realised it would be some time before she could leave with a clear conscience.

Without Toni at Zamzum, there were no innovations, just a continuous round of routine labour. She was the only one except Esther without a fiancé and even Esther had her best friend Leah to share her worries, even more so now Toni wasn't around. At least she could still write to Ruth, the person who knew most about the Peter episode and, although Ruth didn't know about Shai, Dalia suspected she knew more about her political activities than she ever let on.

During one of the long summer lunch breaks, while most members of the brigade dozed in the dormitories, Dalia, armed with fountain pen and writing pad, remained in the canteen. The only other occupant was Esther, busy drawing up a duty roster for the next three months.

Dalia wrote to Ruth, telling her what had happened between her and Dov.

As she wrote, she thought of Ruth and Uri, both so confident in their love for each other, and envied them. She thought too of Patsy, who had married her childhood sweetheart and had become a doting mother despite previous protests that she didn't like babies. She thought of Maftur and the proud look on her face when she spoke of the husband she had schemed to marry despite her parents' original resistance.

If only she too could be certain of being in love, but perhaps friendship and good physical relationships were all she was capable of experiencing. She picked up her pen again.

I think I did a stupid thing, Ruth. I liked Dov and was comfortable with him. I was happier with him than I was with Peter but I still couldn't swear that I loved him, not the way you and Uri love each other.

Talking of marriage, is there any news of Uri's demob date yet? I am looking forward to being your chief bridesmaid, so give me all the warning you can.

She then changed the subject and wrote about happenings at Zamzum and the news her mother had passed on from Bereisheet.

With her letter to Ruth finished, she started her monthly report on the project's progress to Shimon.

Shimon,

Shalom from the Negev.

Nearly all the plants survived the three day khamseen we had here at the end of May, thanks to the shade Toni thought up and his irrigation system. You can tell your mother her old sheets did sterling duty. Toni's left us now as the Agency needs him elsewhere. We all miss him and his innovative ideas.

The water in the tank should see us through the summer, thanks to the rains in April. However, rainfall here is so hit and miss, a dry winter would land us in real trouble. We could do with you coming home and starting piping water from the Jordan as you promised. How long before you are demobbed?

Across the table, Esther gave a deep sigh.

Dalia looked up. "What's the matter?"

"All these romances, that's what. We need three people for each market trip, two to market, and one to do our shopping, collect the mail and handle Hod. We can't afford to send more, but everyone still wants to go with the person they've got themselves engaged to. That was fine while Toni always made up the third. I'm grateful to you and Leah for filling in for Toni so far, but when it's Leah's turn our team always arrive at market late. Leah says she wouldn't mind driving a Jeep if we can ever afford one but nothing in the world is going to teach her to handle Hod."

"I don't mind making up the third, permanently," Dalia offered, "although I'm nowhere near as good with Hod as Toni was."

Esther put down her pen and rested her chin on her fist as she ruminated. Eventually, she said, "If you're sure about that, I'll promote you to post mistress, assistant transport officer, and purchasing officer. You can keep the record of purchases up to date and I'm sure Dov will be only too willing to re-arrange his clinics so he's free to give you lunch on market days."

Now was as good a time as any to announce that she had broken with Dov. She needed the news to get around before he announced his engagement to Clara. It was easier, somehow, now she had already put it in writing to Ruth.

"Esther, Dov and I have split up, all very amicable. He wanted to marry and settle down and I didn't." She gave a little laugh that sounded artificial even to her own ears. "It hasn't taken him long to find a more satisfactory substitute."

Esther put down her pen, her eyes rounded in concern. "I'm so sorry, Dalia. I wouldn't have accepted your offer to go to Beersheba every week if I'd known. I assumed it would be an ideal way for you and Dov to have time together. Do you still want me to put you on the roster?"

"Absolutely."

"Then you can start your postal duties by making a letterbox. That way everyone will know what to do with their letters, instead of thrusting them into the hands of whoever's going to Beersheba."

Six weeks later Dalia could have made the walk to and from Beersheba in her sleep, and knew exactly which stalls sold the items required by the community for the following week. Now in Beersheba, after a breakfast purchased from the nearby falafel stall and strong, black coffee poured from the brass pot of an itinerant vendor, as usual she left her companions to pack away unsold goods while she posted Zamzum's letters and collected mail from their PO Box, just one of a bank of brass boxes occupying a whole wall.

She went outside and sat away from the noisy dusty market on a bench in the shade of a pepper tree, by a circular bed filled with plants displaying leaves of dark red velvet. There she sifted through the mail and found two letters addressed to her. She read the one from her mother first.

Dalia, my Dalia, such great news! Uri is coming home on leave. By the time you read this he should be here!

You must hurry back. I need you now to help with the wedding.

Your father will drive to Beersheba to pick you up. Is that Dov of yours ready to marry? We could have a double wedding. It will be so good to have both my children settled.

Tell me that you are the same size still and I will get your bridesmaid dress made. Ruth will tell me the colours. If you and Dov decide to marry you shall have my wedding dress but I will have to ask Thelma to help me alter it, since you are such a giant. Praise be that your Dov is tall too.

We have had no answer from the Red Cross yet, so your grandparents won't be here in time for the weddings.

Dalia put the letter down, too overwhelmed to think straight. It was wonderful news to have Uri home unwounded. Ruth would be over the moon.

She must go home at once even if it meant letting her parents know her liaison with Dov was over. Her mother's irrational optimism regarding her grandparents, however, disturbed her.

Grandfather, not being Jewish, was more likely to have survived the war than her grandmother, but he knew her parents' address. He would have contacted them if he were still alive. Perhaps by refusing to face facts, her mother was merely attempting to keep up her father's spirits. She hoped that was so. Her mother wasn't much more than fifty. It would be awful to discover she was slipping into early senility.

Dalia continued to sit while she thought things through. She was entitled to a three week vacation. Did she need to return to Zamzum? The other two would welcome the chance to walk back on their own. Hod always behaved on the journey back to the stable. Her best clothes were still in Bereisheet. She had a little money and her cheque book on her. She could hitch to Jaffa, draw money out of Barclays, buy a few underclothes and some shirts and shorts, (she needed new ones, anyway, after ten months in the wilderness). From Jaffa she could get a train to Hadera and hitch from there.

She went back through the market to the Zamzum stall. The eagerness in the two pairs of eyes, as they assured her they would be fine going back on their own, brought back nostalgic memories of how she and Dov had treasured similar opportunities to be alone. She returned to the Post Office to book a reverse number phone call to Bereisheet and was lucky enough to be put through immediately. She asked the nurse to fetch her mother.

Uri would not be in Bereisheet until the day after next, her mother said once she had got over the excitement of hearing her daughter's voice. Dalia told her she would be hitching home.

"No. You stay where you are at the Post Office," her mother cut in. "Your father will fetch you from outside Beersheba Post Office."

"But, Eema, if I'm lucky I could get home quicker by hitching than waiting for Abba."

"Oi, and if you are unlucky?"

Her mother handed the phone over to her father. He was firm. "No arguments, Dalia. I will be outside the hospital at Beersheba by five o'clock. I'm setting off now."

Dalia returned to the others and found they had sold all their produce. She fetched water for Hod, and fed him more barseem. Before joining the others in a siesta, she wrote a note to Esther, apologising for her sudden decision, and placed it in the mailbag along with the shopping change and the community mail. She stretched out next to the others using the postbag as her pillow and wound the end of Hod's tether and the straps of her haversack around her wrist.

They rose at four. By half past they had loaded Hod for the return journey. She entrusted the mail to the others, and waved them off.

She remembered she still had an unopened letter. She had been so excited by her mother's letter she had forgotten. It was from Patsy.

The big news was that Tim had been transferred from Jenin to Sarona and been allocated married quarters.

She heard a car draw up. Her father had arrived.

Part 8

Dutiful Daughter 1945-1946

Chapter 29

Preparations for Uri's wedding were the usual mixture of chaos and organisation, the signing of the contract a prime example.

Before they set out, Dalia checked that her mother had a hammer in her bag, that Uri had collected an old plate, and that her father had the pen with a gold-plated italic nib.

Jack Goldstein read the contract written impeccably in elegant calligraphy. Her father and Reb Cohen signed the contract, without smudge or ink blob. Uri put down the plate to be smashed and her mother let out a shriek.

"Not that one, Uri!" She held out her arm to ward of Miriam Cohen's hammer.

Uri looked bemused. "But it's old. We've had it ever since I can remember."

"Not that kind of old, I meant, you idiot. That's part of my father's wedding present."

"Trudi," Miriam Cohen rebuked. "You want to bring bad luck on this wedding? Uri brought this plate. We smash this plate."

By this time, Dalia was at the door sprinting home. She snatched up a less precious plate and raced back to the synagogue.

Her mother and Miriam were glaring at each other. Reb Cohen was holding the disputed plate beyond reach of Miriam's hammer.

Dalia placed the substitute on the table. Her mother and Miriam set upon it with such vigour that shards flew like arrows in all directions. One hit her father on the arm, piercing his shirt sleeve and producing a copious flow of blood.

"Phone for an ambulance," her mother yelled.

Nurse Bornstein, one of the spectators, gave the wound a quick inspection, pronounced it a minor injury, and borrowed plaster and iodine from the first-aid unit in the kindergarten corner.

Her father was shaking so much with laughter he had difficulty keeping his arm still as the nurse applied the plaster. Everyone else was laughing too, now, even her mother and Miriam.

After the ceremony, Uri went off to pack his haversack to stay at Cousin Elsa's to ensure he didn't see his bride before the wedding.

With Ruth returning to Bereisheet in two days' time, Dalia reflected, wedding fever would infect everyone. Before that, she needed a respite. She found Patsy's telephone number and went up to the nurse's house to make a call.

Patsy exclaimed. "Dalia! Is that really you? I thought you were buried in the wilderness!"

"No. My brother's on leave. We're in the middle of wedding preparations but I'm taking a day off tomorrow to save my sanity, and go shopping in Tel Aviv. Could we meet for lunch and go swimming afterwards? I so much want to see Johnny."

They agreed to meet at the cafe they had frequented when on their wireless course and arranged to go on to Nathanya beach for the afternoon in Patsy's car.

After replacing the receiver, Dalia stretched her arms and imagined herself lying out on a towel with nothing to do except relax.

While she was dawdling back across the oval, a motorbike screeched to a halt outside her house. A Post Office courier delivering a telegram? From her grandparents, after all? She quickened her pace. The driver remained on his bike with the engine ticking over. As she drew nearer, she saw he was an officer from the Jewish brigade. Her heart beat faster. He removed his goggles. It was Shimon Mabovitch. She ran forward. Uri sprinted out of the house carrying his haversack and climbed onto the passenger seat. Her parents stood in the doorway waving. Shimon waved back, replaced his goggles and started the engine.

Uri caught sight of her. "I knew my best man wouldn't let me down," he shouted. "We'll see you next week."

She watched the motorbike recede.

"Now perhaps we can all relax and conduct this wedding in an orderly fashion," her father said.

"I'm taking tomorrow off to meet up with Patsy Craine," she told him.

"Patsy Craine?" her mother exclaimed. "The British girl who stayed with you at al-Tira when that nice Arab girl had to leave because her father-in-law was assassinated? You're still in touch? They must both come to the wedding."

* * * *

The next afternoon, Dalia, wearing a broad-brimmed sunhat, lay stretched out on a towel in the sun drying off on a beach that was busier than it used to be. It was her turn to watch over Johnny while Patsy took a dip.

Johnny sat a few feet behind her on a flat rock in the shade of the overhanging cliff, filling his gaily painted tin bucket with dry sand.

Her mind turned to the wedding. It had taken on a different dimension since she knew Shimon was to be best man. She wondered if there would be an opportunity for a private chat. She had so much to tell him, but he and Uri wouldn't be returning to Bereisheet until the evening before the wedding. On the wedding day she and Shimon would be tied up with wedding duties. The following day was the last of Shimon's leave and, unless he had developed a death wish, he would have to spend it with his mother, despite having already spent almost all his leave at Rohovot. Her only chance to chat was at supper the night before the wedding.

The small dot that was her friend's head moved back through the double row of breakers. She watched Patsy wade through the shallows to firm sand. Before pulling on her sandals she bent down to pick something from the flotsam left by the last tide.

Before drying herself, she squatted down to show Johnny a large shell bearing a ribbed spiral pattern in rust red on the convex side, but lined with glowing mother-of-pearl on the concave.

Johnny took it from her hand and promptly put it in his mouth.

Dalia gasped in horror.

"It's too big for him to swallow," Patsy reassured her, "and the sea's cleaned it of germs."

As Patsy reached for a towel, Dalia said, "What a pity Maftur and little Raffy can't be with us today. When did you last see her?"

"VE Day. We had dinner at my mother's and went to listen to the band outside the King David. Now I'm settled in, I must invite her down. Ismail's teaching her to drive, but I'm not sure if she's yet confident enough to drive as far as Sarona."

"Do you think she and Ismail would accept an invitation to Uri's wedding? My mother suggested it when I told her I'd be inviting you and Tim."

"I'm sure she'd love to come if she can. She already knows you, Golda and me. Ismail is pretty cosmopolitan but Raffy's only seven months old. Maftur might feel it's a bit much for him. It would be wonderful to see her again though."

Chapter 30

Dalia was seated opposite Shimon and Uri at the pre-wedding supper.

Her mother ladled out chicken noodle soup while saying, "So, Shimon, you've broken your mother's heart and signed up to stay on in the army."

Dalia looked up startled at the unwelcome news.

"I should have known Eema would phone you," Shimon replied.

Her mother glared. "And so she should. Why have you done this to her? You've found a good Jewish girl there, perhaps, so why not tell her?"

Dalia concentrated on keeping her spoon still in a hand that wanted to tremble.

"No such luck!" Shimon replied. "I've been far too busy."

She lifted the spoon with no difficulty.

Uri spoke up in Shimon's defence of his friend. "Eema, he's doing sterling work in Italy. He spends his off-duty time preparing DP survivors of concentration camps for life in Palestine. He teaches Hebrew to both children and grown-ups. You want to stop him?"

Dalia broke in. "Shimon, you'd be better employed building a water pipe to the Negev since the British are keeping DPs out."

"They may try," Shimon replied, "but we're smuggling DPs in. We've already collected enough money to hire a boat."

"The Irgun are doing that too," her father commented.

"Yes, but they're only bringing in people capable of fighting the British. We're taking children, old people, and anyone who wants to make Aliyah, regardless of whether they can fight."

"That's a good thing you are doing," her mother admitted. "I'll tell Cousin Elsa she should be proud."

Although Dalia agreed, she still wished Shimon had made

bringing water to the Negev his priority. It would deprive the British of the excuse that there was no room in Palestine. She hoped to have a word with Shimon in private but as soon as the meal was over he disappeared to organise the details of Uri's Tish.

The next morning Dalia put on her bridesmaid's dress of blue silk before going over to see Ruth. She and the other bridesmaids dressed Ruth in the lace bridal dress that Miriam had worn on her wedding day.

Despite the heat, Ruth insisted on wearing the American nylon stockings Uri had bought her. Everyone ran their fingers up and down Ruth's legs. The nylons fitted magically, even better than real silk. Dalia and the other bridesmaids wore white sandals without stockings.

They spent the rest of the morning arranging Ruth's hair, plucking her eyebrows, applying Max Factor lipstick, and varnishing nails. After that, they attended to their own hair and makeup, before snacking on cold meat, bread and tomatoes sneaked from the wedding feast that Miriam and the other ladies of the moshav were preparing. Uri and his friends were safely out of the way, conducting their Tish in one of the tractor sheds before the bridesmaids conducted Ruth onto the oval, brown and hard as concrete with just a few tufts of brown grass remaining from spring's lush green. The men had erected a low platform beneath the shade of a clump of eucalyptus. With the bridesmaids holding her train, Ruth mounted the platform and seated herself on a throne-like chair.

While the women of the settlement danced in front of the platform, Dalia allowed her mother and Miriam to take her over to admire the Chuppah they had erected outside the synagogue. Four wooden poles, each bearing a Tilley lamp, stood in green painted gas tins that in spring Miriam had planted up with blue flowering convolvulus. In between the convolvulus, women from the moshav had tied sprigs of sweet-smelling citrus blossom. White parachute material embroidered with blue cross-stitch formed the canopy. Blue and white tassels hung from each corner. A small baize-covered table stood in the centre of the Chuppah.

Dalia heard the rumble of a heavy engine and turned to look. A coach was drawing up on the edge of the oval, the Rehovot party.

The two mothers, joined by her father and Reb, both wearing festive kippas, walked over to the coach. While the parents welcomed the guests, Shimon and Dalia stood side by side.

"Where's your Dov?" Shimon asked. "I was hoping to meet him."

Dalia stared at him in surprise. Surely wedding fever hadn't been so rampant in Rehovot that all other gossip had been forgotten.

"He and his fiancée are celebrating their engagement party in Tel Aviv this week."

Shimon widened his eyes. "But I thought…"

"Well, you thought wrong."

The parents finished their welcome speeches.

Dalia led the Rehovot women and their children to the dance and tried to concentrate on her duties instead of analysing the expression on Shimon's face when he discovered she and Dov were no longer a couple.

The dancing had only just got back into swing when Patsy's car pulled up by the tractor sheds. Four people clambered out. She presumed the man who emerged from the driver's seat was Patsy's husband, Tim. Shimon sprinted off to greet the newcomers. By the time she arrived, Shimon and Patsy's husband were embracing. She went up and hugged Patsy and Maftur. To her surprise, she heard Shimon greet Ismail warmly by name. She hadn't known those two knew each other.

"Dalia," Shimon said in English, "why didn't you tell me your brother had invited Ismail?"

"You didn't tell me you knew Abu Rafiq," she retorted.

"Abu Rafiq, is it now? Congratulations, Ismail. Dalia, Ismail and I were on an officer's training course together at Acre."

Ismail introduced Maftur to Shimon.

"Ah," Shimon exclaimed, "the beautiful wife from Haifa.

The reason Ismail was never with us when we went on the razzle. I'm pleased to meet you at last."

Maftur placed her hands together in formal greeting, and replied in English, "Any friend of my husband is my friend too."

"Thank you. You may not continue in that frame of mind, though, because I am about to steal your men." He winked at Patsy. "I promise, though, to keep Tim in slightly better order than I managed at his stag party."

While Shimon took off Tim and Ismail, Dalia conducted Maftur and Patsy over to the dancing.

The two mothers came over. "Welcome, Patsy and Maftur," her mother said in embarrassingly accented English. "This is my friend and neighbour, Miriam Cohen, the bride's mother. We are both honoured to welcome you to our children's marriage celebrations. Please feel happy to watch for a while, if you do not know the steps, but then, please, you must both join in."

Maftur was dancing within minutes but Patsy was still standing on the fringe half an hour later. Dalia gave her a challenging look. Patsy smiled weakly but joined in and before long was dancing confidently.

The sun grew low in the sky. Dalia was wondering whether the men were enjoying each others' company so much they had forgotten the point of the day, when Uri burst out of the shed carrying a veil. Shimon and a crowd of men playing musical instruments followed him.

Uri stepped onto the platform. Ruth stood to face him. They gazed at each other in the last glow of the setting sun. Dalia felt a stab of regretful nostalgia as Uri placed the veil over her best friend's head. Things would never be the same again.

From the corner of her eye, she noticed Shimon racing up to the Chuppah and lighting the Tilley lamps.

Uri took Ruth by the hand and led her off the platform. Both sets of parents stepped in line behind them. She and Josh followed. When Shimon returned and took his place beside her, the bridal party set off. The guests followed singing and dancing towards the Chuppah.

She smelt the orange blossom attached to the poles. The crowd hushed and stood still. A single male voice sang into the silence. Uri stepped beneath the canopy, drew a shawl over his head and shoulders, and swayed backwards and forwards as he chanted a prayer. Ruth followed him onto the Chuppah and, while Uri continued to pray, circled him seven times.

It was dark now except for the stars and the Tilley lamps casting their yellow light. A violin resonated through the still air.

Reb Cohen stepped beneath the canopy holding a glass glinting blood red in the lamp light. He placed it on the table and began to recite. When he had finished, Ruth and Uri drank from the glass.

Dalia and Josh joined the bride and groom. Uri took a ring from his pocket and placed it on Ruth's finger while reciting again.

Her father entered the canopy next, carrying the contract. When he had finished reading, her mother, Miriam and Shimon joined them under the canopy. Leaving Ruth and Uri together in the centre of the Chuppah, they clustered by the table where the chalice stood and, in turn, each recited one of the seven blessings.

Uri and Ruth broke apart and took turns to sip from the chalice. When the glass was empty the groom placed it on the ground and stamped on it to shouts of "Mazel tov".

The band struck up again. The guests divided by gender and formed a semi-circle to dance the wedding party into her parents' house. She and Shimon served Uri and Ruth a meal in the dining room and left them on their own.

Later that evening she broke away from the celebration to check that everything was all right. She studied Ruth and Uri, the centre of attention. She had never seen Ruth so beautiful or Uri so ecstatic. Everyone else seemed happy and relaxed too, even her mother and Miriam Cohen. Bereisheet, she reflected, had been luckier than many settlements when it came to war casualties. It was good to see all her old school friends together with their children.

As she refilled jugs she remembered Uri and Ruth's engagement party three-and-a-half years earlier when she had felt alienated from both family and friends. Now she felt she belonged here and, to some extent, always would. All the same, she sensed Bereisheet was not where her future lay.

* * * *

The day after the wedding Dalia was in the kitchen sorting borrowed crockery with her mother and Miriam. She was due to return to Zamzum the next day. While the others chatted she tried to work out her future plans so she could discuss them with her parents before she left.

She knew it was time to move on. Soon Uri and Ruth would take over the running of the small holding and her parents would immerse themselves in grandchildren. There was no room for her here. This was why her father had bought her the citrus groves but if she went to live in al-Tira before her manager retired, she would only get under his feet. Why did she have this feeling there was something she had to accomplish before she settled down?

Thelma shouted "Shalom," and bounced into the kitchen. "Trudy, I brought your post."

Her mother held out her hand for the envelope, took one look at the return address and covered her mouth. In a muffled voice so low it was almost a whisper, she said, "Dalia, fetch your father. It's from the Red Cross."

Her heart thumping, hoping for a miracle but not expecting one, (after all less than 1.5% of German Jews had survived) she raced towards their top field where her father was driving Bereisheet's noisy combine harvester.

She took off her apron and flagged him down. He switched off the engine.

"The Red Cross have replied."

They ran back to the house together. Her mother handed her father the unopened envelope. They watched as he tore it open and drew out a type-written sheet. He scanned it. Slowly, he raised his head, handed the letter to her mother and left the kitchen. They heard the bedroom door slam. Dalia's stomach felt heavy. Her mother read the letter, passed it on to her and followed her father out of the room.

Dalia read it. The contents came as no surprise, so why did her legs feel as if they no longer wanted to support her weight. Miriam and Thelma stared at her, their eyes sympathetic but curious.

"My grandmother was last seen in Auschwitz," she told them. "No one saw her after the summer of nineteen forty-four."

Miriam said nothing. She returned to sorting dishes.

Thelma shook her head, muttered "I'm sorry," and helped Miriam with the sorting.

Dalia joined in without breaking the silence, pushing grief to the back of her mind, while she revised plans. She would have to stay and support her parents at least until Uri and Ruth returned. There was no need to mar their honeymoon by sending them a telegram.

The crockery was all sorted. Thelma picked up her pile but before she left, she asked the question Dalia had been dreading. "No news of your grandfather?"

If she told Thelma that the Red Cross had discovered her grandfather had been summoned from retirement in nineteen forty-one to work at the mint in Hamburg, Thelma would know he was a Goy. The Red Cross had surmised that her grandfather was one of the thousands of unidentified victims who had died in a giant fireball in July nineteen forty-three following an air raid by two hundred allied bombers.

"They don't know what'd happened to him," she replied truthfully.

"So you still have some hope," Thelma said to console her.

* * * *

Uri and Ruth were still on honeymoon when another letter arrived—this time from the Romanian illegal immigrants who had been working on the Leitner's small holding since Uri had joined the army. It was to inform her parents that they had decided to stay on in Northern Israel since so many of their fellow countrymen already worked there.

Dalia offered to stay on in Bereisheet until Uri was demobbed.

Her father rejected her proposal. "You've been a great comfort, Dalia, during these last few days but creating a settlement in Zamzum for holocaust survivors is the best way to honour your grandmother. With Ruth's help, your mother and I can cope until Uri returns."

So when Ruth and Uri returned from honeymoon, Dalia returned to Zamzum and settled back into the daily routine, not with her original joyous enthusiasm but with solid determination until the war in the East ended with a horrifying superblast.

There was no talk of going home to celebrate this time. Esther summoned everyone to a formal meeting to discuss their immediate aims. All agreed that, given the plight of the Jewish DPs in Europe, the British would have to allow Jewish settlement in the Negev. Dalia persuaded them to create in Zamzum a memorial community to the relatives they had all lost. Whether it be moshav or kibbutz would be up to the new immigrants.

With renewed zeal, they levelled land and cleared the route to the main road ready for wheeled traffic. Instead of easing restrictions on immigration, however, the British tightened them. They even re-opened the infamous detention camp at Athlit, filling it with Jews desperate to leave European countries that had betrayed them.

In Zamzum, as in every other Jewish community in Palestine, grief over lost relatives transmuted into rebellion.

One night in October, Haganah underground radio announced that the Palmach had raided Athlit and freed over two hundred detainees.

Although Dalia joined in the cheering with the rest, her joy was tinged with regret that she was no longer a member of Palmach and so could not take part in such daring exploits.

After a sleepless night, she told Esther that she had

decided the time was right for her to leave. She wrote to Yitzhak Sadeh, who was still in overall command of the Palmach, asking if she could resume training, and told him she would be staying with her parents at Bereisheet until she heard from him.

Chapter 31

Her father came in for coffee after fetching a tractor from across the oval. Dalia set out four mugs

"You'll help with the potatoes, Dalia? Your mother says she can spare you."

She had intended to spend the day in the kitchen helping her mother and Ruth transform a pile of cabbages into kegs of sauerkraut. Her mother's acquiescence to her father's request emphasised the fact that Ruth had taken over her traditional role. She turned her face to the sink, scrubbing the base of an already clean cup while she attempted to embrace the positive side. A strenuous day in the top field would prevent her going soft.

Miriam Cohen came in from next door as she was prone to do at this time of the morning now her daughter had moved in.

Dalia took down a fifth cup.

"Have you heard the news?" Miriam asked.

"Oi!" her mother replied, giving the cabbages a baleful glare. "We have time to listen to the wireless? We should be so lucky."

Miriam threw up her hands. "So, you cannot work and listen to the wireless at the same time? You think there is nothing outside Bereisheet? You do not care that the whole of Palestine is cut off from the rest of the world."

Abba got up and turned on the wireless. The official radio channel merely confirmed that there had been trouble overnight. To Dalia's amazement, her father switched to the underground channel. She hadn't realised he knew where to find it.

A distinct note of triumph tinged the announcer's voice as he spoke of 'The Night of the Railways' when Jews from all three underground movements, working in unison, had blown up train-lines and bridges across Palestine.

Again, deep beneath her overt pleasure at this incredible

act of defiance, there lay that spark of resentment. Why hadn't the Palmach allowed her a role in this operation?

"I never expected Haganah to descend to terrorist tactics," her mother commented.

Dalia's resentment flared into anger. "And how else do we show the world that we are united?" she shouted. "Any organised sabotage is more effective than a hundred protest rallies."

Her father shook his head. "Calm down, Dalia. Everyone is sick of fighting. We should be talking, not throwing bombs. What use is this new United Nations organisation if we don't take our disputes to it?"

"You think DPs want us to wait while we find out if talking works?" Dalia retorted.

All the same, she consented to go with the rest of the Bereisheet residents to a peaceful protest meeting of five hundred thousand people in Tel Aviv's Kiryat Meir parade ground.

The next morning Miriam Cohen joined them for midday coffee, bringing a freshly-baked seed cake with her, ready as usual to pass on the early morning news.

"Oi, weren't we all lucky yesterday?" she started. "I know we grumbled at the bus driver but we should be grateful now that that he parked where he did. People going the other way, they walked into real trouble. It said on the news that three people were killed in the riots."

A cheery 'shalom' in the doorway stopped her in full flow. Golda Kaminer came in.

"Hey, Golda," Dalia greeted her as she stood to get an extra mug. "What are you doing this way?"

"I cycled over with a letter for Reb Cohen. He told me Miriam would be with you and if I called in you might offer me a cup of coffee."

Ruth filled Golda's mug and Miriam gave her a generous slice of cake while Golda regaled them with more details of the riots.

"Mobsters from the Carmel market used the rally as an excuse to create havoc, more interested in looting than anything else. When the police arrived they shot over the heads of the crowd but killed a boy standing on a balcony."

Miriam gave a gasp of horror.

"The mob didn't disperse," Golda continued, "so the police shot at the crowd's legs, but one boy was so small they hit him in the stomach. He died. Someone else was killed too but I'm not sure how."

After the coffee break, Dalia led Golda into the vegetable field she was weeding. "So what was in the letter you gave Reb Cohen? I assume it wasn't citrus business?"

"Actually, my father did ask me to deliver this year's export arrangements at the same time, but as you've guessed, that's not the real reason I'm here. Haganah want the settlements making preparations to take in more refugees. If you promise not to pass it on, I can tell you more."

"I promise."

"Haganah are bringing in two hundred and fifty DPs from Europe."

Before Golda could pass on further details, Dalia's mother called out from the kitchen door. "Dalia, go and fetch your father. Reb Cohen's calling a meeting."

"That was quick," Golda commented. "I'll be on my way."

Inside the synagogue, which doubled as the community meeting room, Reb Cohen asked for volunteers to house displaced people at short notice. He allowed time for private discussion. The Leitners and Cohens conferred and agreed that Ruth should return to her parents until Uri was demobbed. That would leave the Leitners with two spare rooms, Uri's and the one they had prepared for her grandparents.

Other households with sons or daughters, still waiting demob, volunteered rooms. The community also agreed to prepare a barn as a reception area and overspill dormitory.

For the rest of the day, they abandoned all except essential work, buckling down to making straw mattresses and improvising blankets from old curtains and coats. The women ransacked wardrobes for clothes.

An hour after midnight, over a week later, two settlers

from Givat Hayim escorted twenty tired sea-soaked and hungry European Jews into Bereisheet. The whole community left their beds and set to work in the prepared barn providing the newcomers with dry clothes, warm drinks, and food.

Dalia noticed Jack Goldstein take a young lad of about twelve—by the look of him—over to her father and wondered why. Jack went off.

Her father beckoned her over. "This young man is Arvon Platter. He has brought two notes with him, one for you and one for me."

"I am fortunate to still to have these," Arvon said in heavy-accented Hebrew. "I promised Shimon I would get rid of them before I allowed anyone to capture me. The British captured our boat but I was off it by then." He held out two envelopes.

"Do you recognise the handwriting?" her father asked.

She had seen it often enough so replied confidently, "That's Shimon Mabovitch's scrawl."

"Arvon, you must change into dry clothes and get some food," her father said.

Dalia couldn't wait to open her letter.

Dalia,

I know you and Dov have split but hope you are still talking. Can you ask Dov to help Arvon Platter, the bearer of this letter? He is a young Austrian Jew. I worked with him when I was in Italy in nineteen forty-four and came across him again more recently in a DP camp. He's obsessed with becoming a doctor like his father. When we were in the resistance, he managed to steal enough books to continue his education. Tim Craine taught him some English and I have taught him some Hebrew so he should hold his own in secondary school. Can you ask Dov to find him a decent school and digs? Dov will know ways of squeezing the necessary funds from the Agency. I wish I could do it myself but can't leave my work here. If Dov can't manage this, could you ask him if he knows of any other doctor who can?

P.S. I wish I had known that you had split with Dov when I saw you at Uri's wedding. Are you seeing anyone else? Is there any chance that the work I am doing here will raise me sufficiently in your esteem to be considered a candidate for your affections?

Shimon, the Penitent.

She stood, letter still in hand, wondering if Shimon, the arrogant, meant what he had written in the last paragraph, or was it just his peculiar sense of humour. She had been so certain that she had lost him forever over the Patria affair.

Her father's voice interrupted her turbulent thoughts. "Dalia, Shimon wants us to keep Arvon Platter with us. I'll check the boy into Uri's old room and ask the Haganah people, before they leave, if he can stay instead of having them drag him off to a kibbutz or agricultural school."

Dalia had to milk the cows in two hours' time but, before returning to bed, she sat down and scribbled a note to Dov and Clara.

* * * *

Dalia was teaching Arvon how to muck out a cowshed when Golda entered, balancing three enamel coffee mugs and three bagels on a tray. She handed one of each to Arvon, who looked at Dalia.

"I take a break now?"

Dalia nodded. Arvon pulled a Hebrew grammar from his pocket and took himself over to the other side of the barn.

Dalia picked up a mug and sank onto a clean bale of straw. Golda found her own bale.

"It's always nice to have a chat," Dalia said, "but what's behind this visit? If you've come to take Arvon, my father wants to speak to you first."

"I've just delivered another letter to your muhktar, and thought I'd cadge coffee off your mother before setting off again. I have to visit a number of other settlements."

Golda left. A few minutes later Eema opened the shed door. "Arvon, can you carry on here by yourself?"

The boy looked up. "Yes, Trudi Leitner."

Dalia smiled. She had succeeded in training Arvon to refrain from calling Eema Frau Leitner.

Her mother turned to her. "Dalia, you have to come down to the house right away. There's another community meeting."

This time the Jewish Agency wanted able-bodied adults from every settlement in the Hefer Valley to take part in a protest march in support of Kibbutz Givat Hayim, which was refusing to allow in the police. They were to hike to a well-known beauty spot between Ein Hahoresh and Givat Hayim, and picnic there.

"We're not to carry arms," Reb Cohen said, "or anything that can be used as a weapon. No banners, passive resistance only and we leave our identity cards behind so everyone, not just refugees, are without papers. If the British interrogate us, our only reply must be, 'I am a Jew of Palestine'. Anyone joining the march must be ready in half-an-hour with food, drink, and warm clothes. Every household, though, must leave someone to feed the animals. We don't know when we're returning."

"Adults only," Dalia told Arvon a few minutes later, as he pushed into the queue collecting sandwiches.

"But I am an adult," he assured her. "I was fifteen in July."

"And I am Golda Meyerson," Dalia retorted, looking down at the slight figure.

From behind, her father said, "Nu, the lad is telling the truth, Dalia, but Arvon, even fifteen doesn't count as grown-up in Bereisheet and, anyway, we need you to look after our animals."

Arvon Platter scowled. "But I am a good fighter. I have had much experience against the Germans."

"We're marching, not fighting," her father replied, "but I'm glad we're leaving a good fighter to protect our home."

Two hours later, the Bereisheet contingent reached the popular beauty spot. Dalia looked beyond it to the open gates of Givat Hayim. The kibbutz was surrounded by British soldiers lying on their stomachs, feet pointing inwards, rifles pointing outwards. Judging by the shouts, a scrimmage was taking place inside the settlement, presumably a battle to which the army had not yet been invited.

A row of empty army trucks lined one side of a lane

leading to the main road. On the other side the military had erected a row of the infamous wire cages used in joint police and army's 'Surround and Search Operations'. Beyond the cages, a group of Red Shield drivers and nurses leant against the trunks of eucalyptus trees beside ambulances parked in the shade. If anyone inside Givat Hayim had been badly wounded no one was bothering to bring them out.

Hikers from other settlements were converging on the arranged meeting place. There must be over five hundred of us, Dalia thought, as she stared around. Nearly all her married school friends had taken part in the hike. They formed a circle, a little apart from the rest, and settled down to picnic and exchange news and gossip. They had to shout to make themselves heard above the roar of an RAF plane circling overhead.

Dalia's nearest companions were Ruth and a woman named Naashom, who had been a close school friend of them both at school. After leaving, Naashom had trained in Tel Aviv as a nurse but was married now with three children.

"This makes a pleasant change from the daily grind," Naashom commented. "Don't mistake me, I love my kids dearly, but it's nice to be me once in a while, instead of just Eema."

A volley of shots from inside Givat Hayim's perimeter fence had everyone jumping to their feet and packing away food and drink.

"Marching ranks!" The order came from a young man she had never seen before.

A group of older settlers, including her father and Reb Cohen, created a close-knit front line. Dalia and her year group positioned themselves in the second rank. To their indignation, a group of local Palmach members pushed their way in front.

A short, slightly-built stranger slipped in directly behind Reb Cohen. "Kadema!" he ordered.

Everyone marched towards the British soldiers who trained their rifles on them. A machine gun on a mound, protected by sandbags, also pointed at them. What would happen, Dalia wondered, when they reached the soldiers? Were they expected to step over them?

A jeep drove towards them. A youthful lieutenant, standing in the front passenger seat, revolver in one hand, and megaphone to his mouth, shouted, "Stay right there or we shoot."

They were near enough to the line of soldiers now to see they all had their fingers on the triggers. The older men in front hesitated. Her line stood still as did the others behind them.

"Kadema," the stranger behind her father repeated.

The march continued.

The officer lifted his arm, fired a shot into the air, and suddenly bullets whizzed towards the soldiers from shrubbery at the side of the field. Dalia turned in surprise, but could only see a flurry of quivering leaves.

The machine gun swung an arc, barking as it turned. Dalia, along with others Haganah-trained, dived flat, covering their heads with their arms. She pulled Ruth down with her.

On the other side of her, Naashom clutched her stomach and screamed as she fell. Men in the front ranks crashed to the ground. The grass turned from winter green to scarlet. The smell of fresh blood and the stench of fear saturated the air.

The majority of marchers sprinted off, shrieking in terror, either to shelter behind tree trunks or to rush back to the picnic area. The machine gun stilled.

Her father was the only man in the front row left standing. He stared in surprise at his arm hanging useless and spouting blood. Beside him, Reb Cohen sprawled, blood pouring from a leg.

Ruth yelled, "Abba," and sprang up, tugging a first-aid bag from her haversack. Dalia ran to her father. She used a handkerchief from his top pocket as a tourniquet.

She heard Reb Cohen saying, "See to the woman behind. Her need's more urgent."

While Dalia tightened her father's tourniquet, she watched Ruth pull down Naashom's shorts and apply a wad of cotton wool to a heavily bleeding wound in her side.

All around, the unwounded amongst the Haganah were

heaving themselves up and checking the fallen. Red Shield ambulances drove over from where they had been lurking. Their crews jumped out bearing stretchers and carried off Naashom and Reb Cohen along with many others.

Dalia led her father over to an ambulance reserved for walking wounded. While it waited for more patients, she watched police herding groups of kibbutzniks into wire enclosures.

Patsy's husband, Tim, directed operations. She felt an overwhelming surge of anger.

Later, while a nurse in Bellinson Hospital put a plaster cast on her father's arm, her mother and Miriam Cohen arrived at the hospital, looking as if they would both fall if they stopped supporting each other.

She ran to them, hugged them both, and tried to keep her voice cheerful as she helped them into chairs.

"It could have been so much worse," she reassured them. "A bullet cut through an artery in Abba's left arm and broke his bone but his wound has been stitched and his arm set. Reb Cohen has two comparatively minor injuries. A bullet went through the flesh of his right thigh and he sprained an ankle while falling. Ruth is with him. The police have interviewed them and say they can both leave once they have been treated."

She didn't mention that twenty settlers were more seriously injured than either her father or Reb Cohen and that there would be eight funerals in the Hefer Valley that week.

Chapter 32

The whole valley attended the funerals of the eight killed in the Givat Hayim incident. Reb Cohen conducted the service on crutches and pleaded for everyone to work towards a peaceful solution. They listened with respect but paid no heed. Dalia's mood, in keeping with the vast majority, was virulently anti-British.

She decided to give Yitzhak Sadeh three more days to answer her letter before visiting the Jewish Agency in Tel Aviv. A few days after the funerals Dov arrived in response to her letter about Arvon.

Her mother, obviously excited at the thought of a reconciliation, left them together in the kitchen saying she needed to go up to Thelma Goldstein's bakery for another loaf, although they already had a whole freshly-baked loaf in a cupboard.

"When Clara and I received your letter," Dov told her, "we considered taking in Arvon ourselves, but, if he wants to be a doctor, he needs a city school. Luckily, I've a widowed aunt in Jerusalem, a lovely woman. I know she'll treat him well. Since I have to go to up to a medical conference in Jerusalem this week, I thought I'd collect Arvon on the way and find him a suitable school."

What a good person Dov was. Dalia hoped that, when she was old, she wouldn't regret not marrying him.

"Dov, I'm so glad. According to Shimon, Arvon's had a horrendous childhood. I'll take you up to the top field. He's weeding under Abba's supervision. You heard what happened to Abba, I guess."

"Yes, I was so sorry to read about it. A dreadful business."

"At least Abba has an adult refugee to help him until the Agency sorts out their permanent billets. He will miss the boy and not just because he's a good worker. Come to that, Arvon will miss my father too, but I know he's keen to start. I gave him all my *Bagrut* course books and he's been working on them every evening."

An hour later they were waving an excited Arvon goodbye.

"I'm sad to see him go," her mother said, "but the way things are, he'll be safer in Jerusalem. Trouble like we have now, I never expected to see again. Goodness knows how Miriam and I will run our farms when the illegals leave next week. If only Uri and Josh were demobbed already."

A few hours later Golda Kaminer cycled over to talk to the refugees about their permanent billets and Dalia feared that she was stuck in Bereisheet until her father and Reb Cohen had fully recovered.

However, Golda visited for coffee when she had finished with the refugees and told Miriam and her parents that the refugees working with them had each received a special letter asking if they would stay on at Bereisheet until Albert Leitner and Reb Cohen were fit to work. They had both agreed.

Dalia experienced a profound sense of relief. She was free to leave whenever she needed to.

Message delivered, Golda shrugged off her official aura and leaned back. "You'll never guess what happened in our part of the world."

Her mother and Miriam leaned forward. Reb Cohen and her father remained straight-backed, indicating they were above listening to gossip.

"It was quite heartening," Golda said. "The most important Arab effendi from Hadera plus the Muhktars from neighbouring Arab villages visited Givat Hayim."

"Why?" Dalia detected a sharp note behind Reb Cohen's question.

"To convey their sympathy and sorrow over the recent troubles."

"Hypocrites," her mother snarled. "After they shot at the British."

Dalia couldn't buy into the commonly held belief that Arabs had hidden behind the shrubs near Ein Hahoresh and fired at the soldiers. The only way the snipers could have escaped detection was by mingling with the fleeing settlers. Despite the chaos, someone would have spotted Arabs in their midst. The culprits were more likely to be members of Irgun or the Stern Gang deliberately stirring up trouble.

She left it to Golda to refute her mother's statement. "My father knows the local Arabs well, Trudi Leitner. They are good customers of ours. He says the sheiks wouldn't have stayed to feast with the settlers after their declaration if their words were false. My father was checking on the citrus crop at Givat Hayim when they visited. He was quite moved when one Sheik told the Muhktar of Givat Hayim, 'Armies come and go but neighbours stay on to live together. We must remain friends'."

* * * *

Dalia had to postpone her visit to the Agency. It was their family's turn to borrow the tractor, but both refugees had been summoned to a Hebrew language course.

She was ploughing the top field in pouring rain making it ready for a crop of wheat, when she heard a motorbike enter the village and stop on the oval.

It couldn't be Shimon, Josh or Uri—they weren't due for leave. She concentrated on keeping a straight furrow until, a few minutes later, her mother walked up the path accompanied by a man. As they drew nearer she recognised Toni Huss. She suspected Leah had written asking him to persuade her to return to Zamzum.

She stopped the tractor and slid down to the mud, pondering her answer. Since she had received no answer from the Palmach, perhaps she should go back.

"Dalia," her mother called, "Toni needs to speak to you but don't take too long. We have to hand the tractor on to Jack tomorrow and I don't want your father trying to drive it."

"Is everything all right at Zamzum, Toni?" she asked, as her mother hurried on to the orchard where her father was using his good arm to pick oranges.

"Yes, Leah says everything's fine and she's coping with

the wireless but they could do with more members now they've expanded the crop area."

"And how are you doing?"

"Been transferred again." He looked around as if spies might be hiding in the empty field and lowered his voice. "I'm working with the United Resistance Movement now. It means co-operating with thugs like the Irgun and Stern Gang, but I guess the means justifies the end."

Dalia clenched her fists and schooled herself to remain outwardly calm while inwardly seething. Why hadn't the Palmach recalled her to active service?

"So, the Resistance Movement needs your services so badly you can take time out for a social visit?"

"It's not a social visit. I've a message from the Agency."

Dalia raised her eyebrows. If Zamzum had taken their troubles to Agency level, they must really need her.

"Yes?"

"The Agency wants you in Jerusalem, Dalia. You've been assigned to a group code-named 'Rabbit'."

"Part of Palmach?"

"No, something so hush-hush they won't trust me with details. You'll leave after Hanukkah."

"I don't want a job with some obscure unit. I want to be part of the Palmach."

"I told them that would be your response. They said to tell you Rabbit needs you more than the Palmach does."

Dalia rubbed her shoe in the soil, leaving a scar in the damp dirt path. "Just what does Rabbit do?"

"They've given me no details. It's too hush-hush, but I get the impression it isn't routine secretarial work."

Part 9

Rabbit 1946 – 1947

Chapter 33

On a fine winter afternoon in early January 1946, Dalia stepped off an Egged bus at its terminal on Jaffa Road in Jerusalem, joining shoppers and soldiers thronging the pavements outside banks and offices. She would have liked to wander through the more elegant shops and lunch at an up-market café but felt out of place in settler garb amongst people dressed in stylish winter wear.

She stopped at a milk bar and treated herself to a chocolate milkshake and a cheese sandwich. The milkshake recipe was back to pre-war standards, but with so many British soldiers walking the pavements and armoured jeeps parading the road, it was hard to believe the war was over. Everything was so different from the peace and calm of Zamzum or Bereisheet.

She glanced at her watch and was relieved to find it late enough to seek out her new digs. She hoped to find a letter there telling her where to report for work.

The gloomy entrance hall of the four storey stone-built apartment stank of urine. A large barrel of it stood at the foot of the stairs. Surely, the Agency hadn't billeted her in a block of flats with no mod cons? She didn't mind roughing it out in the wilderness, but in the closely packed confines of a town, she had hoped for more civilised facilities.

A hand-written list of tenants stuck to the brown painted wall informed her that Itka Rabinowitz, her landlady, occupied the fourth and top floor.

She climbed worn marble stairs and knocked on an imposing mahogany door. A female voice on the other side asked her name. There was much rattling of chains before the door opened onto a thickly carpeted foyer hung with gilt-framed oil paintings.

A plump but diminutive woman of at least fifty dressed in tightly fitting green silk faced her, a welcoming smile on her round face. "Shalom, Dalia Leitner." Itka Rabinowitz's Hebrew, Dalia noticed, had a strong Polish accent.

She followed her landlady through the lobby into a large dining cum living room filled with heavy furniture similar to that of Dalia's childhood home in Munchen. Heavy net curtains kept out an excess of sunlight. Bowls of sweet-smelling potpourri littered occasional tables. A door at the side led to another lobby.

Itka opened one of the three doors in the lobby to reveal a room containing a double bed with an eiderdown of maroon silk. A rose-patterned porcelain wash bowl and ewer, matching the wallpaper, stood on a marble wash-stand that could double as a desk.

Dalia walked over to a large window framed by rose velvet curtains and looked down onto a busy street far below. Opposite were more tall apartment buildings. So many strangers all squashed together. How many other lungs had breathed this air?

Itka relieved her anxiety over the sanitary arrangements by revealing a washroom complete with flush toilet. A showerhead hung over a drain in the tiled floor. She noticed both hot and cold taps.

"Why the barrel downstairs?" she asked, as they left the washroom.

Itka wrinkled her nose. "A disgusting local custom. The landlord pays the male tenants and sells the contents to soap makers. If this place were not so conveniently situated for work I would have moved into the suburbs long ago."

"Where do you work?"

Itka glanced at her curiously. "The same bookshop as you."

Dalia put her hand to her chin as she stared at Itka in dismay.

"It is okay," Itka said. "I know nothing about your job, except that I've been told to introduce you to Ludwig Mayer tomorrow."

"Ludwig Meyer?"

"Yes. The owner of Jerusalem's best-known bookshop. A very nice man."

The next morning Itka escorted Dalia to the shop in Princess Mary Avenue and used a key to let them in. A man in a grey suit faintly chequered in red, bending over ledgers open on the counter, presented a ring of curly grey hair surrounding a balding scalp. When he straightened to greet them, she saw he was taller than average.

"Here is Dalia Leitner, Ludwig," Itka told him. "You have been expecting her?"

"Indeed I have," Ludwig Mayer replied. "Come with me, and I'll show you our work place."

He led her past double-sided bookshelves, into a stone-slabbed room furnished as a basic staff kitchen with a stone sink, cups, primus, and kettle. At the far end a flight of stone steps led down to a rough wooden door. Ludwig knocked on it five times.

After much rattling of bolts, the door opened to reveal a slim wiry man in his early thirties with a freckled face and shock of springy, ginger hair.

"Meet my son, Herman," Mr Mayer said. "Herman, I leave Dalia Leitner with you."

Herman gave a welcoming smile. "Welcome to Rabbit, Dalia."

He ushered her into a cave-like cellar where a man with earphones and a woman with a pencil and notepad sat facing a large wireless set, a later model than the one she had worked on in Zamzum. The man with the earphones had his finger on a dial and was dictating to the woman.

"We're a new unit, answerable to Shai," Herman said. "Our task is to monitor police activity."

"How many in your team?"

"Four wireless operators plus myself, but I spend much of my time at the Agency. I've organised three overlapping shifts of nine hours each. Oh-seven-thirty hours until sixteen-thirty hours, fifteen-hundred hours until twenty-four hundred hours and twenty-three hundred hours until oh-eight hundred hours. The Agency also loans us their trustworthy shorthand typists to make transcripts. I gather that you are an expert in wireless maintenance, so you will spend some of your duty hours on technical duties. Mostly, though, you'll be locating police channels, and translating Morse code and police jargon to the scribe. We send the transcribed police messages to the Jewish Agency. We keep tabs on several types of police channels, mostly from JOP and LOP but occasionally from HOP."

"HOP, LOP and JOP?" she asked, wondering if Herman's childhood reading had been dominated by Beatrix Potter.

"Operational Patrols," Herman explained. "JOP for Jerusalem, LOP for Lydda, which includes Jaffa and Tel Aviv, and HOP for Haifa. Patrol cars use radio telephony for distances of up to twenty miles. For distances over twenty miles but less than forty miles, they use carrier waves, Morse code and Q code."

"Q code?"

Herman handed her several sheets of paper. "Q code consists of groups of three letters all starting with Q, usually transmitted in Morse code. You must learn these off by heart before you start work tomorrow. Now, for the other part of your job." He pointed to a wall cupboard. "That's where we keep the radio manual."

Dalia replied, "I'd rather look through the manual after I've mastered the code."

She wrestled with Q code for the rest of the day and into the small hours. By the following morning, she felt competent to start her first shift.

As she got into the swing she realised how useful this project would be to the United Resistance Unit. Her own assessment was confirmed when Shai allocated them two more wirelesses and trebled their staff.

Mostly, Rabbit monitored tedious traffic information and location reports from cars on escort duty. Dalia found day shifts cooped underground hard to bear. At least night duty allowed her some daylight between sleep and work.

Her social life was better than she had expected. Every evening, except when on the middle shift, she met Toni and other old comrades from her Palmach days in a cafe in Jerusalem. There they argued politics and planned the future. The main topic of discussion was how to persuade the British to let all displaced Jews into Palestine. As much as she and her Palmach friends disagreed with the tactics of the Irgun and Stern Gang, they reluctantly admitted the necessity of co-operation in the Jewish Resistance Movement.

* * * *

At the beginning of February Dalia received two letters forwarded from Bereisheet. The first contained two silver printed cards with scalloped edges, one in English and one in Arabic. The Arab one invited her to Suzanna's women-only pre nuptial ceremony in Jenin, the one in English to the wedding proper the following day in Nablus. She placed the invitations on her dressing table and made a note to request time off. She wasn't sure whether she would actually enjoy either occasion but felt she had to accept the invitations.

The second letter was from Shimon.

Dear Dalia,

I hope everything in Bereisheet and Zamzum is going well and that your father has recovered from his injuries. I have missed your progress reports on Zamzum so I am addressing this to you in Bereisheet in case you are still helping your father.

Here in Italy, army life is quiet but my so-called leisure time is surprisingly productive, as I hope you gathered from Arvon Platter.

Have you heard from Arvon recently? He wrote to say he was doing well in lessons. If you ever get up to Jerusalem do you think you could take him out for an ice cream or something after school?

Dalia put down the letter feeling guilty. She had been in Jerusalem for over a month and had not once thought to visit Arvon.

She picked up her diary, noted which days the following week she would be on night shift, and wrote to Arvon inviting him to meet her in a cafe in Ben Yehuda street the following Wednesday.

She arrived at the cafe first and watched the door. When he came in she nearly didn't recognise him in his neat town clothes. He had grown considerably during the last two months, and had filled out too. He looked much more like a typical sixteen year old. He accepted her offer of an ice cream parfait, however, with juvenile enthusiasm. He waxed enthusiastic about his school curriculum, but admitted he was finding it hard to make friends.

"The other guys all belong to Gadna Youth Club," he explained, "so I'm an outsider."

"Why don't you join Gadna?"

He lowered his voice. "It's run by Haganah."

She couldn't keep the indignation out of her voice as she demanded, "What's wrong with Haganah? They brought you over, didn't they?"

Colour drained from the boy's face. He looked around the cafe in terror at the ladies at the other tables, all seemingly interested in nothing but cakes and family conversation.

"Haganah is in my heart," he whispered. "I wish I could explain but I may not, you understand?"

She didn't understand but didn't pursue the subject. She asked if he had heard from Shimon recently.

"Yes, I have had three letters since I was here. I wish I could meet with Timateo too."

"You can't do that, Arvon. Tim's in the police now. If he discovers you're an illegal immigrant, he will send you to a detention camp."

"No, Timateo is my comrade."

"Never trust an Englishman, Arvon."

"You are wrong, Dalia. I trust Timateo with my life," a statement Dalia was to recall often in the future.

She met up with Arvon regularly after that first meeting, and reported to Shimon on his progress.

His English has improved beyond all recognition and he's getting top marks in biology, chemistry and physics. You should be proud to have helped him. It worries me that he keeps on about Tim. It's such a shame

Tim joined the Palestine Police after you all worked together so closely in Italy. I have nothing to do with Patsy and Tim, now. How could I mix socially with someone who herded innocent members of the Yishuv into cages like cattle? Tim is as bad as the Nazis.

Chapter 34

Dalia enjoyed herself in Jenin at the all-female pre-nuptial ceremonies, not too dissimilar to those of her own family. Different music, granted, but essentially the same rites. She joined in the dancing in honour of Suzanna who sat on a throne, wearing a wide sleeved cream tunic elaborately embroidered in crimson. Before sleeping that night she, Leila and her sister sat on their shared bed drinking night caps of cardamom tea laced with honey and gossiping about the doings of Arab, Jewish and British police officers. Even on this peaceful occasion, however, there was no respite from the tense political situation.

Suzanna's Aunt Melia, who had been listening to the wireless downstairs, came up. "You girls will be interested in this. That police superintendant who you liked so much when he brought work into your office from Nablus, the Irgun ambushed his car in Haifa."

Leila gave a gasp "Did they kill him?"

"No. He escaped. Only his skilful driving saved him from a hail of bullets, the announcer said."

"Praise God, he is all right," Suzanna said "He was so kind to little Evie Shepard when she spent a week with his family."

Dalia said nothing. She would be the only one with mixed feelings. Rumour had it that the superintendent had authorised the cages at Givat Hayim. If it were true, he deserved to be punished. She knew Tim was also on the Irgun's death list because of Givat Hayim, but although she never wanted to have anything to do with him and Patsy again, she didn't want him dead.

The next morning, while the bridesmaids dressed Suzanna, she offered to help Suzanna's aunts pack the picnic baskets the servants would put on the coaches taking the guests and bridal party to Nablus. By the time they had finished, Suzanna and the bridesmaids were back again in the wedding hall for a last dancing session. By the time she and the aunts arrived, Suzanna occupied the same platform as the previous day, but this time in a western-style satin wedding dress complete with a wide lace veil covering her face. Dalia wondered if the bedecken had already taken place in a private ceremony. She noticed a puzzling detail. Suzanna wore a pair of stout walking shoes beneath her delicate gown.

The dancing was quieter than the previous day and the bridesmaids exuded an air of expectancy.

Then the hall doors burst open and, to her horror, a man waving a terrifying Turkish scimitar above his head charged in, followed by others uttering loud war cries. The first man bounded onto the platform, seized Suzanna by the wrist and dragged her out of the hall. The bridesmaids screamed loudly. Dalia rushed forward to rescue Suzanna but Leila grabbed her, whispering, "Suzanna's guardian and the bridesmaids go first."

Dalia realised then that the abductor was Sa'eed and this was just a normal part of the family's wedding rites.

Suzanna's uncle, who must have been lurking in a back room, chased after the marauders. Leila and the other bridesmaids, still screaming, rushed after him and everyone, Dalia included, followed.

Shivering in a biting wind, with mud splashing her best shoes, Dalia realised why Suzanna had worn sensible shoes. She watched Sa'eed and his rowdy friends hustle Suzanna into a waiting coach and place her on a seat set up as a throne. Suzanna's uncle and the bridesmaids banged on the coach door. The men let in the women, but refused entry to Suzanna's uncle.

A second coach drew up. Suzanna's uncle climbed in and sat behind the driver. Dalia boarded it with the other guests and the two coaches hurtled along the twisting road, horns tooting all the way.

In Nablus, they drew up outside a small church surrounded by the soap factories. A few desultory snowflakes floated down. A priest wearing a tall black hat stood outside the church door. Suzanna's uncle left their coach and approached the priest. Sa'eed joined him. After a brief conversation, the priest signalled to the bridesmaids, who brought out Suzanna, now wearing a pair of spotless high-heeled white brocade shoes. The bridal party followed the priest into the church. Everyone else remained in the coaches out of the freezing wind.

The woman sitting beside Dalia explained, "We have to wait while the priest conducts the vestibule ceremony. Someone will tell us when the entrance is clear."

When at last the guests entered the church, Dalia recognised the interior as being similar to ones she'd seen depicted on hundreds of postcards sold at souks and tourist shops, with wall paintings, chandeliers, hanging ostrich eggs and gilded wooden icons, such a contrast to the dingy Second Chosen hall she and Peter would have been married in. There, anyone attending a service sat still on seats and only opened their mouth to sing hymns or insert loud "Amens" into pauses during a sermon, but here the guests stood around chatting. Apart from the bride and groom, bridesmaids, and others intimately involved in a ceremony at the far end of the church, everyone behaved as if this were an ordinary social occasion, but with the bridesmaids all occupied she felt isolated. She listened in on the chit-chat around her, mostly in rapid Arabic. It seemed to centre on the weather. A man said it was snowing hard in Ramallah.

"Dalia, I'm so pleased to see you." The words were in English. She looked over her shoulder and there was Patsy Quigley. She turned her back on her, walking the length of the church to stand in front of the platform alongside the few watching the wedding proceedings.

Suzanna and Sa'eed wore elaborate metal crowns and they already had wedding rings. Presumably, that was what the hold-up in the lobby had been about, a ceremony involving the putting on of crowns and the exchange of rings. She watched the familiar ritual of the couple sharing a glass of wine but missed the smashing of wineglasses and shouts of "Mazel Tov". There was also something familiar when the bride and groom circled a table, even if the table held a Christian bible and a cross.

When the service was over, everyone left the church and headed for a hall over the road. Dalia followed slowly, making sure she didn't overtake Patsy. She was surprised to see Maftur standing outside the hall until she remembered Maftur's Ismail owned an agricultural estate outside Nablus.

Maftur saw her, and called out, "Dalia! How wonderful to see you."

"Maftur," she shouted back, and was about to go over when Patsy joined Maftur. The two women talked, neither looking happy.

Dalia hesitated. Was Patsy telling Maftur how she had snubbed her in church? She had no quarrel with Maftur. It wasn't her husband who had herded Jewish settlers into cages. What should she do?

Maftur saved her having to decide by running across the road. "Dalia, you haven't seen Abu Rafiq, and Tim, and Mrs. Quigley, have you? Patsy says her mother and Tim haven't arrived and they were bringing Abu Rafiq because I used our car yesterday when Patsy and I brought the children down."

Dalia felt a surge of panic. "Tim and Mrs. Quigley were bringing Ismail?"

"Yes. Tim and Patsy live in Jerusalem now. Patsy said she wrote to tell you. Tim left the Police Mobile Force after what happened at Givat Hayim. I know she was terribly upset about your father."

"Whose car were they using, Mrs. Quigley's or Tim's?"

"I am sure Tim would prefer to drive his own car, it's safer on those bends."

It would be Tim's car the Irgun would target, Dalia thought, and her chest pounded. She thought back to the weeks of agony Patsy had suffered when Tim had gone missing, believed killed in 1942. Maftur wouldn't know that Tim was on the Irgun list, although Patsy would. She didn't want to frighten Maftur.

"Someone said it was snowing in Ramallah," she said. "Perhaps the weather has slowed them down." She looked around. "Where are Johnny and Raffy?"

"Back at the house being spoilt by my mother-in-law.

They're a bit young to appreciate weddings. It's not as if it's family."

"You and Patsy aren't doing yourselves any favours standing out here in the cold," she said. "Let's all go into the hall and get warm."

They crossed the road.

Patsy, despite her obvious worry about her husband, gave her an embarrassed smile. If the scenario she feared had occurred, now, Dalia thought, was not the time to continue her own vendetta. While Maftur walked to the corner to see if there was any sign of Tim and Patsy's car, she said to her former friend, "I'm sorry about just now, Patsy. I've not been myself recently."

"With all that's happened to you and your family, I am not surprised," Patsy said.

There was an awkward silence until Maftur came back and they walked into the hall.

Dalia hid her own worries. The thumping in her chest subsided to a vague ache as she worked hard to keep up Maftur's spirits. There was no sign, though, of the three missing persons by the time the bridesmaids whisked Suzanna away to prepare her for the marriage bed.

Maftur said she would try to telephone Jerusalem from a café on the off-chance that Ismail was still at home. Dalia volunteered to accompany her. They left Patsy in the hall in case the missing trio turned up.

At the café, Maftur spoke to the owner in Arabic. Dalia heard him say the phone was out of action but he was speaking too fast for her to follow the rest of the conversation.

A British police officer entered the cafe and asked in English if they belonged to the wedding party at the hall opposite. When they replied in the affirmative, he asked, "Do you know if there is a Mrs. Craine there? I have a message for her."

Dalia's heart pounded again. She tried to reply but her mouth felt paralysed. She heard Maftur say, "Yes. Follow us."

Inside the hall, Dalia watched Patsy look towards them stiff and white-faced.

Dalia was trembling so much she couldn't stand. She found a chair and sat down. Maftur and the policeman walked on. Maftur had her back to her. The policeman hid Patsy from sight as he delivered his message. She forced herself to stand and walked over to where she could see the two women's faces. They weren't looking happy, but neither were they in shock or in tears. She went over.

"Oh, Dalia," Maftur said. "Tim's used the police radio channels to send us a message. The roads out of Jerusalem are impassable. They've had to turn back and go home."

Once again Dalia felt faint, but this time with relief. She sank into the nearest chair.

"But how are you getting home, Dalia?" Patsy asked.

She hadn't thought of how the snow would affect her.

"I don't know," she said. "I'd ordered a taxi back to Jerusalem. That won't be happening now."

"Stay the night with us with us," Maftur said. "The roads will be back to normal tomorrow and I'll be able to give you a lift back if you don't mind being squashed."

By the time they had gossiped half that night away, she and Patsy were once again on good terms, although Dalia was glad Tim wasn't with them. She still hadn't forgiven him.

* * * *

That spring of 1946 when she was on late shifts, Dalia often joined Patsy and Maftur in a lunchtime picnic. She looked forward to playing with the toddlers, and revelled in the name *Aunty Dalia*.

She explained away being free during the day by telling them office staff had agreed to do night shifts to make sure there was always someone to sound an alarm if the building was attacked.

One day in April when orange ranunculi had taken over the task of painting the mountain sides and the air was warm but still fresh, Dalia was on the Mount of Olives with Patsy, Maftur, and the two children. While Patsy and Maftur set out the picnic she played peek-a-boo with Johnny and Raffy behind gnarled olive trees.

While they were enjoying egg and cress sandwiches, Patsy said, "Dalia, would you like to join Maftur and me on a jaunt to Ramat Gan tomorrow? A good friend of mine who is married to a police inspector in charge of the Tegart there has had a second baby quite recently."

She was tempted to accept the invitation. Herman would give her the day off in return for a report on the station and layout and its security. However, since the mess she had made in Haifa, she had vowed never to abuse her friendships for political ends, so she refused, saying she had to be at work because it was going to be a busy day.

As she settled in front of her wireless next morning, Dalia spent a couple of boring hours listening to traffic reports in Jerusalem in clear speech, but there was one from Ramle in Morse ordering Inspector Murphy of Ramat Gan to take a squad to deal with a land dispute. She thought of Patsy and Maftur with their two children well on the way to Ramat Gan and wished she was with them instead of being stuck in a gloomy cellar.

A message came through in Morse from Lydda division traffic police. Two culverts under the main road in Ramat Gan had collapsed, causing traffic jams. She hoped Patsy and Maftur weren't stuck in traffic with two restless youngsters, but they should be at the Tegart by now.

Another message from the traffic police. "Culvert collapse—possible sabotage. No officers free to investigate."

A sergeant at Ramle reported, "Callout to land dispute a hoax. Inspector Murphy with squad en route to investigate culverts."

She intercepted a weird message from a traffic sergeant. "It's like the flying Dutchman here. No sign of drivers or passengers in fifty cars abandoned on each side of culverts."

Then a Ramat Gan Tegart call sign, "Attack, attack." No message ending, just the sound of gunfire.

Dalia felt her heart thump in shock.

"Unbelievable," Herman exclaimed. "An attack on an urban Tegart in broad daylight!"

The Petah Tikvah Police Headquarters call sign next, "Message received, Ramat Gan. Inspector Murphy and squad on the way."

Everyone except Dalia cheered. Her thoughts were still on Patsy, Maftur, Johnny and Raffy.

The other wireless operator intercepted a signal from Inspector Murphy's squad, reporting delays due to traffic jams.

Herman jumped up and down in excitement. "Nu! What superb organisation. They'll get away with it."

Get away with what? Dalia thought. Burning down the Tegart, her friends in it roasting alive? It was too dreadful to contemplate. Around her, the others urged on the daring unit.

She intercepted another message from traffic police. "Drivers and passengers of abandoned vehicles located at local cinema."

Next from Inspector Murphy, "Abandoning van. Making way on foot."

No fresh information from Ramat Gan for almost an hour. Dalia grew more and more worried.

Police reports from Ramat Gan at last. Raiders had escaped in a lorry, taking the contents of the police armoury, leaving one dead raider and one severely wounded who had been sent to hospital. An unarmed Arab supernumerary had also been killed.

Dalia breathed a sigh of relief. No news about her friends had to be good news.

Herman turned on the ordinary wireless. The Irgun claimed to have executed the raid. They named the wounded prisoner, Dov Gruener, a demobbed war hero.

Patsy and Maftur were full of their involvement in the incident the following week when Dalia met with them. Patsy had even used one of her friend's sterilised baby nappies to clean Dov Gruener's horrendous facial injury.

"A wasted effort, that," Maftur commented. "After the Irgun shot down that poor lad in cold blood, they have to execute Gruener."

"It wasn't Gruener who shot the supernumerary," Dalia pointed out.

"Under British law that makes no difference," said Maftur, with all the authority of a woman married to a qualified attorney.

Chapter 35

One evening soon after the Ramat Gan incident, Dalia was in the Palmach's favourite cafe listening to Toni Huss.

"Dalia, how would you like to spend tomorrow working for Palmach?"

Surprise and hope battled for supremacy. "Is that an official request?"

"Semi-official. I need a partner."

"Doing what?"

"Going for a ramble and taking photos of birds. The Palmach will lend you binoculars."

She smiled. "No guessing where they found those."

Toni's grin confirmed her suspicion that they would be stamped OHMS.

"You'll need a camera, though," he said. "Do you have one?"

"Only a Brownie."

"That'll do. I'll get the rolls of film."

"Where are we going?"

"The Adamia Bridge."

The main users of the Adamia Bridge were truck drivers bringing in fruit and vegetables from Transjordan. She assumed the Palmach were planning to bring in illegal refugees from Iraq via that route. A load of watermelons could hide a whole family.

She wondered if she would get a ride on his motorbike. "How are we getting there?"

"We hitch a lift on a vegetable truck. The driver has a permit allowing him to drive during curfew. However, we'll have to dodge the police patrols to reach it. Another truck will bring us back. Are you game?"

A whole day away from Jerusalem's crowds and winter cold! Dalia would have jumped at the chance, even without the added incentive of knowing she'd be helping refugees.

She set out before dawn the next morning. She hadn't

gone far when the rumble of an armoured car had her dodging into a doorway, making herself as small as possible to fit into the darkest shadow. She drew in her breath. That resulted in an intense desire to cough. By the time the vehicle had passed she had almost choked. Keeping a wary eye open for foot patrols, she carried on and met up met with Toni on the Jaffa Road. They clambered under the tarpaulin of the waiting truck. It drove off. They lay still until the driver announced they had left the curfew area. Then they sat up and watched the sun rise over the dark Moab Mountains, tinting golden the Dead Sea far below.

The truck took the steep route through the rocky wilderness to Jericho and turned north onto a road running parallel to the Jordan. The driver dropped them off on a crossroad at the eastern end of the Al-Farah wadi.

"So what are we looking for now?" Dalia asked.

"The best escape routes from the bridge."

Dalia frowned.

Why, if trucks had succeeded in carrying people across the boundary, would they unload them by the bridge? However, it was not her place to question tactics that doubtless had had a full airing at squad meetings. She should consider herself fortunate just being allowed to play a small part in a Palmach project.

Toni pulled a sketch pad from his forage bag and a section of the official OS map. He pointed to the map. "We're here, on the Nablus road about three miles from Adamia Bridge. There's marshland to the north. We're looking for signs of dry season paths through the marsh."

Dalia thought of the police tracker dogs that had traced the saboteurs from Kiryat Vitkin to Givat Hayim. "Not dry paths. You need water to foil dogs."

"You're right!" Toni exclaimed. "I'm glad I asked you to come."

A while later they were walking along shady tree-lined paths, examining small fields, some green with wheat, others already glowing with ripe barley. It was hard to believe that this fertile wadi was in the middle of barren wilderness.

"Who owns these fields?" she asked.

"Arab villagers," Toni answered, "but they don't work at night."

They reached the stream responsible for this miniature paradise.

"Do we wade all the way down to check where it joins the Jordan?" she asked.

"That might arouse suspicion. I'll canoe it later."

They turned back. Close to the road leading to the bridge, they sat under an olive tree enjoying a meal of cheese, bread and onion. The only thing that could have improved this day, Dalia reflected, would have been a genuine lover by her side. Would she ever be able to fall properly in love like Toni and Leah, and if so, would any man she fancied return that love?

She dragged her thoughts back to the purpose of the day out and inspected the landscape. The road dipped into a ravine and remained hidden until it re-appeared in Transjordan across the river. She wondered what people making Aliyah Beth would think of this first sight of the promised land.

"Why drop the immigrants by the road? Why not drive to a kibbutz?" she asked.

Toni looked at her in surprise. "Immigrants? Where did you get that idea? We're not bringing in immigrants. We're blowing up the bridge."

If they had been exploring the area round the Allenby Bridge she would have realised. "Why this one? The Allenby has more traffic."

"We're planning to destroy all bridges linking Palestine to the outside world and all on the same night."

She bit savagely into her pitta bread. If only the Palmach had trained her in sabotage instead of sending her on a wireless course back in 1942, she could have played a starring role in this glorious operation. However, she mustn't spoil this special day by wallowing in envy.

Toni picked up his haversack and left the main road to explore a parallel goat track. She followed, eager to get a first glimpse of the famous river Jordan. She'd heard that it flowed through a three hundred metre wide jungle where wild boar, lynxes and wolves still roamed.

She was bitterly disappointed. The word jungle had conjured pictures of soaring trees covered with liana climbers but, apart from the occasional date palm, the tallest trees lining the Jordan were willows and fluffy-flowered tamarisks. The so-called jungle consisted mainly of shoulder high thistles and tall reeds supporting bird nests that resembled straw-coated ostrich eggs.

As they pushed their way through dense reeds, birds, large and small, shot up with loud squawks and a heavy flapping of wings. It would be impossible for a squad to reach the bridge in silence along this route. They returned to the road and approached the bridge by the more conventional route. Her heart pounded as they strolled past two rifle-bearing policemen, one wearing a kalpak, the other the flat British cap. A female police searcher in uniform similar to the police sat in a booth with the bead curtain drawn open to let in air. She smiled at them as they passed. It took all Dalia's will power to smile back in a natural fashion.

At the Transjordanian end of the bridge, British soldiers guarded a roadblock. The Palmach couldn't saunter onto this bridge to lay their mines. "Another job for my canoe," Toni whispered.

She and Toni leaned over the parapet searching for appropriate spots to attach bombs. The loud flapping of a crane flying past disturbed her. She looked up to watch its flight north towards distant stretches of the river that resembled a crinkly green thread from unravelled knitting.

Once Toni had decided on the most likely spots, they proceeded to photograph each other in the most outlandish postures, giggling loudly but making sure the photos included portions of the bridge's underside close to spaces invisible from above.

The police officer with the astrakhan kalpak approached them. Dalia forced herself to carry on giggling while she snapped photos. As the man drew nearer her heart beat so hard she was afraid he would hear it. Then she recognised him as the policeman Leila's sister, Michelle, had married and greeted him in Arabic, enquiring after both Michelle and Leila. Handing him Toni's camera, she asked him if he would be kind enough to photograph her friend and herself together. He good-naturedly complied.

Once they were well away from the bridge, Toni congratulated her on her presence of mind.

She smiled. "The time I spent working for the police wasn't wasted after all, but I've been thinking. Wouldn't a raft be less conspicuous than a canoe in the dark? Punting it would make less noise than a canoe's paddle and saboteurs would balance more easily while placing the mines."

"You're more than a pretty face," Toni responded. "I'm glad you agreed to come with me. Leah would be proud of you."

They had used up all their film but Toni was satisfied with the day's work.

When their truck arrived, Dalia stretched her legs on rolls of Persian rugs the driver had added to his cases of tomatoes. She had enjoyed her glorious day in the open air and wished once again she was in the Palmach and didn't have to return to the sunless cellar next morning.

Chapter 36

Dalia usually finished a night shift by tuning in to Haganah's underground radio. Early one morning in mid-June, she was finishing a last shift before taking a week's leave, when a triumphant presenter announced that the Palmach had sabotaged every border bridge. Palestine was cut off from the world. A cheer went up in the cellar but the atmosphere became more sober when the presenter added that there had been Palmach casualties, with some bodies so damaged they were unidentifiable.

"The British are as bad as the Nazis," her scribe exclaimed.

Dalia thought back to that idyllic day in April when she had stood by Toni watching a crane fly over the tamarisks. Cheerful, ingenious Toni Huss. Please don't let him be a casualty. She pictured everyone at Zamzum listening to the report. Did Leah know her Toni had been involved? She ran through a mental list of other Palmach members.

Dov? He had no time for planning sessions and practice runs with the Palmach while working all hours at Beersheba and the outreach clinics.

Uri? He was still in the process of being demobbed so wouldn't have been available.

Shimon? Beavering far away in Italy, well out of it.

Josh? Her stomach took a dive. Ruth's brother would have been available. Which bridge would he have worked on?

She jumped up. No point dawdling here. She would learn more when she reached Tel Aviv.

She bade farewell to her colleagues, picked up the rucksack that doubled as an overnight bag, and set off for Cousin Elsa's surprise sixtieth birthday party.

As she walked to the bus station, excited at the prospect of a whole week of normal domestic activities, she noticed youngsters surreptitiously attaching notices to trees and lamp posts. She read one.

The body of one of the dead Palmachs has been identified. His name is Yehiam Weitz, son of Joseph Weitz of the Jewish National Fund. The police have released his body and his funeral will take place in Jerusalem this afternoon.

A crude diagram of the funeral route accompanied the text.

She dithered. She should stay to pay her respects but she had promised her mother to help with Cousin Elsa's birthday party.

Family won out. Dalia took the last seat on the Jaffa bus next to a young man in a smart grey suit. Even before she had sat down, he was telling her he sold the world-famous Katab fountain pens. By the time they set off he had opened a sample case and started on his sales pitch. She snapped that she already owned a fountain pen. He lit a Palestinian cigarette. Her eyes watered as the malodorous smoke drifted across her face.

Three children, equipped for their sea-side holiday, occupied the seat in front of her. A boy, aged about two, stood facing her banging the top of the seat with his wooden spade, narrowly missing her face. Two girls, slightly older, clashed their tin buckets together while chanting a song without recognisable words. Their mother, immersed in conversation with another young woman with her own quota of noisy children, took no notice. The sooner this journey was over, the better.

They hit a traffic jam. The police had set up a roadblock at the city boundary, checking traffic in both directions. The bus inched forward. Eventually, they showed their identity cards to armed police who, struggling through the standing passengers, checked all luggage.

"So that's out of the way," said the driver when the police eventually moved the cement-filled oil drum to let him through. He slammed his foot on the accelerator. "I'll drive as fast as I can to make up for lost time, but we're still going to arrive behind schedule!"

The wheels shrieked.

"Oh! Koos Em—Em—Em—Em—EM ek!" the driver

swore, stamping his foot on the brake, narrowly missing the last car in a second traffic queue. A middle-aged woman standing in the aisle lurched against the boy with the spade, knocking him off the seat. He bawled loudly enough to interrupt his mother's conversation.

A roadblock outside Givat Shaul proved the cause of this fresh hold-up.

"Two roadblocks in one kilometre!" the fountain pen salesman complained to a policeman struggling through standing passengers to check identity cards. "What's going on?"

The policeman shrugged. "They tell me nothing."

The middle-aged woman said, "It'll be this afternoon's funeral in Jerusalem. The way these police are acting, rioters have killed some of their own."

The young mother who was examining her son for injuries said, "I hope they have. The more of those manyaks they take out the better."

A murmur of agreement all round.

The small boy wriggled out of his mother's grasp and continued bashing the top of the seat.

"You want your children brought up in a country without law and order?" the middle-aged woman demanded.

"*I* provide the law and order in my family," the young woman retorted, and continued her conversation with her friend.

The little boy thumped Dalia's hand with his spade. She pressed it to her mouth, partly because it hurt but mainly to stop herself swearing aloud.

The driver set off again and drove at insane speed down the Seven Sisters. People sitting held on to their seats, those standing clung to the roof straps.

Another roadblock at the junction of the Jaffa and Qalqilya roads brought them to a standstill again. By this time, what with squabbling children, families late for lunch, and businessmen missing urgent meetings, everyone was irritable.

Matters grew worse as they approached Jaffa. Another roadblock at Wilhelmina and four more inside the city boundary. The bus finally arrived two and a half hours late.

Dalia sprinted across the highway that divided Jaffa from Tel Aviv, passing long queues spread along pavements outside grocery shops, butchers and dairies. Billboards held government notices announcing a curfew of indefinite length starting at five a.m. the next day. Below the government notices, resolutions from the city council condemned terrorist attacks in both Jerusalem and Jaffa, and ordered abductors to release five kidnapped British army officers.

At least there was no curfew that night, so the restaurant Shayna had booked would remain open and her parents could return to Bereisheet in time to milk the cows.

When Dalia arrived, Shayna shrieked with delight. "Thank goodness you've come. Eema will be here any time. We haven't started on the balloons and flowers. Because we've a curfew tomorrow, I had to queue at the dairy for milk and butter. Hadassah and Ephraim are still queuing at the bakery. Goodness knows when the shops will open again. I knew we should have held the party at Rehovot, but how then could we keep that a surprise for Eema?"

Dalia couldn't understand Shayna's panic since she had enough flour and evaporated milk in her cupboards to stand a month's siege.

She dug out Shlomo, who had retired to his study away from the fuss, and organised him into blowing up balloons, while she set to work arranging flowers. Luckily, Cousin Elsa and Uncle Moshe were late, having also been held up by police roadblocks, so she had arranged the flowers and Shlomo had hung up the balloons by the time they arrived, although the children were still out queuing. However, everyone was back and dressed appropriately in time to walk to the restaurant.

With no sign of trouble on the streets, they reached the restaurant without incident. Dalia stopped in the doorway over-awed by the magnificent buffet. Watermelons and olivewood had been carved into a huge arch with the numerals six and zero fixed to double gates. Moulded gefilte fish gaped up from a sea of chopped ice. Palaces of humous and pyramids of olives in various hues of green and purple surrounded layers of pastrami shaped into a herd of cattle. In the place of honour, a plantation of round-fruited chillies aped a miniature citrus grove. In the midst of all this stood a marzipan model of Moshe and Elsa Mabovitch's house in Rehovot.

Elsa clapped her hands in appreciation.

"The chef here," Shayna told Dalia, "learnt his trade in Berlin in the twenties."

"I wish the British government was here so we could rub its nose into Palestine's horn of plenty," Dalia replied. "We could easily manage to feed one hundred thousand refugees."

"Dalia, you're even worse than my brother!" Shayna exclaimed. "Don't you ever think of anything except politics? Relax! It's my mother's birthday."

* * * *

Sabbath evening was normally uneventful, so only one wireless operator was on duty. Tonight was even more peaceful than normal—nothing out of the way happening anywhere. No bombings, no ambushes, no fights, no phone calls from the Agency. Police operation patrols communicated their positions precisely on time. Cars on escort duty ran smoothly and reported regularly. After a while, Dalia gave the wireless only half her mind and used the rest to contemplate the demob party her mother was organising for Uri.

At four-thirty a.m. a correctly coded knocking on the door surprised both herself and her scribe partner.

"Whoever it is, it can't be the boss checking up on us," the scribe said. "He goes home for seder long before curfew."

Dalia jumped up to unbolt the door. Ludwig Mayer and Herman came in accompanied by the wireless operators and scribes from the previous shift that had slept through the curfew in the loft.

Ludwig burst out, "What are you getting?"

Taken aback, Dalia remained silent.

"Nothing!" her fellow wireless operator responded. "It's exceptionally quiet tonight."

Herman folded his arms. "So! Then why is there a plane

circling so low overhead it's almost scraping the rooftops? Why are police trucks cruising the streets, ordering people, even those with curfew passes, to stay indoors?"

Dalia handed him the headphones. "Listen for yourself. There's nothing here. The British never do anything too serious on the Sabbath, nor do the Irgun."

"Go upstairs to hear what's happening for yourself," an off-duty wireless operator offered. "We'll take over."

"Make sure you don't turn on a light," Ludwig warned.

As soon as Dalia opened the door to the stairs, she heard the roaring engines of the low flying plane and a strident amplified voice growing louder as it grew nearer. Something big was happening.

Just how big that something was they didn't get to hear until seven a.m. when the Palestinian Broadcasting Service came on air with a statement from the High Commissioner. The British military had raided the Jewish Agency buildings in Jerusalem and Tel Aviv and arrested most of the executive.

Dalia's gut feeling of *The British can't do this*, was overtaken by *but they have*. Nothing made sense anymore.

"What will happen now?" she asked more to herself than anyone else.

Herman answered, "The Agency will take it to the United Nations."

One of the scribes, a secretary from the Agency, shook her head. "With all the chief officers arrested who is left to go to the UN?"

They soon discovered it wasn't just the Agency that had suffered. The army had arrested over two thousand Palmach members and were searching not only Jewish settlements but even city synagogues. They found dozens of weapon caches, including a huge one hidden in Tel Aviv's Great Synagogue.

* * * *

Three weeks later Dalia arrived at the bookshop for the morning shift in a better frame of mind than she had been since *Black Sabbath*.

Haganah had called on the United Resistance Group to cease action while talks were going on in London. The weather wasn't as hot as usual for July. The previous evening she had received a letter from Esther with exciting news. Observers from the Anglo-American Committee of Inquiry had visited Zamzum and enthused about the hard work and perseverance of pioneers in the Negev settlements.

"We've won the Negev for Eretz Israel," was Esther's triumphant conclusion.

At midday Dalia was listening to JOP's steady stream of routine patrol commands while munching on a cucumber sandwich, when she heard an order for all police in West Jerusalem to get to the King David as quickly as possible.

Herman clattered down the stairs and banged the code. "The whole facade of the King David's south wing has collapsed."

As she listened to messages with devastating details from rescue teams, Dalia felt none of the exhilaration she had experienced in previous acts of sabotage. The list of civilian casualties from the British Secretariat grew steadily, many of them Jewish women from the Secretariat's typing pool. The people setting up the bombs knew Jews worked in Palestine's civilian administration, many of them only there to smuggle out information for Shai or the Irgun.

This had to be an Arab venture, although everyone had thought that all Arab groups with the ability to organise on this scale were too occupied with internecine assassinations to have time to attack British or Jews.

A few days later, however, to her consternation, the Irgun declared responsibility for the bombing. What, she wondered, had happened to the principle that Jew did not deliberately kill Jew? The Irgun claimed the British were accountable for the high death toll because they had ignored warnings to evacuate.

Hermann pointed out that if the hotel had activated their evacuation plan, the death toll would have been even higher. The Postmaster General had been walking up to the building close to the designated assembly point when the bombs exploded and his head had landed up across the road as a gargoyle on the YMCA's west wing.

Soon after the Irgun announcement, the presenter on Kol Israel read out a message sent by the General in Command of British Forces in Mandate Palestine to his officers.

"I have decided that with effect on receipt of this letter you will put out of bounds to all ranks all Jewish establishments, restaurants, shops, and private dwellings. No British soldier is to have social intercourse with any Jews. I appreciate that these measures will inflict some hardship on the troops, yet I am certain that if my reasons are fully explained to them they will understand their propriety and will be punishing the Jews in a way the race dislikes as much as any, by striking at their pockets and showing our contempt of them."

Dalia's eyed filled with tears of anger. Never, never again, she vowed, would she mix socially with anyone British. They had revealed themselves in their true anti-Semitic colours. It had been weakness getting back together with Patsy after the Palmach's weapons had been confiscated.

She determined to forget her former friends and concentrate on working towards Jewish Independence, but she would miss little Johnny and little Raffy.

Chapter 37

Because of the frequent night curfews, Dalia spent more time at the bookshop than at her digs, so she had asked her parents and Ruth to address their letters there.

A few days after the King David bombing, Itka handed her a letter from her mother. She opened it during a lull in police messages.

Dearest Dalia,

Such awful news! Soldiers came into Shayna's flat with their rifles the morning of Tel Aviv's daytime curfew. They searched every cupboard, pulled out every drawer, and tipped out her jewellery. The ruffians even searched through her underwear. They ruined all her pickles and jams, opening them up and stirring them with the same fork. Can you imagine?

Of course they found nothing. Can you imagine Shlomo belonging to a terrorist group? So they went away but came back in the afternoon with a policeman, a Jewish policeman, one of Shlomo's friends even. He carried a warrant for Shlomo's arrest. What for, you ask? On suspicion of Shlomo being involved with the King David bombing. Shlomo! Are they mad?

They put him in a cage in the local park with no shade and Cousin Elsa says they wouldn't even allow him to take a bottle of water with him, and you know how hot it's been this week.

Dalia put the letter down, her stomach knotted in shock. Shlomo, in one of those iniquitous army cages, without shade, without water! Shlomo, one of the least political people she knew.

They must get rid of the British who treated them like interlopers in their own country as fast as possible.

She picked up the letter again.

Later, children, but only children, were allowed to take in water. Hadassah took her father a large bottle but one of the soldiers guarding the gate drank a whole lot of it. Hadassah was so angry when she came home after seeing the British treat her father and all the other people in the cages so badly she says she's going to join the Irgun because they are the only ones who will stand up to the British. Shayna is really worried about her.

At least Shlomo is home now, with no apologies from the British, though.

I'm so glad, my Dalia, that you are keeping out of politics. Working in a bookshop is such a nice, peaceful occupation in these terrible times.

Your loving mother.

Dalia sympathised with Hadassah's feelings. She hoped, however, Hadassah didn't join the Irgun. They were just a gang of brutal criminals. If it hadn't been for them blowing up the King David, Shlomo wouldn't have been put into a cage in the first place.

She seethed all through her shift which finished at three, and walked briskly back to her lodgings wondering if she could do something more positive to bring a real Jewish state into existence. She wished Shimon would give up his naive ideals that Jews didn't need a totally Jewish-run state. Perhaps with his sister's husband being so badly treated, Shimon might change his views.

She wanted to discuss the latest situation with her Palmach friends, most of whom were still in prison.

She opened the front door of the apartment building. The stench from the barrel in the hall seemed to get stronger every time she returned home. She was beginning to hate everything about her life in Jerusalem, this building, her job, and most of all her non-existent social life.

On the landing outside Itka's apartment, someone sat huddled on the floor. The figure jumped up. She stepped back startled, and just saved herself from falling backwards down the stairs. Then she recognised her niece and panic set in.

"What are you doing here, Hadassah?"

"I want to join the Irgun."

"So my mother told me." She unlocked the front door. "You'd better come inside. Does your mother know you're here?"

"I left a note to say I was coming, but didn't say why."

Dalia shut the front door behind them. "And just why have you come?"

"You're the only person I know who belongs to Irgun, and don't tell me I'm too young to join, Cousin Dalia. I'm fourteen now."

The reply left her speechless. She went into the kitchen and filled a kettle. Eventually, she asked, "What makes you think I belong to the Irgun?"

"Eema said…" Hadassah stared at the ground.

"Your mother said what?"

"That you were brave, and a good Zionist, but there were things about you we mustn't talk about."

"That doesn't mean I belong to Irgun, and I can assure you I do not. Now tell me, why do *you* want to join Irgun?"

"So I can kill the British, of course. You didn't see what they did to Abba, and there was this woman in the park. They kept her in a barbed wire cage, all by herself. My father said she was still there when he left. The British are worse than the Nazis."

With that she burst out crying, so Dalia put her arms around her. She took a deep breath and pounded down her own anger. It wasn't going to help this confused adolescent.

"Hadassah, what the British did to your father and that young woman wasn't right. I understand why you are so angry, but…" to her own astonishment she found herself defending the British "…believe me, the British are nowhere near as bad as the Nazis. If they were, they wouldn't have let your father come home, and you, your mother, and Ephraim would all be in cages as well. The British are so horrible now because they're angry. Many British civilians were killed when the Irgun blew up the King David, but remember, seventeen Jews died as well and Irgun didn't care."

"That was the British fault, Jews dying. They didn't tell people about the warning."

"Hadassah, if the British had done so, even more people would have died."

She debated as to whether she should give Hadassah any gruesome details but decided against it. The child was in a bad enough state as it was.

"Unless you live in Jerusalem, Hadassah, you have no

idea what those bombs were like. They were far worse than the bombs the Germans dropped on Tel Aviv when you were little, and they were bad enough."

She heard Itka's key in the lock and, almost immediately after it, the wail of the curfew siren. She would save a lecture on the wisdom of Haganah's recently re-embraced policy of restraint for another occasion.

The most pressing needs were to explain Hadassah's presence to Itka and, after that, to put a call through to Shayna, who was probably in the same state as Cousin Elsa would have been.

Later, before turning out her light, she looked down at the sleeping half-woman, half-child sharing her bed and wondered how many other adolescents were trying to join Irgun after visiting caged fathers. It was almost as if the British were deliberately shooting themselves in the foot.

As she lay in bed she considered the violence being committed in the name of Eretz Israel. When she had first joined Haganah, they had talked around campfires about creating a new kind of state, a model for all others, where reason and hard work prevailed and there was no aggression, only skilled defence. Could present day Zionists ever resurrect their former idealism?

* * * *

Coming off duty but unable to go home because of a curfew, Dalia was conducting a low conversation with one of the scribes and only half listening to Kol Israel, Haganah's underground radio station, until two names caught her attention. She switched her attention to the wireless, as the speaker piled up damning evidence that a British Police Officer, ASP Craine, had abducted and murdered a young Jew, Arvon Platter, only recently arrived from Europe.

She sat there stunned. Poor little Arvon Platt dead, and killed by a wartime comrade? Despite the compelling evidence, she found it difficult to accept that Patsy's husband was a murderer until she recalled Tim herding kibbutzniks into cages at Givat Hayim.

Her mind wandered further back to that other Palestine Policeman she had known, Peter, allowing his squad to bury two Arabs on a lonely mountainside, leaving their families to wonder where they were.

At her digs, she watched Itka cheer after Kol Israel's jubilant announcement of the arrest of Assistant Superintendent Craine.

She should be cheering, too, but images of little Johnny stopped her. Whether or not Tim was guilty, Johnny was losing a father. Patsy must be going through hell.

"The British policeman they're talking about, he's the husband of your friend?" Itka asked.

She recalled the occasions she and Patsy had worked together during the war and their more recent outings with Maftur and the children. She jumped up. "I must write to Patsy."

"You think that's wise? It's a terrible thing her husband has done."

"It's not Patsy's fault."

"Would she have written to you, in such circumstances?"

No, Dalia thought, Patsy wouldn't have written. She'd have come banging on her door asking what she could do to help.

She went to her room determined to write a supportive letter but, since she couldn't believe in Tim's innocence, found it difficult.

Eventually, it was just a short note, not mentioning Tim, just asking Patsy how she was and sending her love to little Johnny.

She wrote a longer letter to Shimon.

Dear Shimon,

I don't know whether you have heard of Tim Craine's arrest. If you haven't it will come as a shock to learn he is charged with the kidnapping and possible murder of Arvon Platter. The evidence seems irrefutable.

Did I tell you Tim still has to use a walking stick? Witnesses saw a police car park near Arvon's digs. Two men in police uniform and a man in plain clothes answering Tim's description left the car. The uniformed police brought Arvon out of his digs, struggling wildly to escape. The police bundled him roughly into the car and sped off. The plain clothes man dropped his walking stick in his hurry to get into the car. One of the witnesses retrieved it. It has Tim's name inscribed on the silver nameplate. The police deny ever arresting Arvon.

Poor lad, such a terrible childhood and now just when everything seemed to be going right for him, his life is over. All he ever wanted was to be a doctor like his father and save people's lives.

All the same, I feel sorry for Patsy, as I am sure you do.

A week later she received a note from Shimon with an enclosure.

Shalom Dalia,

Thank you for letting me know about Tim. Unlike you, I am convinced of his innocence. I suspect Arvon is still alive but in hiding from the Irgun. I am enclosing a letter I hope you can forward to Tim.

Do write and keep me up to date with everything that happens.

Shalom again,

Shimon

That autumn everyone in Palestine seemed to be in a prison of some kind.

Senior members of the Jewish Agency, along with thousands of Palmachniks, languished at Detention Centres. Arabs were locked behind bars of custom and tradition. The British had herded themselves into a concentration camp centred on the Russian compound and Patsy Craine's Tim was locked away in Acre awaiting trial for the murder of a lad he had befriended.

One damp November morning after a few hours' sleep on a camp bed in the staff's improvised loft bedroom, Dalia stumbled blearily down to the cold shop floor intent on making coffee. Looking through the plate glass doors, she was astonished to find barbed wire rolls doodled along the whole street, leaving only a narrow pedestrian path on the nearer sidewalk.

The telephone rang. The Palestine Post. "Your papers will be late. Our van can't negotiate your street. We'll send them in a wheelbarrow when we get hold of one."

"Why's our street blocked?"

"No one's said, but rumour is it's not temporary."

Prison walls closing tighter each day. She asked without hope, "Any good news for a change?"

"Yes! According to sources in London, the government are freeing all detainees except those facing criminal charges. Not definite, but there's hope."

"I'll believe it when I see it."

She made the coffee by the saucepan method, speedier than the percolator but just as effective, and took it down to the cellar.

Towards the end of the afternoon, she tuned in to the underground radio. To everyone's astonishment, the presenter announced that all the detained, both Agency leaders and the majority of Palmach and Haganah members, had been released, free of charges. In addition, the Government had lifted curfews throughout Palestine.

They stood and cheered, delighted the Yishuv had won so significant a battle.

"I'm off to the Agency to welcome back the detainees. We're unlikely to hear anything worth monitoring today," Dalia called.

She ran upstairs and peered into the shop. As usual at this time in the afternoon, it was empty, shoppers having left for home and office staff still at work. She shouted the news to the shop staff. Itka turned the door notice to 'Closed'.

Bouncing along the narrow path between rolls of barbed wire, risking laddered stockings and torn skirts, they merged with crowds heading towards the imposing buildings in Rehavia's tree-lined boulevard.

They managed to secure a prime position close to a balcony overhanging the courtyard. They had a two hour wait in the jam-packed enclosure but at least it had stopped raining. The convoy carrying released detainees from Latrun entered the gates. Photographers flashed cameras. The crowd cheered and waited again.

Eventually, the top executives came out onto the balcony. The crowd spontaneously broke out into the HaTikvah.

Later that evening, while celebrating at her favourite cafe

with returned Palmach friends on this first curfew-free night for months, Dalia wondered whether Patsy would be rejoicing that her former Palmach colleagues were free, or seething at their release while her Tim remained incarcerated.

In December, Dalia received another letter from Shimon.

Dear Dalia,

Happy Hanukkah!

I hope you have changed your mind about Tim being guilty. I am enclosing a copy of a statement I sent to the Jewish agency. I know that statement will count for nothing in a courtroom but hope it will influence you.

She read the enclosure.

Statement by Captain Shimon Mabovitch of the Jewish brigade re Trial of ASP Craine

During the war, Tim Craine, Arvon Platter, and I worked together with a partisan group in Italy. Throughout that time, Tim treated Arvon like a favourite younger brother and Arvon hero-worshipped Tim. Our group in Italy helped Arvon make Aliyah and found him a school place. Since Arvon's return to Palestine, he has spoken in glowing terms of ASP Craine. I am positive this accusation against him is Irgun mischief. Arvon bore a grudge against Irgun because they had promised him a place on one of their boats but gave it to an older lad who had collaborated with Nazis.

Dalia read and re-read the letter. Arvon had spoken warmly of Tim when she had spoken to him in Jerusalem but she didn't realise they had met up. Shimon knew Tim much better than she did. Perhaps she should give Tim the benefit of the doubt!

She rang Mrs. Quigley's number several times, but received no reply. She then rang Maftur, who told her Patsy was confined to Ramat Gan Tegart for her own safety, unable to receive visitors, but she and Johnny were staying in Aileen's flat so they wouldn't be on their own over Christmas.

Dalia wrote to her manager at al-Tira and asked him send a box of oranges in her name to a Mrs. Craine at Ramat Gan She enclosed a letter to Patsy and Johnny for him to tape to the box.

After New Year, she was relieved to receive a letter from Patsy thanking her for the oranges and telling her the date for

Tim's trial in Jerusalem.

She agonised over whether to attend the trial. If she did, her Palmach friends would expect her to sit with them. Being seen sitting with Tim Craine's wife would ruin her reputation. Eventually, she wrote to Shimon telling him that she would attend the trial to support Patsy.

On the first day of Tim Craine's trial, Dalia arrived at the courthouse in the Russian Compound by a path flanked by barbed wire but still open to the public. An ATS sergeant guarding the entrance led her into a booth and subjected her to a humiliating body search before allowing her inside.

Tim sat between two warders in a raised area but she wouldn't look directly at him. She stood at the back of the courtroom searching the crowd until she spotted Patsy sitting between Maftur and a plump woman in a row near the front. She passed Herman who pointed to an empty space beside him. Giving an apologetic smile, she walked on and stopped by Maftur. Patsy, so much thinner than when she had seen her last, was talking to the plump woman.

Maftur smiled and nudged Patsy. "Look who's here!"

Patsy gave a tremulous smile, stood up, and burst into tears. Maftur pushed back to let Patsy through.

Dalia felt Patsy trembling as she embraced her, saying, "Thank you so much for coming, and for forwarding Shimon's letter. Tim was so pleased to get it." She called out to the plump woman, "Aileen, this is Dalia Leitner, the one who sent us those Jaffas at Christmas. Dalia, this is my friend Aileen Murphy. She's been so good to me. I don't know how I would have coped these past weeks otherwise."

A British police constable came up. Dalia stood ready to stand her ground if he ordered her away.

"Constable Tell," Maftur said, "Any chance you can persuade those people at the end to move over to give our friend room?"

The policeman smiled reassuringly and went off. Dalia squashed herself in next to Maftur.

The clerk to the court banged a gavel for silence. Everyone stood as the black-robed, bewigged judge entered and mounted the steps to a pulpit-like seat. After the preliminary proceedings, the prosecutor gave convincing evidence of Tim's guilt. As she left the courtroom on that first day of the trial, Herman came up and congratulated her on placing herself in the best place to research the British stance. He would take over her shifts at Rabbit so she could continue attending.

On the third day of the trial the defence lawyer made a great deal of the fact that Tim's surname was misspelt on his walking stick. He brought in Tim's British secretary who, unfortunately for Tim, under cross-examination by the prosecutor, reluctantly admitted that her boss's spelling was atrocious and while she was sure ASP Craine's cane hadn't been engraved before he lost it, she couldn't swear to it.

The prosecuting lawyer elicited the fact that she had been off duty when Arvon was allegedly kidnapped so could not substantiate ASP Craine's claim to be working in his office when Arvon Platter had allegedly been kidnapped.

While the prosecutor was cross-examining, a clerk handed the judge a message the desk sergeant brought in, testifying to Tim's presence in the CID building on the day in question. The desk sergeant said that ASP Craine had ordered no one to disturb him and admitted under cross-examination that there was a handy fire escape from his office.

Dalia couldn't see how the jury could fail to find Tim guilty, but didn't voice that opinion when Maftur whispered, "They're bound to acquit Tim now. The prosecution's case is based on purely circumstantial evidence."

When the desk sergeant left the witness box, the judge addressed the court. "For security reasons, the last witness will give evidence on camera. Guards, take the accused back to the cells. Ushers, clear the court."

Dalia couldn't bear talking to Patsy's other friends, all so confident that Tim was innocent. She collected their nearly empty water bottles. "I'll get these refilled."

The queue at the fountain snaked around the public sector of the compound, but she was glad of the excuse for delay. The task eventually accomplished, she was making her way back when a Major wearing sunglasses and sporting the badge of the Jewish brigade moved out from the shade of a cypress and touched her arm. She looked up and gasped, "Shimon!"

He beckoned her to follow him behind the tree trunk, out of sight of the guards. "Just stand still, so I can look at you and remember the image," he said. "I can't stay long. I told the ushers that I had to get a breath of fresh air. I'm not supposed to speak to anyone but I've spent the last five minutes looking for you."

"What are you doing here?"

"Proving Tim's innocence."

"But how…?"

He put his finger to his lip.

"Is Arvon alive?"

"Tim is innocent and no more questions, please. Tell no one you've seen me, and that includes my mother. If anyone asks, as far as you know I've been in Italy since Uri's wedding. There's one thing I would like you to do, though. Keep in touch with Patsy if she leaves Palestine?"

"Why don't you speak to Patsy yourself?"

"I can't. Let me repeat. No one must know I've been in Eretz Israel."

"Can't I even tell Ruth?"

"No, no one at all. I have to get back now."

"Can we meet up somewhere after the trial?"

"No, they're rushing me back to Italy, but I had to see you."

He bent down and kissed her on her forehead. "Please keep writing and, please, don't hate me when I tell you that I love you."

And he was off. She watched him show his pass to two British soldiers and slip through a small door. Had he really been there and had he really said he loved her? As she stepped from the shade into the heat, she felt dizzy. She stood still for a moment, composing herself. It was not the most appropriate time to return with a broad smile on her face. Then she hurried back to distribute the water bottles. Patsy looked so nervous.

She wished she could tell her of her encounter with Shimon.

The ushers opened the courtroom doors. She watched Patsy force an encouraging smile for Tim's benefit.

Once again the usher called for them to stand.

The judge re-entered the courtroom followed by the lawyers. He looked around at the crowd. "Fresh evidence has been presented that contradicts evidence already produced. I cannot, for reasons of national security, disclose this evidence but, because of it, I must advise the jury that there is no case to answer."

Loud boos sounded from all around the court. Policemen rushed around trying to nail down the culprits.

Patsy burst into tears again and asked, "Does Tim have to go through the whole process again?"

The judge rapped his gavel. "If there is any more commotion, I shall judge the perpetrators guilty of contempt of court. The accused is free to leave. Ushers please clear the court."

She watched Patsy push past Aileen towards Tim, but instead of freeing Tim, the guards hustled him down to the cells. Tim struggled against them while looking back at Patsy in desperation. The door behind him closed.

Patsy pushed her hands through her hair, knocking off her hat. "What am I supposed to do now—just walk off without him?"

Constable Tell came to Patsy's side and took her arm. "Come with me, Mrs. Craine." His official manner softened. "You may say goodbye to your friends."

In the now empty aisle they managed a four-way hug before the constable led a drooping Patsy to a door at the back of the court room.

Dalia, however, almost danced out of the courtroom with Maftur and Aileen, but her joy wasn't altogether connected to Tim's acquittal.

Shimon's last words rang through her head.

Chapter 38

Only three days after that brief meeting outside the courthouse, Itka handed Dalia a letter from Italy as she passed through the bookshop on her way home. She tore it open as soon as she had negotiated the barbed wire path to the open pavement on the next street. She stood in ecstasy as she read the greeting.

Dear Darling Dalia,

She couldn't read this walking along the street. She almost ran home and flopped down in her room to read the letter slowly, stopping when her eyes blurred with tears, sometimes of joy, sometimes with sadness, for lost opportunities.

Shimon confessed that he had been in love with her ever since her early Haganah days, only, he told her, that he had felt she was too young to fall in love and had been afraid of winning her in her puppy stage only to lose her when she matured.

Once she was settled in Haifa, he had considered the time right to declare himself. Only recently had he realised that it was his own immature insensitivity to her feelings when Uri was on trial, and his inexcusable masculine pride, that had created the barrier between them. Did he have any chance with her now?

Dalia didn't know whether to laugh or cry but was determined not to mess up this time. Although she wanted to run out in the streets and shout to the world that the man she had always loved, loved her too, she felt she had to be as open with him as he had been with her, so sat down and wrote her own confession.

She told Shimon about the photo she had stolen when she was twelve and admitted that for years her feelings for him had been hero worship, not love. He was quite right to assume she was still too young to be seriously in love when she joined Haganah. It was different now. Her hero worship of an outstanding Zionist had matured into love for the caring man he had become, as shown by his devotion to rescuing DPs from the camps. She understood why he had to stay in Italy and would wait for him patiently.

She explained her guilt feelings when repulsing him on Mount Carmel and admitted that if she had been older she would have considered his feelings as well as her own. She explained that she had gone out with Peter, in the first instance, as part of her work for Shai, but had allowed herself to become emotionally involved when he, Shimon, had become engaged to Yael. As for Dov, she told Shimon of her pact with him.

She ran out and posted the letter and waited in trepidation for the reply. When it came it started *Dearest Dalia*, and could only be described as a love letter.

They wrote mushy love letters, only of interest to each other, every day. Only the thought of her future with Shimon kept her sane during the stuffy months in the cellar and the escalation of violence throughout Palestine.

In between the mushy bits, she continued to keep Shimon posted on the progress in Zamzum where they both hoped to work when Eretz Israel became a state.

He told her of a plan for sending so many illegal immigrants to Palestine the government wouldn't have enough space in the detention camps.

In April she wrote sad news. The current drought in the Negev was about to end the Zamzum project, and asked if there was any way he could persuade the water board to hasten the process of bringing water to the Negev.

He replied that he had suggested to the Agency that, as a temporary measure, they could pipe water from existing wells further north.

* * * *

The four people on duty at Rabbit were listening to Kol Israel telling them about a ship leaving France for Palestine carrying four thousand five hundred DPs with no entry visas.

"Since the British know about it!" Dalia exclaimed, "they're never going to get past their navy."

Her scribe for the day, private secretary to a senior member of the Jewish Agency, tapped her nose. "That's the whole point! Four thousand five hundred detainees will present the British with an insoluble logistical problem now all detainee camps in Cyprus are full."

A coded knock interrupted conversation. Herman entered, anger seeping through his habitual calm. "Those Irgun maniacs and the British idiots have surpassed themselves this time. The Irgun have snatched two British sergeants from Nathanya as hostages for their three members under sentence of death. The British have retaliated by cordoning off Nathanya plus several settlements in the Hefer valley right at the height of the holiday season and fruit harvest. The cordon stays in place until the Irgun release the hostages. Thousands of our people face economic disaster. Haganah has to find those hostages as soon as possible and needs all the volunteers it can get." He looked across the room. "Dalia, your brother's in charge of a local search team and your moshav's just outside the cordoned area so we needn't waste time this end getting you a permit. Your brother can sort that out."

Being part of a search team in the open air was far more to Dalia's taste than sitting in a stuffy cellar, so her response was instant. "Consider me volunteered."

Uri was out searching when she arrived home.

"How do I get a permit to cross the cordon?" she asked when he returned.

"You don't need one if you're part of my team. We've a group pass allowing us to search inside the cordon."

She glowered. "You're collaborating with the British?"

"Only to help people whose livelihoods are at risk."

That was why Dalia found herself tramping through the moist shade of citrus groves, searching winter stables and sheds filled with harvest equipment. The task gave her plenty of time to wallow in fond thoughts of Shimon while reminding her of the many outings she'd once enjoyed with Haganah. In several groves they found the neglected Heath Robinson style irrigation systems had already stopped working, putting crops at risk. She persuaded her brother she would be more useful to the Yishuv checking pumps and repairing them while the rest of the team carried on the search without success. As a result of all the bending and stretching that the repairs involved, she returned home in the evening stiff, weary and sunburnt, realising how unfit she had become while employed by Rabbit.

She relaxed during the familiar family evening talking about farming, listening to local gossip and discussing the political situation, but towards the end she beckoned Ruth to follow her outside.

"Ruth, we haven't had a chance to talk properly. Can you spare a few minutes in the cow shed?"

As soon as they were settled on bales of hay, Dalia told Ruth her news, being careful to make it sound as if everything between Shimon and her had happened by post.

Ruth was so delighted she wanted to rush down and tell everyone, but Dalia stopped her.

"You're the only person I've told. Neither Shimon nor I want Eema or Cousin Elsa presenting us with wedding plans set in concrete the moment Shimon returns home."

Ruth saw the point. "I promise not to tell even Uri, although," she added, "I wouldn't be at all surprised if Shimon hasn't already got in touch with him and sworn him to secrecy as well."

Later in her room, Dalia wrote a long letter to Shimon about the day's happenings as she was to do every night she was at Bereisheet.

The next few days followed the same pattern as the first with no sign of the sergeants anywhere. Increasingly, however, family discussion in the evening revolved round the progress of the DP ship, now renamed *Exodus 1947*.

When she and Uri returned home on the fifth day of the search, Ruth greeted them with, "Guess what? The captain of the Exodus will broadcast off the Gaza coast tomorrow at seven-thirty a.m."

Uri hastily rescheduled the following day's search so the whole squad could listen to the broadcast at the Leitner's house.

Her mother, loving every minute of it, dished out coffee and cheese sandwiches to the whole team, as the young American captain gave a detailed account of the difficulties the ship had encountered since leaving the USA. He made an emotional appeal to the United Nations to force Britain to scrap the White Paper. The broadcast finished with a children's choir on board singing first the Palmach signature song in Hebrew and then the Hatikvah. The sound of those innocent voices stayed with her throughout the day.

The next morning Ruth and her mother again served breakfast to the whole team, as they listened to Kol Israel. The British had attacked the Exodus 1947 during the night and were escorting the ship into Haifa. People had been killed, many more seriously wounded.

The Captain broadcast again. The Exodus would reach Haifa by mid-afternoon. He urged the whole Yishuv to make their way to Haifa docks to protest against the British action.

The squad, however, had their job to do. Nathanya, vital to the economy of a future independent state, was still cut off from the rest of Palestine and on the verge of bankruptcy.

Ruth and Thelma Goldstein were going, and promised to report back.

Chapter 39

High fences and securely locked gates prevented protesters seeing what was happening on the dockside when the British took everyone off the Exodus, Ruth told the family when they returned from Haifa.

"So all we could do was stand chanting at the back of a huge crowd waving our flags," Thelma added.

"But somehow people in front of us seemed to know more than we did," Ruth said. "They told us the British had deliberately rammed cabins at sea and had killed many women and children while forcing them off the ship, and then left the passengers standing on the quayside in the full blaze of midday heat without any water."

"I'm surprised the British behaved so brutally in front of UNSCOP," her father commented.

Reb Cohen raised his eyebrows. "UNSCOP were there?"

"I heard the news on the wireless while shaving. The chairman and the Yugoslavian delegate had a grandstand position on the dockside along with the foreign newspaper correspondents."

Uri grinned broadly. "That will help our case no end."

Their mother turned on him. "How can you smile when women and children are being beaten, and men killed?"

The next morning at breakfast, however, her mother asked, "Ruth, why did you say the British killed women and children? The wireless reported only four people died and those were all men, one of them a British sailor, even."

"Three Jews killed is three too many," Dalia retorted, "and what about all the wounded? Over thirty in hospital! And no one being allowed to stay in Palestine, when we've made homes for them here! After what's happened, I don't care if the Irgun hang the sergeants. I'd stop searching for them if it weren't for the people of Nathanya."

She slipped out, using the excuse of fetching the newspapers, to post the previous night's letter to Shimon.

On her return, her father turned to reports in the Palestine Post. "Let's see what it says here." He skimmed the article. "The Palestine Post reporter talks of women and children carrying their luggage and lining up patiently to disembark."

Uri looked up from his own Hebrew language paper. "This says passengers were kept on the quay all afternoon in the heat, and several people fainted because their water and food was taken while their luggage was searched. They'd nothing to eat until they embarked on the ships taking them to Cyprus."

"If the Exodus didn't make port until four o'clock," her father reasoned, "and they took a long time to disembark, they couldn't have been on the quay in the full heat for long. The worst is over by five and it gets dark at seven. It says here the older children were laughing and playing."

Dalia begged a turn at the papers and read conflicting reports of the sea battle. An American Christian minister, described variously as a crew member and an observer, claimed a destroyer had deliberately rammed the ship. According to the British commander's log, however, the captain of Exodus1947 had steered his ship erratically as he tried to escape and had damaged both his own ship and two destroyers in the process.

She couldn't make up her mind what to believe, except that four people were dead, many seriously injured, no refugees had been allowed to enter Palestine, and they were still searching for the missing British sergeants.

* * * *

Thirteen days after the kidnapping, Dalia took a call from Golda while preparing breakfast.

"Dalia, a message from the Agency for Uri. The British have called off the search for Irgun's hostages and withdrawn the cordon round Nathanya. Nathanya's Mayor is panicking, sure the British intend to go ahead with hanging the three Irgun men. He is certain the Irgun will hang their hostages from his town's lamp-posts and Nathanya will suffer the consequences. Uri's squad is to patrol Nathanya to stop the Irgun doing anything stupid."

"The British are abandoning their sergeants?" her mother exclaimed in an incredulous tone when Dalia relayed the message.

"Maybe they've already rescued them," Ruth suggested.

Dalia shook her head. "They wouldn't keep that secret."

Uri drained his coffee. "Enough chat! Dalia, round up our squad. Tell them the change of plan, while I phone Nathanya's mayor."

Two days later the British carried out the death sentence on the Irgun convicts. While Uri's team made themselves deliberately conspicuous patrolling the streets of Nathanya, non-Hebrew speaking journalists added to the palpable tension by accosting residents and asking what they knew of the missing sergeants.

The next day the Irgun announced they had hanged their hostages. Apprehensive residents of Nathanya moved to Tel Aviv or neighbouring settlements, fearing retaliation by British troops. The streets were empty apart from Uri's men. With no one else to pester, the journalists focussed on Uri's squad, most of whom had only a limited command of even standard British English, let alone the variety of English accents and dialects used by international journalists.

Dalia feared members of the team would lose their tempers and antagonise journalists whose support they needed.

Uri obviously had the same fear. He took her aside. "Sis, our task here is to look tough and keep the Irgun at bay. Six foot tall brawny men look more threatening than an attractive woman so, although I know you're as capable of handling yourself as well as any member of our team, I'm picking you for the task of getting rid of the journalists."

"How do you expect me to do that?"

"Any way you like so long as you get them away."

It didn't take her long to come up with an idea. She ran to a nearby school, deserted except for the caretaker, grabbed crayons, paper and drawing pins and concocted multiple copies of a notice.

OFFICIAL JEWISH AGENCY PRESS RELEASE 1PM OUTSIDE MAYOR'S RESIDENCE.

She ran around the town sticking sheets of paper to notice boards and lamp-posts, before making her way to the mayor's house. She cut his telephone wire before ringing the door bell, and took a deep breath before speaking to him.

"Mr. Mayor, the Jewish Agency wants you to meet the press at one p.m. today outside your house and give your views on the kidnapping of the two British sergeants. I have been appointed the official press officer and interpreter for Nathanya and the Hefer Valley so you may make your speech in Hebrew."

To her relief the mayor was more than eager to make a speech.

By one o'clock a large crowd of foreign correspondents had gathered outside the residency.

The mayor delivered an impassioned speech defending his townspeople against all involvement in the kidnapping and death of Clifford Martin and Mervyn Paice and vigorously condemned the real perpetrators, pausing to let Dalia translate each sentence into English. When he had finished, Dalia informed the journalists that she would make herself available to the press at Tulkarem police station where Martin and Paice had been based. Any official news would be announced there first.

She cadged a lift to Tulkarem with a jeepful of journalists, promising them a behind-the-scenes account of the unsuccessful search on their journey.

The journalists waited outside the police station, but by dusk there was still no news. Promising to return to Tulkarem at first light, Dalia hitched a ride home with a French reporter eager to hear her views on what should happen to the passengers from Exodus 1947 who were currently refusing to disembark at the French port where the British had returned them.

Her mother treated the visitor to coffee and a slice of her famous chocolate cake. The journalist left swearing eternal friendship.

The next morning at Tulkarem after several more hours of inactivity, Dalia was at her wits' end on how to prevent the journalists from returning to Nathanya when a motorcycle screeched to a halt in front of the station. A member of the settlement police jumped off and ran into the station. The journalists, with Dalia in their midst, raced into the building.

"We've found the bodies, sir," the gaffir shouted at the stolid duty sergeant.

The British officer asked in a level voice, "Have you disturbed them?"

"No, sir. The Irgun warned us the area had been mined."

The sergeant picked up a phone. "Put me through to the superintendent."

The journalists rushed to their vehicles in preparation for action. Her friend from the previous day offered her a lift.

From the rear of the building, police and military armoured cars followed the station superintendent as he sped onto the main road. The journalists gave chase.

The cavalcade took to the road and came to a halt close to Nathanya. The superintendent stood, surrounded by his squad armed with rifles, against a backdrop of citrus trees. The journalists crowded around.

The superintendent, Dalia thought, kept his temper remarkably well. He raised his hand for quiet and told the crowd that they could follow, so long as they observed complete silence and stayed well to the rear of his men. He waved a hand at two soldiers bearing mine detectors. "Keep to the path cleared by the minesweepers."

The police squad set off, preceded by the two soldiers sweeping the ground in front of them. Dalia noticed a third soldier, a captain, carrying a long pole to which a knife had been attached.

Inside the shade of the citrus grove the only sounds were the faint thumping of heavy boots on soft ground, the humming of insects and the clacking of tin cans from the irrigation system. Ten minutes on and citrus grove gave way to a clump of eucalyptus trees. Dalia felt her stomach lurch as she saw, hanging from lower branches, two bodies surrounded by black clouds of buzzing flies.

The journalists kept back as the soldiers swept the ground around the bodies.

"All clear, sir," one said at last.

Dalia and the journalists crowded nearer, many already frantically scribbling in notebooks.

Dalia stared at the scarecrows, so recently confident young policemen.

"Take them down," the superintendent ordered.

The captain with the long-handled knife cut a rope.

BANG!

Fragments of putrid flesh hit Dalia in the face.

Chapter 40

Esther wrote giving better news. Piped water from wells to the north had arrived in time. The UNSCOP representatives had been impressed by their healthy crops and technological knowhow in such contrast to the famine and primitive conditions in the nearby Bedouin camp.

"I felt terrible after all the help the Bedouin gave us," Esther admitted, "but if it saves the lives of DPs, I suppose we're justified."

After Esther's letter, Dalia waited even more impatiently for UNSCOP's final report. When it came out in September, the commission recommended partition.

What excited her most was the recommendation to include the whole of the Negev south of Beersheba, apart from Gaza and a small coastal strip, into the area allotted to Jews. Her brigade could build homes for DPs.

To her irritation, her Jerusalem friends appeared indifferent to the inclusion of the Negev. They were furious because Jerusalem was nominated an international city.

"Calm down, everyone," Hermann said, when they were arguing at work. "Once we have a state, we can change boundaries."

"How?" Dalia challenged.

"Either through diplomacy or military means, whichever proves more appropriate."

Dalia could hardly believe he had said that. "You mean if diplomacy fails, we seize land by force?"

"Nu, Dalia, change that face. The Arabs will strike first. If we fight a war we didn't start, and improve our borders, who's to blame?"

The rest laughed. Dalia turned her attention back to searching the channels, feeling miserable. If the UN voted for partition she would leave Rabbit and return to Zamzum.

The end of November, and the United Nations were voting on Partition. It was late evening in Jerusalem but only mid-afternoon in New York. Like her colleagues in the cellar, Dalia, with her hands gripped tightly together, was listening to the public wireless bulletins, concentrating on the voting which still hung in the balance.

Outside, someone tapped the correct code. She turned around and bellowed the password challenge. A muffled voice gave the correct answer. She undid the bolts but kept the chain in place and peered through.

"Shimon!" she shouted and pulled out the chain.

Before she had time to realise what was happening, he had her in his arms. She stood, pressed against him, her head on his chest, feeling as if that was where she had always belonged.

He bent his head and whispered, "Dalia, oh Dalia."

Under normal circumstances her colleagues would have goggled, perhaps even cat-called, but all were too engrossed in what was taking place in New York to spare her and Shimon a second glance, except for Herman, who called out, "Shalom, Shimon. You've returned for the fight?"

Shimon tightened his grip around her waist but lifted his head. "Oi, what fight?"

"The one that follows this vote."

"So you know the result already?"

"It makes no difference. If it's partition the Arabs will make war on us. If its federation, we'll make war on them."

"There are other options but we'll argue afterwards. For now, may I listen with you?"

Dalia led Shimon to her bench. That day's scribe smiled knowingly and moved away.

Shimon dropped down and put an arm around her shoulder. She noticed for the first time he was out of uniform. Her happiness notched up another degree. "Demobbed?" she whispered.

"Yes. I hitched straight from the airport to find you."

She wrenched her attention back to the wireless. The votes were swinging first this way, then that, but, on such a charmed day, nothing could go wrong.

Well past midnight the announcer declared in an excited

shout, "The General Assembly of the United Nations has voted for the partition of Palestine."

Shimon's lips came down against hers. She spiralled into a state of ecstasy, only dimly aware of the yells bouncing against the ceiling. "We have a state! We have a state!"

Herman put his arms around both of them. "Enough. I'm locking up. We're off to the Agency."

Her scribe thrust white flags decorated with a blue Star of David into their hands. With their arms around each other's waists and waving their flags they raced upstairs, out into the moon-silvered street and ran, crabwise, down the narrow barbed wire out onto the Jaffa Road.

People, some with clothes hastily drawn on over pyjamas and still wearing slippers, crowded pavements, shouting and cheering. Cars raced by, horns blaring. Buildings lit up, bars and cafes opened. She and Shimon, still clutching their flags, linked arms with strangers dancing a hora.

A British JOP car drew close. Dalia's arm tightened around Shimon as a group of students swarmed over the police vehicle.

"Please," she gave a silent prayer, "no violence, not on this, the most magical of all nights."

Her prayer was answered. The students merely flung their arms around the shocked officers and kissed them on the cheeks. The British, recovering swiftly, embraced them back.

Shimon broke into the Hatikvah. Others joined him, but another group near them sang in Polish and another further back in Russian. Yet they all danced on in unity towards Rehavia and the fortress-like structure of the Agency building, lit now by blazing searchlights, and all the while Dalia was conscious of her arm around Shimon's warm back and his strong arm around her waist.

She watched the blue Star of David climb up the Agency Flagstaff and cheered more loudly than she had ever done.

Dumpy, middle-aged Golda Meyerson appeared on the balcony. The crowd grew quiet. This woman had devoted her whole life to bringing about Israel's independence. She addressed them now in triumph, finishing with a final, "Mazel tov."

Everyone cheered and the dancing began again.

Dalia allowed Shimon to pull her into a side alley away from the crowd. He bent his head to place his face against hers and kissed her. During the prolonged kiss it felt as if they were creating a single soul from the union of two. When eventually they separated, he put his arm around her and they returned to her digs, shoulders and hips touching. Inside the apartment, they tip-toed quietly to her room, so as not to disturb Itka.

The coming together that followed was like nothing that she had ever experienced. Sex with Dov had been just two good friends collaborating in de-stress exercises. This was unity. It was, she realised as she screamed in exaltation, the goal for which she had been searching for so long.

Later, after Shimon had fallen asleep, his warm chest against her back, Dalia lay awake, adrenalin still high, conscious that she was not only fulfilled on a personal level, but her main ambition had also been fulfilled. Her people would, for the first time in almost two thousand years, have a state of their own.

Gradually, however, twenty-three hours without sleep took their toll. Apprehension, born of physical exhaustion, bled into her elation. How long before new griefs counter-balanced this present happiness? She made a determined effort to reject negative thoughts and think rationally. After all, if the universe really consisted of a yin-yang balance of fortune and misfortune, surviving inmates of concentration camps would be living in palaces, not refugee camps.

She turned her head towards the window. Dawn had already robbed the sky of last night's stars but the sound of singing in the road outside told her people were still celebrating. It was as well she hadn't been able to sleep. Much as she wanted Shimon to remain in her bed, protecting her with his love, he had to be on the living room sofa before Itka rose. She wriggled around until she could kiss him on the lips. He kissed her back even before his eyes opened. She removed her lips reluctantly, withdrawing her head until he could see her whole face. She smiled and whispered, "Time to move, darling!"

He came fully awake, slid his legs to the floor, hauled himself to his feet, and pulled on his underpants. He collected clothes strewn across the floor, came back to give her another long kiss, and was gone. She reached under her pillow for her neglected night dress.

Six hours later she woke to the aroma of brewing coffee and stretched her arms, no longer apprehensive.

Shimon, now fully dressed, entered carrying a tray bearing two glasses of orange juice, two cups of coffee, and a plate of bagels.

She held her arms wide open. Shimon put the tray down on her bedside table and bent to give her a long kiss.

When he straightened, he picked up the glasses and handed her one. "I squeezed the oranges from that big sack in the kitchen. Are they from Bereisheet?"

She said, without thinking, "No. from my orange groves at al-Tira."

He laughed. "You own your own orange groves? My mother never passed on that piece of gossip."

"Probably because *my* mother never told her." She drained her glass and kissed him again. "My father, unlike yours, is proud of working his own land without Arabic help, but when we first made Aliyah he was old-fashioned enough to believe a father should provide a daughter with a dowry. I was fourteen when he gave me the groves. Your father would have teased mine without mercy if he had known my father kept on the Arab who had been managing them for years. When I came of age I kept him on, too, so I could go off and do real pioneering farming."

Shimon burst out laughing. "I can't wait to tell Abba!"

She kissed him again as she picked up a bagel. "You dare! We don't want our engagement party ruined by a full-scale political argument."

Shimon suddenly looked panic stricken. "We must phone Rehovot before anyone else tells my mother I'm engaged and in Jerusalem."

Fancy someone with Shimon's military record cowering

at the prospect of upsetting his mother! She would make sure they didn't live close to Rehovot once they were married.

She hoped she would never become as bossy as Cousin Elsa, but for now it was time to take charge of this situation.

"Phoning our parents, my darling, needs careful planning. If either Eema or Cousin Elsa thinks the other received our announcement first, our lives won't be worth living." She took a sip of coffee. "This is how we'll do it. We'll go straight to the bookshop. I'll ask Herman for a week's leave. We'll phone our parents simultaneously using separate phone boxes." She picked up a bagel. "Do you need to go to Rehovot straight away, sweetheart, or can you come to Bereisheet with me and ask my father for his blessing?"

Shimon kissed the top of her head. "I'll let you know when I've spoken to my mother."

Could she have expected any other answer?

In the street, blue and white flags decorated every lamp-post. More flags hung from apartment windows. Looking up, she was pleased to see Itka had draped a flag from their kitchen window.

At the bookshop, they told Itka of their engagement and received excited congratulations. Waiting until there were no customers, they sneaked down the cellar steps and she gave a coded knock.

Herman opened the door. "Dalia! I wasn't expecting anyone in today after the all night celebrations. I'm so glad you brought Shimon. I need to speak to him urgently."

Somewhat taken aback by his response, she explained that she needed to spend time in Bereisheet to celebrate her engagement and had only come in to request a week's leave.

If she had expected Herman to trot out the traditional congratulations she was disappointed. "If you really feel you have to go I can't stop you, but I'd advise against it. Arabs are assaulting our buses. Now please wait upstairs while I have a quick word with Shimon."

She wondered what Herman had to say that was unfit for her ears but she left Shimon no time to satisfy her curiosity. When he rejoined her, she pointed to the nearest cafe. "Get over there and phone your mother. I'll meet up with you after I've talked to my mother on the phone here."

At the cafe a quarter-of-an-hour later, she asked, "How did it go?"

"Eema was ecstatic. Said how fortunate Yael had broken off our engagement because you make a far more suitable wife now you're grown up, but we'll have to marry at once before you're too old to have children."

Dalia smiled. Her mother had said much the same thing, and had added, "Whatever you do, make sure you stand up to that dragon you're getting as a mother-in-law." She suspected Shimon had held back a similar remark from Cousin Elsa.

"What did your mother say about asking for my father's blessing?"

"I was to go home with you."

Dalia blinked her surprise.

Shimon added, "She said that would give her time to organise the joint demob party and engagement party, and we were both to return to Rehovot by the first bus after your father gave me his blessing."

"I think my mother might have something to say about that," Dalia retorted.

"Let's just watch the battle from the sidelines," Shimon suggested. "We don't have to take part."

She looked at him affectionately. "In some ways you're an awful lot like my father."

"Most girls marry men who take after their father," Shimon said.

She didn't ask if most boys married women who took after their mothers.

"We'd better get going straight away," she said.

Shimon took both her hands. "We've missed the last bus for today, darling, and," he lowered his voice, "I have a couple of things to tie up for Beth Aliyah, so I'll meet you at the bus station tomorrow in time for the first bus. Meanwhile, go straight home and have an early night. If you pick up any post, don't read it. Just stick it in your bag. No questions now, please, just trust me."

Her first instinct was to protest, but this was the man she loved and who loved her back. He wouldn't ask her to do something against her interest. She curbed her natural curiosity.

As she walked back to her digs, she noticed Arab shops displaying notices that they would be shut for three days in protest against the UN decision.

On the corner of her street, however, a group of Arab youths were smiling as they watched Jewish girls dancing.

Part 10 – Escalation

November 1947 – May 1948

Chapter 41

Dalia found a note slipped under the front door as she was leaving the next morning. The urge to read it was almost overwhelming but she slipped it into her rucksack. When she arrived at the depot the bus was already at the stand with the driver behind the wheel. A guard, presumably supplied by Haganah, stood beside the open door checking passengers before allowing them on board. Shimon was in the crowd moving towards the bus. She pushed her way through and held his hand.

In front, two women were in the middle of an argument.

"I tell you, Zirma, we should turn back. You heard that man – two buses attacked near Wilhelmina, six people killed, and thirty wounded."

"You're telling me now to go back after getting me up before dawn? Are you nuts? We're safer in Jerusalem surrounded by Arabs? I tell you, in Tel Aviv we can forget these troubles."

They reached the door of the bus. The guard blocked their way. She let go of Shimon's hand to hold out her ticket.

"Why are you leaving Jerusalem?" his tone truculent, as if accusing them of deserting their posts.

"It's no business of yours," she responded.

"It is if you belong to Haganah."

She couldn't believe he had said that aloud so everyone could hear him. What had happened to their vows of secrecy?

"What's it to you if I do?"

She heard Shimon laugh. "Hush, Dalia," he said and held up an official-looking document. "Special orders."

The guard looked embarrassed and let them through. There were no seats left. They would have to stand all the way.

The bus was jam-packed and there was still a crowd outside when the guard slammed the door shut behind him, picked up a rifle hidden beneath a seat, and took up position behind the driver.

The driver started the engine and manoeuvred the bus out onto the Jaffa Road. When they were nearly at the city boundary the guard raised his rifle into action position.

"This good place for ambush," a man explained in broken Hebrew to his neighbour. "Is mostly Arab country now. You keep your nut down."

Dalia looked around and saw most seated passengers had already placed their heads below window level.

The standing passengers, squashed as tightly as grapes in a bunch, had no way to protect themselves. She clung to Simon. If they died, let them die together. Every time the bus rounded a corner Dalia waited for a hail of bullets, but in the long descent to the coast they suffered nothing more dangerous than Arab children throwing stones which bounced off the sides of the bus. The guard dispersed them by firing his rifle over their heads.

She remembered the letter she had picked up before leaving home. In the confined space she had difficulty removing it from her rucksack but managed at last to retrieve the letter. It ordered her to remain in Jerusalem and await further orders.

She showed it to Shimon. "You knew I would be receiving this order."

He nodded. "I wasn't going to let anything interfere with placing an engagement ring onto your finger."

She glowered. "Yael's cast-off?"

"No, my grandmother's ring. My mother's idea."

That could only mean Cousin Elsa was genuinely happy to have her as a daughter-in-law.

Dalia leaned in to Shimon and clutched his hand—easy to do inconspicuously in the packed bus. He gave it a squeeze. Briefly, she forgot about the danger they were in, but was brought back to reality when the seated passengers cowered even lower as they passed the side road to Wilhelmina where intense police activity still surrounded yesterday's wrecked buses.

When they finally arrived at the Jaffa terminal, cheers broke out when the bus drew up intact. Two women even rushed up to kiss the guards. Passing Arabs, though, cast hostile glances.

She saw her father wave. Disappointingly, he was on his own.

"Couldn't Ruth come?"

"I dropped her and Uri off at Nathanya," her father replied. "Someone from our family had to go to the funerals."

"Passengers from yesterday's Nathanya bus?"

Her father nodded. "You can imagine your mother when she heard the news, but it was too late to stop you coming."

The drive home was uneventful apart from an unusual amount of police activity. On arrival at Bereisheet, her mother ran over and embraced her, dripping tears onto her blouse. "Oh, Dalia, you're safe! And you, Shimon, are to become my son! Come, sit down both of you and have some chocolate cake."

Her mother dished out enormous portions of the chocolate cake for which she was famous throughout the district and reported that she had won the battle over the engagement party's location, although the demob party quite properly was to be held at Rehovot which would be a much smaller affair.

Bereisheet had an unfair advantage, Dalia reflected. Their huge, new community hall had space to accommodate all her school and work friends in addition to as many coach loads of Rehovot residents as Cousin Elsa could wish to invite.

When Shimon went off with her father, she settled down to a baking session with her mother. They listened to the wireless while they worked. The news was not good. The surrounding Arab nations were threatening to invade. More Jews were being killed in ambushes.

Her mother turned it off again. Dalia knew she would not be happy until Ruth and Uri arrived home safely.

Her father and Shimon came back chatting amicably

about irrigation systems.

Shimon winked at her as he accepted another cup of coffee.

Uri and Ruth returned.

Ruth ran over and hugged her. "Oh, Dalia, I'm so happy for you. It's like a fairytale breaking into the middle of our troubles. As soon as I get you alone I want to hear all about Shimon's proposal."

Before that they had to settle for more cake and coffee.

"The funerals were so sad," Ruth said. "One was for a woman going to Jerusalem to get married."

Her mother exclaimed, "Dalia, you must not return to Jerusalem."

Dalia kept quiet, determined not to spoil the evening by quarrelling with her mother, but she would return to Jerusalem as soon as the engagement party was over.

* * * *

Luckily, the demob party at Rehovot was a joint one for several members of the settlement so it was easier than expected to resist Cousin Elsa's last ditch attempt to turn it into an engagement party, especially as the hall was far smaller than the new one at Bereisheet. The Bereisheet contingent left early to prepare the engagement party. Uri acted as the armed guard on their coach. Dalia felt sad to leave Shimon behind.

On the big day her mother smiled as she watched rain pelting against the kitchen window. "Just imagine a party as big as ours having to dance outdoors at Rehovot in such a downpour."

Dalia thought of a more cogent reason for being grateful for rain. It was the best deterrent against Arab terrorists.

She heard a vehicle pull up outside the gate and ran to the front door. Surprise, surprise. Leah, Toni, Esther, Dov, and Clara were jumping out of a Jeep.

"We picked up Toni from Rehovot," Leah said, when they were all in the kitchen. "You've heard he deserted Zamzum for the Ayalon Institute?"

Her mother nodded. "The Ayalon Institute, that's where they train people to run kibbutzim."

"That's right," Toni answered.

"They chose my Toni because of all the new ideas he put into practice in Zamzum," Leah said.

Dalia wondered whether Leah was aware that in reality Toni worked in a bullet factory hidden beneath the Institute's laundrette. She only knew because Herman had once asked her to radio Toni a message warning of the imminent arrival of CID after the Irgun had derailed a train right outside the Institute.

She looked around this seemingly carefree bunch. How many different kinds of secrets was each keeping?

After the inevitable coffee and cake session, Dalia's mother insisted the Negev group had a couple of hours' rest before the party began.

Later that afternoon Dov railed against the murderer of Arvon Platter and the judge who had set him free, but finished up by saying, "I know some people blame you, Dalia, for sitting next to Patsy in court, but she was our comrade-in-arms. You had to stand by her, whatever crime her husband committed. It must be terrible for her to be married to him."

Dalia clenched her fist, wishing she could argue. To change the painful subject she asked Dov if he'd been called up.

"No, the government employs me so they're keeping me on the reserve list."

While her father and Uri went off to see to the cows and goats, Dalia, Ruth, and Miriam continued to help her mother. Listening to dire news on the wireless again, Dalia felt guilty. She and Shimon should be preparing to defend Eretz Israel, not wasting time on a party.

She put aside her misgivings, however, and donned a wide hostess smile when her mother called out that the coaches from Rehovot had arrived. Shimon jumped out first and came over to hug her. There followed not only all Cousin Elsa's friends and neighbours but a large contingent of recent immigrants who'd known Shimon in Italy.

"Your Shimon, he is the most wonderful man in the world," one wizened man assured her as he helped a limping white-haired woman off the coach. "It is thanks to your fiancé that my Elise and I have come to Eretz Israel. I am so honoured to be here to witness his betrothal and to such a beautiful woman."

Shimon, being so conspicuously a hero, seemed almost to have compensated Cousin Elsa for her son's engagement party being held at Bereisheet. She was affability herself to her mother and even gave her a private showing of the engagement ring.

Later in the evening, Shimon broke off from the dancing to drag her to a mini platform. In front of everyone, he placed his grandmother's ring on her finger. Loud cheers from every corner of the hall rang out when she held up her finger to display a braided gold ring inset with a sparkling clear diamond. She experienced a moment of absolute happiness as she gazed up at Shimon before turning to flash a smile at her parents, then caught an unexpected glimpse of sadness on her father's face before he turned it into a great grin. She realised he had been wishing her grandparents had been there to see her.

It was dawn before she flopped into bed, only to be woken an hour later by a screech of brakes followed shortly after by a loud masculine 'Shalom'. She threw on her working clothes and went into the kitchen to find Shimon drinking coffee with a Palmach commander.

"Sweetheart, I have to return to Jerusalem right away. We've an urgent problem with the water supply."

"I'll be back in Jerusalem myself tomorrow," she promised.

"No!" Her mother's head shook a firm refusal.

Shimon stood up and led Dalia outside. He kissed the top of her head. "It would make life easier for me, sweetheart, if I knew you were here."

"No, where you go, so do I. Let's get married as soon as I'm back in Jerusalem."

Shimon laughed. "What? And do our mothers out of a proper wedding? Neither of them would ever speak to us again." He tilted her face. "Darling, believe me, I want nothing better than to settle down with you and raise a family but there's going to be a war. I'll be away fighting and you'll be on comms night and day. That's no way to run a marriage." He looked down at the ground "Besides, if anything happens to me I don't want to leave behind a child who will never know its father."

Chapter 42

The following day Uri started the car engine ready to take her to Jerusalem.

"Please don't go," her mother urged, clinging on as Dalia kissed her goodbye. "A job in a bookshop is not worth your life."

"Eema, would you have deserted Abba just because being with him was dangerous?"

Reluctantly, her mother stepped back.

Once they were alone in the car, Uri told her, "Haganah are calling me and Josh up next week, sis. I haven't told Eema yet. Abba and Reb Cohen have been offered illegals to replace us, so Abba knows. He says he'll tell Eema for me, if I like."

"Best to tell her yourself," Dalia advised. "She'll blow up, of course, but will get over it more quickly than if she hears it from someone else."

When they reached the bus station, she was relieved to find Haganah had improvised armour for buses running the Jerusalem route, though the boards covering all windows except the driver's windscreen were a constant reminder of unseen danger. The only compensation—there were plenty of empty seats.

Nerves were stretched to the limits as they wound their way up the Seven Sisters past Arab villages, but they were in luck. An army convoy happened to be travelling in front so they reached the Jerusalem boundary unmolested.

Shimon was at the bus station to meet her but had to dash back to work after a quick kiss and cuddle in the doorway of a closed Arab shop.

Dalia couldn't believe the difference a few days had made. Jerusalem was a shambles. Although the UN had designated it an international city, Arabs were attempting to take over Jewish zones without interference from the police, still officially in charge of law and order until May fourteenth. The British police, however, were under orders not to interfere with incidents that stemmed from the UN vote.

The postal service still functioned. When Dalia arrived back at Rabbit, Itka handed her several letters. She turned over one postmarked Jerusalem and found the return address.

Mrs. Quigley,
The Nurses' Home,
Russian Compound.

She remembered Patsy had written asking her to keep an eye on her mother. She opened it, read the message, and leaned on the counter to stop herself from falling.

"What's the matter?" Itka asked in alarm.

"It's little Johnny. He's been killed."

"How?"

"A gas explosion in his grandmother's house."

"And he went there because England was a safe haven."

There was a letter from Patsy but it had been written before the accident so Patsy sounded her usual self, passing on news that Maftur was expecting a second baby but Ismail had been recalled to the Jordanian army.

She wrote to Patsy immediately but knew her words were inadequate. If Uri had been killed nothing anyone said or wrote would have comforted Eema.

She phoned the Nurses' Home, but Home Sister said Sister Quigley had flown to England.

The weight of Johnny's death crushed her spirits. It didn't help that she couldn't talk to Shimon in private. He was working an eighteen hour week. Very occasionally, he popped into the cellar for coffee between jobs and sat by her while she worked. He looked exhausted.

She had to work twelve hour shifts herself now because the Agency had transferred two colleagues to other duties. When she slept it was to the accompaniment of gunfire and explosions in almost every quarter of the city.

One day, Shimon asked Herman's permission to take her out of the cellar for ten minutes as he had some private news. Sitting on a camp bed in the attic with Shimon's arm around her shoulder, she listened while he told her he had received a letter from Tim. Before she could tell him she already knew about Johnny, but hadn't wanted to make life any more difficult for him than it was already, he kissed her gently and told her Tim had said Patsy wouldn't be up to writing letters for a long time. Any letters of condolence should be addressed to him. There were circumstances that couldn't be broadcast that made their situation even more difficult.

They sat silently cuddling each other for a few minutes, while Dalia tried to imagine Patsy's agony.

* * * *

It was gone mid-December now. Hanukah in Jerusalem would be bleak this year. Jewish shops were almost empty because wholesale suppliers from Tel Aviv and Haifa were reluctant to risk ambushes. There was an even greater shortage of fuel. Drivers refused to make journeys through Arab territory while carrying inflammable goods. Jewish shops, prone to incendiary bombing, were just as reluctant to stock them.

In common with other Jerusalem residents, Dalia and Itka took to carrying a kerosene pail wherever they went, on the off-chance of meeting a donkey-drawn kerosene tanker.

Just when she was feeling at her most depressed, Shimon turned up at Itka's flat in hiking gear with a rucksack full of freshly dug potatoes, carrots and a chicken.

"Don't ask!" he said when Itka wanted to know where he had obtained them. "I've come to beg a place on your sofa and please may I join you for the first two days of Hanukkah?"

Dalia picked up a wicker basket. "I'll hunt for greens to go with those root vegetables. Are you coming, Shimon?"

She led him to a deserted plot of waste land where they enjoyed half-an-hour of passionate privacy before scouring the ground for the weed now widely known as Jerusalem spinach. They found enough to fill half the basket.

Itka produced a hoarded packet of pearl barley and a bottle of white wine, and they set about preparing the traditional feast of potato fritters and barley soup.

Shimon recited the Hanukkah prayers. She and Itka held

the lighted candles. It was a wonderful Hanukkah after all.

The food situation, bad as it was before, became much worse by the end of January. A notorious Palestinian Arab leader, exiled since before WW2, returned in secret and organised Arab villagers, along with armed guerrillas from Iraq and Syria, into ambushing all Jewish traffic on the Jerusalem to Jaffa road.

The Jewish Agency commandeered all stocks of food from both Jewish shops and private houses, and issued ration books.

Grocery shops opened mornings only. When on night shift, Dalia queued at the grocers with the ration books in the mornings. When she was on day shifts, Itka had to take time off.

Fresh vegetables, milk and eggs were non-existent. She and Itka grew mustard and cress on their windowsills and co-operated with other residents in the apartment block to grow mushrooms in the basement. They envied nearby neighbours with balconies who grew tubs of potatoes.

One lunchtime, she and Shimon managed to meet up at one of the few restaurants still open. The only item on the menu was meat-flavoured fritter.

"So what have you been up to that's been keeping you so busy?" Dalia asked.

"Storing water. We're done now. The food situation may be bad but it's water that will decide the issue." He drew on the table with his finger. "The mains run through the Arab sector first, so as soon as the British leave, the Arabs will cut off our water. Fortunately, the British brought in regulations years ago that all new buildings in Jerusalem must have rainwater cisterns. We've been storing enough mains water in them to last until we create an alternative water system. Luckily, the British haven't noticed the surge in water consumption."

"Ah, that's why I saw two men running a hose pipe into our rainwater cistern last week!"

"And they'll have locked and sealed your hatch. But that job's finished now so I'm leaving Jerusalem."

She gripped the edge of the table. "They're calling you

back to the Palmach?" The Palmach were fighting Arabs down on the coast. Was she fated to lose Shimon almost as soon as she had won him?

"No. I've another job with the water board. Very hush-hush. Don't worry. I shan't be travelling along any main roads."

"When will I see you next?"

He shrugged. "I'll be back as soon as I can, sweetheart."

A few days later Dalia found the wireless in front of her wavering. Darkness swamped her peripheral vision. The next thing she knew, she was staring up at Itka's concerned face.

"Can you hear me?" Itka was saying.

"W-what are you doing here?" her voice came out slowly.

"Herman came and said you had fallen off your chair. Can you stand?"

She tried but sank back. Her eyes closed. She heard Itka saying, "Call the Agency for an ambulance," as she sank into swirling darkness. She revived sufficiently to feel her body being lifted and her arms and legs tied down.

"I'm a parcel," she mumbled as she felt herself tilted and jolted. "Who's carrying me?"

Cold rain fell on her face. She opened her eyes to see barbed wire passing by—closed them again and retreated into the churning darkness.

She smelt cooked onions and opened her eyes.

A nurse stood beside her. "You're in hospital," she said. "The doctor says you just need food and rest and you'll be as good as new. I've brought soup."

The soup, chicken and barley as well as onion, was the best she had ever tasted.

"How did you get it?" she asked the nurse when she had cleaned her bowl.

"The Agency allows patients special rations. If you're finished, your friend Itka wants to see you."

"Dalia, I've talked to Herman and he agrees that you should have a break from the cellar. The agency is transferring you to a day job."

She hoped she that meant work on a kibbutz with the

Palmach. Instead, the Agency placed her in the specialist communications department at their Jerusalem headquarters.

She felt safe working in the Agency compound. With all their heightened security measures, there was little chance of the British ever again entering unannounced, and even less of sabotage by Arabs. As a bonus, the communications office in the semi-basement had long windows at ground level, protected by heavy bars.

The one drawback was the nature of the job, telephoning Arab householders advising them to leave before their homes were blown up. She protested to her new boss, a wiry, gnarled man.

He leaned back in his chair, pursing his lips in a smile that reminded her of her German grandfather, arguing against accompanying them to Palestine.

"Nu," her boss said, "you would prefer us to blow up houses without warning?"

"But we're not really intending to blow them up, are we?"

"So, suddenly it is a bad thing that we do not damage property?"

She refused to be put down. "These Arabs I have to phone, they are doctors, hotel keepers, teachers; not terrorists."

Her boss turned serious. "If Jerusalem is to be part of the Jewish state we have to have a majority here. The Arabs are trying to force our people to leave so we are trying to force theirs. The winners in this war will be the ones who keep their nerve and stay in their homes."

That night she was woken by three even louder than usual explosions. She turned over and tried to go back to sleep until loud banging on the front door returned her to consciousness.

A minute later Itka burst into her room. "There's been a gigantic explosion in Ben Yehuda Street. It's destroyed half the buildings. They've asked me to help in the hospital. They want you digging for survivors."

Dalia jumped out of bed, flung on her oldest clothes, and ran downstairs onto the street. At the corner of Ben Yehuda Street she peered at the damage through dust-filled air that clogged her nostrils. She heard crashes of falling stone, and the scrape of spades moving rubble.

She had experienced bombing in Haifa during the war, had seen the wreckage in Tel Aviv after the largest air-raid Palestine, had known and had witnessed the destruction of the King David hotel, but she had never seen street destruction on this scale. She gazed at a hole where a well-known cafe had stood, at apartments where remnants of bedroom floors sloped almost vertically, at piles of rubble covering the road. A volunteer fire brigade hosed burning buildings using RASC mobile water tanks. Rescuers carried loaded stretchers to both Red Shield and army ambulances.

An elderly man guarding a collection of tools stood by a large hand painted notice that read, *Silence, so we may hear the wounded.*

He shoved a spade into her hands, pointed towards a block of flats, now little more than a pile of rubble. "The teams there have found twenty bodies already," he whispered. "Help them."

She joined a team of four clearing rubble, beneath which a child kept crying that his Eema and Abba were hurt.

Dalia dug. She dug until her arms felt as if they no longer belonged to her, she dug until she was vomiting as she worked, but she carried on digging until her team had succeeded in clearing a hole large enough for a rescuer to crawl through.

While others only yards away were rewarded with nothing but dead bodies, her team pulled out three people still alive, two adults, unconscious but not fatally wounded, and a miracle child able to walk out into the open, unaided.

After watching the two adults leave on stretchers, Dalia slumped to the ground. An elderly woman led her to a mound of rubble beyond the 'Silence' notice and handed her a glass of water. Dalia drained the glass at one go.

"Rest here for at least fifteen minutes," the woman ordered.

An armoured Jeep carrying a squad of British police negotiated its way over rubble and stopped by the notice. A sergeant jumped out and told the old man, "We've been sent to help."

The old man spat at him and yelled in Hebrew, "So now, after driving the trucks that caused this, you want to help?"

A few of the nearer rescuers gathered round and threw chunks of rubble at the Jeep. Others threw stones at the sergeant. Too tired to move out of the way of the impending riot, Dalia watched the sergeant retreat to the police vehicle, and order the driver to reverse. Jeers broke the silence until a Haganah officer ordered everyone back to work.

She looked down the street. The fires were out now and the RASC mobile water units were gone. The army ambulances had departed with their patients.

A hand settled on her shoulder. With an effort, she opened her eyes and saw Shimon, hardly recognisable beneath a layer of filth.

"I hate Arabs." The words tumbled out of her mouth before she realised she was saying them. Shimon squatted beside her and laid an arm around her shoulder.

"Because of this?" he asked, waving his arms at the chaos. "So how do you think Arabs felt about Jews after the Jaffa Gate barrel bomb?"

"That was not Haganah's doing."

Shimon shrugged, dislodging a fine spray of dust from his hair and shoulders. "You think the Arabs care two hoots whether it was Haganah, Irgun or the Stern Gang? To them it's all Jews, just as you blame all Arabs when you look at this lot."

He rubbed a filthy hand across his eyes. "You realise the method used here was the same as in Jaffa Gate?"

"How do you mean?"

"Stolen police lorries, drivers in British police uniform, barrel bombs rolled off the back, only these barrels were even bigger than at Jaffa Gate and filled with stronger explosives."

She hauled herself to her feet, kissed the top of his grimy hair, and picked up her spade.

Chapter 43

More than a fortnight later, Dalia was still in the Jewish Agency, making telephone calls to Arab households warning that their houses were due for demolition, but after the Ben Yehuda Street bombs, she pursued her task with more enthusiasm.

As she put the receiver down on an engaged signal, a shadow fell across her desk. She looked up to see a grey-green Ford saloon parked.

A colleague on the next station commented, "That car from the American Embassy is here again!"

Before Dalia could dial the next number on her list, the loudest explosion she'd heard yet occurred outside the nearest window. As glass flew across the room she dived under her desk and rolled into a ball. She watched her nearest colleague collapse to the floor, blood flowing from her neck, her mouth open. Dalia could hear no scream and realised she could hear nothing at all. A bank of cubbyholes spewed out paper and slowly toppled in eerie silence. Falling stone and plaster turned her vibrating desk into a miniature cave and shut out the light. She couldn't stop sneezing. The desk vibrated again but the solid oak held firm. She attempted to free herself but as she pulled one piece of rubble away, another fell into its place. She merely succeeded in reducing the size of her cave. Her hearing gradually returned. She heard the rasping of her own breath but nothing else. To conserve what air she had, she forced her body to stop its violent shaking and relax her shoulders.

Aeons later, she heard scraping. She tried to shout but could only produce a hoarse whisper. A piece of rubble moved, letting in light, glorious air, and Shimon's voice, "We've a live one here."

The hole became larger.

"Thank God," Shimon shouted and knelt down to place a tin mug filled with water to her lips.

She hadn't realised how dry her mouth was until she

began drinking.

Shimon and other rescuers moved more rubble. She stuck her arms through the hole. Shimon knelt down, pulled her out and she found herself in his embrace.

Someone exclaimed, "A miracle. No injuries at all."

"How many people in your office?" Shimon asked.

Her voice was stronger now. "Four."

"We can go on to the next room, then," someone said.

"I'm accompanying this one to hospital," Shimon declared.

"But I'm not injured."

"We can't be too careful." He led her to an empty Red Shield ambulance.

"The others from my office?" she asked.

He looked as if debating whether to answer but eventually said, "I'm sorry, Dalia. We uncovered three bodies in your office before reaching you."

She began to shake again. After a brief examination in the hospital, Shimon walked her home. What would she have done without him? She clung to him all evening, begging him not to leave. Itka, despite her strict notions of propriety, took pity and allowed Shimon to stay in her room.

Before dawn, she woke, slowly emerging from a fading nightmare of black throbbing nothingness. Wonderingly, she found herself still in Shimon's warm arms. She poked him to make sure he was real and lay back again. When she next woke, it was daylight. Shimon insisted she stay at home.

The day after, however, she took herself back to work. Shimon came with her as far as the still intact reception foyer.

A harassed official interviewed her briefly. The disaster had, of course, he explained, destroyed the communications systems and the lists. She was an expert at firearms, wasn't she? She had kept up her drill, yes? Good, the youth group, Gadna, needed another full-time instructor.

* * * *

Gadna was Haganah's recently formed youth group,

consisting of youngsters between the ages of fourteen and sixteen. It trained future Haganah members in military drill and firearm practice.

Their training ground lay on the outskirts of Jerusalem. Like so much else since the end of the previous November, the British ignored its activities.

Today, Dalia stood by the targets, observing her current squad making a right balagan of falling in, their sole apparent aim being to position themselves between their best mates. The previous half hour's fire practice had revealed that over half the latest recruits had never handled a rifle. Judging from this performance, they were also deficient in basic drill.

Each successive squad passing through her hands was younger than the last and she was given even less time to train them before they joined the Haganah troops currently battling to gain control of the Jerusalem-Jaffa Road at Latrun. She would have relished the challenge if she were not conscious that many of her pupils would die in battle, and their deaths would serve no purpose. Haganah alone would never defeat the Arabs. The only hope for victory, much as she hated the idea, lay in the resurgence of a united Jewish Resistance.

Around her, the Judean hillsides were pink with flax. Nowadays, however, she was only concerned with any plant's culinary qualities. Fragile Linum Pubescens, however pretty, did not produce the edible seeds of its more robust blue cousin. The coming evening, however, she would not be foraging for food. Shimon had invited her for supper at an apartment a friend had lent him.

On the dirt track outside the gate a car and a truck drew up. The occupants clambered out. The Gadna organiser strode down the path trailing two senior instructors, one a middle-aged school teacher whose right leg had been shattered during WW2, the other an aging owner of a garage.

She had come to know the garage owner well. During her half hour lunch break he taught her car maintenance and how to get the best out of Haganah's armoured cars and trucks. That was the favourite part of her day, racing a car around the training ground to cheers and cat-calls from her squad as they lounged on the grass eating their meagre packed lunches.

She was especially pleased to see the charismatic organiser Yehoshua Arieli. He would only have to look at the current squad to understand why they needed extra training time. She gave a cheerful shalom, and was taken aback by a curt response.

"Load your squad into the truck. Ensure they keep those rifles."

Before she could protest, he had turned on his heel and walked off.

Seething with anger, she obeyed orders. With only half an hour's rifle instruction, these children would be worse than useless in any battle.

"What's going on?" she asked the instructors.

The retired schoolteacher replied, "I'm not sure, but it must be something bad if it's upset Yehoshua."

By the time they reached the gate, Yehoshua Arieli was seated in the front passenger seat of the car. The instructors climbed into the back. A junior instructor named Yakov sat in the truck's driving seat, the engine switched on.

Dalia supervised her squad as they climbed jauntily into the rear, only their trembling rifles betraying inner terror. She fastened the tailgate.

"Over here, Dalia," Arieli ordered. "You are to drive the car. Yakov, you are to follow us in the truck."

"Where to?" Dalia asked as she turned on the engine.

"An Arab village just inside the Jerusalem boundary."

Five kilometres west of the old city, by Shaul Givat, Arieli told her to draw up. He leapt out, flagged down the truck, and ordered the puzzled youngsters out and to wait until required. They clustered under the dappled shade of almond trees, looking like any well-behaved class on a school outing, apart, of course, from their rifles.

Arieli motioned the instructors to follow him. From the other side of a ridge, they saw a hillside village, rather more gentrified than Dalia had expected. Large houses surrounded by well-tended gardens lined a wider than usual dirt road. "What's the village called?" she asked Arieli.

"Deir Yassin."

Deir Yassin! That was where Maftur lived!

Arieli led them uphill towards the village entrance. Close to, they received the first whiff of the unmistakeable stench of death. Dalia felt her forehead break out into sweat although the day was pleasantly warm rather than hot. She forced herself to remain outwardly calm and professional, even when they had their first glimpse of bodies strewn across the road surface, each with its own buzzing swarm of flies. As they drew closer, she realised that the bodies were those of children, women, and old people.

Arieli, his shoulders bowed, his hands to his face, muttered something indistinguishable. He took his hands down and faced them all.

"I was with the British army in Greece during the war and saw what Nazis did to villages there. I never thought to see horrors like that committed by my own people in my own country. We cannot let the children see this. We will work in twos."

He paired Dalia with the crippled schoolteacher and addressed them again.

"Be respectful when you carry the dead. Lay them neatly. Cover each body. If you find survivors, take them to the truck and let the children care for them. We have been sent here to discover what happened, so be observant."

As Dalia and the schoolteacher approached their first body, an elderly woman with a bullet wound that had shattered her skull, the stench became unbearable. She removed the scarf protecting her head from the sun and tied it across her nose and mouth. Together, she and her partner brushed the swarm of flies from the woman's face but could do nothing about the maggots attacking the eyes.

"This lady was shot at close range from the front, would you agree?" the schoolmaster asked.

"Yes," Dalia said, bending down to hold the woman's legs.

Between them, lurching slightly because of her partner's limp, they carried the woman to the edge of the road, laid her down and straightened limbs which had already lost rigor mortis.

As they stood up, Dalia looked around at the other bodies, dreading to find one she knew. She saw a dress she thought she recognised and ran over. Beside the dress a male child sprawled on the ground, his face covered in dried blood, a pool of blood beneath his head. The woman wearing the dress lay face upwards, her stomach bulging, her chest smothered in blood even though the bullet hole through it was surprisingly small. Maggots crawled on torn ear lobes, but the face was unwounded. Despite discoloured, puffy skin, Dalia recognised the once beautiful Maftur. The child at her feet had to be Raffy. Before she could stop herself, she gave a loud wail.

Arieli came running up. "Please," he said softly, "I know how distressing this is, but we have a job to do."

Dalia clenched her fists. Her voice came out in a scream. "You don't understand. That was my friend and that," she said, pointing to the child, "was her little boy."

Arieli opened his eyes wide in shocked sympathy. He bent down and gently picked up the child's body. Almost blinded with tears, Dalia helped her partner carry Maftur.

As they laid her down the schoolmaster exclaimed, "The bastards were even callous enough to rip out her earrings."

She watched Arieli examine Raffy's body, and heard him say to the schoolmaster, "There's powder marks around the bullet wound in this child's back. I suspect mother and child were killed by a single bullet."

"She was pregnant," Dalia said. "One bullet killed three, not two."

A numbing calm spread though her body as her mind anaesthetised itself against further horror. From a distance, she heard her own voice say in a matter of fact tone, "We need sheets."

Accompanied by the schoolteacher, she walked calmly through the open doorway of what she presumed was Maftur's house. Furniture lay overturned on ripped tapestries and curtains. A geometry exercise book lay open on the floor next to an upturned table, its neat diagrams stamped with the pattern of a man's boot. No sheets here.

Upstairs. That is where she would find sheets. The bedrooms were in the same state as the living rooms. Drawers pulled out, contents strewn across the floor, topped by empty jewellery boxes with broken hinges. Mattresses ripped and, more importantly, sheets missing.

While the schoolteacher gathered torn curtains, she went down to the kitchen – yet another body, one with a smashed skull. Ishfaq, Raffy's nursemaid.

Sheets first, she told herself and went through the back door.

Beside a pair of bullet-scarred children's swings, flies swarmed over another body with torn ear lobes. Blood stained the front of a green checked school uniform. Nearby, an overturned basket spilled out withered spinach.

The sight of this unknown schoolgirl slashed through a barrier protecting her sanity. Invading madness flooded her mind with dangling earrings, ruby, emerald, and sapphire, covered in blood, floating, falling in piles, turning into jewelled guns for the defence of Eretz Israel.

Someone shook her shoulder gently. Her partner, carrying a pile of ripped curtains. "We'll cover the bodies with these."

The glass box of calm enclosed her again. Her mind concentrated on sheets. She walked away slowly, following a path beyond a clipped laurel hedge. On a washing line, sheets hung dry.

She was carrying the white linen across the front garden when she heard the rumble of approaching vehicles. She stood still, thinking she should do something but unsure what or why.

A convoy filled with armed men and women appeared and halted outside the garden. A man stepped down from the lead car. She was sure she should know him.

"Report, Dalia Leitner," the man commanded in a cold voice and she recognised him.

Jerusalem's deputy Haganah commander Yeshurin Schiff. She had been on Palmach courses with him. From the look on his face, she realised he thought she was looting Maftur's house. Her face burned with shame, her eyes watered. She couldn't speak.

Arieli stepped into her silence and explained the situation but the feeling of disgrace wouldn't leave.

The Haganah leader ordered out his troops. "And you," he said waving his hand at the Gadna instructors, "Follow quietly."

She ignored the instruction and continued on her way to replace the torn curtains covering Maftur and Raffy with her clean white sheets.

The young instructor, Yakob, came running back. "Yeshurin wants to know where you've got to. Come on."

There was no more she could do for Maftur right now. She followed Yakov uphill until they reached the top of the hill. She heard voices and mad, loud laughter, male and female.

In front of her Palmach troops walked stealthily downhill, peeling off to the right and left, under Shiff's directions, to encircle a eucalyptus grove.

Arieli and the other instructors stood to the side. She and Yakov caught up with them and saw the Palmach had surrounded a group of khaki clad men and women sprawled under the eucalyptus trees, all with guns of one kind or another slung casually over their shoulders.

"Lehi," Arieli whispered.

So the Stern gang were responsible for Maftur's death!

She watched as Schiff stepped into the open. One of the dissidents stood and squared his shoulders, although his gang, studiously ignoring the Haganah commander, carried on with crude banter. The Palmach emerged from hiding, and trained their rifles on the lounging group. She willed them to mow down Maftur's murderers, but they held fire.

Schiff spat on the ground. "My men have surrounded your animals. Command them to surrender their arms."

His opponent curled his top lip. "And just who gave you the authority to order us about?"

"Surrender your arms."

"No."

Schiff ordered the Palmachniks. "Keep your guns trained on this scum while I radio HQ. If anyone raises a weapon, fire at once." He marched back over the brow of the hill.

Dalia, along with the rest of the instructors, slumped to the ground. Images of Maftur, Raffy, Ishfaq, and the young schoolgirl raced through her mind while the Lehi continued their incongruous banter.

Schiff returned. "You," he said to Arieli, "take your instructors and look for anyone left alive. Drive them to hospital." He glared at the Stern Gang leader. "And you, remove the corpses to the quarry. Pour on kerosene and burn them until only ashes are left. Then tidy the houses."

"No," Dalia screamed. She raced up the road towards Maftur's house, but everything started to blur at the edges. Where was this place? Why was she running?

Someone came up to her.

"Where's Maftur?" she asked and somehow found herself sitting in the front passenger seat of Arieli's moving car. "What happened?"

The Gadna organiser shrugged. "You tell me. For the past hour we've heard nothing from you except, 'Where's Maftur?' and 'Where are we?'"

She looked out of the window. A plume of black smoke rose from the quarry. Even from this distance, she could smell burning meat. Maftur and Raffy going up in smoke. Was this Auschwitz?

She tried to order her thoughts. She could remember nothing between running up the hill and being in the Arieli's car, and yet it didn't feel odd sitting there. She didn't feel as if she had been unconscious, just that there was time she couldn't remember.

Why was it that she could remember things she didn't want to – the stench of Maftur and Raffy's bodies, the maggots, but nothing after? She tried to remember the lost hour but there was nothing except a blurred central image surrounded by a ring of darkness – a patch of grey soil and a grey spade digging into it.

"Did I bury Maftur and Raffy?" she asked.

Arieli didn't look at her as he changed gear. "No, but we did. You watched us, remember, from the swing?"

She looked out of the window and the view seemed normal, no dark edges and no blurring. He stopped the car in front of the Agency and told her to wait. She sank back and tried to remember more but couldn't.

Arieli came out carrying an envelope and started the car again.

"Where are you taking me?"

"To Shimon's apartment. Itka said she thought you would rather go straight there. He's expecting you."

Arieli stopped the car in King George's Street and gave her the envelope. "Take that to the Jewish Agency when you feel ready to return to work. I've recommended you for a spell of office duty."

She put the letter in her pocket and climbed the stairs of the apartment block. Her feet felt so heavy she could hardly lift them from one step to another.

At her knock, Shimon opened the door and put his arms gently around her. "Arieli phoned," he said. "We won't speak of what happened until you've washed and we've both eaten." He showed her the bathroom. "My friend's shower has an electric water heater and the electricity here is back on again."

"Oh, Shimon, I haven't had warm water since leaving Bereisheet."

"And here is something even better." He handed her a sliver of perfumed soap, a fluffy towel, a bottle of Cousin Elsa's famous homemade hair conditioner, and a clean pair of men's pyjamas.

She saved the water from her shower to scrub her clothes.

When she came out, dressed in Shimon's pyjamas, she found him in a kitchen with an electric cooker.

He looked up and smiled approvingly. "I've boiled a kettle. I can't offer you proper coffee though, only the acorn stuff. I'll know we've won the war for Jerusalem when we have proper coffee, but just look what we have for supper." He opened a cupboard and showed her a tin of baked beans. "My friend left it for me when he went off to Latrun and I've saved it to share with you. I have my bread ration, too, so tonight we'll feast on beans on toast."

After supper, she lay in his arms and sobbed. "How could they do it?" she kept repeating. "There were women soldiers there too."

Shimon said nothing but continued to hold her protectively until, at last, her tears stopped. They made love, gently and sadly. When he lay back, she began weeping again.

Shimon got up and made her another hot drink. He put it down beside her and sat on the bed. "Darling, do you know where Ismail is?"

She put her hands to her cheeks. How could she have been so selfish as to forget about Maftur's husband? "He's in Jordan. I think. Patsy wrote. They called him back to his regiment. He won't know what has happened. If only Tim were still here. He'd know how to get in touch."

"I'll write to Tim and enclose a letter for Ismail. He's bound to know someone who can find out where to send it."

"I ought to write to Patsy."

"No, you mustn't do that. Tim can break the news. I'll get Ismail's address from Tim. Thanks to you, I'll be able to tell him that Maftur and Raffy had a decent burial and are lying at rest by the swings."

"Those dissidents are monsters."

Shimon shook his head. "Those fighters at Deir Yassin, Dalia, have received no training in military discipline, nor have they been taught the principles of restraint, so it's hardly surprising they succumbed to the blood-lust of battle. They will have to live with the guilt of what they did all their lives." He kissed her gently on the lips. "Some day, sweetheart, we'll tell our children how war affects victors as well as victims. For now, though, for the sake of Jewish unity, we say nothing. To win our War of Independence we must join forces with both the Stern Gang and the Irgun. If our soldiers despise the comrades they fight alongside, we may lose Eretz Israel."

Dalia clung more tightly. "Shimon, even if we have to keep secrets from the whole world, we must never keep secrets from each other, promise?"

Shimon kissed her again, long and not so gentle this time. "I promise."

Chapter 44

The next morning, Shimon attempted to dissuade Dalia from going to the Agency. "You need at least one day in bed. I wish I could stay here with you but I have an urgent defence meeting at ten."

"If I stay in by myself, I'll go mad. I have to be with people."

"If you insist on going in, you'll need a change of clothes. I have time to walk you to Itka's, before we go on to work."

After she had changed into her office dress and shoes at her digs, and picked up the kerosene bucket, they set off for the Agency.

She was amazed to find the wreckage in the compound cleared. Shimon left her in the lobby and ran upstairs. She showed Arieli's letter to the Chief Administrator, who asked, "Can you do shorthand?"

She admitted to being qualified.

He beamed. "We can use you. We're desperate for telephone monitors."

Telephone monitoring, she discovered, was similar to wireless monitoring, except it involved fewer skills and the person who monitored the calls also transcribed.

The supervisor, a stern-faced, middle-aged woman with tightly curled, shoulder-length auburn hair, equipped her with paper, pencil and a pair of earphones with an attached lead. She pointed to a chair next to two women scribbling away on a narrow bench in front of a board punched with holes that ran the whole width of the room. Green lights flashed above several empty holes. The women's earphones were already jacked into holes with red lights.

"Sit there," the supervisor ordered. "Place your jack into the nearest flashing light and start transcribing. Be prepared to transfer your jack on my command."

The concentration this required kept nightmare thoughts of Maftur and Raffy at bay. Unlike her previous job at the calling office, the task did not involve her emotions.

Shimon met her after work and carried her bucket. Halfway back to the apartment they found an Armenian kerosene seller who filled Itka's bucket while Dalia and Shimon stood by his donkey stroking its nose. She felt her luck had turned.

That feeling was enhanced when Itka's front door opened while she was still fumbling for her key, and Ruth flung herself around her neck. If there was one person in the world she wanted to be with almost as much as Shimon, it was Ruth. She couldn't believe she was seeing her. No Haganah convoy had broken through from the coast all week.

"How did you get here?" she asked as she hugged her friend.

"Dalia," Itka shouted from behind Ruth, "come, see what your friend has brought. Now, if we only had kerosene we would feast tonight."

Shimon held up the full bucket. Itka let out a screech of joy and led them into the kitchen where she was in the process of filling tins with flour, sugar, baby milk, and South American coffee. A can of olive oil stood on the dresser.

"And look at this," Itka said reverentially. She took from a cupboard a cooked chicken covered in netting weighted with blue beads.

Dalia's mouth salivated. "Ruth, you brought all that with you!"

"Your mother and mine insisted."

"You still haven't said how you got here."

"A British army friend of Uri's is doing the swan run this week. I hitched a lift."

"But why? Jerusalem's not currently a top tourist attraction."

"Hospitals are desperate for staff. The Agency ordered me to report to Mount Scopus tomorrow morning."

Dalia was to remember that evening as an oasis of normality in the desert of war. They ate appetising food and exchanged news. Josh had been wounded during the fighting around Latrun but was well on the way to recovery. Uri was with a Palmach unit in Galilee fighting Jordanians. Dalia said nothing about Deir Yassin. She would tell Ruth about it eventually but not on this special evening.

Long after midnight, Ruth yawned. "I must get to bed. The weekly convoy to Mount Scopus leaves early. I'm looking forward to travelling with more VIPs than I've ever seen before. All the top consultants are returning from an international conference."

Shimon stood up. "There's no curfew tonight so I'll be off."

The next morning Dalia accompanied Ruth to the convoy of ambulances and buses waiting outside the Agency compound.

"It will be good spending time together," Ruth said as she hugged Dalia. "There's a transmitter at the hospital. I can let you know, via the Agency, when I have time off."

Dalia watched Ruth greet a group of nurses before hurrying into the Agency building.

"Guess what!" someone shouted soon after she had taken up her post. "A convoy from Tel-Aviv has reached Jerusalem."

Everyone burst into a spontaneous cheer.

Her elation was short-lived, however, when a few minutes later her neighbour announced, "Arabs have ambushed the convoy to Scopus."

The supervisor sent the report to Jerusalem's Haganah commander and switched her neighbour's jack.

Dalia had the British colonel's line. He came on the phone to say he was leaving to assess the situation. Her neighbour reported that the Jerusalem Haganah commander had asked the Tel Aviv convoy commander if he could borrow his armoured cars, but the commander had refused because the drivers were under orders to return to Tel Aviv as soon as they had unloaded.

Dalia's pencil dug through the paper of her writing pad as she transcribed inconsequential calls. How dare the Tel Aviv convoy commander turn his back on world-famous doctors, patients, nurses and, in particular, her friend Ruth?

She relaxed a little when the woman at the end of the line reported that the local Haganah's three armoured cars, each carrying fourteen Palmachniks, were on the way to the ambush site.

Almost immediately she intercepted the colonel's call to British Command.

"An Arab mob has taken over more houses lining the road to Mount Scopus. Our cease-fire order is being ignored. The people in that convoy are in extreme danger. Request half a troop of guards with armoured cars, an observation officer to arrange the shelling of Arab occupied houses, permission to use mortars."

The British were doing something at last! Or so everyone thought until the military British Command responded, "Half troop will be sent, requests for observation officer and use of mortars refused."

Just as well, she reflected, that the Palmach were on their way.

The colonel radioed his base, his voice thick with rage. "Get me a truck and a bloody half-track. Unless something's done quickly no one in that bloody convoy will come out alive."

To her disgust, the supervisor changed her jack, but her irritation dissipated when she found herself listening to a Haganah field telephone.

Gunfire and yells of "Deir Yassin" drowned out the report of the Haganah officer in charge of the three cars.

She managed to hear when the Haganah officer reported again. One car, damaged by gunfire, was heading for Jerusalem with the wounded.

Dalia closed her eyes. Was Ruth amongst the wounded? She had no time to brood before transcribing the next message. A second armoured car, loaded with dead and wounded, was heading for Jerusalem. Her feet thrummed the floor. It was bad enough imagining Ruth wounded, but supposing it was worse!

Another report from the same Haganah officer. A mine had blown the front wheel off his car. Only one person alive in the convoy's lead car and he was badly wounded. Fighting to keep control, Dalia carried on transcribing. During the long radio silence that followed, she practised calming techniques, without, it appeared, too much success, because the supervisor tapped her on the shoulder.

"Are you all right?"

"Yes," she snapped, immediately ashamed of herself.

The supervisor switched her jack back to the British colonel talking to Government British Command.

"Sir, requested troops have not arrived. My gunner's been killed. The people in the buses refuse to transfer to the half-track while Arabs are firing. They say they are waiting for Haganah to rescue them."

But Haganah had nothing left to offer. "Ruth," she whispered to herself, "if you're still alive, please, please transfer to the British half-track."

Then came the most unbelievable order yet—from military British Command.

"Fire on Haganah if they intervene."

The operator on the other end of the bench let out a wail. "No, no! My father's on one of those buses."

I mustn't break down like that, Dalia thought. She concentrated on her breathing.

The colonel reported the arrival of the military armoured cars. Five minutes later, he phoned again. "Gunner in lead car dead. Request to fire mortar."

As the clock ticked ever more loudly, they waited on the reply. Half an hour later, British Command gave the colonel permission to fire mortars. "But no other intervention."

The colonel reported the arrival of yet more Arabs and requested permission to shell the adjacent houses.

Permission refused.

The day dragged on. No one took a lunch break. The supervisor ordered the other two to switch jacks but left Dalia listening in on the British. Eventually, the colonel reported Arabs setting light to petrol soaked rags and hurling them at the buses. Dalia found a cup of coffee beside her but it was stone cold.

The woman at the end of the bench intercepted a request by the commander of the British armoured cars for smoke cover while he attempted to rescue people from the burning buses. She let slip another wail.

Not until three thirty that afternoon did the British command authorise intervention.

At three-forty-five she heard the colonel again. All six survivors had been rescued. They were on their way to Mount Scopus.

She slumped. Six out of a whole convoy? What odds on Ruth? The woman at the end of the bench sat rigid, her fist pressed against her mouth.

The supervisor used the internal phone to request that the list of survivors be delivered to their department. When the messenger appeared, neither Ruth nor Dalia's colleague's father were on the list.

Dalia was not conscious of returning to the apartment until she groped for her key and missed the lock twice. The door opened from the inside as it had the previous day and again Ruth was hanging around her neck, but this time she was sobbing.

Dalia also burst into tears. "Oh, Ruth, I thought you were dead, I thought you were dead."

Ruth gave a huge sniff to clear her nose. "I should have been. If I had been on a bus I would have been."

"You weren't on a bus?"

"No, I met a friend on the end ambulance." Ruth dabbed at her eyes with her handkerchief. "I joined her. A mine blew up in front of us. We turned back, black smoke behind us. Arabs were cheering, and chanting. It sounded like, 'Deir Yassin', whatever that means. Oh, Dalia! All those famous doctors! The hospital director, his wife. Why didn't the British rescue them?"

* * * *

It was the last day of the mandate. Dalia stood sideways to a window in a second floor apartment on Jaffa Road, her finger on the trigger of a rifle aimed at Arab snipers in buildings opposite. This was the first occasion she had fired against human beings, not a task she relished. She heard a fresh burst of gunfire and risked peering out. The shots were directed down to the street.

Jim Shepard in a wrinkled business suit, briefcase chained to his wrist, zigzagged at a trot towards Barclay's Bank. He entered the bank unharmed, which said a lot about either the quality of the Arabs' weaponry or their firearm skills.

"What kind of fool was that?" Shimon exclaimed from the next window.

"The assistant engineer from the Post office, collecting his men's wages before leaving."

"Hush," Toni called from the back of the room where he was working a wireless.

Dalia waited for Jim's return dash to Bevingrad. He made it back without a scratch.

Knowing him, Dalia thought, he'd probably spend the rest of his life using the incident as an example of the way His Lord protected his own.

The wireless stuttered into life. David Ben Gurion announced the formation of the state of Israel.

"But the mandate doesn't end until midnight," Dalia commented.

"It's Friday," Shimon said. "Ben Gurion won't upset the religious by celebrations that break the Sabbath."

"Celebrations!" Toni grumbled. "All very well for people safe in Tel Aviv. They don't give a damn for us, starving and fighting to win them Jerusalem."

Epilogue – 2012

Dalia opened her laptop, pulled a file from her draft folder and checked what she had written so far.

Dear Patsy,

Thank you for contacting me on Facebook. I can't believe we are both ninety this year It doesn't seem sixty-four years since we met.

I was sorry to lose contact with you when you went to Kenya.

She took her eyes off the screen. That last sentence wasn't strictly true. She had lost meaningful contact with Patsy long before the move to Kenya. She had written but received no answer. It was only years later when Shimon finally told her the true story behind Johnny's death, that she understood why.

She continued writing.

I heard that you have made a name for yourself in palaeontology but didn't realise you still live in Kenya. I loved the photo of your great-grandchildren picnicking by Lake Turkana. It must have given you great pleasure when your grandson took over your farm. I wish I had known you had called your eldest daughter Maftur. I would have found some comfort in that.

That was where she had left off last night. She wasn't sure whether Patsy knew what had happened to Ismail. The story had filtered through that he had been shot by his own superior officer after disobeying a command to cease fire when settlers from Kfar Etzion came out waving a white flag. It was reported that he had continued chanting Deir Yassin in time to his machine gun fire. It was not a story she wanted to pass on.

So far, she realised, all she had done was comment on Patsy's email. She should say what she herself had been doing but so much had happened. She couldn't write it all.

Her fingers went back to the keyboard.

Shimon and I moved into the house at al-Tira when we found we were expecting our first child, Moshe. We had to wait to regain possession. The Palmach had evicted my manager and allocated the house to refugees as the Agency hadn't realised I owned it. We spent many happy years as citrus farmers until our children grew up.

> *By 1973 we were about to hand over the business reins to Moshe, the only one of our children interested in farming, but he was killed in the Yom Kippur war.*

Dalia stopped again as she thought of Patsy's own loss. Which was the more painful, to lose a child still dependent, as Patsy had done, or to lose one like Moshe who had been part of her family for twenty-two years? If only she and Patsy could talk face to face! Well, there was a way.

I would love to have a video chat with you. There's so much I want to tell you but I don't think I can do it all by email. My Skype name is GrannyintheNegev.

Meanwhile, here's the rest of my potted history:

The next few years were difficult running the groves with hired help and supporting Moshe's wife and children. Al-Tira was not the place it had been. Our new neighbours had no memories of Eretz Israel as it was when you and I first knew it and had no interest in agriculture. Most of the old orange groves had been built over. We hung on until 1980 but then sold up and moved to Zamzum.

I can honestly say that the last thirty years here, far from crowds and constant traffic, have been the most contented of my life. We still have clean air, wide views, and live life at a slower pace.

She sat back. Was it just crabby old age that made her resent modern Israel taking its rightful place in the world as a fully fledged business-based state with all the moral compromises that entailed?

The initial Zionist idealism couldn't be expected to last when the current younger generation had only the mundane task of protecting boundaries their parents had already drawn. Was it any wonder that some tried to expand those boundaries? Were those modern settlers she disliked so much really so different from her own generation? Or were they just unlucky enough to be born in an era with different views on international morality?

She went into the kitchen, pressed the button on the coffee grinder, and switched on the kettle as she reflected on her last paragraph. It made her sound like a right refusenik but she was not against all things modern. She enjoyed having piped water. She enjoyed having her rubbish collected, but most of all she loved her computer. It made the frailties of old age bearable and had repopulated the barren fields of widowhood even if it didn't remove the pain. She was proud that her own children, thanks to their father's philosophy, had found journeys so very different from her own. Who could say that the paths they had taken in science and medicine wouldn't lead to greater contributions to the well-being of all humankind?

She made her coffee and took it back to her desk to finish the email.

I'm so glad Shimon was able to enjoy the last years of his life in peace. I was lucky to have had such a wonderful husband.

I do hope, now that you have contacted me, we can keep in touch,
Shalom Dalia Mabovitch.

She pressed *Send*.

About The Author

Margaret spent her childhood in Palestine during the 30s and 40s of the last century.

During the pre-WW2 Palestinian Arab Rebellion, she watched her father strap on a revolver before leading night squads off to repair sabotaged telephone lines. When WW2 started, she watched police and army struggle to rescue passengers from the capsized SS Patria. Later, she and her mother spent an anxious few weeks when her father, covertly recruited by Eastern Mediterranean Intelligence Centre, disappeared in Bulgaria. He turned up in Athens weeks later, after escaping from a rural Bulgarian prison, and joined the last allied convoy from Greece. Fifteen months later, with the Axis poised to invade Palestine, her father, due to a domestic crisis, left her in sole charge of a fake army camp set up to deter Germans from landing on a beach near Haifa. After the war, when the Irgun blew up the West wing of the King David where her father worked, she sat in front of the radio biting the back of her hands while awaiting further news. At the end of the mandate, her father gave her the last Union Jack to fly over Jerusalem. These experiences left her with a lifelong interest in the British Mandate of Palestine and the turmoil the land has experienced since.

Nowadays, when people ask which side she is on in the conflict, she replies – it depends on which character I am currently writing.

Lightning Source UK Ltd.
Milton Keynes UK
UKOW02f1214220116

266922UK00001B/6/P